Also by Nicola Cornick
HOUSE OF SHADOWS

# NICOLA CORNICK

## _The_ PHANTOM TREE

GRAYDON
HOUSE

GRAYDON
HOUSE

Recycling programs
for this product may
not exist in your area.

ISBN-13: 978-1-525-80599-8

The Phantom Tree

First published by HQ, an imprint of HarperCollins Publishers, Ltd., 2017

This edition published by Graydon House, 2018

This edition published by arrangement with Harlequin Books S.A.

For questions and comments about the quality of this book, please contact us at
CustomerService@Harlequin.com.

BookClubbish.com
GraydonHouseBooks.com

**Printed in U.S.A.**

*For old friends, and remembering Flagstone Farm and an evening of remarkable plotting.*

# The
# PHANTOM
# TREE

# ONE

*Alison, Marlborough, Wiltshire, the present day*

SHE SAW THE PORTRAIT QUITE BY CHANCE, OR so she thought.

It was eight weeks to Christmas and the rain-sodden streets of Marlborough already glistened in the gaudy light of the decorations that were strung from buildings and lampposts. The wind was strong that night and the illuminations swung back and forth scattering shadows and shards of colour over the late-night shoppers below. A Victorian market was being held in the town square and the air was thick with the smell of grilled sausages and hot soup. It made Alison feel hungry.

She put her head down and increased her pace against the fine rain that slicked the pavements. She hated this sort of *faux* historical event, with rosy, smiling stallholders dressed up in costume. Beneath the crinolines and jackets they had on their thermal vests and long johns to guard against the cold. They had waterproof boots and raincoats. They thought this play-acting was fun, a jolly celebration of Christmases past.

She remembered past Christmases very differently; the bone-sharp cold, the damp, the chilblains and the hunger that had hollowed her stomach. Even though she had been trapped in the present day for so long now that time had started to blur, some of her past she could remember with utter clarity. Pain, sickness, violence, death had been a raw reality. Someone thrust a toffee apple under her nose in an invitation to buy, and she shuddered and turned away, picking up her pace along the pavement.

There was a creaking noise high above her, a flap as the wind caught the edge of an inn sign and set it swinging.

*The White Hart.*

She stared at the image of the majestic white stag as it swayed backwards and forwards in the wind. Its head was raised proudly. Around its neck was a golden crown. It was strange how the most potent and magical of Savernake Forest's symbols survived into this brash and modern world. There were traces of history everywhere; in street names, on inn signs, in old tracks and ancient hedgerows, buried walls and tumbled gravestones. Scratch the surface and it was there.

Alison had seen a white hart in the forest once. Her cousin Edward Seymour had said that the Queen had wanted to come to hunt it, the hart being the ultimate hunter's trophy and Elizabeth being a queen who collected such things. Perhaps she had come to Wolf Hall after Alison had left. She did not know. There was no record of a royal visit but then so much fell through the cracks of the past.

The fresh blast of air from the Downs to the north brought with it a softer scent of mingled herbs and flowers, wild garlic, basil and lavender, taking Alison straight back to a long-lost summer in the garden at Wolf Hall and the smell of sun-warm brick and hot grass. She had not been happy in those days but still the sense of loss and dislocation hit her fiercely and gave her no time to prepare. There was too much that was familiar here in Marlborough—the town, the inn, the memories. She should have realised that coming back to Wiltshire was a bad idea. But she had had so little choice.

*Breathe. Accept. Wait.*

The wave of dizziness and nausea retreated a little. Alison found she was leaning against a wall between two shops, rather like a drunk steadying himself as he tried to weave his way home late at night. Awareness returned to her, the smooth coldness of a drainpipe against her clutching fingers, the chill sting of the rain and the heavy, greasy smell of the street market.

She was standing in front of a shop she had not seen before. High Street shops came and went, of course, and it was a good ten years since she had been in Marlborough, maybe more. She tried not to count most of the time.

The shop was actually an art gallery, all high-tech lighting and huge windows, its modernity blaringly incongruous in the middle of Marlborough High Street's olde-worlde charm. Most of the paintings Alison could see through the window were equally strident, highly coloured, swirling patterns in oil with huge price tags and no artistic merit in her opinion. Not that she knew much about art. She drew for pleasure and had done so since she was a child, but she had no training and no technique to speak of.

To the right of the enormous bow window was a pastoral scene with a spotlight trained on it. It might have been an antique. Alison could not really tell. Below the canvas ran a broad white shelf that stretched along the full length of the showroom. There were a number of smaller paintings displayed there, mainly portraits, and she knew at once that they were old, sixteenth century, to judge from the style and the type of clothing. There was King Henry VIII, painted at the moment his glorious, golden youthfulness was changing into something more watchful and inimical. When Alison had been a child, his name had been used to frighten them all into obedience: "Behave yourself or old King Hal will come to get you." When she had been young she had had no idea what he had looked like but her imagination had supplied the image of a monster. She had seen hundreds of pictures of him since, of course. The English were proud of their infamous, spouse-murdering monarch. Distance had lent the sort of affection to his memory that had never been felt in her own time.

It was odd seeing Henry now, a relic, a throwback to her past. It unsettled her.

Alison's gaze travelled on to the next portrait on the shelf, that of a woman, standing, her hands folded demurely in that style so beloved of artists who wanted to persuade the viewer that Tudor womanhood was modest and decorous. The display light cast a shadow across her face. Alison strained closer to see. This was no one as instantly recognisable as Henry and yet there was a familiarity about her. It was a face she knew.

*Mary Seymour.*

Alison's breath stopped. There was a tight pain in her chest and a buzzing in her ears. Mary. After all this time.

She had never given up hope. It wasn't in her nature to despair, although she had come very close to it so many times. All the history books—those that mentioned Mary Seymour at all—said that she had died as a child. Alison had known that was not true but she had never discovered what had happened to Mary after she had left Wolf Hall.

*"Help me,"* she had said to Mary all those years ago. *"Help me to find my son. I'll come back for him. Leave me word…"*

She had not begged precisely; her relationship with Mary had been too prickly to allow her to show that vulnerability. She had phrased it as an order, but Mary had known. There had been a bargain between them. She had helped

Mary escape Wolf Hall and, in return, Mary had promised to help her.

Mary was the key to finding Arthur. She always had been and so Alison had held tenaciously to the belief that one day she would see Mary again.

And now she had.

Suddenly she felt faint with shock, trembling, tears pricking her eyes.

"Are you all right?" Someone was addressing her, a woman with a plastic rain hat and an anxious expression. She spoke in the tones of someone who feels obliged to offer help but sincerely hopes it isn't going to be needed. Alison forced a smile.

"I'm fine, thanks. I tripped over the edge of the pavement and winded myself for a moment."

The woman's sharp gaze scanned her face.

*She thinks I'm drunk*, Alison thought. She took a deep breath and pinned the smile on tighter. "No harm done," she said. "Thanks for stopping to check."

"Well, if you're sure…" The woman was already moving away, duty done.

Alison found that her hand was resting against the windowpane as though reaching out to touch the portrait within. She let it fall to her side and straightened up, pushing open the door and stepping from the dark street into the bright interior of the gallery. For a moment the harsh light dazzled her. Out of it came the figure of a man, summoned by the bell on the door. He was elderly, greying, with a stoop and leather elbow patches on his tweed jacket, but his eyes were bright, vivid blue, and he seemed to crackle with life and energy. Alison felt it at once, that force of personality that some people seemed to project effortlessly, lighting up everything around them.

"Can I help you?" He sounded surprised that anyone should have dropped in on a wet December evening.

"That portrait of a lady," Alison said. "The Tudor one…"

"Beautiful, isn't it," the man said.

Alison was taken aback. Had Mary been beautiful? Perhaps she had, although Alison had never thought so. She was the one whom men had admired. She had been curves to Mary's angles, rose to her sallow. She looked at the portrait again, trying to be dispassionate and to ignore the stirrings of old jealousy. She had never liked Mary. In the beginning she had hated her with a child's simple hatred. That had grown into a more complicated set of emotions as she grew up, but they had never been friends. They had been too different and too far apart.

The woman in the picture had features that were neat rather than beautiful: a long nose but delicate and not disproportionately so, arched brows above eyes of an indeterminate dark colour, a slight smile on the pursed pink lips. There was only the faintest hint of the hair colour beneath her Tudor gable hood though Alison knew it to be red-brown, like her mother's. Mary's gown was of sumptuous gold and green velvet embroidered with pearls. She looked to be a woman of substance. There were pearls on the hood too, and a space where one was missing. That was typical of Mary. She would not have noticed.

She realised that the man was waiting patiently for the question she had not yet articulated.

"It's lovely," she agreed. "The artist must have been very talented."

She saw him smile and realised that she had not quite been able to repress the spite. Mary, grown up, or at least on the cusp of womanhood, made her as jealous as Mary the child had once done.

She sighed. None of that mattered. What was important was that Mary had survived. Thrived, in fact, by the look of it. And that was good because Mary was the key. Mary had promised to leave word of Arthur for her, and Mary never broke her promises.

Alison felt it again then, the dizziness that was a mixture of hope and terror. She could not let herself believe that this time she would find Arthur. The crash of despair that had followed each time she had failed had been almost too much to bear.

"…unidentified." She realised that the man had been speaking all the time that she had been lost in the turbulence of her thoughts.

"Sorry," she said. "Did you say that the artist has not been identified or the sitter has not been identified?"

Now he was looking at her with concern. She caught a glance of herself in the mirrored wall behind the sales desk, all wet rat's-tails hair and pallid complexion. No wonder he was fidgeting with the display in front of him, fussily moving an ugly ceramic vase two inches to the left whilst he waited for her to take herself off. She could hardly fit the profile of a potential customer.

"The artist is unknown," he repeated patiently. "The sitter is Anne Boleyn."

"No," Alison said. She cleared her throat. "Sorry, but that isn't Anne Boleyn. It's Mary Seymour."

"It is Anne Boleyn." The man was still smiling in a rather determined fashion. He was charming. She didn't deserve such tolerance. "Tudor portraits aren't my forte," he said, "but I do know that this is a newly discovered portrait of Anne, authenticated only recently." He pointed to the background of the painting. It was dark and the shapes drawn there were difficult to decipher. "Can you see the box?" he asked. "It has her initials on it." Then, as Alison frowned, leaning forward to peer into the depths of the picture: "AB. For Anne Boleyn."

The box. *Her box.*

Alison could see it, now that he had pointed it out. It sat on a ledge to the right of Mary's head, only the very faintest sheen on its patina showing in the dark background. It would have been easy to miss, this clue, this promise.

*"See, Alison, I did not forget you. I have your workbox here, safe for you."*

She looked back at Mary's painted face, at the slight sideways glance that led the viewer's gaze to the wooden box and the bold initials. It had been made of walnut, she remembered, worn smooth over the years by the touch of her fingers. She had loved that box, storing any number of inconsequential items in it: her thimble, a length of ribbon, and a scrap of lace. She might have kept Edward's love notes in it had he written her any, but he had not.

"My godson could tell you more about it," the man said. "He was the one who discovered the portrait. He's written a book about it. He's speaking at the festival tomorrow night."

"Festival?" Alison said. She tried to get a grip. She felt strange, jittery. Although the shop was almost aggressively modern she felt closer to the past than she had done in years, disorientated and confused.

"There's a literary festival running all week," the man said. "Adam—my godson—is talking about the painting and about the Tudor court." He nodded towards Mary, serene under the dazzling lights. "It's all very exciting. Apparently, there aren't many portraits of Anne Boleyn."

"And this isn't one of them, I'm afraid," Alison said. Rain was seeping down her neck, making her shiver. Or perhaps the shivers were coming from elsewhere, somewhere far deeper inside.

There was a pile of flyers for the talk spread in an artful fan on the white shelf beside the portrait. She bent to pick one up.

"Adam Hewer," she read. "'Historian author and presenter, unveils the face of Anne Boleyn. Don't miss this exciting event, exclusive to the Marlborough Festival.'" There was a picture of a book cover for *Discovering Anne Boleyn* and a photograph of the author.

*Adam.*

Alison sat down abruptly in a flimsy-looking white plastic chair that she thought was probably part of an art installation. It creaked.

"You look quite done up," the gallery owner said kindly. "Can I get you a cup of tea? It helps, you know."

"I'm fine," Alison said automatically. "Just a bit tired."

Odd that it should be Adam, of all people, who should be the one to lead her to Mary. Or perhaps it was not odd at all. That sense of time shifting, the lure of the brightly lit window, the portrait… It had not happened by chance. When it came to fate and time she did not believe in coincidence.

She needed to think. She had to get away from the bright lights that were making her head ache with the buzz of too many discoveries, made too quickly. She dropped the flyer back down on the shelf where the edges curled up slightly in the heat of the lights.

"Thank you," she said. "You've been very kind but I'd better go now."

"Alison?"

Adam's voice stopped her when she was two steps away from the door. She turned slowly. It had not occurred to her that he might be there, listening, and now she felt a prickle of annoyance that he had not made his presence known sooner.

He looked older than she remembered, but not by much. It was a good ten years since they had met, but annoyingly Adam seemed to have aged better than she felt she had. He was tall, well built, with brown eyes that were a startling contrast to his fair hair, and had an air of restless energy that was familiar to her. With a sudden tug of the heart she realised he had become the man she had glimpsed in the boy she had known.

After they had split up, she had shied away from following Adam's career, although she did know that he was one of the new generation of TV historians, celebrity academics who travelled to exotic places to present the past in new and vibrant ways. As a breed they were young, good-looking, photogenic and formidably bright. Apparently, they made history accessible. That had always felt a painful irony to her. History was not accessible at all; at least she did not find it to be.

Adam came out of the office at the back and into the bright lights of the gallery, casual, hands thrust into the pockets of his trousers. "I thought it was you," he said. "How are you?"

He was smiling. Alison remembered the public-school charm, so like that of his godfather, which could smooth over the most awkward of encounters. It had bowled her over when first they had met reminding her painfully of the life she had left behind. She had clung to something that felt familiar in an alien world only to find that there was no similarity between Adam and the men she had known in her past.

Now she felt a disconcerting echo of that teenage confusion and she was cross with herself because there was a flutter in the pit of her stomach and a whisper of what might have been. Stupid, because what might have been had already happened: a youthful affair that had burned itself out.

"I'm good, thanks," she said, matching his effortless courtesy with what felt like abject gaucheness. "Just down here for a few days. I work in London now. But you—" She gestured awkwardly towards the flyers. "You're doing well. TV shows, writing…"

She knew she sounded inane but he merely inclined his head. "Thanks."

"It's what you always wanted."

She saw a flicker of expression in his eyes then, gone too quick to read. He said nothing. Alison was starting to feel hot and anxious. It had been a stupid thing to say. She knew nothing of what Adam wanted these days. She had barely known him ten years before and if she had realised she was going to meet him again today she would have been better prepared.

Butterflies fluttered again, trapped, beneath her breastbone. She needed to give herself some time and space to think. Adam's godfather—in an unusual breach of courtesy, Adam had not introduced him—had moved away, pretending to rearrange the paperwork on the sales desk, but she knew he was listening, wondering.

"Well…" She waved a vague hand towards the door. "I really must go. Good luck for the talk tomorrow. Not that you'll need it, of course."

"I heard what you were saying," Adam said, ignoring her words. "You don't think this is a portrait of Anne Boleyn."

Alison felt a sharp pang of disappointment, followed swiftly by a sort of anger at her own obtuseness. This was why Adam had come out to speak to her. It was not because he had wanted to see her. It was because she had raised questions about his work. The anger pricked her into speech.

"It's a portrait of Mary Seymour," she said, "the daughter of Katherine Parr and Thomas Seymour."

Adam paused for a moment, studying her face. There was a tight frown between his brows now. Alison waited for him to contradict her. She was already regretting her words; she should have gone back to the hotel, thought about what had happened, decided on what she should do next, rather than blurt out a statement that would only make Adam want to know more.

"I thought Mary Seymour died as a child?" Adam said.

Kudos to Adam, Alison thought. Most people had never heard of Mary Seymour, let alone knew what had happened to her. She did not know herself. Until tonight her search for Mary had drawn a blank. She had hunted her through books, archives, museums and galleries and had found next to nothing. Mary's had been a life almost completely lost from history. But the one thing that Alison did know was that Mary had not died as a child.

She shifted, aware of Adam's acute gaze resting on her. "She definitely survived into adulthood," she said.

"I assume there is evidence to support that?" Adam leaned against the edge of the sales desk and folded his arms. His tone was not disbelieving, but there was more than a hint of challenge in it. Alison felt a flutter down her spine. This was precisely the sort of conversation she should have avoided until she got her head together.

"I've seen other portraits of Mary," she said. "I know a bit about her. I researched her for some work I was doing…"

She could sense Adam's puzzlement. One thing he did know about her was that she was no historian. When they had met at summer school in Marlborough, she was a sullen teenager with a sponsored place on a tourism course. He had just accepted an offer to read History at Cambridge.

"Genealogy," she said quickly, forestalling his next question, making it up as she went along. "I was looking for some stuff on my family tree and found Mary. There's a distant connection between us."

She felt as though she was digging herself in deeper rather than out.

"Genealogy," Adam repeated. His gaze was narrowed intently on her now. He looked as though he didn't believe a word. "You never talked about your family," he said slowly. "You told me you couldn't leave them behind fast enough."

"That's how I felt at eighteen," Alison said. "People change." She fidgeted with the strap of her bag. "Look, forget I mentioned Mary at all. You've got a talk and a book…"

"And a TV programme," Adam said dryly. "All based on the premise that this is a portrait of Anne Boleyn not Mary Seymour."

Alison felt a flicker of sympathy for him. The discovery of a new portrait of Anne Boleyn was quite a coup and would bring Adam lots of publicity. She had planted a seed of doubt in his mind now and even though he knew she was not a professional historian, he could not risk making a highly visible mistake.

"It was authenticated," Adam said now, almost to himself. He straightened and pushed away from the desk, taking several strides across the gallery before turning back towards her, all repressed frustration and energy. "We found it with some other Tudor artefacts," he said. "There was no doubt about the dating. Then there was the box with the initials on it…"

"The box still exists?" Alison cut in quickly. "The one in the portrait?"

Adam stared at her. "Yes. Why?"

"Oh." Alison moderated her tone, realising she had sounded too eager. "I thought there might be something interesting in it, that's all. Something to do with Mary, I mean."

Adam was still watching her. It was unsettling. She had always thought she was a good liar but now she was starting to doubt it.

"There were some items inside," he agreed. "If that is indeed Mary Seymour in the portrait, I suppose they might have some connection to her." He did not elaborate and Alison knew it was deliberate. There was no reason why he would satisfy her curiosity.

Her heart was thumping. She could feel herself shaking. She knew she should not push this now but desperation was driving her harder than she had ever known it. Mary seemed only a breath away. And Arthur... What clues had Mary left her to Arthur?

"Where did you find the box?" she asked, and she could hear the quiver in her voice.

Adam shook his head. There was a faint smile playing about his lips now.

"I'll trade you that information—and more," he said, "to see the genealogical research you've done on Mary Seymour."

There was a small, deadly pause.

Alison knew she was trapped. She could not see any way that she could show Adam the work she had done on tracing Mary without disclosing her own history. He had been right: she had not told him a single thing about her family. She had never spoken of them. But they were all there on the pages of notes she had so painstakingly compiled. The Seymour family tree linked them together, tangled as the roots of the old oaks of Savernake Forest. They were all there: she, Edward, Mary, Arthur...

The silence stretched out whilst her mind scrambled for a solution, but then Adam shifted and smiled a condescending smile that made her itch to smack him.

"I thought not," he said pleasantly. "There is no research, is there?" He ran a hand through his thick, fair hair. "Look," he said, "I don't know why you've suddenly turned up after all this time, Alison, but there's really no point. I moved on a long time ago—"

"What? Wait!" Alison drew back. "Are you implying I'm here because I wanted to see *you*? I didn't even know about your talk!" She threw out a hand, narrowly missing the ceramic vase. "I came in because of her," she said, pointing at Mary's picture. "It was nothing to do with you—"

"Whatever." Adam raised one shoulder in a half shrug. "I'm not interested."

"Fine," Alison snapped. "Then I hope you don't find that some other person more academically credible than I blows your Anne Boleyn theory to smithereens."

She pushed open the door of the gallery and stepped out into the driving rain. She thought she heard Adam call after her as she slipped out into the dark but she did not wait, pulling up the hood of her jacket and hunching deeper inside it when the wind caught her with its icy edge. The disconsolate re-enactors were closing down their stalls and heading to the pub. A woman was wheeling a pushchair erratically across the pavement and was dragging a small child along with her other hand. He had toffee apple smeared across his face and was screaming.

Emotion pierced Alison deep inside where the hurt and the loneliness were locked away. She shuddered, blocking out the child's scrunched-up face and the mother's harassed scolding. Only fifty yards further along the wet pavement was her hotel. A small bay tree stood shivering in a planter on each side of the door. She hurried inside.

She'd chosen somewhere modern and exclusive rather than one of Marlborough's more traditional places to stay. She'd always found that embracing the present was the best way to keep the past at bay. Except that in Marlborough tonight the past had swept back in like a dark tide.

She was still shaking. She knew that rationally she could not blame Adam for thinking that she was only trying to stir up trouble, but rationality had nothing to do with the fury and frustration that welled up in her now. She felt the hot prick of angry tears against her eyelids. She had waited so long for word from Mary, each time she failed to find her, absorbing the blank wall of silence and the bitterness of defeat. And now here was Mary—and the box—and Adam was thwarting her attempts to get closer.

The winter storm was gathering, sending litter skipping along the gutters, dimming the Christmas lights with a fresh downpour of rain but, inside, the hotel was warm, opulent and lit discreetly by lamps with striped beige and cream shades. A smiling receptionist handed Alison her key. So often, Alison found light and warmth—the most basic trappings of modern life—gave her comfort and made her feel safe. Tonight, though, they only served to emphasise her sense of dislocation. So did the impersonal luxury of her room.

She dropped her soaking jacket on the floor and lay down on the bed, staring at the orange glow of the streetlights beyond the windows. She knew she did not have much choice. Adam had information she needed. He had the portrait, the box, possibly other artefacts connected to Mary. She had been waiting for five hundred years for news of her son. She could not let the chance slip now.

# TWO

*Mary, Wiltshire, 1557*

ALISON BANESTRE AND I WERE COUSINS OF A kind. We were both orphans. There the bond between us began and ended: Alison, my enemy.

We made a bargain, she and I. She helped me to escape; I helped her to find her son. It is entirely possible to bargain with an enemy if there is something that you both want and so it proved. Thus we were bound together through time.

We met at Wolf Hall. I came there in the summer of fifteen hundred and fifty-seven, in the fourth year of the reign of Mary the Queen. I was a Mary too, cousin of the late king, Edward, daughter to one dead queen and niece to another, with a famous name and not a penny to pay my way. I was ten years old and I already had a reputation for witchcraft.

"The child is possessed, your grace," the cook at Grimsthorpe told the Duchess of Suffolk when, at the age of five, I was found sitting under a table in the kitchens, holding a posset that had curdled. "That cream was as fresh as a daisy only a moment ago."

"Mary broke my spinning top!" one of my Seymour cousins wailed one day when the wooden toy was found to have split neatly into two halves like a cut pear. "She put a spell on it!"

That was the first time I realised that I possessed the magic. He had been tormenting me and I had hated him; the anger had boiled over within me and I had wanted nothing more than to teach him a lesson.

I did not want such power though. I wanted no more than to be ordinary, accepted. My mother, many years before, had been within inches of arrest for heresy. Witchcraft was but one strand of such blasphemy and dissent and the thought of following her fate terrified me. Yet I could not escape. It came with me to Savernake, the whisper of witchcraft, wrapped like a cloak about me, for I was different, other, an outsider, whether I wished it or not.

My name is Mary Seymour. I was born at Sudeley Castle but have no recollection of my nursery there, hung with red and gold, for almost as soon as I came into the world my mother left it. I'm told that my father had never anticipated that she might die in childbirth, which is odd since it is a common danger, particularly for a woman such as my mother, Katherine Parr, who was past the age when it was wise to have a first child or perhaps a child at all. But she was giddy for love of him and he was giddy for love of himself so I imagine they gave little thought to the consequences of their infatuation.

I was born. My mother died. My father professed himself to be so stunned by grief that he could not think straight. However he knew enough to realise he did not want the burden of a baby daughter, so he took me to London and abandoned me in the nursery of my aunt and uncle, the Duke and Duchess of Somerset, where I might have cousins with whom to grow up. It was a good plan, if a self-interested one, and it might well have turned out quite differently had it not been for his overweening ambition, which toppled over into treason.

My earliest memory was of being unwanted.

"What is to become of the Lady Mary?" My governess, Mistress Aiglonby, was the only one who, in the chaotic aftermath of my father's arrest for treason, pressed for my family to continue to care for me. I can still hear the wail of her voice rising above the sound of my belongings being packed away into boxes. I had no real sense of what was happening. I remember tipping my set of skittles out of the box again, spilling them all over the floor and tripping the nursemaid up as she ran about trying to fold my clothes into a bag that was too small. She was red of face and flustered, and looked near to tears.

"Lady Mary cannot stay here." It was my aunt, the duchess, who spoke. She had no warmth in her, least of all towards me.

"I agree it would be difficult to explain to her in the future that her uncle signed her father's death warrant." Dearest Liz Aiglonby. She could be tart when she chose. She had been one of my mother's maids before she became my governess. Her family were ambitious for preferment at court but that did not prevent her from defending me like a lioness.

"That was not my point." The duchess's tone had chilled still further. "Let her mother's kin take her in."

"The Parrs do not want her."

*No one wants her.*

My skittles had been a present from my father. They were carved into the shape of men, painted to look like sailors. I took one in my fist and neatly struck off the head of another with it. Or so I am told. In truth, I probably remember nothing of this, being too young, although it feels as though the memory is real.

"Lord Seymour suggested her grace of Suffolk…" Mistress Aiglonby sounded hesitant now and my aunt gave a brusque bark of laughter.

"Why would he do that? I thought he liked her?" Her voice changed. Malice rang clear as a bell. "Mayhap the rumours are true and she did refuse him and this is his revenge."

"Her grace was a close friend of the late Queen."

"Which does not mean she would wish to be saddled with her penniless child."

Yet to the Duchess of Suffolk I was sent, like an unwelcome gift, trailing my retinue of nursemaids, rockers, laundresses and servants.

Lady Suffolk was renowned for her piety but this did not mean she possessed generosity of spirit as well.

"The late Queen's child is too expensive for me to keep," she told anyone who would listen, but no one *was* listening, not really, not even parliament, which eventually restored to me all that was left of my father's property. This was practically nothing. So my expensive household was dismissed but for a few servants, and Lady Suffolk sent me to her castle at Grimsthorpe in Lincolnshire since I could live more cheaply in the country than in London.

I loved Grimsthorpe. The castle had been neglected since the visit of the old king Henry some ten years before and its rooms smelled of stale air and damp and secrets. There were locked doors and tumbledown walls, rambling gardens and endless woods under wide blue skies. Best of all, no one cared what I did so no one interfered. One of Liz's brothers came to tutor me sometimes, and Liz herself tried to instil in me the skills and lessons appropriate to a lady, but I was a stubborn child and had no interest in learning. I think that the Duchess of Suffolk might have tried to betroth me young had I even the smallest dowry, but as I had nothing but notoriety she knew no one would want to wed me.

How long my idyllic life at Grimsthorpe might have continued I do not know, for when I was eight years old the duchess and her fierce Protestantism fell foul of the Bishop of Winchester and she vowed to leave England for fear of persecution. There was no question that she would take me abroad with her. For a couple of years, I was shunted from pillar to post, from London to the country, from north to south, from court to church and back again. I was a nuisance. Queen Mary declared that I should be sent to one of my father's manors. Liz Aiglonby staunchly maintained I was too young, that I was the Queen's ward and her responsibility. Mary said dryly that the Seymours had begat me so to the Seymours I should go.

My uncle Somerset had followed my father to the executioner's block, so it was left to my cousin Edward, as head of the family, to provide for me. He and I were united in disgrace, the Seymours fallen further than they had ever risen.

It was then I first heard the whisper of that name:

*Wolf Hall.*

My first sight of the place was on a day of bright sunlight, but once we were within the forest of Savernake the sun vanished into darkness and the track seemed interminable and lonely. It felt as though we were arriving at the end of the world.

"What sort of a name is Wolf Hall?" Liz asked, as she placed my clothes in the big bound chest in the chamber I was to share with my cousin Alison. We had been welcomed warmly enough on arrival with bread, a little butter and some fruit although it was closer to dinner than breakfast time. Dame Margery, the housekeeper, had then shown us to my bedchamber and had vanished, although Cousin

Alison had remained. She sat in the window where the pale light seemed to shimmer on her flaxen hair. I had never seen anything so pretty in my life.

Liz sounded suspicious, I thought, as though she expected a wolf to appear from behind a tree and gobble her whole. She disliked the country and thought its inhabitants unruly and unpredictable, whether human, feathered or furred. Nor did she like Wolf Hall itself. The rambling old manor was even more run down than Grimsthorpe had been and here I was less than no one, and Liz, consequently, was nothing at all for all her London connections and service to the court.

"Wolf Hall is nothing to do with wolves," Alison said. She sounded faintly patronising. "It comes from the ancient Saxon name for the estate."

"Saxon!" Liz said. Her family had come over with the Norman King William. Her sniff of disdain left no room for doubt that she considered the Saxons even more barbaric than the present inhabitants of Savernake Forest.

Alison smiled, tossing her golden plait over her shoulder. She looked very Saxon herself with her cream-and-roses complexion and her blue eyes. There was a look of the late Queen Jane about her, or so I was told. Except that Queen Jane was pious and demure and Alison was never that.

Alison and I were only distantly related, but at Wolf Hall, I had already discovered that we Seymours were all jumbled up together, called cousins regardless of our relationships, abandoned here because there was nowhere else for the sprawling offshoots of the family to go. There were half a dozen of us children and I never worked out how we were connected other than through rejection or loss. There were two babies in the nursery; whose they were I never discovered. Closest in age to me was a boy of seven, but from the lofty heights of ten years, I considered him negligible. Then there was Alison, two or three years older, and above her in the pecking order, a sullen youth who boasted that he was soon to be sent away as squire in a knight's household.

Liz had turned her back as she laid out my linen shifts in the trunk. These had been worked with fine white lace and I saw Alison's gaze narrow on them and something cold and hard and inimical come into her pale eyes as she looked back at me. She could not have looked less like meek Queen Jane then.

"Those are very beautiful linens indeed," she said.

"The Lady Mary is dressed as befits the daughter of a queen," Liz said.

Alison's cornflower gaze swept over me. "Only beneath her gown," she said.

Even though I was only ten years old I was adept at reading what went on in the minds of men—and women—for my fate had often depended upon it. I knew that Alison resented me; that for all my notoriety and poverty, she was jealous because I had fame even though it was not of my own seeking. I was also adept at smoothing over discord so I slid from my chair and went over to her.

"Would you show me the forest?" I asked.

She looked scornful. "It would take days for you to see the forest." Her sharp gaze pinned me down. "We are forbidden from venturing there. It is dangerous."

"Why?"

There was a sudden silence and I realised that she did not know. She had never asked.

"It just is." Her head was bent. I could not see her expression. Her busy fingers were sorting through the skeins of thread in her workbox. She put aside the ones that drew my gaze—the red, the gold, the blue—and selected the brown and the black. "Besides we have no time for idleness here.

We clean and cook and sew and tend the garden and dairy and a thousand other things beside."

"Are there not servants to do such tasks?"

She gave a snort of laughter. "So speaks the Queen's daughter. No, *your highness*—" her mouth curved into a sly little smile "—we do not have that luxury here, at least not when Sir Edward is away. In his absence we make shift for ourselves."

I bit my tongue before I could make reference to Cousin Edward. Already she found me presumptuous. I would do nothing to antagonise her further. Instead, I slipped out of the bedroom when Liz's back was turned. I knew Alison would tell her she had no notion of where I had gone and if I got lost in the dangerous forest she would not mourn me.

I had not been at Wolf Hall long enough to know which chamber was which, but I ignored the blank doors staring at me and trod softly down the stair. Patterns of light and shade speckled the steps. The wood creaked beneath my feet and I hesitated, but no one came. I was accustomed to sliding away on my own, gone like a ghost. Although I had been hedged about by servants from the earliest age, I still managed to be a solitary child.

To my left was the Great Hall with its sloping stone floor, swept clean this afternoon and smelling sweetly of rushes. Behind me the chapel door, heavy studded oak, forbidding, warning of retribution within. But ahead was the passage and, at the end of it, the door was open into the garden and I was drawn irresistibly outside.

The gardens at Wolf Hall proved a delight, a tangled land of enchantment full of overblown roses and secret paths. Beneath the trees of the orchard I could see a harassed-looking goose girl trying to round up her flock. She was flapping as much as they. Over in the stable yard, I could hear the chink of harnesses and the murmur of voices. The air was full of scent and heat, and I wandered at will, lost in the pleasure of it.

The garden led to the wood. There was a half-open gate covered in ivy and a path beyond. Naturally, I followed it. I say naturally because I am drawn to the forest. I don't know why; people say it is a lonely, lawless place, but to me it is a safe haven in which to hide. One path led to another and another, some overgrown tracks, other wide avenues lined by trees that looked like the entrance to a manor far more majestic than Wolf Hall. I went where I willed, following a butterfly here or the sound of water there, running through the dappled shade, discovering new delights.

It was growing dark. I realised it suddenly, knew I had been out for a long time because I was hungry. There was a damp chill settling on my skin. The trees that had enchanted me now threw long shadows. The rustle of the leaves sounded too loud. The air felt still and watchful.

I had no notion which way was the road back.

Distantly, I heard the sound of hoof beats. My hopes lifted, for where there was a horse and rider there might well be a track leading to Wolf Hall. I scrambled through the under-growth, pushing aside bracken and nettle and grasses, fighting my way towards the noise. With each step the night seemed to close in. The hoof beats were growing louder and, as I stumbled out of the clutch of the thicket and onto a wide av-enue, they seemed to fill my head and make my entire body pulse. The earth shook. I fell, dizzy and sprawling, and lay there in terror, waiting either for the shout of fury from the rider or the crush of the horse's hooves.

Neither came.

The beat in my head eased a little and I dragged myself up onto one elbow and stared into the engulfing shade. Down

the long avenue, I could see the white shadow of a horse galloping hell for leather. In the saddle swayed the figure of a
woman. She looked as though she were about to fall at any
moment. Her cloak billowed out behind her, a fine velvet
cloak laced with silver thread, and on her head… But she
wore no hat and she had no face because above the line of
her collar she had no head, nothing but white bone, gleam-
ing in the last light, and deep red splashes of blood.

There was a jumble of light and voices about me. I was
not lost in the forest but lying in a bed. The tip of a feather
pricked my cheek and I turned my head against the pillow.
There was candlelight. It was night, and I felt hot and sickly
and wretched.

"Already nothing but trouble…" The lamentation floated
far above my head. I recognised Dame Margery's voice.
"Only here for two minutes and already we have had to
send out a search for her, and pay for a physician—"

"Pass me the bowl and the cloth." Liz this time, sounding snappish. "You heard what he said. She has the fever."

"She has only herself to blame, wandering around the
forest alone! She's like her father was, reckless and foolish.
She does not think about the consequences of her actions."

"She is a child who got lost, that is all." Liz was starting to
sound frayed. I thought it unlikely she would defend my father, whom she had never liked. It was my mother to whom
she had been devoted.

"Babbling about phantom horses and headless women!"
Dame Margery was not so easily appeased. "It sounds like
witchcraft to me."

"It's fever, no more," Liz repeated. I heard the rustle of
cloth as she stood. "I need fresh water."

"I'll come with you." Dame Margery sounded hurried

now, as though she did not wish to be left alone with me for fear of enchantment. "Alison can watch over her for a moment."

I had not realised that Alison was there. I opened my eyes a crack. She saw the flicker of movement and immediately she was at my ear.

"I hope you are satisfied, your highness." She smelled of peppermint and sweat. Her whisper was fierce. "Thanks to you, I have to share a chamber with the babies now whilst you lord it in here alone. I wish they had not found you!" Her face hung over me like a big red angry moon.

"It's true, there are phantoms in the forest," she said. "I think it was the black shuck you saw, a huge dog that brings death and madness to all that see it."

"It was a horse." My lips were dry. I felt hot, feverish, and my head was full of the nightmare but I was still stubborn. If I were to be terrorised by a phantom at least let it be the right one.

"A horse and a dead woman?" She laughed. "Mayhap is was Queen Anne Boleyn you saw then. If it had not been for *your* Aunt Jane she would not have lost her head. Maybe she is coming for you in revenge."

The sound of voices and the lifting of the latch warned her. She scrambled away and when Liz and Dame Margery re-entered the room she was sitting on the window seat all prim and quiet.

"She sleeps," she said sweetly. "May I go now?" And with that she slipped from the room leaving me with my feverish nightmares.

Darrell came to me that night as I was tossing and turning in my sleep. Darrell had been my companion, from the earliest time. He was more than a daydream or an imaginary friend. I knew from the start that he was as real as I; that we could talk to each other in images and thoughts and ideas. Such things are natural to children. We do not question. I did not know who he was. I assumed we must be related in some way, such gifts so often connecting members of one family, but I had so many relatives and when I looked around at the sprawling network of my Seymour cousins not one of them felt right. He told me his name was Darrell and even though he knew I was called Mary he called me Cat because he said I was small and fierce. I loved him; it was simple and comfortable because I had always known him. He felt almost like another aspect of myself, closer than close.

*"Cat. Are you there?"*

The words came to me, as they had always done, as a whisper sliding into my mind, calling me. From earliest childhood it had happened like this, first in blocks of colours and images in my mind and then, as I grew older, in words and emotions.

*"Where are you?"*

I ignored him, turning a shoulder as though he was in the room and I was shunning him. When I had been obliged to leave Grimsthorpe, I had called to him for comfort but he had not replied. I had been hurt, needing him and the comfort his presence brought. Yet sometimes it had been like this. He slipped back and forth through my life and sometimes when I needed him, he was gone. This was the first time he had spoken to me since I had left Lincolnshire and it was contrary of me to sulk when he was the one person who could make me feel better.

*"Cat?"*

*"I am at Wolf Hall."* I was short with him.

I felt his puzzlement before it cleared like rain clouds running from the sun.

*"Savernake? Why?"*

*"They sent me away again."* I was sick and feeling sorry for myself. I felt him laugh. Unforgivable.

*"Poor Cat."*

I sent him the mental equivalent of a rude gesture I'd seen the servants make and felt him laughing harder.

*"Such a lady."*

*"Go away."*

He sobered at once, sensing the genuine misery beneath my ill temper.

*"I'm sorry. Is it very bad?"*

This time I sent a shrug, a hardy sort of a feeling. It was bravado. He knew I was homesick and lonely and unhappy. He could sense it. I could not keep him out even when I wanted to do so. Yet I also knew that not so many years before he too had been sent from home. I had sensed his loneliness and isolation. I had tried to get him to tell me about it—had he gone to another household for his education? It was the way life ran for the sons of noble households and sometimes the daughters too. He would tell me nothing about himself, though, not then, not ever. He was a mystery to me.

*"There's the forest to explore. You love the forest."*

The thought felt eager and so like a boy, trying to offer solutions. If only he knew how much the forest had cost me already. Nevertheless, I had softened towards him. I could not help myself. He always made me feel better. There was comfort in his presence and I no longer felt so alone.

*"Yes. I suppose so."*

He sent me a boy's hug, clumsy, affectionate. I smiled. The warmth of it soothed me, lulling me back into sleep.

*"Goodnight, Darrell."*

*"Goodnight, Cat."* Goodnight, goodnight...

I slept.

# THREE

AS SOON AS MY FEVER HAD GONE, ALISON CAME back like nettle rash, irritating, never leaving me in peace. Of course I would not be ten years old for ever and Alison and I would not always be at daggers drawn, but just then it felt as though we would. For a little while we rattled around together like two cats trapped in a box, hissing, scratching each other, fighting on occasion, but over time we learned to live with each other. We kept a wary distance, although life at Wolf Hall did not make it easy to avoid her.

We were up at five, whether it was summer or winter. In the summer this was no hardship for dawn had crept into the room long before, but in winter I clung to the warmth of my bed for as long as I could. Naturally, Alison called me lazy. In order to eat we had to work, and the work started early. There was milk to be churned, pottage to be boiled, flax to be spun and carded, rushes to be peeled to make lights and rooms to be swept clean. I preferred working in the kitchen in the winter. At least there was a fire, whereas the damp chill of the forest crept like a ghost through the cracks and crannies of the old house. There was no idle chatter to accompany our work. This might be a nobleman's household, but whilst my cousin Edward Seymour lived the life of a courtier in London, we followed the older rules of life in the country.

I was lucky. I had time given to learning: languages, reading and needlework. So did Alison. The idea, I imagine, was that we should be settled creditably in marriage when the time came. Alison had no interest in book learning and neither did I really, but there were two things that kept me at my studies. The first was the knowledge that my mother had been a well-educated woman and I felt in some obscure way that I would be letting her down if I were to abandon my lessons. The second was more practical. I knew that time spent in study was time not spent washing, cleaning and pickling fruit, which I liked even less than book learning.

Going to the market in Marlborough was our treat. It was not permitted often, which made it all the more exciting. We had no need for the eggs, butter and cheese on sale there since we made our own, but Dame Margery would purchase meat and fish to augment our stocks and we would browse the stalls selling leather purses and belts, nails, knives, dead pigeons and coneys.

The day would start with the long cart ride into town, jolting over the rutted forest tracks. Dickon escorted us. He had fought alongside the late Sir John Seymour, Edward's grandfather, many years ago. On bad days, when his bones pained him, he would grumble that all he was fit for now was acting as nursemaid to a parcel of women. On good days, when the sun shone and the birds sang, he would whistle tunelessly as he rode beside us.

I loved the market for the noise and colour, the gossip and drinking, the smells and the sense of a bigger world beyond the brick walls of Wolf Hall. It mattered not to me that the cobbles of Marlborough ran with blood from the carcasses that hung on the pegs on the stalls, or that the sweet sickly smell of them mingled with the scent of ale and burning until Alison pressed her pomander to her nose and threatened to retch. When Dame Margery took her eyes off us I would slip away between the booths. The shouts and calls of the traders crashed like waves above my head as I wriggled between chickens in their cages.

"Good day, Lady Mary." It was the barber surgeon, pausing in the removal of a tooth to greet me.

"Hold still," he instructed the groaning man in the chair. "Take some more spirit to dull the ache."

The scent of cloves, the heat of a fire, the man screaming in pain: that was the world of Marlborough market as I remembered it. After a few hours, Dame Margery would round us up like sheep and take us back to the cart, where Dickon lounged with a flagon of ale, and we would jolt our way home. Dame Margery would be mellow and smell of meat pasties. I would doze as she regaled Alison with the gossip from the town.

One trip was different though. It was a hot summer day, too drowsy to do much except sleep. None of us wanted to exchange the cool shadows of the forest and the scented gardens of Wolf Hall for the rotting smells and flyblown stalls of the market. Dame Margery insisted, however. She was in a bad mood and was determined the rest of us would be unhappy too and so we took to the rutted roads, the journey almost shaking the cart apart, and arrived in town in the blazing heat of midday.

It was curiously quiet. There was no business for the barber surgeon, no business for anyone save the stalls selling ale. Dame Margery and Alison disappeared off to buy some gold and silver thread to embroider a shirt for Cousin Edward. He was due to visit Wolf Hall soon, a rare occurrence, and there was much excitement at the prospect. I wandered listlessly between the stalls where the vendors did not even trouble to glance my way. Some snored in the sun, others were drinking, everything was muted and still, and over the top of it all was the smell of the dung and the meat and the rot, strong enough to make my head spin.

I stumbled out of the crush of stalls and found myself a few paces down from the White Hart Inn. And there was Alison, poised in the tavern doorway, looking as though she were about to run inside. She was clad in a cloak of orange tawny, and her fair hair was dark with rain and I realised that I could feel the water on my face too. I was soaked to the skin and shivering, and the sky was dark grey and the wind was cold. I called her name and then I felt a touch on my arm. Her face swam into focus; she was shaking me.

"Hush! What is the matter with you? You sound crazed!"

The sun was burning hot and the sweat was running down my face, splashing on my gown. I blinked it out of my eyes. There was no orange cloak and no rain. People were staring. Alison looked furious.

"I swear you are a simpleton, Mary Seymour," she hissed, dragging me away, towards the cart.

"I saw you," I said. "At the inn. In an orange cloak."

"She is taking another of her fevers." Dame Margery was on my other side and between them they half lifted, half pushed me up so that I rolled across the floor of the cart like an ungainly barrel. "Either that or she is bewitched."

She made the sign of the cross.

"More likely she is a fool than a witch," Alison said, but she was looking at me very thoughtfully indeed.

*"Darrell."*

I reached out to him that night, tired, lost and lonely, but there was no response. I knew he always came back. But I needed him now and I sent the thoughts out through the dark, but received nothing back but a faint, lost echo.

I was in my twelfth summer when Alison started to disappear. One night I woke to discover that she was missing. Assuming that she had merely gone to the privy, I rolled over and fell asleep almost immediately. It happened again a few days later, and then again, and this time I forced myself to stay awake to see how long she was gone. I lost track of time; the moonlight crept across the ceiling, the floorboards creaked and settled, the mice scratched and I fell asleep waiting. In the morning Alison was asleep in bed beside me and made no reference to her absence the night before.

How long we might have gone on in this vein, I do not know, for Alison never explained herself and I never asked. I was not even sure she knew that I knew. One night, though, about a month in, the pretence unravelled. My curiosity had got the better of sleep at last and when I heard the sound of murmured voices outside I slipped out of bed and tiptoed across to the window.

It was high summer and the casement was wide, letting in soft air and starlight. Down on the terrace I could see two shadows merging. I heard a sigh, and laughter, quickly hushed. One figure broke away then and the other disappeared into the darkness of the garden. A door closed softly below; the dogs did not bark. I made a dash for the bed, bumping into the table and knocking the china jug to the floor in the process. It fell with a clatter that broke like thunder through the quiet house and rolled across the floorboards to smash against the wall. The dogs began barking then.

The chamber door flew open. Alison stood there, fear in her eyes. She cast a hunted look over her shoulder for behind her there was a babble of voices and the sound of footsteps. She was about to be discovered.

"Quick!" I hissed. "Into the bed!"

She leaped fully clothed and shod under the covers and pulled them up to her chin. When Dame Margery appeared, candle in hand, grey braids trailing, Alison was doing a creditable imitation of someone who had just been woken from sleep.

"What in the name of all that is holy is going on here?" Dame Margery looked like a terrier, brindled and growling.

I dropped a submissive curtsey. "Your pardon, Dame Margery. I knocked over the jug on my way back from the privy."

Dame Margery looked suspiciously from the pieces of broken china in my hand to the dark corners of the room, as though she expected to see some devil lurking. Again I saw her making the sign of the cross in my direction, a hasty and furtive guard against witchcraft.

I bit my tongue hard. I was no witch; I did not choose my gift and wanted none of it. It scared and angered me that she labelled me so. But my position at Wolf Hall was precarious beneath the veneer of my fame and status. I could not afford to anger Dame Margery.

"You may tidy it in the morning." She was brusque with me. "Back to bed now, and try not to cause any more trouble."

The door closed. The light was doused. I climbed back into bed.

"Why did you do that?" Alison's hissed whisper reached me out of the dark. "Why did you help me?" She sounded annoyed rather than grateful.

I decided to take it literally. "If I had not you would have been found out."

She was silent for a moment. I had not answered her question and I could feel her puzzlement.

"Don't tell anyone or you'll be sorry," she threatened.

I turned a shoulder and drew the covers up over me. I had already proved that I would not tell. There was no need for further words.

I heard her slipping off her shoes and the rustle of clothes before the mattress shifted and she lay back down. A few minutes passed.

"Did you see him?" she asked suddenly.

"No," I said.

She gave a sigh and a little wriggle. "He's lovely." Her voice had softened. "Oh, Mary, he is so handsome! I love him." She rolled over so that she was facing me. "Shall I tell you about him? About what it is like when I am with him?" Her voice was eager. I knew she wanted to talk but I did not want to hear it.

"No!" I said. "Tell me nothing. That way I can't be made to tell anyone else."

There was silence. I could feel her withdrawing from me. It had been our one chance of friendship and I had rejected it. She said nothing else but I felt her coldness.

Despite that, she was all glowing and bright through those hot summer nights, slipping off to meet her lover more blatantly now that she knew I knew and would say nothing. In the daytime she was dreamy and softer than she had ever been, almost kind. She looked buxom and ripe and she seemed always on the point of bursting into flower. I saw the way that the men looked at her and she saw it too and liked it. I was twelve years old, skinny and small and quiet. No one looked at me and I made sure it stayed that way. Not for me, midnight trysts in the garden or a tumble behind the orchard wall. I thought Alison foolish beyond measure.

Disaster came to her very quickly. One day I was called away from my duties in the stillroom and into the parlour. The page was voluble and excited, the courtyard swarming with men and horses.

"Sir Edward is here!" He told me as I followed him, wiping my hands on my apron in a hasty attempt to rub off the smell of oil. "He wants to see you at once."

As the parlour door swung shut behind me, I saw that there were four people in the room. Dame Margery was there, her long face sunk into grim lines I had not seen before. Beside her sat Liz Aiglonby. I looked to Liz for clues but for once her expression gave me nothing.

The two men were unknown to me. The elder was large, careless in his dress, with a high complexion and, I judged, a short temper. Already he was tapping his fingers impatiently. I did not care for the look of him.

The other was indeed my cousin Edward Seymour. Throughout my time at Wolf Hall, Edward had been an elusive presence, often rumoured to be about to visit us, but never appearing. Our house of misfits and orphans had been beneath his notice. But now he was here.

My cousin Edward had gloss. He had been brought up with the Boy King Edward, our cousin, and it showed. He was only a young man but confidence cloaked him. He was handsome too and, as I entered the room, he stood and he took my hand and kissed it in courtly fashion.

"Lady Mary. Cousin. I am happy to meet you."

I could have pointed out to him that he appeared to have been in no great hurry to do so but I did not, bobbing a curtsey, which gained a nod of approval from Liz.

"Sit. Please." He led me to a chair that was placed directly before the circle of inquisitors. "Dame Margery and Mistress Aiglonby are known to you, of course." His smile was charming. "This is our uncle Sir Henry Seymour."

"Lady Mary." Sir Henry inclined his head with a wintry smile. I could tell at once that he thought me of no account, being a woman and a plain one at that, but because of my name and our kinship he was prepared to show courtesy at least. There were men who said that Henry Seymour lacked the ambition of his brothers, my late father and uncle, but since they had lost their heads for it whilst he had garnered lands and offices, he was self-evidently the wisest of the three. He was certainly too grand and too important to have visited Wolf Hall during my time there. Now I felt his shrewd gaze assessing me.

"An ill-favoured maid to be the child of so handsome a man and so gracious a lady," he said now.

I saw Liz poker up with outrage but I felt nothing but amusement. Nothing could please me more than to be considered undistinguished. Notoriety had served my parents ill. Invisibility would suit me best.

"Mary will grow to be a beauty," Liz said stoutly, although she sounded less than certain.

I settled myself in the chair, folding my hands demurely in my lap. Dame Margery's frown deepened; she knew my docility was assumed and it was another reason she disliked me. She thought me sly when I was simply careful.

"Lady Mary." My cousin Edward sat forward, pleasantries over. "You share a bedchamber with Mistress Banestre?"

I nodded. His gaze grew sharper. "Does she ever bring anyone else to your chamber?"

"A man," Sir Henry snapped. "Has she brought men into her bed?"

I saw Edward shoot him a look of irritation. "Gently, sir. Mary is but a little maid—"

"No," I said bluntly, interrupting, "she has not."

"Have you ever seen her with a man?" Edward asked.

I thought of the night when I had seen Alison and her lover kissing on the terrace. I had seen nothing but shadows, no man.

"No," I said.

Liz sat back, the tension in her shoulders slackening. "See?" she said. It was directed more at Dame Margery than the men. "She knows nothing of it."

"Does Mistress Banestre ever slip out at night?" Sir Henry demanded. His colour was vivid now, like spilt red wine. He was drumming the fingers of one hand on his knee.

I hesitated.

"She does!" Sir Henry said triumphantly. "I knew it!"

"Since she is four months gone with child," Edward said with exasperation, "we all know she must have done."

Liz was watching me and saw the shock reflected in my eyes. "You did not know, did you, Mary?" she said gently. "You did not know that Alison was *enceinte*?"

"No," I said for a third time. I hesitated again. I knew little of pregnancy and childbirth but I was not completely ignorant. I had grown up in the country. I had seen farm animals mating and knew that people did it too. I had also been with the others to the Midsummer Fair, where maids and men would slip away with much giggling and touching and disappear into the bushes together.

"Has she been sick of a morning?" Dame Margery asked sharply.

"No," I said, once again. "Not that I am aware."

Dame Margery gave a snort of disgust. "It seems you have seen and heard nothing! All manner of things might have occurred but you would be in ignorance of them."

"Which is precisely as it should be," Liz said sharply.

"Has Mistress Banestre told you the name of her lover?" Edward picked up the questioning again. "Has she mentioned any man's name to you?"

I realised then that Alison must have refused to disclose the name of the child's father to them. She had told me that he was handsome, and that she was in love with him, but she had never told me his name.

"No," I said.

"You are a woman of few words, Cousin," Edward teased me. "Or perhaps you are a loyal friend."

"Alison and Mary are not friends," Dame Margery said, as though it gave her pleasure.

"Then she knows nothing," Liz said. "If it please you, sir—" she glanced at Edward "—she should be allowed to go."

Edward nodded. "I will see you at dinner, Coz," he said. "We have much to talk about."

But it was apparent that both he and Sir Henry were far too busy and important to stay to dinner for less than an hour later they were gone in a spatter of summer dust and clatter of hooves, their entourage with them, and silence settled on Wolf Hall once more.

I found Alison up in our chamber, dragging clothes from a chest and throwing them furiously into a smaller travelling box. She did not look so radiant now. Her face was puffy and tearstained.

"They're sending me away," she said briefly, answering my unspoken question. "I have to go to my aunt in Kent until after the baby is born."

"I didn't know you had an aunt in Kent," I said.

"I don't." She shrugged. "I made her up. I was damned if they were going to tell me what to do. I'll go where I please."

It sounded like bravado to me but I held my tongue. Alison in this mood was brittle and dangerous. I sat down on the edge of the bed and watched her take out her anger and frustration on her smocks and petticoats. "That disgusting old man—" One of the smocks ripped in her busy hands. "Sir Henry. He wanted to beat the name of my baby's father from me. He said I would scream it soon enough if they stripped me and whipped my back."

I winced. I had sensed that streak of prurient cruelty in Sir Henry.

"Why will you not tell them?" I asked.

For a brief second she looked utterly desolate. "I cannot. You don't understand. He…" She hesitated. "I promised him I would not."

"Is he already wed?" I asked. It seemed the only reasonable explanation, otherwise Cousin Edward would surely find the man and oblige him to marry Alison.

"No, he is not," she said.

"Then…" I waited. What barrier could there be then to marriage? It did not make sense to me. What sort of man, for that matter, would take his pleasure and then abandon Alison to the consequence?

"He is a great man." She spoke in a rush. "A lord. He cannot marry me. I am not—" She stopped but it was as though she had said the words aloud.

*I am not good enough.*

Her defiance returned: "It is no matter. I can manage on my own."

I said nothing. Could she? Alison was clever but she was a gently bred girl. It seemed unthinkable that she could survive alone. However, I had learned not to voice such opinions. They never seemed to find favour even if they were often true.

Alison finished packing the box and slammed down the lid, drawing the buckles on the straps tight. Then she stood looking at me a shade awkwardly.

"I don't know if I'll see you again," she said.

"No," I agreed.

She frowned. "You're a strange one, Mary Seymour," she blurted out. "Do you care for no one and nobody?"

I was taken aback. I'd never really thought about it. I cared for Liz. She had always been a part of my life and it felt impossible not to love her. I cared for Darrell too, with a sweet sharp pang of possessive pride because he was my secret. Yet beyond that I formed no real friendships and made no ties. Because I was rootless somehow I had understood instinctively that it was safer to remain so against the time when everything would change again.

"I'll miss you," I said, not sure if it was true but needing to find something to appease her.

She looked scornful. "Like a thorn in the side."

"Even so," I said.

"Liar," she said. All the same, she almost smiled. There was a moment when I thought she might even hug me but in the end she did not.

"Goodbye, then, Mary Seymour," she said, and she walked out of the room without a backward glance.

That night I lay alone in the bed I had shared with her. It felt strange. I did miss her.

I lay awake staring at the ceiling, the cracked plaster and the moving shadows. I wondered about Darrell. I had always thought he must be a cousin of mine, sharing the same gift as I, inherited in some distant past. I wondered if he could be Cousin Edward. It seemed impossible though; that distant, glittering figure, too fine for all of us at Wolf Hall, could surely not be my mysterious companion and friend.

Tentatively I whispered his name and felt the familiar pattern come through in return, the warmth, the love, the friendship.

*"Are you Edward Seymour?"* I asked.

I felt his laughter but he did not answer me.

# FOUR

*Alison, 1559*

"WHERE TO, MISTRESS?" THE CARTER ASKED.

They were bumping along the rutted track through the forest in the company of turnips and with the stench of manure. Alison drew her cloak closer about her face but it could not block out the smell, only make the world darker.

"Anywhere," she said, "as long as it is away from here."

She hated the forest. She hated Savernake. She hated Wolf Hall. Most of all she hated Edward Seymour with his lies and his hypocrisy.

"I will always love you," he had told her. "I will never forsake you."

What sort of fool was she to be so taken in?

"Bastard," she said aloud, but the words had a desolate edge. She had been taken in because she had allowed herself to be. She had dreamed a dream of marriage and restoration to her place in the world. She had loved. She had hoped.

She saw the carter casting a look at her over his shoulder before he coaxed to horse from walk to amble.

*Careful.*

He would talk, in his cups, about the pregnant wench from Wolf Hall who had been sent away in disgrace. Likely he knew of her already. She had to follow the plan proscribed for her or word might get back to Edward. Not that he would care. She was off his hands now. The entire Seymour family were good at picking up and discarding their relatives as it suited them.

"Marlborough," she said, with a sigh.

"The castle?"

"The White Hart."

The tavern was the place where the coach sent by her aunt was supposed to be waiting to convey her to Kent. There was no coach, of course, just as there was no aunt, but it had pleased her to pretend to Edward that she did not need his help. He had given her guilt money, enough for the journey and more. She could survive on her own. She had done so after both her parents had died of the pox and her brother and sister with them. Both the manor and the village of Hartmere had been decimated. It had been weeks and weeks before anyone had ventured to look for survivors and found her, foraging for food whilst her family rotted upstairs in the fetid heat of summer. She had been six years old.

Now she was sixteen but the emotions were the same; the fear so great she could only look at it out of the corner of her eye in case it would swallow her whole; the determination that the fear would not win no matter how monstrous. Now she had something else to survive for too: the babe growing inside her. She had to be strong for her child.

At first she had thought she might get work making lace or pins. There was plenty of industry in Marlborough, though most of it was too crude for her, the tanning of hides and the spinning of coarse cloth. But she had a talent for embroidery and sewing and she had been well taught. Then she had realised that it was too dangerous; someone would see her. Edward would hear of it. But the world was a big place and she should have bigger ambitions. There was Salisbury, or Bath, or London, where she could lose herself amongst the thousands of others. London appealed to her; she had heard that a man—or a woman—could make a fortune in that febrile, exciting society that felt so different from anything she knew.

She would be able to keep the child if she was brave and followed her plan. Her hand strayed to her swollen belly. She had tried to hate the baby for ruining everything but to her surprise she had failed. Accustomed to thinking herself cold, she had found nothing but maternal warmth towards the unwanted child. It was hers and she loved it fiercely. If she were honest with herself, and she had no wish to be, she had loved its father as well. Loving him had been a mistake but perhaps she was not as strong as she liked to imagine herself. That, however, was no way to think when she was facing the future alone.

She thought of Mary then. Mary was lucky and the thought turned Alison's stomach sour as it always did. Mary might be an orphan, but her status as the late Queen Katherine's daughter would protect her for as long as there were people to remember it. Even if they did not care, the Seymours had to be seen to do right by her. They would provide her with a dowry, or the Queen would grant her an estate, or perhaps two. Alison closed her eyes and rested her head against the hard wood of the side of the cart. The Seymours might once have provided *her* with a modest dowry to encourage some rustic squire to take her to wife, but not now. She told herself she was glad and swallowed the bubbles of unhappiness that rose in her throat.

The cart crossed the river by the stone bridge, turned right into the high street and rolled past the town cross, weaving across the street to avoid a pile of brushwood stacked haphazardly in front of a house. Craning her neck, Alison could see the mound, with its tumbledown castle atop, cutting the skyline to the west. The castle belonged to Edward too, but since his father's fall from grace he did not have the funds to restore it and it had been slowly decaying for at least a hundred years. It was said that the mound beneath contained the body of the wizard Merlin, which Alison thought was a ridiculous idea. People were very credulous. Never had she believed in magic. Dame Margery babbled about witchcraft because she was frightened of life, of those matters she could not explain. Alison had always considered life to be mundane and without any sort of enchantment except perhaps of the sort she had briefly found in her lover's arms.

This was the end of the town where the tannery was situated and Alison drew a fold of her cloak across her face, trying in vain to blot out the smell of dung and urine and blood. Her stomach lurched with sickness. She had eaten nothing and so there was nothing to bring up; a blessing perhaps.

"We are at the White Hart, mistress."

The cart had stopped. The horse waited patiently, the carter less so. He had errands to run. He did not offer to help her down and when she jumped, it was awkwardly, hampered by her pregnancy and the full skirts. She gave him a penny and no thanks.

There was no waiting coach in the inn yard. For all his haste, Alison could feel the carter pausing to watch her so she walked nonchalantly under the arch of the gatehouse and through the open door into the hall. It was dark enough to make her stumble after the light outside and the smoke from the open fire caught in her throat. A woman was standing by the hearth, stirring one of the pots that was hanging over the flames on an iron frame. A wooden hourglass stood on the table to the right of the fire. The sand in it had almost run through.

The woman glanced up as Alison came in. "There's no work here. Not for the likes of you." Quick to judgement. Her gaze flickered over Alison's stomach making her meaning explicitly clear. Like the carter, she knew. She had heard about the Seymour cousin, who was no more than a trollop.

"I am waiting for a coach to London," Alison said haughtily. "I will sit if I may."

The woman tossed her head. "Sit if you want."

*Go to hell if you want,* Alison thought.

The woman offered no refreshment.

The bench was of wood but made slippery by the cushions balanced on its narrow surface. Alison sat gingerly. What now? She was waiting for a coach that would never come and, judging by the sly look in the landlady's eye, the woman knew it.

A sudden clatter from the yard outside, the sound of voices in some imaginative curses, the splintering of wood made the woman exclaim and sent her hurrying out of the door towards the buttery, wiping her hands on her stained apron as she went. Quick as a flash, Alison slid off the bench and hurried over to the pot. Beef stew; it smelled good now that the nausea had subsided. She tried a spoonful, then another. Too hot, it scalded her mouth.

There was the sound of a latch lifting across the other side of the hall.

*Caught.*

She turned. The wind blew the smoke sideways, setting it swirling in the draught flowing between the two open doors. For a moment, Alison was blinded by it, eyes stinging, head aching. The world jolted as though she had missed a step in a flight of stairs and tripped over an unseen obstacle lurking in the dark below. She moved instinctively towards the door, seeking light and air and clarity.

The darkness cleared, the smoke disappeared. She was out in the street, but it was a different street in a different place completely. The sunlight was bright enough to make her shade her eyes. The air was full of noises. They assaulted her; shouts, crashing sounds, a roaring she could not begin to identify. Everything was shockingly intense, frighteningly loud and utterly unfamiliar, spiralling outwards into a spinning top of sensation. Her knees sagged. Her heart pounded.

"Are you all right, love?" A woman with a broad West Country accent had stopped in front of her. She was wearing very few clothes, legs and arms exposed, brown as a nut and wrinkled. It was disgusting.

"You should take it easy," the woman said. "You can't go rushing about in the hot sun when you're pregnant, not in fancy dress like that." She pushed something into Alison's hand, a bottle, made of a clear substance, not glass but something lighter.

"Drink it," the woman said. Then, impatiently, meeting Alison's blank gaze. "It's only water, for God's sake. I'm not trying to poison you."

"I…" Alison did not know what she was trying to say but the sound was lost in a roar of noise as some sort of vehicle drove past. Beyond it Alison saw the façade of a house that looked familiar with its jetties and steep gabled roof. Familiar and yet different; the distortion was like looking through a glass window at something she knew and yet no longer recognised.

Alison dropped the bottle on the stone at her feet. It bounced. She turned and ran, back through the door of what had been the tavern. Immediately, the sound died, shut off, the silence so loud it hurt her ears. The landlady was stirring the pot over the hearth. The smoke still stung her eyes.

"There you are," the woman said. "There's a man in the yard outside asking for you. Seymour livery." There was a grudging respect in her tone now.

Alison sank down onto the cushioned bench and raised a hand to her head. She could feel the sweat, sticky and hot, at the roots of her hair. She had no idea what had happened to her; whether she was mad, possessed, or sick. Perhaps those fools who believed in enchantments were not such fools after all. She had seen… What precisely had she seen? She had no notion.

"Mistress Banestre?"

Edward's squire did not look best pleased to have been obliged to come looking for her. He was a dark, surly fellow with a sly expression in his eyes. Alison had seen him before. Edward used him to arrange his amours.

"She's sick," the landlady said, sounding pleased and important. "It's too hot for someone in her condition to be travelling."

The man's gaze flicked over Alison carelessly. It told her that he had seen plenty of light women come and go and her condition was by no means unusual.

"She'll manage," he said, "if she wants to please Sir Edward."

"I was not expecting you," Alison said coldly. "Sir Edward did not mention sending a carriage."

The man smirked. "Aren't you a lucky girl, then? Sir Edward's changed his mind. He's not done with you yet."

He put a hand beneath her elbow, levering her to her feet, steering her towards the stable yard. His grip felt like a manacle on her arm. Suddenly Alison was desperate to escape. She could not give herself to Edward again when he treated her with such contempt.

She threw a glance over her shoulder towards the other door, the one out into the street. What future lay behind that one in a place so foreign and strange? The servant had her in a tight grip, half dragging, half lifting her towards the carriage and, suddenly, now that it was too late, Alison wished she had found out. She struggled but the man only laughed. And then the door slammed and the darkness closed about her.

## Mary, 1560

I missed Alison. It surprised me. I was growing up and the gulf between the younger children and me seemed accentuated by her departure. Wolf Hall was quiet. No new waifs or strays came to take Alison's place. My lessons with the chaplain and with Liz Aiglonby continued and, in between, I avoided Dame Margery and spent any spare moment in the forest.

I had never been afraid of the forest despite the nightmare that had been my introduction to its secrets. Forests were full of concealment and surprise and I had known that from the beginning. I took delight in exploring Savernake. It was by no means an empty land. It seethed with people: Sir Edward's rangers, the foresters, the villagers whose pigs grubbed for nuts in the undergrowth in the autumn, the poachers who risked their lives to take the Queen's deer, the thieves, gypsies, runaways, witches. I saw them all and avoided them as much as I could, slipping between the trees like a wraith, like a hind.

Now that I had a bedchamber to myself, it was easy enough to slip away at night, simply by climbing down the ivy that covered the old brick wall of the manor. I knew every ancient oak in the forest now including the one that marked the boundary of Edward's land with its huge bulging belly. It was rumoured to be the oldest tree in the woods, already ancient when the Conqueror had claimed Savernake along with the rest of the kingdom, a tree in possession of old magic. I had heard Dame Margery whispering to the scullery maid, with many gestures to ward off evil, that the witches sought its power to summon the devil. I could imagine that they did and I shuddered to think of it. Old magic was dangerous and unpredictable. Even though I had never dealt in it myself, I had an instinct for it, never knowing where my knowledge had come from, only knowing that I saw and heard things that others did not. However, the threat of heresy, of witchcraft, haunted my every step. I thought of my mother and longed for an ordinary life, free of visions, untouched by magic.

One day, when I had tired of my lessons with the chaplain, who was even more tedious than usual, I asked permission to visit the privy and rather than return to the schoolroom went instead out into the garden and through the orchard gate into the forest. It was high summer, hot and heavy. The closeness of the air made me want to sleep. I followed a track through the dreamy woods, until I came to the top of hill where another of the old oaks grew, the Duke's Vaunt, named for my uncle Protector Somerset, who had liked to hunt here. From there the view was wide out across the tree-tops and down to the cottages below, where a number of youths and maids cavorted naked in the pond, their shrieks of excitement and pleasure floating up to me. What I saw of their sport made me feel even hotter and I plunged back into the woods feeling that I was spying. Instead, I found a warm clearing used by the charcoal burners for one of their kilns. The sun cut through the trees and the wild raspberries grew and I sat down to eat some. They were sweet and burst on my tongue like sunshine and I ate too many, greedy for them, until my tummy ached.

I must have fallen asleep after that, although I don't remember. I do remember waking because it was sudden and frightening and there was a pain in my head that felt like a shout.

*"Cat! Wake up!"*

It was Darrell.

*"Danger to you. Run. Hide..."*

I didn't question. Already I could hear it, the clash of steel on steel, brutal, closer by the second. I dived through brambles, cowering behind the widespread roots of a nearby tree, shaking.

They had reached the clearing. There were only two men, for all the noise and fury, but they fought with a ruthless intensity that was terrifying. I watched through the veil of bracken and nettle. The light glanced off the sword blades in a run of fire. The crack of metal on metal bounced off the trees. It was not like anything I had seen before; I'd seen men fight, in practice, as a game, even in earnest when blood ran too hot, but it had not been like this. These men were dressed strangely and their swords were like none I had ever known.

The conflict was as brief as it was brutal. The shorter and stockier of the two men was lighter on his feet than his bulk might have suggested. He parried a blow aimed for his neck and counter-attacked, dancing forward on the balls of his feet, beneath the guard of his opponent to slide his blade between his ribs.

Blood spurted. The stench of it made me want to retch. I had seen wounds before. I had even seen death in my short life. It was ever present in the pecked corpses that hung from the gibbets at crossroads to the beggars dying in the filth of the gutter. It stalked childbirth and shadowed every step we all took. It had taken both my parents before I was a year old. Yet to witness such violence in death was still unusual for me.

The murderer looked around quick, furtive, and then dragged the body roughly towards the kiln. As I heard the crack of bones, I stuffed my hand into my mouth, biting down on my knuckles to crush my screams. He was trying to push the corpse into the furnace, which glowed with the sullen light of old burning, but the body would not fit. Finally, with much cursing under his breath, he managed to wedge it inside. Grey smoke belched suddenly from the open roof. Soon, I knew, it would start to smell of burning flesh.

Despite my attempts to keep still and quiet I must have made a sound. I was shaking, my hand pressed to my mouth to keep the sickness down. The murderer's head came up. He turned slowly, like a hunting dog scenting the air. I saw his face clearly then, the lank hair darkened with sweat and his narrowed blue eyes. He withdrew his sword from the corpse, cleaning it with great deliberation on the grass. Then he took a step towards my hiding place and I flattened myself even closer to the roots like a cowering mouse. There was no sound but the slam of my heart against my ribs as I waited for him to find me. I could feel Darrell with me. He was afraid also, but there was anger in him too, and frustration, and despair. His feelings seemed to sweep through mine, merging with them, flowing like a tide. Any moment now I knew we would be discovered.

The ground vibrated the same way it had when I had seen the apparition of the woman on horseback only this time the noise was louder, the vibrations more intense. The man's head snapped around. His breath hissed in on a fierce whisper.

"King's men!"

He ran.

The air was full of noise now, the thunder of hooves raising dust from the track. I saw the flash of men through the trees, cavalry, with buff coats and crimson sashes, a whole column of them. I waited until they had gone and the world had turned quiet and then I waited some more. I could not have moved had I wished it. I was paralysed with terror and confusion.

Stiffly, I stood and stretched, feeling the tension slowly leach from my body leaving me exhausted. Darrell had gone. I felt light-headed, as though my mind was empty.

*King's men…*

Yet we had a queen now, Elizabeth, and before her another queen. There were no king's men in England any more and had not been for more than a decade.

I walked home very slowly along the track. It didn't occur to me that the riders might return. I made no attempt to hide. The forest was in one of its silent moods when it felt as though nothing lived, nothing moved in it. I felt dizzy and drained of emotion. I placed one foot in front of the other and thus I got back to Wolf Hall.

"You imagined it, lovey," Liz said later. I was lying on my bed and she was stroking my hair, soothing me, as though I were still a child. "Doubtless you were asleep and dreaming. Raspberries can give you nightmares."

All the raspberries had given me was an ache in my stomach. However, I said nothing. When I had arrived back at Wolf Hall I realised for the first time that my skirts were in shreds and that there were leaves in my hair and dirt on my face. I had had to come up with some explanation and I thought it best to stick as closely to the truth as I could. So I said that I had witnessed a fight in the woods and seen a troop of soldiers, and had run from them in terror.

I had not, however, foreseen the consequences of my words. There was uproar. The foresters were called out and word was sent to raise the villagers to arms. The whole of

Savernake was scoured for these intruders who threatened the Queen's peace.

I knew they would not find them. I knew they had not been from our time. Like the nightmare vision of the galloping horse and its headless rider they were apparitions from another present, one that I could not explain, but no less dangerous for all that. Such spirits would have been sufficient, indeed, to set Dame Margery off crossing herself and muttering against the devil but fortunately she was occupied in making sure that there were sufficient provisions for the men hunting my ghosts.

"There are no soldiers," one of the foresters groused as they came in late in the afternoon, hot, angry, spoiling for a fight. "The maid imagined it all. The kilns are all cold and there is no body of a dead man half burned."

I was in disgrace. I did not care as I wanted to be alone to talk to Darrell, but when I tried to find him he was not there. My call to him echoed emptily through my mind with no reply. Perhaps he thought I would nag him with questions, for there were so many things I wanted to ask; how had he known I was in trouble, had he seen what I had seen? Disconsolate, I put my head down on my pillow and closed my eyes.

*Thank you.* I sent the message to him anyway and felt the faintest of acknowledgements, so brief it was like a flutter across my mind, yet as warm as an embrace the same. I had the sense not to ask for more. I smiled and fell asleep.

# FIVE

---

*Alison, 1560*

SHE AWOKE TO FIND EDWARD TOUCHING HER. He insisted that she sleep naked for this very purpose, so that she was always available to him, even though sometimes she lay awake for hours shivering in the cold. Even when he did not come to her she was obliged to remain uncovered in case he should decide to visit her bed after a night spent carousing on the town. He would roll in, his breath smelling of wine, and demand that she open her thighs for him. No preamble, no words of love. At least when he was not drunk he made some pretence at arousing her first.

His hands swept over her breasts and down across the curve of her stomach. She felt nothing, nothing but an anger that grew with each day. She wanted to go to the privy but she did not dare leave the bed.

She had been such a fool. She should have run away when she had the chance that day in Marlborough. She would have survived somehow. At the time she had told herself it was all for the best; as Edward's kept mistress she lacked for nothing.

She had had the baby to consider as well. It was vital that she protected them both. She had thought Edward would do that.

How she regretted her weakness now she was so demeaned, helpless, of no account. Edward rolled on top of her. It was all over quickly and clumsily. With the amount of wenching he indulged in, she would have expected him to be more proficient by now. Odd how it had all seemed so enchanting before Arthur had been born. She had been in love with him then though.

He stood up, leaving her lying splayed on the bed, the cold air washing over her.

"You return to Wolf Hall today," he said.

She gaped at him.

He shrugged on his robe and poured wine for himself, refusing to look at her. Outside, the chatter and clatter of London was all around but Alison heard nothing of it. Her head buzzed.

"I am to wed." He was still avoiding her gaze. A line of colour stung his cheek beneath the beard.

She felt as though she could not breathe. Had she really thought that he would marry her? Had she still dared to hope for it? How much more of a fool could she be, when he had refused to acknowledge her, hidden her away, bound her to silence, taken her son away?

She dragged the covers over her, her entire body chilled. "Who is she?"

He shook his head. "I cannot tell you. It is a secret."

More secrets. They ruled him. She wondered if he had asked the Queen's permission or if that was where the difficulty lay.

Stubborn hope lifted in her heart though. Perhaps this was a political match and after a little while he would send for her again. In the same moment she felt fury, with herself, with him. How much more misuse would she accept? She could no longer fool herself that this was best for her—or for her child.

"In a few months I will find you a husband too, give you a dowry." He was looking eager now, almost pleading. "Someone who is…" He stopped.

Not too particular? Alison thought savagely. Prepared to accept his discarded mistress if the pill was sweetened with enough money? She could not pretend any longer. There was a bitter taste on her tongue. She had chosen this, humiliated herself for a security for herself and her son that had proved an illusion.

"What about Arthur?" She made herself ask although she already knew the answer. Arthur had been taken from her as soon as he had been born. For a little while, Edward had indulged the pretence that she would see him again when he was weaned. It was the way things were done, he said. She was a lady not a wet nurse.

The truth was that he had wanted her all for himself. She had been his plaything and the child had been a nuisance. Now Edward no longer wanted either of them. So she had go.

"Arthur stays with me," Edward said.

Alison clutched the sheet a little tighter.

"But I will see him?" she said. She could hear the begging in her voice.

"It's better you do not."

Her fingers ached from her grip on the sheet. She did not notice. Her head ached too, a sharp stabbing pain behind the eyes, but she blinked it back trying to concentrate.

"Better for whom?"

Edward looked surprised. "For Arthur, of course. I will place him in a noble household when the time comes. He will want for nothing."

*Except a name and a mother's love*, Alison thought. The pain had spread to her throat now. It felt like a blade that threatened to cut her if she swallowed. Her chest was too tight.

"It will be better for you too." Edward refilled his cup. Some wine splashed, red as old blood. "It will be a new start."

Fury spurted up in her that he thought her memories, her love for her child, could be so easily discarded. The callous arrogance of it stole her breath.

"You mean that my new husband would hardly want to be saddled with another man's by-blow as a constant reminder of his wife's lack of chastity," she said.

Edward looked shocked, more so at her crudity than the sentiment. He did not reply.

Alison sat up and reached for her robe, needing to protect herself against the thought, against her lover, against her own weakness. She felt powerless. If she went against Edward's will he would throw her out onto the street as carelessly as a pile of rags, justifying his actions by accusing her of ingratitude. But she would never give Arthur up. As well rip her heart out. Nor would she marry a man of Edward's choosing. She had absolutely no intention of being parcelled off to some yeoman farmer in order to tidy her away. She was a gentleman's daughter even if he was long dead and she had come down in the world.

Now was not the time to show defiance though. She would need to be cunning and bide her time. And she would need to be brave too and show more backbone than she had done so far.

"It will be pleasant to see Wiltshire again, I suppose." She forced the words out. "Though I shall miss you, my love."

He looked gratified and bent to kiss her. The contempt rose in her throat. He was so gullible.

"I shall need some new clothes." She pressed her advantage.

"You will have a trousseau ere long." He was not as much of a fool as he looked.

"Just one new gown for winter." She busied herself about the room, looking, planning. How much could she take with her to Wolf Hall? Edward would probably be quite generous if she were prepared to go quietly and would overlook the odd item that went missing, though her thefts would have to be small. A few silver dress pins, the pomander encrusted with emeralds, perhaps even his gold crucifix since it was a sign of nothing but his hypocrisy. It was not as though he had ever been generous with gifts. He owed it to her. And one day soon it would enable her to make a new start.

She had nothing. She felt her shoulders slump as despair took her. She was less than nothing. But this misery was why she had not had the courage to leave him before. It cast her down when she most needed to be strong. It would not win this time. She had had enough of being used and she wanted something better.

"I shall be ready to leave within the week," she said, and was rewarded with another quick, clumsy kiss, the prize for being complaisant. When he took a purse out of his pocket and extracted a few gold coins, she felt a flash of triumph.

This was where it began. This was where she started to take back.

## Mary, December 1560

That winter, Alison came back. She had changed. I think perhaps I had imagined that she would not return. She had slipped from my mind like a wraith, lost beneath the detail of day-to-day life until suddenly one frosty morning she was standing by the bare hawthorn hedge, one hand on the gate, wearing a new woollen riding hood of orange tawny. She saw me and smiled, half raising a hand in greeting before she pushed open the gate and came up the path towards me.

It was an odd moment. I felt an impulse to run to her and embrace her though I had no notion why. She dispelled that quickly enough, however, offering a cool cheek for my kiss, in the French fashion. She was seventeen years old now to my thirteen and I felt gauche in the face of such elegance.

"You are home!" I said, although I doubted that Alison, any more than I, thought of Wolf Hall as her home.

"Only until I wed." She was examining the stitching on her gloves, not meeting my eyes. "Lord Seymour has found me a husband."

Our cousin Edward had been restored to his earldom the year before and was even more grand now and further beyond our reach. He had been building a new house a few miles distant at Tottenham; Wolf Hall being too old and inconvenient for him. I wondered if the new house, and his plans for Alison, meant that he would be spending more time at Savernake.

"You're to wed." I parroted her words, knowing I sounded simple. There was so much I wanted to ask her but could not. She did not have a child with her. I wondered what had happened to it. Was it a boy or a girl? Where had she been, and with whom? Who had paid for the beautiful orange tawny? Cousin Edward, perhaps, since it appeared he wanted her well turned out for her marriage. Alison's silence prevented me from blurting out any questions though. There was a wall of reserve about her and she had withdrawn behind it.

There was no suggestion this time that Alison and I should share a chamber. Suddenly she had become an adult, elevated above me. She was excused any work and spent much of her time in a huddle with the other women, talking about mysterious matters ranging from the assembly of a trousseau to the management of a household. Perhaps Liz might have thought it would be useful for me to listen and learn but, often as not, I was not invited. Dame Margery and Alison were still close as two peas in the pod and since neither of them liked me much, I was left out. I did see some of Alison's new clothes: the scarlet wool petticoats, soft and warm, which I envied, and the fragile silk-lined slippers, which seemed a pointless extravagance. Alison's future husband was a well-to-do yeoman but there was no question that she would need practical clothing in which to work.

"Do you like Master Whitney?" I asked her one day. We were in the solar and it was raining, the water running down the diamond panes like tears. For once, I had been included in the group. We were trying to embroider in the dim grey light of winter, with only one sputtering candle to aid us. My eyes smarted.

Alison let her hands rest in her lap as she looked up. "He is well enough. Liking has nothing to do with marriage."

"He likes you." Dame Margery dug her in the ribs, letting loose a raucous laugh. Alison gave a pale smile in return. It did not seem to please her that her future husband lusted after her but Dame Margery was right. Even I had noticed the hungriness in his eyes when he watched her. I could not have borne for him to touch me. There was something perpetually angry about him and it felt dangerous. I'd heard he had an uncertain temper and I thought Alison was making a mistake. Not that she had a choice.

"He is wealthy and of good standing," Alison said. "I could not hope for better."

There was an odd silence. She had sounded almost wistful.

"But you are a gentleman's daughter," I said. "Surely…"

She looked at me hard, though she said nothing, and I knew that she was thinking of the scandal of her pregnancy.

Yes, I had been tactless. Not many men would have been prepared to wed her when her chastity was so clearly compromised. I wondered if Edward had paid Whitney handsomely to overlook it.

"You will find," she said, after a moment, "when it is your turn, that being the daughter of a queen and a gentleman avails you nothing if you have no fortune or…beauty…to speak of. You will take what is on offer and be glad of it."

I knew I would not.

"I do not wish to wed," I said hotly. "I cannot see that it makes anyone very happy, so why do it?"

Dame Margery's mouth fell open in shock at such heresy but Alison simply shook her head. "You are so determined to be naïve, Mary Seymour," she said. "Can you truly be in such ignorance of how the world works?"

I was not, of course. I observed the lives of others even if nothing happened to me. Yet it was true that I could see little benefit for a woman in marriage. If it were a love match, it would end in betrayal or death or both. One only needed to look at the example of my parents, or old Queen Mary, to see that. If it was a marriage for profit, then it seemed to me the advantage was usually on the man's side for the price exacted on the woman was very high.

"Her Majesty the Queen has not wed," I pointed out.

"She will," Dame Margery said. She cut her thread neatly with a little pair of silver scissors. "She needs an heir."

Queen Elizabeth, I realised, was exactly like a man in that respect.

"Perhaps Lord Seymour will find you a husband at the hunting party," Alison said. "It is not just about my betrothal; there is business to be conducted."

Thus I learned something else new. Events that were called one thing so often had a quite different purpose. I had heard that there was to be a grand celebration of Alison's betrothal, a week of feasting and hunting in the forest. The household was already buzzing with the preparations. Yet it seemed it was not about Alison, or even about her forthcoming marriage.

"I am too young," I said, to offset the chill of disquiet that touched me. "I am not yet fourteen."

"Old enough to be promised," Dame Margery opined. She stood up, wincing a little. "Ach, I'm aching all over."

"Take some of my juniper oil," Alison said. "It will ease your bones." She smiled at Dame Margery and I saw with surprise that there was genuine affection between them. I had never seen Alison offer kindness to anyone before. Nor had I thought of Dame Margery as anything other than an old woman given to small spites. Alison was right; life was not always the way I saw it.

Once Dame Margery had left the room and Alison and I were alone, I expected more of her provocation but instead we sat in silence for a while as we worked. Or rather I did. Looking at Alison, I realised that her hands were resting on the material in her lap again and she was staring into space.

"I haven't seen my son since he was a few weeks old," she said, suddenly. "They took him away and gave him to a wet nurse." She looked at me and her eyes were such a bright blue with unshed tears that I felt shocked. "His name is Arthur."

I stared at her, uncomprehending. Why was she telling me this? Why now, when she had not spoken of the baby at all since her return to Wolf Hall? I could sense pain in her: huge, ungovernable pain, but I did not understand why she felt it. I had not known my mother at all but even had she lived I would have been consigned to the care of servants. She would not have raised me herself. My father had taken me to London with him as though I were just another piece of luggage, left in the hallway of his house for someone else to find and deal with. Why should Alison's son be different?

She had seen the blankness in my eyes.

"I would not expect *you* to understand," she said bitterly.

"I..." I grasped after something to say. "Surely when he is older you will see him again? It's only whilst he is nursing—"

She gripped my wrist so suddenly and so sharply that I winced.

"No," she said harshly. "I do not even know where he is. They will not give me any news. They say it is better I know nothing of him and he knows nothing of me and so it will remain for ever."

I understood now and was struck dumb by the finality of it. She had lost her child or rather he had been stolen from her. I wanted to lie to comfort her, but the words would not come and anyway there was no comfort in lies. We both knew that her fate was to wed and provide lawful heirs for her husband. No one would speak of Arthur again. Her future children would not even know their half-brother existed.

Alison stood up, made clumsy by her tears, and the embroidery fell unheeded to the ground. I picked it up when the door had closed behind her. It was exquisite; a piece of pure white linen with a perfect rose embroidered on it in white thread that glowed with all the beauty of the flower itself. She was a very talented seamstress. I folded it carefully and put it in the wooden box where she kept her needles and thread. There was a very fine gold crucifix in there as well, and some silver pins and her pomander, smelling faintly of orange and cloves.

I had a dream that night. It was not a vision in the sense I normally saw them though it was no less vivid for that. I was outside, in a landscape quite different from the woods and fields of Savernake. This was high country with a wide blue bowl of a sky and tracks as white as bone. I could feel the sun beating down on my head. In my hand was Alison's box. The shining walnut was dazzlingly bright, the initials AB bold and black. The sun-warmed wood felt hot against my palm.

It was a beautiful day but in the dream I felt uneasy. There was a flutter in my chest as though time was running out.

*I must be certain to leave word safely for Alison*, I thought. *Before it is too late.*

White dust was rising along the track. Someone was coming. My heart leaped, and then plummeted again. Something was wrong. I felt it so strongly through the dream, that sense of growing dread and a fear that clawed at my throat. Standing outside of myself, I saw the box fall from my hand and open, scattering its contents across the grass—a coin, a carved wooden chess piece, a sprig of rosemary that smelled sweet and fresh.

I woke up suddenly, gasping for breath. The room was icy cold but I was drenched in sweat. I lay racked by shivers, trying to shake off that huge, smothering sense of horror, but it clung to me like cobwebs. Then Darrell:

*"Cat? What's happened? What's wrong?"*

*"Nothing. A bad dream."*

I sensed his relief and the clumsy hug he sent me. It made me smile and eased the horror. Even so, the dread still lingered at the corners of my mind and I did not sleep again that night.

I had a new outfit that winter, less extravagant than Alison's trousseau but still very fine. It was green velvet with gold and a matching hood trimmed with pearls. It was too big for me, though Liz said that I would grow into it fast enough. I had wanted to wear it for the first day of the hunting party but Liz had laughed and said it was not that sort of gown so I was obliged to wear my dull old crimson velvet instead.

Wolf Hall was in a positive fluster over so important an occasion, although I noticed that whilst Alison was supposed to be the focus of celebration, she, and indeed the rest of the women, seemed largely forgotten. Cousin Edward rode in with a whole host of cronies—men strutting like peacocks in their finery, attended by servants, surrounded by a cacophony of dogs and a host of hunting falcons.

I didn't like hunting, but I sat a horse well enough and was given no option other than to join the party when they rode out in the frosty morning of the following day. There was to be a grand breakfast later, but as I shivered deep in my crimson velvet, I could think of many things I would prefer to do on a cold December morning.

The forest was full of pale light and misty glades that morning. At the back of the group the women hung back, chattering, but almost drowned out by the call of the horns and the baying of the dogs. The Queen was a keen hunter, as her mother had been before her, and many noble ladies enjoyed the chase, but none of us had the bloodlust on us that day. Early on, I caught a glimpse of a white hart and the dogs picked up the scent almost as fast. I willed it gone with all my strength and felt enormous relief when it disappeared into the mist. No one else was happy. The dogs sniffed around, running in disconsolate circles. The riders and the footmen grumbled as they waited for another scent. The excitement of the morning slowly fizzled into disappointment.

It was a subdued party that sat down to eat a couple of hours later, but the ale and the wine, the cold venison pies and the roasted chicken soon helped to assuage the bad mood. One of cousin Edward's squires came to sit beside me, a merry fellow with laughing black eyes and a mop of black hair, who introduced himself as Harry Stapleton. I saw Alison watching me, as though to say, "I told you so," but Liz was smiling on us benignly and after a little I forgot to be suspicious that Edward wanted to marry me off too because I liked Harry Stapleton. He made me laugh.

Suddenly it seemed everyone was laughing. The sun came out and the day felt almost warm. There was anticipation in the air again, and merriment. Alison had coaxed Dame Margery up onto her betrothal gift from Master Whitney—a highly bred white palfrey with a red and gold leather saddle. The horse had an uncertain temperament, like its master, but Alison was praising it lavishly, casting a glance at him under her eyelashes as she did so. Whitney was red and raucous from all the wine he had taken and put a clumsy arm around Alison's waist. I heard his voice ring out:

"I'd rather my own filly, even if she has already been had by other stallions first, than the old grey mare!"

There was a horrible silence, all talk, all laughter suspended. Someone tittered; a couple of Whitney's men, as drunk as he, roared their approval of the jest. Alison had dropped the reins and stood looking pale and stricken. Whitney tried to kiss her again, but she turned her face aside and so he slapped her, the sound shockingly loud in the quiet. In the moment that followed I noticed several things at the same time. I saw Alison's body jerk with the force of the blow; I saw Edward take a step forward, as if to intervene, his face a mirror of uncertainty. He stopped and did nothing. The sound of the slap echoed about the clearing, so loud it raised the birds from the trees.

To me it seemed as though the silence that followed lasted hours although it could only have been a moment. I knew with a horrible clarity what happened next; I had seen it before.

The palfrey bolted. I heard Dame Margery scream and saw her make a grab for the pommel, knuckles white. Everything happened very quickly then. The horse crashed across the clearing, sending food, wine, platters and flagons flying, knocking over one of the footmen who tried to catch the reins, trampling the skirts of one of the women who screamed like a fishwife.

There was a low branch blocking the path from the clearing. We all saw it. A number of us shouted a warning but it was too late. It hit Dame Margery across the throat and severed her head as neatly as any executioner.

The last thing I remember was seeing the white palfrey galloping away down the track with Dame Margery's headless corpse still swaying in the saddle and her silver-trimmed cloak flying out behind, a horrible repetition of the vision I had had on the very first day I had come to Wolf Hall.

# SIX

ALISON STOPPED THE CAR AND CUT THE ENGINE, looking about her at the picture postcard neatness of the village green, the ducks on the pond, the tumbledown wall of the churchyard and the lichened gravestones beyond. This was not what she had expected when she had set out from London to visit Diana, her former counsellor. Diana had always seemed such a vibrant person, active and fizzing with energy. The setting of a quiet old village seemed far too staid for her.

Diana's cottage was chocolate-box perfect, set along a path beside a stream. A wooden gate gave access to a handkerchief-sized garden that in the summer Alison imagined would be filled with hollyhocks, sweet peas and old-fashioned roses. Now it looked straggly and neglected, dead leaves gathering in the cobwebbed hollows of the steps that led up to the door, bare stalks straggling over the whitewashed walls. Not even the cheerful black and white shutters that framed the leaded windows could add much zest to the scene.

Diana herself looked much the same as she had always

done, elegant in black trousers and a black jumper, the severity of the outfit lifted by a brightly patterned scarf about her throat and a cluster of silver bracelets on the right wrist. Alison could detect little sign of the illness that was killing her until she leaned in to kiss Diana's cheek and realised how brittle and hollowed-out she felt. Perhaps that was why Diana had settled here, Alison thought, with the quietness and the graveyard over the wall. Perhaps she had accepted her mortality and was simply waiting. The thought made her shudder. She almost wished that she had not come.

It had been a surprise to receive Diana's email. Her message had been diffident, unlike her normal confident style as though she was stepping beyond the agreed parameters of their relationship. She had something to tell her, Diana said, something important. And so Alison had come.

"How are you?" she asked, holding out the bouquet of crimson roses, gerbera and rosehips that she had brought with her. She knew it was an empty question; Diana was dying and nothing could change that.

"I'm doing fine," Diana said lightly. Her eyes lit up as she took in the flowers. "How beautiful! Thank you." She gestured Alison to a seat. The cottage had one long, open room with a huge inglenook fireplace at one end where a fire burned, red and hot. The other end of the room had full-length doors that opened onto a small, enclosed courtyard. The ceiling was low, the timbers matching that of the huge beam across the top of the fireplace. Although it had been completely gentrified, Alison recognised it as the sort of labourer's cottage that in her childhood would have had a dirt floor and held an entire family and their animals as well.

"Oh dear." Diana was watching her face. "I should have thought. We could have met in a coffee shop somewhere."

"No." Alison pulled herself together. She had seen the

tremor in Diana's hand as she grasped the back of her chair and heard the catch of her breath as she lowered herself into it. She imagined it was difficult for Diana simply to move, or even to breathe. When they had last spoken, the tumour had been in danger of cracking Diana's ribs and Alison could see that the colour in her cheeks was hectic rather than healthy. If ignorance was not always bliss, Alison thought, knowledge could be a curse. These days there was so much information available to everyone on any subject from particle physics to medicine. It was stark and graphic and so often it left no space for hope.

"There's coffee." Diana gestured towards a smart little cafetière in a flowered cosy that sat beside two flowered cups on a matching flowered tray. It was precisely the sort of chintzy design Alison usually hated but here it just made her feel sad, seeing Diana so determinedly cheerful amongst her flowery cups. Even though she had not seen Diana in three years, she had always felt like a constant in her life. It was Diana who had kept her sane in the days when she had first arrived, listening to her as she poured out her story, explaining to her that what she had experienced was bereavement, a loss of her old life. Alison remembered sitting in Diana's room at Marlborough College, taking in the blandness of the beige chairs and the inoffensive pictures on the walls, a safe space, she supposed, for all manner of disclosures. It was unlikely though that Diana had ever heard anything like her story before.

"I don't want to be here," Alison had wept. "I'm trapped and I hate it. I want to go home."

Even after the counselling was over and Alison had moved away, they had kept in touch sporadically, Alison sending cards and updating Diana on the things that were happening in her life, Diana always acknowledging her messages but never stepping over that boundary counsellors maintained with their clients. It wasn't a friendship. Alison knew that. To start with it had hurt and angered her that Diana hadn't wanted her as a friend. She knew and understood the reasons why counsellors maintained a distance, but that had not changed the sense of rejection she had felt. In the end though it was Diana's integrity, a quality that had been absent more often than not in her own life, that had forced Alison into a grudging respect and from there to admiration.

They talked about Alison's work for a while, the trip she was making to Namibia in the spring, the roof terrace she had created at her London flat, her friends, her plans for Christmas. The coffee was delicious and Diana produced some shortbread to go with it. Alison had already decided not to tell her about seeing the portrait of Mary. Diana wasn't her counsellor any more and it felt like taking advantage. Even so, she was tempted. Their relationship had not been like this, the idle chat of acquaintances. She valued Diana's opinion. On a more selfish level, she wanted to talk about it. However, it was Diana who had asked her to come and Diana who would tell her what she wanted in her own time.

"I'm spending Christmas with my brother and his family," Diana said, pouring them a second cup. Alison watched her struggle a little to grasp the handle of the milk jug. She wanted to offer to help but she knew Diana would not welcome that.

"They insisted," Diana said. A shadow crossed her face. "I'd rather be alone. It's noisy, you know…" She gave an apologetic smile. "Grandchildren. They're lovely, but…" Her voice trailed away. Alison could see the lines of fatigue on her face.

"It's tiring for you, I expect," Alison said. She hadn't

known anything about Diana's family other than that she was divorced. An awful lot of counsellors seemed to be.

There were no photographs of family or friends in the cottage. It felt a little empty, as though Diana had already gone. Then there was the click of a cat flap opening and a very handsome marmalade and white cat strolled into the room. He stopped when he saw Alison, studied her for a moment with his striking green eyes and then jumped onto Diana's lap purring extremely loudly.

"This is Hector," Diana said. "I'm trying to find a home for him for after I'm dead and gone."

Alison flinched inside at the matter-of-fact way in which Diana spoke. So few people referred to death openly. They skirted about the topic, as though speaking bluntly made it more likely to happen. She wondered when she had become so squeamish. Certainly it had not been in her childhood, when the sights and smells of death had been all around, bodies swinging from the gibbet, beggars rotting at the side of the road.

"I'd have him myself but I don't think he'd like London very much," she said.

Diana smiled. "I didn't know you liked animals," she said. "You never mentioned them."

"The animals I knew were functional rather than pets," Alison said. "Especially the cats. They were there to keep the rats down. They worked for their keep."

Hector looked at her again. She was sure there was contempt in his eyes, as though the thought of working for his keep was utterly anathema to him.

"We're much more sentimental these days," Diana said, stroking Hector's head. Alison watched him close his eyes, luxuriating in the attention.

"You like London," Diana added. It was not really a question but Alison nodded.

"Yes, I do," she said. "I'm never lonely there. In an odd way it feels familiar to me even though I had never been there and it has changed beyond recognition over the centuries."

"Only in appearance, I think," Diana said, "not intrinsically. It's still a melting pot of different peoples and cultures, a place where fortunes can be made and lost, just as it has been for centuries."

She looked up suddenly and Alison almost jumped. Diana's blue gaze was as sharp and incisive as she remembered in the past with no shadow of illness or pain.

"You might be wondering why I invited you here," Diana said.

"I am," Alison said. "I wondered if—" She stopped.

"It was because I'm dying," Diana finished for her. She looked down at her hands resting in Hector's thick ginger fur. She was frowning a little. "In a way I suppose it is," she said slowly. "Normally, as you know, I wouldn't disclose anything personal to a client no matter how long I had known them." Her smile took the impersonal edge off the words. "It's the only way," she added, almost apologetically. "In the room it's about you, not me."

"I understand," Alison said. She reached out; touched Diana's hand. "I know I took it badly to start with when you wouldn't tell me anything about yourself, but I do understand."

Diana nodded. Her fingers clasped Alison's briefly before she let her go. "A counsellor thinks about a lot of things when she is seeing a client," she said slowly. "Obviously, we're supposed to be focusing on that person, but sometimes a discussion brings out our own feelings and emotions as well."

"Transference," Alison said. "I've read about it."

"I always found it difficult to talk to you about your son," Diana said. "About Arthur. I lost my son when I was in my twenties. He went to live with my ex. I wasn't in a good place." Again she made that little dismissive gesture of the hand as though to brush it away. "It was better for him that he should live with Dan," she said quietly and Alison was not sure whether she believed it or was still trying to convince herself.

"I'm sorry," she said. "I never realised."

"I never told you." Diana's words were abrupt. "It was my issue to solve, and I did solve it. I don't think it interfered with our work."

"No," Alison said. She had found so much comfort in telling Diana all about Arthur, pouring out her sense of fury, frustration and bereavement. It was not as simple as overcoming the grief of losing her son. She knew that would never happen. She could not forget him and she would always mourn his loss. With Diana's help, though, she had at least learned to live with the pain from one day to the next, carrying it with her, feeling the sharp edges spike her every so often.

"I shared some of that wrenching misery you felt," Diana said quietly. "It was different for me, though. There was always the chance I'd see Christopher again whereas you... You couldn't find a way back to the past."

"No," Alison said. "I didn't know how to go back and find Arthur." She had been very naïve, she thought, imagining that she could trip back and forth across time as easily as stepping through a doorway. That was exactly what had happened the first couple of times she had tried it, so she had assumed it would always be so. She would step into the hall at the White Hart Inn of the sixteenth century and out into Marlborough High Street in the present. So she had become complacent. Then one day, the day she had planned to go back to find Mary, to trace Arthur and bring him away with her, she had found the way blocked.

The White Hart had been redecorated. She had stepped inside from the High Street confidently expecting to see the old cobbled hall, full of smoke, and the sullen landlady stirring the pot: *"Back again, are you?"*

Instead there was modern wood furniture, a polished bar, big windows looking out onto a beer garden and the hum of quiet conversation as men downed their warm pints and looked at her curiously. Nothing changed. The vision did not falter and re-form into the past. She was rooted in the twenty-first century.

*A woman walks into a pub...*

There should have been a punchline. For her it was that she was trapped in the present when all her plans had been focused on the past. She had gold in her pocket to hire a cart to Wolf Hall—and to pay for the carter's silence. She had plans, plans that caused the excitement to bubble up in her chest. She had found somewhere she could live, she and Arthur together. Mary would tell her where to find him and she would steal him away and take him somewhere no one would ever be able to find them.

"I was so stupid," she said now, feeling the thud of that moment's horrible disbelief as an echo through her body. "So bloody stupid to assume it would always be easy to trip backwards and forwards through time."

"Why?" Diana said. They had had this conversation before. "Why were you stupid? It was a natural assumption to make. You had found a gateway to the past."

"And gateways can be closed."

It had never opened again and that had been close to ten years before.

There was silence. The handsome mahogany clock on the sideboard ticked time away. The cat rolled over and purred.

Diana hesitated. "What I wanted to tell you... It wasn't just that I could empathise with you about Arthur." She seemed uncharacteristically at a loss. "What I wanted to say..." She cleared her throat. "Well, I had another client like you once."

Alison stared at her. "You mean... You knew someone else who claimed to have travelled through time?"

"Exactly," Diana said.

Alison put her cup down very gently in the saucer. Even the click of china sounded loud in her ears.

"Did you think you were the only one?" Diana said. She was smiling a little at Alison's stupefaction.

"Yes." Alison said. She felt her mind seize on the idea like a vice. "Yes, I did," she said, more strongly. "Of course I did. I mean, what are the chances of there being two of us?" She realised that what she was feeling was jealousy as much as shock. She had thought herself unique. It was astonishing to hear that she was not.

"That's what I thought when you came to see me," Diana said. "What were the chances of there being two of you?"

Alison looked at her sharply. "That was why you were so open to what I had to say," she said. She felt the memories click into place in her head. "It wasn't because you believed I really was a time traveller," she said. "You were so accepting because you had already gone through the same experience with someone else."

"I am always accepting of what a client says." Diana's tone was slightly reproving. "What I believe is not important. It's what the client believes that matters."

"Even so, you must have thought I was delusional," Alison said.

Diana shook her head. "That was what I thought when

it happened the first time," she said. Regret laced her voice. "I'd learned to handle it better by the time I met you."

"What happened?" Alison leaned forward. She knew that Diana was breaking client confidentiality in telling her this, which was something any good counsellor always scrupulously avoided. Whatever Diana had to tell must be so important that now, when she had so little lifespan left, she had decided to break the tenets that had ruled her entire career.

"It was three years before you came to see me," Diana said. "I'd only been working in Marlborough for six months." She stroked Hector's head absentmindedly and the cat purred all the louder, opening his mouth wide to yawn and showing sharp white teeth. "A man stumbled into the grounds of the college one day in a state of distress. Security was going to call the police but I persuaded them to let me talk to him first, to try to calm him down." She was not looking at Alison now, but at some fixed point across the room, as though she was seeing the events of that day run past her eyes like a film.

"He was filthy and hungry and dressed in rags," Diana said. "He kept repeating that his name was Reginald De Morven and that he had stumbled into hell."

The name meant nothing to Alison. She sat back a little, feeling disappointment, though she was not sure why. Perhaps she had imagined she would have recognised the name from her own time. But the past was a vast country.

"I thought he was delirious," Diana said. "That, or psychotic. I could barely understand him he had such a thick accent. He said he was a knight, the Duke of Gloucester's man, and that he had been riding from Oxford to join the duke at Salisbury when he had fallen from his horse. When he woke he had found himself in this unknown place full of noise and evil spirits."

"Modern-day Marlborough's not that bad," Alison said.

A smile twitched Diana's lips. "You can imagine why I thought he was delusional, all the same," she said.

"Yes, of course," Alison said. "How could he possibly be telling the truth? It would be ridiculous, fantastical." She took a sip of her coffee. It was cold now and she put the cup down again, grimacing. She had been lucky in comparison, she thought. She had planned her escape from the past and so she had been spared the shock Reginald De Morven had clearly suffered when he had tumbled from one time into another.

"What happened to him?" she asked.

"They took him to hospital," Diana said. Her hands moved sharply in the cat's fur and Hector flexed his claws, disturbed.

"Sorry," Diana said, to the cat. She looked up and met Alison's eyes. "I felt as though I had failed him in some way," she said. "I hadn't been able to help. It preyed on my mind. So I went to the hospital to visit him, to see if there was anything I could do. But..." She hesitated. "When I got there they said he had gone."

"Gone?" Alison repeated. Her throat was dry. "Gone where? You mean he had vanished?"

"No one knew," Diana said. "He simply disappeared. I think he found a way home."

*Tick tock.* They sat in silence again whilst Alison thought about it and the clock marked time.

"Whereabouts was the hospital?" Alison asked.

"Swindon," Diana said. "But Reginald De Morven originally came from Kingston Parva. It's a village about ten miles north of here and a few miles east of Swindon. I looked him up," she added, in response to Alison's silent question. "He was real. He lived in the fifteenth century."

"So somewhere around here there is another place where

the past and the present meet," Alison said slowly, "the way that they used to do in the White Hart Inn. Either that, or there is some means of connecting to the past that I don't understand and, until I do, I'll never be able to make that journey."

Her mind felt engulfed in a blizzard, thoughts and facts falling so hard and fast she could not see clearly through them. There had been another traveller in time, from another place and another past. Unlike her, he had found his way back. And if he could do it, if he could find the way, then so might she...

Diana was watching her. "If you could," she said, "would you still go back?"

"Always," Alison said. "In a heartbeat." She did not need to think about it. "I would do anything I could," she said, "to find Arthur again."

Alison stood in the churchyard at Kingston Parva, hands deep in the pockets of her coat, fingers clenched. Generally, she avoided churches. The older ones were amongst a small number of buildings that were familiar to her in the modern, alien landscape, but she had found early on that they did not give her comfort. On the contrary, they only served to emphasise how far she was from home. She had reasoned that as she had made a new life for herself it made sense to distance that life from the old one so she stayed away from anything that was the same age she was.

Now though, she had come to find Reginald De Morven. Diana had told her that the slender information she had found about him had revealed a man who had apparently died in 1436 and was buried here on what had been his family estate. He was not, however, in the well-kept churchyard. He had a memorial in the Lady Chapel as befitted a knight who had been in the service of Duke Humphrey of Gloucester.

Alison walked briskly up the uneven path to the main door, her boots tapping on the flagstones. Inside the church had none of the musty dampness she had come to associate with modern-day religion. It smelled instead of polish and flowers, and the winter sun cut through the sparkling diamond-paned windows to scatter shards of coloured light on the floor. There was a low hum of a Hoover coming from the vestry on the north side. Alison paused to pick up a leaflet about the history of the church and put a pound in the honesty box. It made her smile; that was something that changed from the old life to the new; in the past she would not have hesitated to take anything she could without paying for it. She was not entirely sure why and how that had changed, except that now she had money she made for herself and that had given her much more than disposable income. Self-respect was something she now realised could be neither taught nor bought.

Reginald De Morven's memorial was not hard to find. It was a great stone edifice, crumbling a little, but still a handsome piece of sculpture. On the carved panel above his head was engraved a skull and three hourglasses in a row, presumably to depict the three decades of his life and the swiftness with which man's allotted span ran out. The inscription was in Latin, which Alison could not read. Unlike boys, girls had not generally been taught Latin in her youth. Probably Mary Seymour had. She grimaced at the thought, wondering why the idea of Mary's book learning still irritated her after so much time had passed.

There was a pile of guidebooks by the church door and Alison picked up the top one. It told her that the De Morven family had been prominent in the local area since the time of the Norman Conquest, holding land from the Crown. They had died out in the seventeenth century when there were no male heirs left and the estates had passed to a distant cousin. Reginald had been a soldier and a courtier who had fought in the French Wars. He had gone missing and had been thought killed in 1435, but had returned to his family some time later, a broken man, and had died the following year. The monument commemorated his great exploits before that sad and ignominious end.

Alison lowered the leaflet and looked thoughtfully at the memorial. She supposed that war was as good an excuse as any for disappearing for a couple of years. A man rode off to fight and returned years later, raving of strange experiences, to all intents and purposes insane. In the fifteenth century no one would have known differently.

She reached out and touched the cold, carved cheek of Reginald De Morven. He had found a way back, but it seemed it had still been too late for him. He had been broken by his journey into the future, driven mad, unable to understand the world he had discovered. He had returned home only to die.

She wondered how she would fare if she ever found her way home. She had changed out of all recognition in this new world. Adapting to the old would be beyond strange. Yet she knew she could survive it because she had no other choice. The memory of Arthur would always drive her on. She still intended to find him and to bring him back. The decision gave her strength and she would not waver.

The drone of the Hoover cut off sharply and silence flowed back. Alison unfolded her brand-new Ordnance Survey map and laid it out on a pew. Kingston Parva was one of the ancient villages that lay at the foot of a line of chalk downs which bounded the Vale of the White Horse. A traveller from

Oxford to Salisbury such as Reginald De Morven might well take a short cut across these hills, especially if he knew the landscape. She wondered where the roads had run in those days. She would need to check. There were plenty of paths and bridleways marked on the map that might be hundreds of years old. She traced them with a finger, the thieves' way, the rogues' way, the sugar road…

"Can I help you?" The vicar, a young woman with a smile and a very fashionably cut cassock, was heading down the aisle towards her. Behind her, Alison could see a man in a pinny putting the Hoover back in a cupboard. It reminded her of the many things she liked about the twenty-first century.

"I was just making the acquaintance of Sir Reginald," she said lightly.

"Oh, Reggie." The vicar smiled. "Our resident saint."

"Was he?" Alison asked, startled.

"Well, not officially," the vicar said. She patted the tomb affectionately. "Apparently, he was everything that a medieval knight was supposed to be: brave, chivalric, generous to the poor. When he came back from the wars speaking wildly of the extraordinary things he had seen, the villagers thought he had been touched by God."

"I suppose that would have been the most obvious explanation in those days," Alison said, "rather than that he had a mental-health issue?"

The vicar nodded. "They thought he had seen miracles. Poor guy."

"What sort of miracles did he talk about?" Alison asked.

"Oh, metal birds and things spewing fire, or something," the vicar said vaguely. "You know, the usual stuff. Lights in the sky, and false suns in the dark of night and sounds like thunder. He must have had PTSD, only they wouldn't have

realised in those days. Instead, they thought he was a vision-
ary and when he died they would come to his grave looking for cures." She pointed to the stone where it was worn
smooth. "So many people touched the monument it's surprising it's still here. It was repaired in the eighteenth century, I think."

"Is the manor house near here?" Alison asked. "The ancestral home of the De Morven family?" She smoothed out the
map, studying it closely. The manor and church were usually located close together but she did not remember seeing
a house as she had driven through the village and there was
no indication on the map.

"It's gone," the vicar said. "Gary—" she called out to the
man, who was untying the apron and wiping his hands on
it. "Where was Morven Hall?"

Gary came up, long, lanky and grinning. "It was over to
the west of the church," he said. "When it fell down the villagers took the stones to repair their cottages so there isn't
much left."

High above their heads the church clock chimed the
hour. The sun had gone and twilight was falling softly in
the church, filling the corners with shadows. Alison briefly
considered looking for the site of the old manor but abandoned the idea. Her boots weren't made for hiking across
fields and if she found a pile of old stone it would not help
her much. What she really needed was to know whereabouts
Reginald De Morven had been when he had found his way
across time. She wanted to see if she could replicate that experience.

The thought made her heart race until she swallowed hard
and deliberately repressed the excitement. In a way, Diana's
information had been a poisoned chalice. It had given her
hope, more hope than she had had in ten years when she had

tried to return to find Arthur and discovered that she was trapped in the present with no way back. Yet she was not really much further on from that. She knew that Reginald De Morven might have shared her experience and achieved what she had not, a return home, but she did not know where or how he had done it.

Slowly, she folded up the OS map and stowed it in her bag.

"We're locking up," the vicar said apologetically. "If there's anything else…"

"No, that's fine, thanks." Alison said. She glanced back at the towering mausoleum. Reginald De Morven lay safe in his stone chamber, untouched by the falling shadows.

"What could you tell me?" she said softly.

"Sorry?" The vicar was sounding slightly concerned now.

"Nothing," Alison said, turning her back on the memorial and walking towards the door. "Nothing at all."

# SEVEN

─────

*Mary, 1560*

THE WHISPERS STARTED IMMEDIATELY AFTER
Dame Margery's death.

*"Witch."*

I did not realise to begin with. I was too shocked, stunned
at what we had witnessed and even more appalled that I had
seen Dame Margery's headless corpse that day in the forest
*before* it had happened. It was one thing, although disquiet-
ing enough, to see ghosts and spectres from the past. It was
another entirely to foresee the future.

It was Alison who told me what they were saying about
me. We had returned to Wolf Hall, distressed, silent, to be
bundled upstairs to our chambers. Liz was tight-lipped on
what was happening. She brought me cold bread and meat
much later than we would normally sup but I had no ap-
petite anyway. All I seemed to be able to see was the whole
terrifying scene replaying before my eyes; the slap of Whitney's hand against Alison's cheek echoed through my head
and everything followed with agonising slowness—the horse
bolting, Dame Margery's scream, the branch like the blade

of an axe... They recurred again and again in front of my eyes by the light of the flickering candle flame.

There was a knock at the door and Alison came in. On her pale cheek the mark of Whitney's hand still stood out in a fierce red line.

"What's happening?" I asked, scrambling to sit up and pushing the untidy hair back from my face. I had heard men's voices raised below, the sound of argument, but Liz had refused to tell me anything and would not let me stir from my room. Somewhere, in the distance, a child was crying, the wail quickly hushed. The whole house seemed to be buckling under the weight of an extraordinary heaviness.

Alison sat down on the bed beside me. Her expression was stunned too, inward-looking.

"They have brought her body back," she said. "She is to be buried on the morrow."

"So soon?"

"The sooner the better, they said."

"No more hunting then," I said, and saw a bitter smile light Alison's eyes.

"It has spoiled their games," she agreed.

"And the wedding?"

"Goes ahead on Friday as planned."

I looked up, startled. "But—"

"Nothing has changed," she said.

"He hit you," I said, stupid with shock and exhaustion.

Her hand crept to her cheek. "Did you think that would make a difference?" she said. "A man may chastise his wife just as he would a dog or a servant."

"It should not be so," I said. "Surely, Cousin Edward should stop it."

She raised her shoulders in a half-shrug. "He of all men is keen for the marriage to proceed." She shook the stupor from her eyes. "It was your future I came to discuss not mine. You are in mortal danger. They are calling you a witch and pressing for you to be tried."

Ah, Alison. Where Liz had hidden the truth from me, Alison would always be honest, whether out of spite or friendship I never was sure. I sat bolt upright, grabbing the covers to me as meagre protection.

"What? Why?"

"You predicted Dame Margery's death." She was not looking at me but was rubbing her fingers over the coverlet, almost as though she too were a little afraid to look me in the eyes. "You spoke of a headless horsewoman and it came to pass right in front of our eyes."

"I did not predict anything!" I felt the familiar rise of panic. I hated my gift. I had not wanted it; it had chosen me and had brought with it nothing but trouble.

"Yes, you did," she said. "It was the very first day you came here to Wolf Hall. You saw a spectre in the forest, a headless woman on a horse. We all remember you raving of it."

The superstitious had long memories, I thought. When all else was forgotten, tales of haunting and witchcraft would persist.

"That doesn't mean I caused Dame Margery's death," I said. "It was just a coincidence. I had a fever. I was ranting about a nightmare."

"You know that isn't true." Alison sounded impatient. She grabbed me by the shoulders, shook me. Her gaze bore into mine. "You did foresee it, didn't you, Mary Seymour?"

I wanted to lie but the truth was already in my eyes and she had seen it. She gave a little hiss of satisfaction and released me.

"That still does not mean that I killed her, or that I am a witch," I said weakly. The words felt a hollow defence even to me. "I had nothing to do with it."

"I believe you," she said. "I think you see images but you do not summon spirits. Not that that will help you."

I clutched her arm. "What do you mean?"

"What I say." I expected her to shake me off but instead she was staring at me earnestly. "The villagers are full of superstition and credulity. They are simple people. They want to take you away for trial, to punish you but also to make sure you cannot curse them further. The forest is alive with rumour. Mistress Aiglonby is even now begging your cousin Edward to send you to safety, but even if he did, it would not serve. It is too late. The moment you set out you would be dragged from the coach and taken away. That is if they did not lynch you on the spot."

"But it's nonsense!" I jumped up, too afraid to be able to keep still. "Anyone who believes I am a witch is a fool."

"They are scared." Alison's steady voice cut across my rage. "Fear makes men savage. They believe you have witchcraft and they will remember your tales of soldiers fighting in the forest and think you have summoned up a legion from the devil." She stood up too and came over to me. "Besides, it is not all a lie. You do have the gift, don't you? You do see the future."

She was watching me and suddenly I realised that this was very important to her. I felt some sort of urgency in her, desperation even.

"No," I said. "It's only dreams, imagination."

"You lie." Her hand was on my arm now, tight like a claw. "You have the sight."

"Why should I tell you?" I said. "You have been no friend to me. You would only betray me."

I was pressed back against the wainscot, the sharp corners of the wood digging into my back through the material of my skirts. Alison was so close I could see the deep lilac blue of her eyes fringed by thick black lashes, the delicate curve of her cheek, the perfect bow of her mouth. I realised she was beautiful and felt a stab of envy. Then I wondered why my mind was dwelling on such irrelevancies now, of all times, when my fate hung in the balance.

"I can help you," Alison said. She sounded sincere. "Your cousin is too weak to defend you against a charge of witch-craft. He will fear contamination, that men will denounce his household as a hotbed of sorcery. He will sacrifice you to save his own skin if I do not stop him. It is the fate of women to be bartered."

I felt cold, shaking. I had no notion whether she was try-ing to frighten me or whether her words were true but there was such vehemence in her tone and a bitterness that rang true even as the sourness of it stung.

"Why would you help me?" I asked. "What do you want in return?"

Her expression registered satisfaction. "So you are not so naive after all. I thought not. I will help you escape Wolf Hall, and in return you will help me by scrying the future for me. I want to know where my son is so that I can find him and take him away."

I gaped. "Scry for you?" I said. "I do not know how to scry! Whatever visions I see come to me of their own accord not at my command."

"Then you had better learn how to command them, little cousin." She gave me a smile that had no warmth in it. "For that is the price of my help." She made for the door, quick, wily, slipping through the gap and turning back only when she had one hand on the latch.

"I will not be long," she promised. "I will persuade Ed-ward to send us both away to safety, to a place of our own choosing."

"You're coming too?" I said, startled. Everything was happening too quickly for me. "But where will we go? And what of Liz—Mistress Aiglonby? Will she not accompany me?"

The pitying look was back on Alison's face again. "You need to grow up, Mary," she said. "Even before this happened, Edward was speaking of sending Mistress Aiglonby back to court. The Queen has offered her advancement. You are on your own now, or very soon you will be."

I gulped back the tears. I was tired and young and my eyes stung with repressed emotion. This was too much. Liz had been with me since I was a baby, one of the few constants in my life, and now she was to be taken from me too. For if the Queen commanded, where did that leave me? It left me nowhere, with no claim and no rights. Worse, I had been blind to what was happening. I had never imagined that Liz would have a life of her own, a future that did not involve me.

For a second I thought I saw pity in Alison's eyes. No doubt she was thinking me a soft fool. She had learned long ago how to deal with the cruelties of life. Perhaps she had been born with more hardihood than I.

"Where am I to go?" I said, more to myself than to her, but it was she who answered.

"What of your mother's kin?" she asked. "The Parrs? Won't they help you?" Then, impatiently, when I did not answer: "There must be someone?"

"No, there is not," I said.

She shrugged as though it was not her problem, which of course it was not.

"Well, you can't come with me," she said. "I have great plans."

I stared at her. "Where are you going?" I asked.

"Somewhere better than this," Alison said, and satisfaction shone in her eyes. "I'm going to find Arthur and then we are going far, far away. And we're never coming back."

# EIGHT

*Alison, Marlborough, the present day*

A BUZZ OF ANTICIPATION WAS BUILDING INSIDE Marlborough town hall's Victorian assembly room as it got close to the start of Adam's talk on 'Uncovering Anne Boleyn'. Alison sat at the back of the room, behind a marble pillar, obscured by a large vase of lilies and the Union Flag. People had given her a few curious glances since she had arrived early and there had been plenty of empty seats with a better view, but she had not wanted to be conspicuous.

There was a big pile of books on a trestle table in the foyer outside. Alison had tried to buy one earlier, only to be turned away by the smiling literary festival assistant who helpfully told her that if she waited until after the talk she could get Adam to sign it for her. Alison had managed to restrain herself from saying that she would rather have a tooth pulled and had shoved the ten pound note back in her purse and decided to order it online. She hadn't wanted to be here but Adam, the book and the portrait were her only clue to Mary and so to Arthur. It was a simple question of what she wanted more.

The microphone crackled as the festival director strode

onto the stage. The buzz of excitement peaked and died away to a murmur as he started to speak. It was clear he viewed Adam's presence as a coup. Alison tuned out the obsequious homage done to Adam's early life and career in the introduction and let her gaze drift around the room.

The combination of Adam Hewer's looks, celebrity and a juicy historical story had certainly lured the audience in. Even the national media were there, as well as a group of people Alison guessed were Adam's family, judging by the shared good looks. When she had first known Adam she had speculated about what they would be like; his parents, she had thought, would be distant and chilly because that was how she imagined aristocratic parents would still be, even four hundred years after hers. His brothers and sisters—she was uncertain how many of them there were—would be like the tumble of relatives she had known at Wolf Hall, squabbling, fractious, requiring the soothing hand of an elder sibling to keep them in order.

But of course it wasn't like that at all. They looked happy and united, and very proud of Adam, cheering and whistling when he stood up to begin his talk. She saw his mouth curve into a smile as he gave them a little wave and she felt the shared intimacy of the occasion, even in a big public hall, and felt also a stab of jealousy. She had never wanted emotional intimacy with anyone. It was impossible with her past, simply something that she could never achieve. Yet in that moment she wanted to be a part of that charmed circle.

Adam held his audience rapt from the start. Although Alison had never seen his television programmes, she could understand why he was so popular. There was an easy confidence in the way he moved and the way he effortlessly established a rapport with his audience. He told the story of his discovery of the portrait and the other artefacts as though it were a page-turning piece of fiction: how he was summoned secretly to an ancient house lost in the English countryside, how the reclusive owner had stumbled on a cache of Tudor relics, the painstaking process of recovering and researching them and the excitement when the team realised they had found a previously unknown portrait of Anne Boleyn. He wove a compelling tale, erudite enough for people to feel they were learning something, light enough not to bore, exciting enough with its sprinkling of history, mystery and celebrity. No hint of doubt ruffled his assurance when talking about the portrait's subject. He was certain of the thoroughness of his scholarship and Alison thought that, to be fair, he had no reason not to be. Experts had authenticated his research. Even though it was sometimes difficult to identify an artist or a sitter, he had no reason to doubt in this case.

When the talk came to an end, there was a rapturous round of applause and a welter of questions from the excited audience.

Where was this mysterious manor house? Could they visit? Was it true that the portrait had been found at Wolf Hall?

Alison shifted sharply in her seat. Wolf Hall, like so many of the places associated with her childhood, was long gone, a Victorian farm of the same name being the only signpost to the past. But the associations of it lived on and possessed people's imaginations. Even the name alone caused a frisson to run through the hall like wind through grass.

She watched Adam smile charmingly and tell the questioner much the same thing, apologising that he could not disclose the location of the finds because the owner of the house had demanded discretion.

Even when she had lived there, Alison thought, Wolf Hall had been a place of ghosts, tumbledown, haunted by her uncle the Protector Somerset and feckless Thomas, Mary's father. Amongst those famous Seymours glided the pale shade of Queen Jane, a previous generation that had cast a long shadow on the living. If she closed her eyes, even now Alison could see the mellow sun-warmed walls and tangle of chimney pots. She had not hated it there. It had not been home; she had known no home since she had been six years old, but it had been a place to live. Dame Margery had almost been like a mother to her. Then Edward had come…

A repeat of the applause snapped her out of the memories. The Q&A had finished and the audience stood up and almost as one made a dash forward, keen to buy Adam's books, to chat with him, even to get his autograph. He was mobbed. There seemed to be a lot of young women with long, glossy hair and very bright smiles, reinforcing Alison's realisation that he genuinely was a celebrity. If she wanted to talk to him she would have to stand in line.

The crowd around the book table was seven deep, reminding her of a particularly busy night in her favourite pub. The assistants from the local White Horse bookshop were working overtime to open new boxes; as soon as the books were on the table they were snapped up.

"Did you wish to buy a copy, madam?"

The crowd had jostled her to the front and now she was being accosted by a slightly harassed-looking young man, who obviously wondered why she was standing still when the world about her was in chaos.

"Oh… Yes, please." Alison grabbed the copy he was offering and fumbled for her purse.

"If you'd like Adam to sign it," the young man said, going slightly pink about the ears in the excitement of using Adam's name, "join that line there."

"I won't, thanks," Alison said, but he hadn't heard her.

Someone else had already claimed his attention, agitating to buy a copy.

She tucked the book, with Mary's portrait on the cover, under her arm and turned to go, but found Adam's godfather standing directly behind her. She had seen him in the hall along with the rest of Adam's family. Adam's mother was now standing slightly to the left of the signing table in animated conversation with a woman Alison thought might be his literary agent.

"Hello again," Adam's godfather said, holding out a hand in a way that made it impossible for her to ignore him. "Adam didn't introduce us yesterday but I'm Richard Demoranville."

"Alison Bannister," Alison said, smiling as she shook his hand. She could not help the smile. It was odd; there were some people—not many—whom she immediately felt comfortable with. Diana Jennings had been one. Richard Demoranville also felt like someone she had known for ever. Perhaps it was that the bright intelligence in his eyes and the restless energy reminded her a little too much of Adam.

"I'm surprised to see you here," Richard said. "I had the impression last night that you weren't persuaded by Adam's identification of the portrait."

Alison didn't contradict him. She thought it would seem disingenuous after what she had said before. "It was still worth coming to listen," she said. "Adam's a great speaker. He knows how to capture and hold an audience."

Richard frowned. "He's been in a filthy mood all day," he said, "worrying about the talk."

"I didn't have Adam down as someone who suffers from stage fright," Alison said.

"He's not." Richard's frown lightened a little. He touched her arm. "Look, could we talk somewhere a bit quieter?"

Alison knew what he was going to say. Her heart sank. "I don't think there's much point—" she began.

"Please," Richard said. Then: "There's a lot riding on this book. A new TV series and—more importantly for Adam—the possibility of a research and teaching post at London University."

*Oh, shit*, Alison thought. She tried briefly to imagine the professional embarrassment and personal mortification that would follow any discovery that Adam had been wrong about the Anne Boleyn portrait. She shuddered at the thought. It would be horrendous, not just for him but for his family with their shiny pride and the hopes they had invested in him. She felt a heel for raising questions in his mind.

But it was too late anyway. The book was out there, and there was no reason why anyone would discover Adam's error. They were not going to have the sort of historical insight that she had.

"If you care about Adam," Richard was saying, carefully, "you might want to consider that."

Alison felt the colour burn her face. "Why would you think I did?" she said.

Richard raised his brows. "Don't you?" he asked dryly.

Alison laughed reluctantly. "I knew Adam a long time ago. I did care for him then." She wondered why she was being so honest. "But, like I said, it was a long time ago. And it didn't end well."

"Youthful infatuations so often end badly," Richard said vaguely. His blue gaze snapped back to her face. "Taking revenge ten years later seems a little harsh."

Alison was stung. "I told him he was wrong," she said. "That's all. I didn't do it to cause trouble but because I know I'm right. If Adam chooses to investigate, he may find the truth for himself—"

"Ali?"

Alison spun around. Adam was standing behind them, hands on his hips, a wary expression on his face. She had been so wrapped up in the conversation with Richard, she had not realised that the crowds had dissipated and only a few people were left standing in the foyer: the booksellers, Adam's agent, torn between concern and proprietary curiosity, and a few diehard fans.

Adam's gaze dropped to the book she was clutching under her arm.

"Would you like me to sign that for you?" he asked. Amusement lurked in his eyes. He extended a hand as though to take it from her.

Alison clutched the book more tightly. "I'm good, thanks," she said.

"A pity," Adam said. There was a definite challenge in his gaze now. "What would be appropriate? Best wishes? Hmm, that's a bit bland, given the nature of our relationship. For old time's sake, perhaps?"

"That's such a cliché," Alison said. "As a writer I would expect better of you."

"We're all doomed to disappointment," Adam said. "That's history for you." He nodded towards the book. "Enjoy. Though you won't find what you're looking for."

"That's fine," Alison snapped, "since you found something and didn't recognise it for what it was."

She turned on her heel and headed out of the big double doors, down the grand staircase and out onto the high street. It felt cold out here after the warmth and light inside. She paused to tuck her scarf into her jacket more securely, huddling down into the cashmere folds.

Squabbling with Adam, scoring points… She knew it was futile and it didn't relieve the misery beneath her frustration but made it worse. There was a sharp pain wedged in her chest. This was so important to her, a lifetime's quest.

The corner of the book dug into her ribs. She longed to throw it into the nearest rubbish bin and vent her frustrations that way. Except that it was her only hope and she clung to that tenaciously. There might be something buried deep within the text that could help her to trace Mary's history. That was the first part of the quest. Find Mary and she would find word of Arthur. She was certain of it. It was just a pity that the plans she had made so carefully all those years ago had gone so spectacularly wrong.

Two girls, laughing and careless, almost knocked into Alison as they sped along the pavement, hair flying. She could see one of them had three copies of *Uncovering Anne Boleyn* clutched to her chest. The books were getting soaked in the rain and so were the girls. They wore no coats even though it was winter. Alison wondered if they even noticed the weather. She felt old all of a sudden. The north wind from the Downs was making her eyes smart so that unwanted tears slid from the corners and chilled her cheeks. Winter these days so seldom involved snow. It always seemed to be cold, stinging rain and a wind that found its way into her bones. It was with relief that she saw the neat box trees that marked the entrance to the hotel and the lighted foyer beyond. She needed a coffee.

"Miss Bannister? Excuse me. You forgot this."

The voice made her pause and turn on the hotel steps. Richard Demoranville was standing a few feet away. He reached into the inside breast pocket of his coat and held something out to her. Alison took it automatically, feeling the wind almost tug the flimsy sheet from her fingers. It was a newspaper cutting.

"I don't think that's mine—" she began, but Richard shook his head once, sharply, silencing her.

"It's the only media report that gave details of the location of Adam's find," he said. "Although the owner of the house wanted it kept quiet, one local paper reported it before they realised. I think you'll find it useful."

He raised a hand in farewell and turned away, vanishing into the shadows before Alison even had time to ask the questions that were forming in her mind. She heard his footsteps recede into silence. The street was empty.

Frowning, she went into the hotel foyer, closing the door carefully behind her and taking off her sodden raincoat as she hurried up to her room. The newspaper cutting was soaking too, almost translucent and too difficult to read. She felt a moment of panic that the ink would run and she would never discover what it said. After flattening it on the radiator, she waited edgily as the paper dried and the words gradually reappeared. When she could wait no longer, she snatched it up and carried it over to the light.

It was from the *Marlborough Mercury* and was dated roughly three months earlier. It was only a tiny square of information at the bottom of an article about the opening of a new recycling plant: "Local celebrity historian discovers lost treasure." She had not thought that Adam was local. She was sure he had told her his family were from Cambridgeshire. She shrugged impatiently and read on:

"Local celebrity historian, Adam Hewer, will be announcing today that he has discovered a significant new portrait of Anne Boleyn, second wife of Henry VIII. Hewer, who has written both a TV programme and book about the discovery, has been working for the last eighteen months to catalogue the contents of sixteenth-century Middlecote Hall, home to the reclusive Smithfield family."

*Middlecote Hall.*

Alison sat down abruptly on the edge of the bed.

She should have guessed. As part of her search for Mary, she had racked her brains, sought out all the places with some connection to the Parr and Seymour families. There had been so many places for her to research over the years: Elvetham in Hampshire, Berry Pomeroy in Devon, houses still standing, houses rebuilt, houses lost. She had not remembered Middlecote though, perhaps because the connection was so tenuous.

There had definitely been some Seymour family connection to Middlecote though. It teased at her memory. Quickly, she ran through the names of the cousins she remembered, then, with a slight shrug, reached for her laptop. All her notes were stored here, family trees, the ones she could not show Adam because there she was—Alison Banestre, born 1543 to Hugh Banestre and his wife Alice, only surviving child.

She flicked to the next page of the family tree, a sideways step via the Seymours to other cousins. There it was: Fenner of Middlecote Hall, Berkshire, a distant connection by marriage a couple of generations before either she or Mary had gone to Wolf Hall.

Fenner. Now, at last, she knew. Mary had gone to Middlecote. So she would too.

# NINE

## Mary, 1560

DARRELL SPOKE TO ME AS I WAS LEAVING WOLF Hall. I did not try to shut him out. I was too lonely and unhappy. Probably that was how he had known something was amiss. When either of us were miserable the other always sensed it.

"Cat."

"Darrell?"

"What's wrong?"

There were times when I thought that Darrell was a typical boy. He did not like talking about emotion. I could sense in those two words all of the reluctant obligation he was feeling and the hope that when I replied it would be to reassure him that all was well.

Had I been less miserable I might have laughed.

"I am sent away again." I made an effort. "Don't fret. It's fine."

Swiftly he demolished my pretence, the answering feeling deriding my lame attempt to fool him.

"It's not. What happened? Where are you going? Why?"

So many questions. It was complicated. I sent thought patterns showing death and blame and danger, accusations of witchcraft, fear and suspicion. I felt him stiffen as though he were there beside me.

*"Cat. No."* Vehement. Then: *"Do they know about me?"*

*"No. No one knows."*

I felt his relief and knew it was for me, not for himself. Darrell had always warned me to tell no one. Not that I needed warning. I knew it was not the sort of thing that anyone would understand. People would see it as yet another sign of my difference, a threat, a hint of witchcraft.

*"Keep it a secret."*

*"Always."*

I felt warmth then, security and love falling like rose petals. Then the moment of intimacy faded and he was practical again.

*"Where are you going?"*

*"I don't know. Some other family manor, I think. They would not tell us."*

*"Us?"*

*"My cousin Alison is with me. They sent us both away. Alison swears she will run off and start a new life."*

I felt Darrell's snort of derision at the thought of a girl being so foolish as to imagine she could forge her own path and for once I was quite cross with him.

*"Why shouldn't she?"*

*"Women don't do that."*

"Whom are you talking to?" Alison's voice cut across our thoughts and I broke away from Darrell instinctively, as though afraid she would read my mind and find out about him.

"I?" I feigned bewilderment. "No one. How could I? There is no one here but you and I."

The coach jerked over a rut and I steadied myself against

the frame. Rain beat monotonously on the leather roof; the chill of it seeped inside and set me shivering. I had half expected Edward to banish me in a turnip cart, sent away under cover of darkness, but whatever Alison had said to him had evidently stiffened his resolve to behave like a gentleman. This was his second-best coach, lined with linen hangings and with the Seymour coat of arms on the side. We had armed outriders too, for protection and to show the superstitious folk of the forest that Lord Seymour's orders should not be challenged.

"Your lips were moving," Alison said. "You were talking to someone in your head."

"I was only talking to myself."

She shrugged. "If you say so."

I wondered how she was really feeling about leaving Wolf Hall. I had asked her the night before when we had sat by the fire and I had tried to read the future for her in its flames as I had promised.

"I am not sorry to go," she had said. "I want respect and I will never find that here or in Whitney's bed. I want to be like a man and determine my own fate."

*Women don't do that.* I remembered Darrell's words. She was braver than I, or perhaps she was foolhardy and Darrell was right. I did not know. But I wanted her to succeed.

"I'm not coming with you," she whispered to me as we climbed up in the carriage that dank morning. "Edward says I am to live with you now but that would never serve. We would drive each other witless within a week."

I was not sure. We had come to some sort of understanding, she and I. It helped that she believed I had seen the future for her when I had pretended to scry the flames the previous night. To add colour and conviction to the experience I had told her to light three candles about us.

"It is the power of three," I had said mysteriously. "Such magic is strong."

Then I told her that I had seen a castle with high grey battlements, flying gold and blue pennants, and her baby in a nursery there surrounded by women who loved and cared for him. As soon as I had said the words I had regretted them for there was a look of vivid unhappiness on Alison's face and I wondered whether she would have preferred me to say that no one loved him. That was the trouble with lying; it was so difficult to know what to say for the best.

She gave a little sigh. "Are you sure they care for him well?"

"He wants for nothing," I said. "I can see him wrapped in a blue blanket." I was warming to my theme now. "He has a tiny gold crucifix about his neck."

"I gave him that," she whispered. "It was one of the few things my mother left to me."

That did surprise me, since I had seen nothing of the sort. However it convinced her.

She smiled at me. "Thank you," she said. Then: "This castle—where is it?"

"That I do not know," I said. "Somewhere north of here."

That left a great deal of the country, but she seemed satisfied by my geographical vagueness for she nodded.

"Livery of blue and gold," she said. "I will find it."

I felt misgivings then and almost told her that I had made it all up, but there was a new serenity about her and I was too much of a coward to crush it with the truth.

Now I could feel her watching me, but she said nothing more, instead turning her shoulder to me as she lifted the window flap to stare out at the rain-drenched landscape.

"We are nearing the bridge at Marlborough," she said. "I will be leaving you soon."

There was an odd note in her voice: tension, excitement, fear. The same emotions were mirrored in her face. She looked half defiant, half terrified. On impulse I reached out a hand to her.

"Won't you tell me where you are going?" I asked. "Is it to find Arthur?"

"Not yet," she said. "I'm going to prepare a place for him. Then when it is ready I will come back and find him." Her voice held a hint of uncertainty but I could see in her eyes how dearly she wanted it to be true.

Suddenly, she grabbed my hands. "If I don't come back—" she said.

"You will." I wanted to reassure her. She seemed so frightened all of a sudden, swinging from confidence to doubt like a weathervane.

"Find him for me," she said. Her grip tightened. "Find out where Arthur is and leave word for me."

I stared at her. I had no idea how to do what she asked. "Leave word where?" I asked weakly.

"Somewhere you know I will find it," she said.

We were rumbling down Marlborough High Street now. The coach had slowed to a crawl. I could hear the familiar sound of the street market, the clucking of the chickens, the shouts of the vendors, all drowned in the steady thrum of the falling rain.

"Give me your promise." Her hands were tight on mine. "I saved your life. You owe it to me."

"I promise," I said.

The coach jerked to a halt. I heard the irritable voice of one of the squires asking what the deuce the driver was doing but then, like quicksilver, Alison had slid out of the door grasping the folds of her cloak in one hand and a small bag in the other. I heard the squire give a shout of warning but Alison slipped like an eel out of his grasping hands and ran.

"Good luck!" I yelled.

She turned towards me, already soaked by the steady fall of rain, her face a pale blur beneath the black edge of the hood. She nodded. "And you."

I saw the dripping market stalls marooned in a sea of mud, the huddled stallholders, the pearly grey of the sky, the endless fall of rain. That was how I remember Alison—a small upright figure in a sea of grey, her hair soaking, wearing the vivid orange tawny as she had in my vision.

She ran for the nearest door. It was the White Hart, the rain dripping from its eaves, a sullen curl of smoke from its chimney the only sign of life. She tumbled over the threshold with one of Cousin Edward's squires in hot pursuit, grasping after her cloak.

Alison had planned this and taken our guards entirely by surprise. Edward's intention was that we should have gone quietly into whatever retirement he had chosen for us. But Alison never went quietly. It was not in her nature.

Her workbox had fallen to the floor when she had scrambled to get out of the coach. It lay on its side, the lid open. I picked it up. It felt smooth and cold against my skin. I knew how precious it was to her and how angry she would be to so carelessly have left it behind.

The box was empty but for a few scraps of material, a pale blue ribbon, some pins with enamel heads and a shred of parchment with a pencil sketch. I turned it around. It was Wolf Hall, drawn in a few spare lines that captured the essence of the place, all higgledy-piggledy roof and jumbled windows. It was very good. Alison always had had a sharp eye and a fair hand.

I looked up as the squire clattered out of the inn empty-

117

handed, palms spread wide. A low-voiced colloquy followed.
I could not hear what he said to the others but the inference
was clear. Alison had disappeared.

I sat in the coach and waited whilst they searched the inn
and the streets around, getting progressively more wet, dirty
and angry.

They did not find her.

# TEN

*Alison, London, the present day*

ALISON FELT BETTER WHEN SHE WAS BACK IN London, more stable, more sane. She had loved the city from the first moment she had seen it, loved everything about it from the lazy curves of the wide river to the multiplicity of people on the streets. She loved the fusion of old and new, the scents and the sights, the buzz of excitement. It was the only place she had ever felt truly at home, where she felt her life click back into place.

With the benefit of hindsight, she could see that the mistake she had made in the beginning was to stay in Wiltshire. It had made sense in an illogical sort of way; she was close to places that were vaguely familiar and she had thought it would be easier to find her way back to claim Arthur. Driven by anger and hatred at the way Edward had treated her, at the way he had treated Mary too, she had made the rash decision to flee into the future. Naturally, she had misunderstood every aspect of her situation. She had been unable to return to the past. She had no idea how to survive in the alien world she had discovered. Early on, sleeping rough, she had tried to barter some of the jewels she had brought with her for food and shelter. The police had been called. She had ended up in care.

It had been the best thing that had happened to her. She was fed, clothed and educated. Beyond trying to discover where she had come from no one asked her anything. She was swallowed up by an incurious system, processed. It gave her exactly what she needed, which was the chance to learn how to speak like everyone else and to observe how this new world worked. She was small for her age and they assumed she was younger than she was. They assumed a lot—that she had run away from home, that she had been abused. It was close to the truth.

She had used the system well, gone to college and studied for a diploma in travel and tourism. She had a real determination to succeed and loved everything that was different about this world from the one she had left—the technology, the opportunities to travel, the significant improvement in the status of women.

She caught sight of a billboard showing a scantily clad starlet promoting online betting. Even after four hundred years there was still some way to go.

She keyed her pass code into the box at the side of a discreet door in Kensington and felt the stresses of the weekend fade away. Up in the office there was chatter and the smell of strong coffee. The familiarity was almost enough to smooth over the memory of the one constant, the nagging ache, the vital thing that she had left behind. Arthur.

"Ali!" Kate, her colleague and friend, paused in exchanging weekend news with one of the other girls. Her face lost its glow. "How was it?"

"Fine." Alison slid behind her desk and accepted the mug of coffee Kate proffered. "Thanks." She took a deep swallow of the scalding liquid and closed her eyes, relaxing back in her chair. "It's good to be back."

"At work?" Kate said.

"In London," Alison said.

Kate's expression cleared. "Yes, well, you're not really a country person, are you? The rest of the world—fine. The British countryside—not so much."

"I grew up there," Alison said. "That was enough."

"How was your friend?" Kate perched on the edge of Alison's desk. Then, as she saw Alison's expression: "Bad?"

Alison nodded. "I'm not sure I'll see her again."

"I'm sorry." Kate touched her hand lightly. Alison did not react. She wasn't a tactile person but Kate knew her well enough to know that she appreciated her friendship.

"I met my ex," Alison added casually.

Kate almost choked on the chocolate biscuit she was eating. "What ex? I didn't know you had any." She dabbed her streaming eyes. "Oh, wait, there was that guy who worked for Deloittes. You went out with him for a couple of months, didn't you? And there was that hot cyclist—"

"Who preferred to spend his weekends clocking up hundreds of miles in the saddle than spending time with me," Alison said dryly. "No, it wasn't him. It was someone I knew a long time ago." She wondered why she had mentioned Adam. She wasn't usually free with the personal information, at least not the sort that was really personal. Trivia was fine— her Facebook page was all about her travels, her friends, the books she was reading, the shows she had seen. But real stuff, stuff that mattered, that was different because it went too deep. She could not be honest about herself, about her past, about the experiences that had made her the person she was.

"You're late." Charles, the MD, had paused by her desk. "Meeting in five."

Kate slid off the desk and gave her a look that said, *Tell me later.*

They all sat around the big oak table in the boardroom. The company, Cleveland and Down, was a young and vibrant high-end tour operator run by a couple of public school dropouts, Charles and his partner Madelin. It was staffed by glossy, public school alumni whose breezy charm and lazy vowels masked a sharp intelligence and laser-like sales ability. Once past its early struggle to turn a profit, C&D had grown exponentially, catering to well-heeled Londoners and their county cousins who wanted adventure holidays, exotic honeymoons and something a bit different. Alison had been with the company from the start, which was why Charles cut her a very small amount of slack over the erratic timekeeping.

Andre, one of the senior account managers started the business round up. "We got the Maitland account," he said. He swung back in his chair, grinning. "Ponta Dos Ganchos, Brazil. Bride and groom plus fifteen guests."

There was some whooping and clapping around the table. Alison took a biscuit and pushed the tin towards Kate, who smiled and shook her head.

"Three honeymoon packages," Kate reported briskly. "Bahamas, Bora Bora and Orkney."

There was more clapping.

"Orkney," Alison said, shuddering.

"It's romantic." Kate sounded defensive, as though Alison had insulted her own personal honeymoon choice. "That sort of environment provides lots of opportunities to cuddle up."

"Alison," Charles cut in, fidgeting with his pen. "Anything to add?"

"Two safari packages," Alison said. Africa was her focus at the moment. "One self-drive for four in Namibia, the other a couple going with a tour group in Tanzania. Plus a potential booking for the wild flower route in South Africa next August."

Charles nodded. "We should push that more. It's a stunning trip."

"I'm on it," Alison said, making a note on the pad in front of her.

"We could make it more of a feature on the website." Janet, the social media manager, leaned an elbow on the table. "The visuals make it particularly appealing."

"Good idea," Charles said. He looked up from his notes. "Now, some news on the open day. Maddy?"

"The programme is almost finalised," Madelin said, scattering some sheets across the table for people to pick up. "It's the usual mix of talks, practical demonstrations and exhibitors. We've got some new and exciting destinations, stuff on health, photography, luxury camping, survival—without scaring people, of course—and, new this year, some culture."

"Andre's going to be leading on developing a cultural programme next year," Charles said. "It's a growth area. So we thought we would launch it at the open day with a keynote speaker."

"I've got a shortlist of potential candidates and wanted your input." Andre drew a list towards him.

"Steve Backshall, Bear Grylls…"

"In your dreams," Kate said.

"He might be too busy," Andre conceded, "but it's worth a try. Adam Hewer is a possibility," he added. "It would be different."

Alison almost spewed the dregs of her coffee. "Sorry," she gasped, rubbing her streaming eyes. "I inhaled at the wrong moment."

"He has that effect on me as well," Kate said, slapping her on the back. "He's super hot."

"But…" Alison struggled. "He's not… I mean, he's all to do with history, isn't he?" She looked around the table. "Is that the image we're going for?"

"He represents history and culture, he travels to exotic locations, he's hugely popular, posh and insanely good-looking," Maddy said. "I'd say that's exactly the image we're going for when we launch our new programme."

The silence felt hostile. Alison had observed over the years that if C&D had a weakness it was that it was so relentlessly upbeat that any dissension was always interpreted as negativity. In this instance she was guilty as charged. It had never occurred to her that her world and Adam's might overlap one day, but she could see that if the company was going to launch holidays touring Ancient Greece or trekking to Machu Picchu then Adam Hewer would be the perfect celebrity ambassador.

"Yes, I see," she said weakly.

"I hope that isn't a problem, Alison." Charles had fixed her with his disconcertingly shrewd grey gaze. "Whilst Andre will be leading on this, we're a small team so we're all going to be involved."

"Not a problem," Alison repeated. "I just wondered…" She was thinking quickly. "Whether it might be more newsworthy to have a female celebrity to launch the programme? It feels as though adventure travel is so male-dominated that we would look really different and cutting edge to team up with someone like Fiona Ellis, for example."

She held her breath for the pause.

"That's a good idea," Maddy conceded. "Yes…" She was warming to the idea. "She's young, talented, she's done a lot of expeditions for charity and there's talk of a reality TV show."

"She doesn't have the cultural credentials Adam Hewer does." Charles wasn't convinced.

"She has a double first from Cambridge," someone said, "as well as a Blue in fencing and rowing."

There were nods around the table and a palpable buzz of agreement.

"I like the fact she's travelled across the Kalahari Desert," Charles allowed. "That fits with our existing itineraries."

"I'm sure she could get up to speed quickly on the new cultural tours if she agreed to be our ambassador." Kate caught Alison's eye. "I think it's a great idea."

"I'll contact her agent straight away." Andre was keen, already half out of his chair wanting to make the call. Maddy cast Charles a quick look. He nodded.

"Great," she said. "Go for it. Good idea," she added to Alison, as they filed out of the meeting room. "This should get us some great publicity."

"I hope she agrees," Alison said.

"She's more likely to be available than Adam Hewer," Maddy said. "He's hot property at the moment, almost impossible to book, I hear."

"Really?" Alison was surprised even though she knew she shouldn't be. She'd seen Adam's popularity for herself.

For a moment she allowed herself to sink back into the memories of how it had been ten years before, when they had first met. It was still so vivid to her that it was like watching a film, rich in colour and texture. It had been summer in Marlborough. A heat haze shimmered over the fields. The River Kennet had run dry, the ducks standing disconsolately in puddles, the mud cracking in the heat and smelling of damp and decay. It was too hot to study, almost too hot to think. She had been at the college summer school, taking a short course in Sustainable Tourism. Adam had been part of an archaeological dig. They had met on her first evening and it had been sweet, hot and had happened fast.

Even now, in a stuffy office in London in the winter ten years later, she could feel the scent of cut grass tickling her nose and hear the distant hum of the mower, and feel Adam's hands tracing patterns over the hot skin of her stomach as they lay together in the shadow of the ruined castle.

She had not loved him the way she had loved Edward. She had wasted the sweetness of first love on Edward in the weeks and months before she had realised that he was using her. That innocence had gone and yet with Adam it had felt more honest and true because she knew that, unlike Edward, he really had loved her. She had seen it in the way he looked at her, felt it in his touch.

Love had been simple for Adam, but nothing was simple for her. She was only nineteen, still adjusting to an alien way of life, still reeling from the loss of Arthur. She had wanted to love Adam too, but it was all too new, too different, too complicated.

Adam was going back to Cambridge after the summer to complete the final year of his degree. He had asked her to go with him. She had wanted to go, but she knew she could not. One day she would find a way back to Arthur; of that she was obstinately determined. She would never be able to explain it to Adam, never be able to be honest with him. So she had pretended it had been no more than a fling, a summer romance, and had ended it when he left Marlborough.

It had hurt at the time. It still hurt to remember it now, even after so many years. She knew it should not and hoped it was only so raw because seeing Adam again had stirred up all the dormant memories and emotions. She hoped so, but was rather afraid it might be more than that. Adam was the one man she did not feel armoured against.

Back at her desk, she surreptitiously removed the newspaper cutting that Richard Demoranville had given her from her bag and typed the name "Smithfield" into her search engine. She had got back late the previous night and hadn't had much time to check out either Middlecote Hall or the family that had owned it. Now she was interested to see that there was very little information on the Smithfield family on the Internet. Jack Smithfield had apparently been an entrepreneur who had made his first fortune in packaging solutions and subsequent ones in any number of diverse enterprises. He had owned Middlecote but had seldom visited. His main home was in Miami and he had died the previous year at the age of ninety-one. His children lived abroad.

Alison rubbed her forehead. So much for her idea of approaching a member of the Smithfield family directly in the hope of gaining entry to Middlecote or learning something of its story. Gisela Smithfield worked in Sweden. Her brother Jack Junior and sister Anna were based in the US. No doubt Adam knew that. Jack Smithfield had invited him to catalogue the contents of the house before he had died. Adam was the only one who had access. Adam was the only one who could help her.

It all came back to Adam.

# ELEVEN

*Mary, 1560*

THE RAIN STOPPED AND THE COACH MADE ITS
way through the sodden landscape, sticking in ruts, skidding
on mud, the driver swearing and the sky becoming darker
as the winter evening set in early. We were left with two
outriders now. One of the squires had ridden back to Wolf
Hall to acquaint Edward with the fact that Alison had run
away. The other had stayed in Marlborough to hunt for her.
I wondered what Edward would do. I already knew he hated
dissent and disobedience, perceiving it as a challenge to his
authority. Yet he was also weak, or perhaps simply lazy. He
might abandon her to find her own way.

I felt lonely after she had gone. Alison and I had never
been friends, our relationship had been too complicated and
prickly for that, and yet I had felt close to her. I thought about
reaching out to Darrell again but my pride stopped me. I was
needy but I did not wish to appear so.

The coach stopped. I lifted the curtain to peer out. We had
passed through a huge archway whose gate piers were topped
with stone wyvern. Torches flared from their mouths. Yet it

appeared that there was no lodge keeper to guide us on our way to wherever we were going; no sign of life at all. After a muttered conversation between the coachman and the escort, we rumbled forward again, down a long avenue lined with trees, their branches bare and dripping.

It was daunting. I shivered.

The house, when it came into view, was another matter entirely. An elegant rectangle around a courtyard, it was built of limestone and flint with a stone roof and impudently arched windows. Tall chimneys stood against the darkening sky.

We drove into the courtyard. The clatter of hooves, which had filled my ears all day, stopped suddenly and all was quiet. There was a chill breeze sneaking into the coach.

I stood up stiffly and pushed open the door. I wanted to wash and needed the privy. One of the squires helped me down, which was good because my legs were trembling with tiredness and apprehension. As I stepped into the courtyard, though, an odd thing happened. The grey of the clouds parted and the last pale light of the sun danced along the roof of the house, lifting the darkness to gold.

A door opened. A girl my age, with long brown hair and pale blue eyes, came running towards me. Behind her, an older woman approached more decorously. The girl grasped my hands in hers.

"You're here at last! I'm so pleased!"

She hugged me and, after the initial surprise, I hugged her back. She was as warm and welcoming as the day had become, the sun glowing on the little house and banishing the grey.

*I have a friend at last*, I thought. Then: *I like this place.* My chilled heart eased a little.

She loosed me. She was smiling, although perhaps I should

have noticed the anxiety in her eyes behind the smile. But I was young and tired and lonely. I took matters at face value.

"Lady Mary." The older woman—her mother?—had come to join us. She was smiling too, but there was little warmth in it—not, I judged, because she disliked me but because she was a very proper woman. It was evident in the pride with which she held herself, the elegance of her dress and the formality in her manner.

"Please excuse my daughter Eleanor's hoyden manners."

I smiled at Eleanor. "It is no matter, ma'am. I am very happy to meet you both."

She inclined her head. Unlike her daughter she had dark eyes, watchful beneath the brim of her hood. "I am Lady Fenner," she said. "Welcome to Middlecote Hall." She looked around. "But where is Mistress Banestre? I thought she travelled with you?"

"She remains in Wiltshire," I said carefully. "I am come alone." I had no desire to launch into an explanation of how Alison had run away. I felt another pang of loneliness, unexpected, unwanted. I must be feeling very tired to be missing Alison, of all people.

I saw Lady Fenner's fine brows, so like the arches of the windows, snap down in a formidable frown. No doubt she had had a room prepared for Alison, and food and other comforts. Eleanor was looking apprehensive now.

"I do apologise, ma'am," I said. "For putting you to such inconvenience."

"No matter," Lady Fenner said, having paused long enough to give lie to the courteous words. "From what I hear of Mistress Banestre, it is perhaps fortunate that she has gone elsewhere. I am not at all sure that she would have fitted in here. We are a very respectable household." Her gaze considered me again and I received another wintry smile.

"You, Lady Mary, are a different matter I am sure. You will find Middlecote much to your liking and I am persuaded we will like you."

The sun had gone in now. I shivered, standing there on the gravel, whilst all about me the servants busied themselves taking in my luggage and the groom and coachman led the horses away to the stables and the steward led Edward's squires away to refresh themselves. It was as though I was just another piece of baggage. Here was another new place, more new people and another new start. Yet I trailed all the ghosts of the past with me: my reckless father, my tragic learned mother and the retinue of relatives who, down the years, had not wanted me. I brought my gift of dark visions and my secret friendship with Darrell. Lady Fenner knew of none of those things nor, I was determined, would she ever discover them. Such secret matters had no place in a respectable household.

"I will show you to your chamber." Eleanor linked her arm with mine. "You will wish to wash and tidy yourself before we eat." She squeezed my arm, warm, friendly. I smiled back, weary and grateful.

*I like this place*, I repeated over in my mind and I tried to persuade myself it was true.

# TWELVE

*Alison*

ALISON ALMOST MISSED THE SIGNPOST FOR Middlecote. It listed at forty-five degrees, pointing down a tiny lane with high banks and close hedges. Gritting her teeth, she backed up and turned the car, narrowly missing a supermarket delivery van that was heading towards her at high speed. Evidently someone must live down this road to nowhere.

She met no other traffic on the lane, nor could she see any houses. Middlecote must be very isolated, as much now as it might have been four hundred years before. She felt a prickle of excitement, overlaid by a stronger wash of apprehension. She wasn't entirely sure what she was doing here. It seemed unlikely any member of the Smithfield family would be living at Middlecote, and if the house had been let, the tenants probably would not welcome her knocking on the door out of the blue. Information on the history of the house had been as hard to come by as information on the owners. Entries in the heritage listings described its architecture as a mix of medieval, Tudor and later. There was a list of the families who had owned it, including the Fenners, whose distant connection to Jane Seymour was noted. There was a Roman villa in the grounds. In the twentieth century, it had variously been used as a school and a private hospital. It was registered as belonging to the Smithfield Foundation, a charity that was based in the Bahamas.

All this screamed privacy and should have deterred her from setting out on a wild goose chase, yet here she was. Feeling the stir of butterflies in her chest again, she shifted in her seat. For so long she had had no word of Arthur. She had had no means of travelling back to find him. Somehow she had lived with that burden of grief, forcing herself to move forward until the time came when something changed. Now it had and the determination gripped her like a fever. The door to the past had opened a crack and she was going to push on it until she found a way.

The plan seemed pretty lame now though, now that she could see that the cast iron gates of Middlecote were very firmly padlocked against visitors. A sign on one of the beech trees that flanked the gates tersely instructed people to keep out. The snarling carved wyverns on the top of the crumbling gate pillars seemed only to emphasise the lack of welcome. Alison drove further along the lane, hoping to find another entrance, but there was none, only a blank-faced wall that encircled the estate.

There were, however, footpaths. She was not a keen walker. She took her exercise at the gym. Nor was she dressed for hiking. But if it was the only way to find out more about Middlecote, Alison supposed she would have to get on with it. She should have thought of this. These days she was so ill prepared for country life. It was impossible to believe that once she had been used to trudging through mud up to her knees, soaking wet and with her hair straggling from beneath a sodden bonnet. That past might as well be no more than a dream. She had become very accustomed to comfort.

Her hands shook a little as she locked the car door and zipped the keys carefully into the pocket of her black quilted jacket. She tucked her hair under a knitted beanie hat and pulled on her gloves. It was cold outside. The cutting edge of the breeze almost stole her breath. Luckily, she had boots on, but they weren't the sort to wear to ramble across fields and her black skinny jeans were too thin for this cold.

Sharp thorns grasped at her jacket as she climbed over the stile and jumped down the other side. Fortunately, the frost had frozen the muddy furrows hard but even so she had twisted her ankle within two minutes. She gritted her teeth and marched on. This would be the moment to pause and appreciate the winter landscape, perhaps; the plume of smoke rising from a cottage across the valley like a feather in the still air, the loud calling of the birds in the bare hedgerow, the way that the frost patterned the leaves with silver. Except that her feet were freezing, her expensive boots were leaking already and she had a tear in the quilted jacket where a particularly malevolent bramble had snagged her.

Why the hell hadn't she just rung Adam up and asked for his help? She needed to accept that she couldn't do this all on her own. She could have spun him some convincing line about her family history research and persuaded him to tell her about Mary's portrait and the box. She was sure she could. He had already refused to answer her questions once but she could have given it another shot. They could have met in London, in a nice warm impersonal coffee shop and that way she wouldn't be slogging across a field, getting colder, dirtier and more annoyed with each step.

The footpath had been descending gently and now it passed through a larch wood and crossed a broader track, a bridleway that ran in a straight line as far as Alison could see before dipping away across the hill. A huge oak stood here, bare of leaf, its branches thick and twisted by age into extraordinary shapes. It reminded Alison of the trees in Savernake. This oak would have been here long before Mary Seymour came to Middlecote Hall.

Again that feeling of stepping back into the past struck her so forcibly that it felt like a step missed in the dark. Drawing her jacket more closely about her she crossed the bridleway and dipped back into the wood, finding that the path ended within a hundred yards in a cast iron gate that matched the one at the main entrance. There was a padlock on this one too but Alison was fairly certain that landowners were not supposed to block public footpaths so she climbed over the gate and found herself in the deer park. A frosty green sweep of grass dropped away downhill, dotted with tall oaks and beech. At the bottom of the slope stood a house.

The clouds were breaking a little overhead, revealing a sky of pale washed blue and a weak sun that picked out the red brick, warming it and sparkling off the leaded windows. Alison caught her breath.

She never visited historic houses, keeping well away from anything that presented what felt to her a sterile past trapped in the present. It had been the only way to survive when she had realised that she could never get back; seeing a facsimile of the past all the time was not comforting. It only made her feel more alienated from Arthur and from her own time.

Now, though, looking at Middlecote Hall, she felt an odd shift in perspective as though she really could simply run down the hill and rejoin Mary Seymour in the past. The sensation was so strong that for a moment she thought she really might have stepped back in time, so easily, so unintentionally, but then she heard the hoot of a horn on the lane behind and the sound of a car, and felt her excited spirits drop.

She started to walk down the path to the hall, beneath the bare, spreading branches of the oaks, where the frozen leaves of autumn crunched underfoot. As she got closer to the house, she could see the neglect. Weeds grew through the gravel of the drive, walls were crumbling and ivy shuttered some of the windows. The neat lines of flowerbeds and parterre were blurred and overgrown.

There was no sign of inhabitation and the impression of warmth and welcome that Alison had felt when she first saw the house had faded now. The blank windows seemed shuttered and secretive. There was something inimical about it.

Her mood tumbled into misery again. She realised that she had come to Middlecote because she wanted to establish some sort of physical connection to Mary, however tenuous, and through that feel comforted that she was closer to Arthur. Instead, she just felt more distant from them, locked out, left behind.

The front door was padlocked just as the gates had been. Alison peered in at one of the downstairs windows and could see absolutely nothing in the gloom inside. Adam had said that he had found Mary's portrait as part of a restoration project but there seemed to be precious little restoration work going on here. A horrid doubt seized Alison that Richard Demoranville had given her erroneous information and sent her off to completely the wrong place.

She sat down on the front steps. The whole thing was too Gothic to be true. Any moment now Mary's ghost would waft across the drive and beckon her inside. Her new boots were ruined, her coat was ripped and she was frozen. She started to laugh.

Looking up, she saw she wasn't alone. A black Labrador—

rotund and with a greying muzzle—was sitting a few feet away watching her with his bright brown eyes. His wagging tail stirred the loose gravel chippings.

There was the sound of footsteps on the drive.

"Monty!" It was Adam's voice, with a shade of irritation. "Where—"

"Your guard dog's here," Alison said, as Monty started to sniff enthusiastically at her boots. "Hello, Adam."

Not even an optimist could consider Adam's response welcoming. He rubbed his chin, his expression closed as he looked at her. Alison felt at an immediate disadvantage and scrambled to her feet, suddenly acutely aware of the mud-spattered boots, the rip in her jacket and her general air of dishevelment.

"How the hell did you know—" Adam said. He stopped, but it was too late. In that moment, Alison knew with total certainty that the newspaper cutting had been correct. She was in the right place. This was where Adam had found Mary's portrait. She felt a rush of elation mingled with terror.

*And so it begins... Time starts to run backwards, the quest is set in motion.*

Adam had changed tack. "How did you know where to find me?" he said.

Alison dragged off her beanie hat and shook out her hair. "I wasn't looking for *you*, Adam," she said, over her shoulder. "I didn't even know you would be here. It was the house I came to see."

Adam didn't reply and when she looked up she could see a hint of a smile creeping into his eyes. She liked that he wasn't too arrogant to believe her despite his celebrity. People must fawn over him all the time these days. She was glad it hadn't spoiled him. Not that it should matter to her one way or another.

"That makes sense, I suppose," he said. "You came because of the connection to Mary Seymour?"

"I traced her to here," Alison said cautiously. She didn't want to give Richard away. She still didn't understand why he had given her the newspaper cutting but she was hugely grateful to him.

Adam nodded. His mouth turned down at the corners. "I had no idea there was a link between Middlecote and Mary," he said, almost to himself, "but last night I found a reference—" He broke off. "Why are you smiling?"

Alison could not help herself. "So you took my claims seriously enough to check them out," she said.

Adam scowled at her. He ran a hand through his hair. "Is that your car parked up the road?"

Alison was slightly thrown by the change of subject. "The red Focus? Yes."

"The farmer's towed it away, I'm afraid," Adam said. He didn't sound particularly sorry. "He gets angry when people block field gates."

"The cardinal sin of the countryside, I suppose," Alison said. "Where is it?"

"In the yard." Adam jerked his head towards the back of the house. "You should have let me know you were coming," he added. "I would have opened the gates and then you wouldn't have needed to climb through hedges to get here." His gaze travelled over her again, measured, cool, and Alison felt herself blush. No doubt she had twigs in her hair and mud smeared on her face. She raised her chin.

"Like I said, I didn't know you were here." She glanced around at the weed-strewn drive and the blank windows. "Do you own the place now?"

"Of course not," Adam said. "A historian's pay can't buy this piece of history." He sighed. "Well, as you're here, I suppose you'd better come in."

"There's no need to sound so eager," Alison said, following him. "Anyway," she added, "if you don't own Middlecote yourself, should you be inviting me in?"

Adam gave her a look. "I have a key because I'm still working on a few bits and pieces of research and as you've gone to such a lot of trouble to get here—" once again his cool gaze considered her mud-splashed boots and trousers "—I assumed you wanted to see the place."

"Fair enough," Alison said. "Thank you," she added.

Monty walked next to her, his stubby black tail wagging. She leaned over to stroke his ears and the dog paused, closing his eyes and putting his head back in a pose of bliss.

"At least Monty seems to like me," Alison said.

She saw Adam's lips twitch into a smile. "I didn't know you were a dog person."

"I don't think the topic ever came up," Alison said.

"I suppose not." Adam had stopped at a battered wooden door with peeling blue paint. He took a key out of his pocket.

"It was all a very long time ago," Alison said.

Adam did not bother to reply.

Alison looked around whilst he wrestled with the padlock on the door. To their right, through an archway, was a coach yard. Alison could see her diminutive red car sitting next to a mud-splashed four-by-four. Adam's, she presumed.

Adam stepped aside to allow her to precede him into the house. She heard him follow her and the door close with an unnervingly final thud. It was so dark in the interior that it took her eyes a moment to adapt.

Black and white marble floor, a huge gallery with a stained glass window that looked more Victorian than Elizabethan, a cobwebbed chandelier… It was the sort of house that looked as though it had been added to piecemeal over the centuries and had ended up as some sort of Gothic horror show. Alison was not sure what she had been expecting but it wasn't this. She felt an obscure sense of disappointment.

It was also dark, cold and quelling. She instinctively wrapped her arms about her to repress a shiver. Monty didn't seem to mind the atmosphere though. He lay down on the marble floor with a heartfelt sigh.

"I thought you said you found the portrait when you were working on a restoration project," Alison said, looking round. "It doesn't look as though you've got far with the work."

Adam snapped on a light switch and the dusty chandelier glowed into faint life. It made everything look much worse, to Alison's eyes; dust an inch thick, elongated shadows and battered panelling all complemented by the smell of damp and decay.

"It wasn't a restoration project," Adam said. "I was only cataloguing the contents of the house. It was Richard who first put me on to it because the family brought a couple of paintings into his shop to be valued."

"Are they intending to sell the place?" Alison asked.

Adam shook his head. "They're not interested in either selling or restoring the property but they did agree to remove all the historic contents that were worth preservation."

"Before they rotted away," Alison said.

"Something like that," Adam agreed. "Though there wasn't much left anyway. It had been sold off down the centuries."

His voice was cold; she had the impression he disapproved of people who let their heritage disintegrate around them.

"Would you like a tour?" Adam said. "I assume that was why you came?" He tilted his head to one side, watching her. "What were you expecting—open house and afternoon cream teas?"

"You never know," Alison said lightly.

"Well, sorry to disappoint," Adam said. "A kettle and some instant coffee is the best I can do. There's no milk, I'm afraid."

"Wow," Alison said. "I won't, thanks."

"This way then." Adam gestured towards a rather unnervingly dark passage. His attitude reminded Alison of someone who was going to the dentist. Get it over with. She wondered why he had invited her inside at all.

She followed him down the shadowed corridor. Monty gave a huff and hauled himself to his feet to patter after them.

"He's Richard's dog," Adam said, "though I borrow him when I'm down."

"He's lovely," Alison said, as Monty gave her a soulful look.

"This is the Great Hall," Adam said, standing aside so that she could see past him into the interior. "It was remodelled in the late sixteenth century but you may recognise the detail in the window since you're such a Seymour scholar." There was a slightly sarcastic tone in his voice.

"One is the Tudor rose," Alison said, following his gaze to the four roundels in the stained glass window. "Then there are the arms of King Henry VIII and those of Jane Seymour and their initials."

"They were supposed to have courted secretly at Middlecote after meeting at Wolf Hall," Adam said.

"I suppose it's possible," Alison said. She thought back over what she had gleaned in her time at Wolf Hall. She had never heard mention of Middlecote, which was why she had not thought of it when she was trying to trace Mary. She wondered if some enterprising owner down the years had made up the story of Jane and Henry's courtship to give the place more importance.

"But you don't think it's likely," Adam said, and she realised how doubtful she had sounded. She gave herself a mental shake.

"The Seymours and the Fenners were related by marriage," she said, "so there was a family connection. And we aren't far from Savernake, as the crow flies. So it is possible." She realised how closely Adam was watching her. His expression was quizzical, not, she thought, because he believed she was making it up but because she sounded so knowledgeable, so convincing. She would need to be careful. It would be easy to give away more than she intended if she lowered her guard.

Deliberately, she broke the contact between them and looked up at the window again with its brilliantly coloured roundels glowing even in the gloom.

"You mentioned that the window is of a later date than Tudor, though," she said.

"Installed by Sir John Hopton, who was inordinately proud of his connection to royal history," Adam said. "Hopton inherited the place from Wild Will Fenner in the 1580s."

*Wild Will Fenner.*

Something stirred in the ashes of the grate, a curl of old smoke released to rise lazily up the chimney. Alison felt the cold inside her seep deeper.

"Have you come across him in your family tree research?" Adam's tone was neutral this time. He was still testing her.

"I've never heard of Will Fenner," Alison said honestly. "But…" She stopped, shrugged. "Sorry, no. The name just seemed familiar for a moment." It did, like an echo down through time or a whisper in her mind.

"He was supposed to have been something of a bad lot," Adam said. "Drink, women, gambling, debt…"

"The usual sixteenth-century gentlemen's pastimes," Alison said.

"Plus highway robbery and murder," Adam added.

"Not so commonplace," Alison conceded. She felt apprehension stir. Mary had come *here*, to a murderer's household? Alison shivered, wondering how she had fared. How could little Mary Seymour, unprotected, honest, inexperienced, guard herself in a place like this?

"What happened to Will Fenner?" she asked.

"I don't know much about him," Adam said, "except that there were endless disputes over his inheritance when he was young. He was always engaged in litigation with his neighbours and family. He died in about 1580, which was when the house went to Hopton. I think he had a fall from his horse, up on the path at the top of the hill, the Thieves' Way. They call the place the Phantom Tree."

Alison's sensation of cold was intensifying now, eating into her bones, rising up her body. It felt terrifying, uncontrollable. With a huge effort of will she fought to break free of the strange sensation.

"This part of the house looks later than Tudor," she said, focusing on the discoloured plasterwork, concentrating on the detail of the panelling to stop herself running from the building.

"It was remodelled in the seventeenth century," Adam said. "Hopton kept the medieval core of the manor but built onto it. What remains of the Tudor mansion is through here." He ducked his head beneath a lintel and led her through another long stone passageway with mullioned windows, which looked out onto a square of overgrown grass. Alison felt disorientated; this sprawling house was like nothing she had experienced. Generations subsequent to her own had altered and added until the familiar lines of a Tudor manor were blurred to her.

Here, though, was something she did recognise: a parlour, with another wide grate and panelled walls, like all the other rooms empty and desolate. She had thought there would be furniture. She had thought there would be *something*, perhaps even something recognisably belonging to Mary Seymour, something she remembered. She realised she had been too optimistic.

Darker patches on the corridor walls showed where pictures had hung. At the end was a stair, turning upwards into the gloom. Adam started to climb it and Alison followed. The oak treads were irregular and creaked alarmingly beneath her feet. The handrail was smooth under her fingers. Mary had walked here yet she could feel no echo of her presence. No voice called out to her. There was nothing but a chill in the air and the scent of decay.

"It's very quelling, isn't it?" Adam had joined her on the landing. "Though it could be stunning again. If they did decide to sell—" He broke off.

"It would probably be bought by a developer," Alison finished for him, "and turned into flats."

Adam laughed. "There's not much romance in your soul."

"There never was," Alison said. An odd silence fell between them, as though they were both remembering. Glancing at Adam, she saw his expression was pensive.

"I thought the house would still be furnished," Alison said, more to break the silence than for any other reason. "It feels so...abandoned."

"It is," Adam said quietly. "That is exactly what it is."

Alison glanced around the landing. In the fading light she could see faint traces of painted walls: vines, leaves and flowers entwined. The floor sloped quite dramatically towards two doorways standing side by side.

"The haunted bedroom." Adam's voice was dry. "The room where Wild Will Fenner murdered his newborn child. Allegedly."

"Allegedly?" Alison said. The doorway of the room yawned open. She felt no compulsion to step inside, rather a dark dread and a sense of utter repugnance returning.

"The legend goes that a midwife was summoned in the middle of the night," Adam said, "and although she was blindfolded she swears she was brought to Middlecote, where she helped at the birth of Will Fenner's child, but as soon as the babe was born, he threw it on the fire."

Alison shuddered. "How utterly grotesque. Why would he do such a thing?"

Adam shrugged. "He was a violent brute. It was his mistress's child so perhaps he wanted to be rid of it. It's said he bribed the midwife to silence but she reported him."

"He should have hanged," Alison said.

"It was unproven," Adam said. "Will Fenner denied it and because the midwife had been blindfolded they could not establish that it was definitely Middlecote she had been taken to. Plus, the judge was one of Will's cronies, our old friend Hopton. It's said he protected Will Fenner from the law in return for being granted Middlecote on Will's death."

There was a cold pain in Alison's head, an ache that made her ears buzz. She found she was standing on the threshold of the room with no real idea of how she had got there. She could see a fire leaping in the grate, hear screams and smell the stench of burning. A baby, consigned to the flames.

The nausea rose in her throat. Suddenly the protective barriers she had erected in her mind were blown apart. It was as though she could feel Arthur in her arms, smell the baby scent of him, see his eyes opening, that deep lavender blue that was the same as hers... Had he died as a child too? How could she ever know? It was all so vivid and so terrifyingly painful that she staggered.

"Ali?"

Adam's hand was on her arm. She could hear concern in his voice. She turned towards him, the vulnerability making her want to fling herself against him for comfort, the last wretched dregs of pride and self-preservation holding her back.

"I'm all right," she said, and did not recognise her own voice.

Adam led her back across the landing to a window seat. It was un-cushioned but she sank gratefully down onto the hard wood.

"Sorry," she said, putting a hand up to her forehead. "I just felt a bit...odd...for a moment."

"You've gone as white as a sheet," Adam said. "Do you need some water?"

"No," Alison said. "I'm fine. I just need to get away from that room, I think." She shuddered. "What a vile man and a vile story."

Adam stood up and offered her his hand to help her rise. She took it, expecting him to let her go once she was on her feet, but instead he led her out onto the landing as though she were a small child, his fingers curled about hers. It was unexpected and comforting and Alison felt some emotion stir inside her and warmth unfurl. She wasn't accustomed to holding anyone's hand. She wasn't sure how to do it. It felt awkward. She never took help; always she managed on her own.

She waited for Adam to precede her down the stair but

he stopped on the landing, turning more fully to face her, leaning against one of the newel posts.

"Why did you come here today, Ali?" he said. "What did you really hope to find?"

Alison felt a shiver go through her at his tone. It felt so intimate, here in the falling shadows.

"I thought there would be something left," she said slowly. "Some sort of clue…"

"To Mary Seymour?" Adam had understood even before she had quite articulated the thought in her own mind.

"I hadn't realised that there was nothing here," Alison said. Hopelessness enveloped her all of a sudden. It had been stupid to come. There was nothing to find here. Her hold on the past, on Arthur, had become so tenuous it hung by a thread. Or perhaps there was no hold at all and her hope was mere wishful thinking.

"It must be very important to you," Adam said, "to send you down here on the off chance of discovering something."

"I'm very tenacious when it comes to my family-tree research," Alison said, "and Mary is key to that." She tried to keep her voice light but the words sounded hollow in her ears. She tried again. "Having no living family, it's particularly important to me to find out where I came from."

Adam seemed to accept that and she felt a rush of relief as she saw him nod. "Yeah, I can understand that," he said. "We all need to feel we belong. I imagine…" He paused. "Well, it must get lonely sometimes being on your own."

Alison tried not to flinch. That hurt her, perhaps more than it should. Once, for a short while, she and Adam had been together, united, sharing everything. Except that she had never really shared the truth of herself with Adam or anyone, except Diana. She could not. They would think she was certifiable.

The silence sat oddly between them, too intimate for her comfort. It felt as though the air was charged, as though they were too attuned to each other's thoughts and reactions.

"Anyway, what about you?" Alison deliberately broke the moment. "Why did you come back?" She watched his face but he was impassive, giving nothing away. Adam had always had that ability even when he had been young. It had infuriated her.

"I think you've got serious doubts about the book," she said suddenly. "I think you really do believe the portrait is Mary's and you came here to check something out."

Adam folded his arms. "Are you done?" he asked, very politely.

"No," Alison said. "You mentioned earlier that you had discovered some sort of reference to Mary Seymour being here. What was it?"

"You tell me," Adam said. "You're the Seymour expert."

Alison hesitated. She knew she had to give him something to encourage him to tell her more. Equally, she could not give away too much. It felt like a game of bluff and double bluff.

"My information says that Mary Seymour grew up at Grimsthorpe in Lincolnshire in the household of the Duchess of Suffolk," she said, "but that when The Duchess fled abroad during the Marian persecutions, Mary was sent to Wolf Hall."

Adam raised his brows. "Wolf Hall? Really? But was it not falling into disrepair during that period?"

Alison remembered the rain dripping through the roof of the solar in the last winter.

"That doesn't mean it was uninhabited," she said. "Mary left there in 1560."

Adam was staring at her. "I would love to know where you got this from," he murmured.

"I'll show you one day," Alison said recklessly. "It's your turn," she added.

Adam nodded. "All right," he said. "There is a reference to 'the late Queen's daughter' living here at Middlecote in 1562. I found it in a letter to William Cecil from Agnes, Lady Fenner."

"The late queen would have been Katherine Parr," Alison said. "There was no one else who could be described in that way."

She put out a hand and grabbed the banister to steady herself. It felt as though the world was spinning too fast all of a sudden. The smooth wood slid beneath her fingers like time running backwards.

"Steady." She could hear Adam's voice. "I thought you said you were okay?"

"I'm fine," Alison said. "Just excited to find there is other evidence to support the idea that Mary Seymour was at Middlecote."

"Just because Mary might have been here later doesn't mean that Anne Boleyn never visited Middlecote," Adam pointed out. "I still think the portrait is of Anne." When Alison didn't reply he frowned. "Okay, I know you don't believe it—"

"No, I don't," Alison said. "And I don't think you do either, really."

Adam frowned. "It's well known that Anne hunted in Savernake with Henry VIII," he said.

"That's pretty tenuous," Alison said. "We're not even in Savernake Forest here. Didn't the costume historians throw doubt on the date of the gown?" she added. "I mean, what was fashionable in 1530 wouldn't be in 1560."

"I'm aware of that," Adam said tightly. "There was some debate. But there was also some jewellery found here, gems from the correct period, a golden cup engraved with the letter 'A,' and a prayer book with the initial 'A' inscribed inside."

"Were they found with the portrait and the box?" Alison said.

Adam was a long time answering. "No," he said, and the word dropped into the quiet of the stairwell like a stone into a pool. "They were listed on an inventory from the early seventeenth century and found in the chapel. The reference said that they had originally been in the previous church, which is a ruin now but was across the field to the east." He thrust his hands into the pockets of his trousers. "I did wonder…" He let the words tail off.

Alison waited.

"The notes in the inventory said that the items had been a gift from Anne Boleyn to the Fenners when she visited Middlecote," Adam said. He was speaking slowly now as though to himself. "I wondered whether it was true or whether that was just Hopton talking the place up again."

"A for Agnes," Alison said. Then, when he looked at her. "Lady Fenner? They could have belonged to her rather than Anne Boleyn."

"I know," Adam said. "But there was the portrait, and the box. My agent got hold of the idea and spoke to the TV people and everyone was really excited about a new painting of Anne Boleyn. Suddenly the pressure was on." He ran a hand impatiently through his hair. "Hell, it's my responsibility in the end, though, and my scholarship. I should have checked it more thoroughly but there were time constraints and I made a judgement call. A bad one, it feels now."

"So you came back here to check on something that had been troubling you," Alison said.

"You're too acute." Adam scowled at her. "All right," he

said. "I'll show you." He took a small flashlight out of his pocket. "This way."

The winter light had been fading as they talked and now Alison realised that the stairwell was dim and full of grey shadows. Suddenly, it was easy to believe that the house was haunted. The inadequate electric light would flicker out, a wind would rise, shrieking along the corridors, and Mary would glide out from one of the darkened doorways, the box clutched to her chest...

"Mind your step." Adam's voice recalled her, shivering, to reality. "There are raised beams across the doorways here."

Looking down, Alison realised that she needed to step over a blackened beam in order to enter the narrow corridor Adam was indicating. She felt claustrophobic all of a sudden; it was a panicky tightness in her chest that made her want to turn and run. Instead, she tried to concentrate on what Adam was saying and to block out the oppressive sense of fear.

"This was known as the 'Dames Corridor,'" Adam said. "The ladies of the house had their chambers here. If Mary Seymour had lived at Middlecote, chances are she had one of these rooms."

There was no electricity here. Bare wires hung from the ceiling and there was a scent of damp and decay in the air.

"It would have been a great deal more pleasant back in the 1560s," Adam said, watching her face in the torchlight. "At least I assume so. We know Lady Fenner had her chamber here, and her daughter Eleanor too, before she married and moved away."

"Will Fenner had a sister?" Alison said.

"And a half-brother," Adam said. "Thomas. He was the son of Will's father's mistress."

"I don't suppose there was much love lost there," Alison said.

"Their lives took very different courses," Adam said.

"Come in here." He gestured with the torch and Alison stepped over the threshold. "I'm not sure which of the ladies had this room as the records don't specify," Adam said, "but this was where we found the portrait—and the box that was in it."

A blinding wave of familiarity hit Alison as she walked into the centre of the room. She could smell the scent of sweet rushes on the floor and lavender from the blankets of the great wooden bed that stood behind her. She could see the benches around the walls, highly polished to a dazzling shine, the fire blazing in the hearth, the tirewoman folding clothes into the chest.

*This was Mary's chamber...*

She blinked and the image vanished and the room was cold and dark again. Adam was standing by the fireplace, shining the torch up into the chimney.

"The box was hidden up there," he said. "The one in the portrait. There's an opening in the wall about two feet deep. The surveyors found it when they were checking the chimneys."

"A chimney isn't the greatest place to hide a wooden box," Alison said. "It sounds like the sort of place someone would put a witch bottle."

Adam gave her a sharp look. "You know about those? Yes, that's exactly it. It was certainly odd; as though it had been hidden in a hurry."

"That's fascinating," Alison said. Her heart was racing again. Was it too far-fetched to imagine that Mary had hidden the box there for her to find, that there was a message in it for her? Adam had said before that there had been artefacts in the box. If only she could discover what they were...

*Leave word for me... Make it a secret... Keep it hidden...* She was back in the coach with Mary, hearing the rain thundering on the leather roof, clutching Mary's cold hands in desperation. She had known she was going to run, that she had so little time, that she would need help to find Arthur again. Pushing aside those memories took enormous effort but she dragged her mind back to the present, raising a hand to rub her fingers over the rough masonry of the fireplace, smelling the old soot and dead burning.

"Where is the box and its contents now?" she asked.

"At London University, undergoing analysis," Adam said. He straightened, running a hand over the nape of his neck.

"Look," he said. "I'll level with you, Ali. I know you want to find out more about Mary Seymour and you think the box and the portrait are linked to her. It really matters to me whether or not you're right. It's important. Like I said earlier, if I've made a mistake I'd rather know than build my career on a piece of historical misidentification."

"Yes," Alison said, "I do understand." They were standing very close together now. For a second she was confused by his proximity, distracted. She wanted to help him. The impulse was strong. Yet she had to remember that finding Arthur was her overwhelming need.

She needed access to the portrait and to the box. Adam could provide that. She had to persuade him to help her. Yet she could not tell him how she knew the things she did or why she needed to know. She never had told him the truth about herself and she never could. She felt as though she was on a knife's edge.

"I can't offer you any proof," she said. "All the stuff I know is hearsay or...or...family myth. You know, stories that have been told for centuries and may have a grain of truth in them."

Adam rubbed the nape of his neck. "Okay," he said, "I tell you what. We'll work on this together. You tell me everything you know about Mary Seymour and I'll find out if it's true or not."

Alison's heart leaped. "I want to see the box," she said quickly, before she lost her nerve, "and all the contents."

Adam's gaze held hers. It felt as though he could see far more than she was telling, that he sensed her desperation.

"All right," he said, after a moment. "I'll get it for you in return for all the information you can give me."

Alison was so relieved and excited that she hugged him, regretting it almost immediately when she felt Adam recoil. His hands were on her arms, holding her away from him, putting space between them.

"Sorry," she said, mortified, "I was just so pleased—"

"That's okay," Adam said. "You took me by surprise." He spoke slowly and there was a tone in his voice that made her look up. There was heat in his eyes, and desire, swiftly banked down. Alison's stomach dropped. Suddenly it felt as though there was no air at all in the stairwell.

Adam's phone buzzed and he reached for it, turning away from her. "Excuse me."

Alison felt firmly excluded. "Hi, Mum," she heard him say. Then: "As though I could forget." There was affection as well as faint exasperation in his tone. He shot Alison a sideways glance. "No, I'm just finishing up here. See you soon." He snapped the phone closed. "Family dinner," he said. "They're wondering where I am."

"People with happy families so often don't realise how lucky they are," Alison said. She thought of his exasperation at being nagged and there was a fizz of anger and resentment in her stomach.

"Woah!" Adam said. "Where did that come from?" He slid the phone back into his pocket. "I can assure I realise just how..." he said, hesitating. Then: "Fortunate I am."

He did not sound angry, only thoughtful, as though he had read more than she had intended into her words.

"Sorry," Alison said, feeling ungracious. "The envy of the orphan, I suppose."

Adam didn't reply. He turned his back to her and set off towards the stairs. "Come on," he said over his shoulder. "We'd better get out of this house of horrors before it gets dark."

Alison followed the wavering torchlight down the corridor and out onto the landing. It was dark now. The shadows curled like serpents around the newel posts and slid towards them across the bare boards.

"Where's Monty?" Alison asked. "I need a guard dog."

Adam laughed. "He'll be waiting for us downstairs," he said. "He doesn't like the place much."

"I don't blame him." Alison was concentrating on putting each foot squarely on the uneven treads so that she didn't miss her step and fall on top of Adam. If she did she was sure he would imagine it had been deliberate.

"Did you find what you came for?" she added. Then, when he threw her a quick, questioning look: "You said you'd come back to check something."

"Oh." Adam stopped. They had reached the ground floor. Above them another huge stained glass window was dark, its colours and patterns hidden by the night. So was Adam's expression. She could not read it in the torchlight.

"I'm not really sure exactly what I was looking for," he said, after a moment. "I wanted to see the place that the box had been hidden. Something about it has always bothered me." He frowned. "It's the weirdest thing, like an instinct, if you know what I mean?"

Alison nodded, and he carried on:

"At first I thought it had been hidden there by someone who planned to come back to retrieve it, a bit like buried treasure." He rubbed his jaw. "But the more I thought about it the more convinced I was that it was deliberately concealed and never intended to be found." His eyes met Alison's. "Don't ask me how I know," he said, "but I think it was hidden to cover up a crime."

# THIRTEEN

*Mary, 1566*

I HAD THOUGHT THAT LIFE AT MIDDLECOTE
would be different from Wolf Hall. I was correct, but not in
the ways I had expected. Both were gentleman's households
but there the similarities ended. At Wolf Hall, we had all
been a bundle of discarded children, abandoned there because there was nowhere else. We had to work to earn our
keep. At Middlecote, I was Miss Eleanor Fenner's companion,
a poor dependent, but a gentlewoman none the less. There
were no trips to market; there was no churning of the butter,
or sweeping of the floors, or making scented soap with the
garden herbs. Instead, there was a soulless round of reading,
needlework, walking in the grounds on fine days and con-
versing with the neighbours. Even our prayers were soulless.
Lady Fenner insisted we attend church daily, but I quickly
perceived that this she did for the same reason as everything
else. She wished to be seen to observe propriety.

Lady Fenner had been somewhat scathing of my lack of
accomplishments when I had first come to Middlecote: the
fact that I had no skill in other languages, my sad lack of pro-

ficiency at the virginals. She had considered my upbringing at Wolf Hall a ramshackle one and she only knew the half of it.

"This is what happens when there is no gentlewoman in charge of the household," she had lamented, ignoring the fact that my mother herself, a most pious and learned woman, had appointed Liz Aiglonby to teach me. The lack was in me and not my education, but I did make great strides under Lady Fenner's tutelage, as there was no other option. If I wanted to escape into the fresh air and the possibilities offered outdoors, I had to do my indoor learning.

Eleanor and I had become firm friends. She was docile and kind, as sweet as Alison had been sharp. Yet too much sweetness could be cloying and I missed Alison's astringent presence. I wondered frequently what had become of her. We got very little news at Middlecote other than sporadic reports from friends and relatives in London, and family news from elsewhere. Alison's name was never uttered; it was as though her very existence had been wiped out yet it was almost as though with each passing month her presence became more real to me, not less. One day, when I had been at Middlecote a month, I was in my chamber reading and looked up to see Alison standing beside the hearth. She was so vivid to me, she looked so real, that my heart leaped with pleasure to see her and I opened my mouth to welcome her. Then I looked again, and she was gone.

One constant in my life was Darrell. There were times when I did not speak to him for a few months and he felt oddly distant from me, as though we were separated by time as well as place. Once, I asked him where it was he went but he parried my questions with affection and humour, telling me that he was a man and had gone away to fight. I was quite angry with him; I felt like the insignificant woman left behind, dropped when something more exciting happened, or worse, a child of no consequence to him. I sulked, just like a child. Yet I could not be angry with him for very long. It felt impossible. He was knit into my life, my soul. He was a part of me.

One day when I was out walking with Eleanor, Darrell had a terrible accident. I knew as soon as he had done it; an agonising pain shot through my arm before he had the control to shut me out of his mind. I think I screamed, which was foolish and unhelpful, because a savage bolt of thought from him silenced me. Eleanor screamed too, simply because I had screamed and scared her, and servants came running and all was confusion.

"It is no matter," I reassured them, winded and afraid, still dealing with the shock and the sensation of Darrell's pain. "I thought I saw a snake, that is all."

After that there was more screaming and running around, which only made matters worse and of course no snake was found. Eleanor retired to her room with a headache. I sought mine also.

*"Darrell."*

No reply. I tried again, gentle, coaxing, hiding the fear that was growing inside me all the time.

*"Cat."*

I had never sensed such weakness in him before, or experienced such pain. I knew he was trying to hide it from me but he could not. It was too great and it devoured him, and when his mind was open to me I was swallowed by it too. I thought he must be dying. I fought the fear but he must have felt it because, despite everything, I felt him smile: reassurance and love and comfort reached me sweetly and softly, edged with exhaustion.

*"Cat. Don't fret. I'll live."*

He was gone then, with apology, too tired to speak to me.

I was in an agony of not knowing for days, weeks after. Each day I called out to him, fearful of losing him, sending my love and consolation, looking for it in return. Gradually, I sensed he was recovering; slowly the spark in him returned and my fears eased, but every so often I would feel the same agonising pain in my arm again and sense frustration coming from him, perhaps because he was not as strong as he wanted to be.

I kept Darrell a secret, of course. I had no wish for the taint of witchcraft to follow me to Middlecote as it had to Wolf Hall. I had had so few visions at Middlecote that I was able to dismiss them as nothing more than vivid dreams. Here I could be as close to ordinary as it was possible for me to be and I welcomed that even whilst I knew that I could never be like other people. But it was only a matter of time. I could try to fool myself, but my gift would find me out. It would not be repressed.

One day, Eleanor and I were in the parlour together sewing our samplers whilst Lady Fenner composed letters in the library. It was pleasant to be without her brooding presence for a space and we had been chatting idly about nothing at all when suddenly my vision clouded without warning and I was drawn into a spiral of darkness. Out of it came a tall dark man on a towering black stallion, galloping up the wide tree-lined avenue towards Middlecote as though all the devils in hell were at his heels.

"Someone is coming," I said. I was cold, shaking. My sampler tumbled from my lap. "Someone is here."

The vision grew, filling my entire sight. The parlour vanished. There was such darkness, such grief. It lapped like a destructive tide. All I knew was that this man brought danger and unhappiness with him and I wanted to run and hide.

There was a loud rapping at the front door followed by a babble of male voices and laughter.

"What's this? No welcome for the master of the house?"

Eleanor, who had been staring at me in consternation, leaped to her feet, her face lighting up and all anxieties forgotten.

"Will!" She ran to the parlour door. "Mama! Mama! Will is home!"

"So I hear." Lady Fenner was already on the threshold, drawn no doubt from her letters by the cacophony. She was a cold woman at the best of times but now I sensed something else in her. I could not pin it down. She did not seem glad that her son was returned. There was a wary edge to her smile.

"You had better show your brother how much you have grown in decorum in the past half-dozen years," she said, but Eleanor had already gone running into the hall, leaving the door swinging open behind her.

Lady Fenner sighed. Her gaze travelled thoughtfully over me, then she nodded slowly as though reassured of something. "Come, Mary," she said, "you must meet my son, William."

It was just as it had been with my cousin Edward, I thought. Here were we, three women, who had lived at Middlecote for the last six years, quietly, efficiently and with little fuss. Lady Fenner ordered the household, received guests and oversaw the lives of her servants and made not the least commotion about it.

Now, though, Middlecote's master was returned and the whole house had taken on a different mood in a matter of moments. It was abuzz. Servants ran and called out to each other as they fetched food and drink. There was noise and activity and a sense of urgency. What manner of man was Will Fenner, I wondered sourly, to stay away for six long years, running up debts in London if the servants' gossip was to be credited, and only now returning to see his family? A bankrupt one, I concluded. A wastrel, a neglectful son, a selfish ne'er-do-well. Was he also a man who trailed evil in his wake, the evil I had felt a moment ago? My vision had steadied now and the parlour was bright with sun. I felt nothing sinister at all.

Lady Fenner was waiting for me. I preceded her through the door, walking slowly and most demurely, as Eleanor most singularly had not. I could hear her voice in the hall upraised in excitement and joy and could not blame her, but Lady Fenner had a face like thunder.

I will never forget how I felt when first I set eyes on William Fenner. He was standing directly in a ray of sunshine from the high windows. It gilded him like an angel. Quite simply, I was dazzled.

He was tall; so tall he would need to stoop to pass beneath all the lintels of the doors in the house, and broad-shouldered with it. He had removed his velvet cap and held it carelessly in one hand. I saw the flash of jewels in the band. A white feather curled jauntily from the brim. Eleanor hung on his other arm, chattering ten to the dozen whilst he inclined his head towards her, an indulgent smile on his lips. Everything about him seemed fine, from his thick dark hair to the rich crimson lining of his cloak. It made me wonder whether under the Queen's laws he was entitled to wear crimson or if he had no care for the law. I know that answer to that question now but at the time it was swept from my head by the look he bent on me and by the smile in his dark eyes.

"Lady Mary." He dropped to one knee before me for which I was completely unprepared, having always been treated like an encumbrance before rather than an honoured guest. He took my hand and pressed a kiss on it and the touch of his lips made me shiver pleasurably. It was an entirely new sensation for me.

"Sir William…" I made an effort not to sound gauche and thought I probably failed. An insane urge possessed me to touch his springy dark hair. I wanted to feel it against my fingers. I turned hot. I had no notion what was happening to me, only that it was heady and powerful, like taking sweet wine on a summer day.

"Please stand up," I whispered, and he leaped to his feet, his eyes sparkling, and swept me a courtier's bow.

"When you have a moment to spare for your mother, William…" Lady Fenner's voice was dry and Will spun around and folded her into a bear hug, releasing her all pink and ruffled. His men were standing around grinning; this then was William's customary behaviour.

"Forgive me, Mama." He sounded contrite but his eyes were still alight with amusement. He held her at arm's length. "You look well and not a day older than when I last saw you."

"Which is all too long," Lady Fenner said sharply. "William, what are you doing here? Lord Kingston wrote from London—"

"Later, madam, if you please." Will's voice had hardened though his lips were still smiling. "The men are sharp-set, as am I. I know you keep the house well stocked. Let us dine and then perhaps this afternoon—" he turned back to include both Eleanor and me in the warmth of his smile "—we may go riding and the ladies can show me the estate."

Eleanor bounced with excitement. I just about managed not to do the same. It felt as though the sun was shining for me alone, for little Mary Seymour who had never in her life commanded the admiration of any gentleman. How dismissive I had been of love, how scathing of Alison's folly. How little I had understood.

Later, as I was preparing for bed after a day packed full of pleasures and delights, Eleanor slid into my chamber and curled up on the bed as she was wont to do. Her expression was troubled but I, brushing my hair before the mirror, was full of nothing but joy.

"How merry it is to have your brother home," I said.

She nodded, but her expression did not change. I carried on brushing. She fidgeted with the embroidered cover on the bed.

"How did you know Will was on his way?" she demanded all of a sudden. "You said he was coming and then he arrived. You cannot see the drive from the parlour, so how did you know?"

I felt a pang of annoyance that she had reminded me when I had succeeded in teaching myself to forget it, and a second spike of anger that she had spoiled the warmth and pleasure I had taken in the day. I was not going to dwell on my visions now. They were nothing to the reality of knowing Will.

"I heard him," I lied easily. "I heard the sound of hoof beats. And I did not know it was Sir William. I just said that somebody was coming."

Eleanor's expression eased slightly although she still looked a little distressed. "You seemed so odd," she complained. "You spoke in a whisper and your eyes were blind."

I turned away from her to hide the wave of fury that possessed me. I could not afford to upset Eleanor and lose her friendship.

"I don't know what you mean," I said carelessly. "I heard horses and told you someone was coming. That is all it was."

"Sometimes," she said, "you seem so strange. What of the time you screamed aloud? I heard you call out the name Darrell."

I felt chilled. I had had no idea that I had done that and the thought scared me. What else might I give away unknowing? I felt guilty too. I had not thought of Darrell all day. His existence had been quite eclipsed by Will's arrival. With a slight sense of shock, I realised I did not need him. Life was exciting now. His appeal seemed to have faded.

"I don't remember that," I said slowly. "I don't know anyone of that name. You must have misheard."

I blew out the candle and left her to find her way back to her own chamber in the dark.

We went out riding every day that followed. The weather was dry so Lady Fenner could not object and if she had I believe that Will would have overruled her anyway. He was not a man who took direction from anyone, least of all a woman. His confidence frequently slid into arrogance but I admired him for it in those days, fool that I was.

Sometimes, Eleanor accompanied us but sometimes she stayed at home and Will and I rode out together with a retinue of servants in attendance like a king and queen. For the first time in my life I enjoyed being on horseback and was glad that I had learned to ride. We ambled along the dusty lanes, the earth baked hard by the heat of summer, beneath overhanging beech, alder and elm where I was shielded from the glare of the sun. Will was an attentive companion. He showed me all the places he had roamed as a boy, the dam he had built across the stream, the tree house in the woods, the tumble of mosaics and walls that was all that was left of a Roman villa built back in the mists of time. We rode west, where there were great grey stones lying in the open fields as though tossed there by giants, and south, where the river ran lazily through drowsy fields and coppices. We never rode north, over the Downs, or into the little town of Hungerford.

"Sir Walter dislikes us," Eleanor confided, when I asked.

"Sir Walter Hungerford," she added, seeing my blank expression. "He is a great knight whose family derive from these parts."

"I see," I said, not really seeing at all. I found it surprising that anyone shunned Lady Fenner socially. She was from a great family herself, that of Essex, and she made sure that everyone was cognisant of the fact. "Why—" I began, but Eleanor shook her head, pressing a finger to her lips.

"We do not speak of it," she said, blurting out almost immediately: "They say that Will seduced Sir Walter's wife."

That, I thought, seemed both entirely possible and a good enough reason to explain Sir Walter's animosity. Even though Will's charm bowled me over I was not stupid enough to imagine I was the only woman who had ever been the recipient of it. He was a man of seven and twenty. Hearing of his worldly experience only added to the allure, though.

"Anne Hungerford was a great beauty once," Eleanor said, "but she is old now, at least thirty years."

At that point I was almost able to feel sorry for poor, faded Lady Hungerford. I was nineteen myself.

It rained that afternoon and so Lady Fenner decreed we should stay inside. Eleanor was writing poetry. She had never shown any of it to me, being so modest about her own work that she would blush if I asked after it and smother it against her bodice in case I tried to snatch it and read it. She was curled up on the window seat, a pot of ink at her side, whilst I sat listlessly at the virginals, picking out a tune with little enthusiasm and no talent. I watched the raindrops run down the windows and wondered how it was possible to have been so happy only the day before and now to feel so out of humour.

The clatter of voices and footsteps in the corridor outside roused me from my torpor, although Eleanor was so engrossed, she did not even glance up. It had to be Will; no one else made so much noise.

The door swung open.

"Eleanor." Will nodded to me then strode across to his sister. "Mama wishes to speak with you," he said. "She deems it urgent."

Eleanor flushed. "I shall be there directly. I just need to finish—" She gestured to the poem, clasped protectively in her hand.

"Leave it," Will said. "Mama wants you now. She is in the Long Gallery."

Eleanor looked ready to burst into tears with no time to hide her precious writing. I wondered if she thought Will or I would pounce on it and read it as soon as she had left the room.

"I'll keep it safe for you, Nell," I said, wanting only to help, but she flushed scarlet and scrambled down from the seat and ran.

"Poor Nell," Will said, staring after her. "No spirit at all." He ignored the sheet of writing, which had drifted down to the floor. He came across to me. All his attention was focused on me and suddenly I realised that we were completely alone. My heart seemed to catch in my throat.

"I wondered if you would care to come with me to the fair later, Lady Mary?" Will spoke softly, as though afraid of being overheard.

I felt elated and swift on the heels of the excitement, utterly downcast.

"Lady Fenner would never permit it," I said.

He smiled at what I had unwittingly given away. "She need not know," he said. "If you wish it, that is all that counts."

I stared at him, not quite believing. "When?"

"Tonight." He took my hand and pressed a kiss to the

palm. My fingers closed automatically as though sealing it in. "What do you say?" His voice was still low, intimate, insistent. "Just the two of us."

I looked into his eyes and saw danger and excitement reflected there. For the first time, I understood why Alison had risked all to steal moments alone with her lover. More practically I wished I had asked how she had managed to slip away unnoticed. I had not thought I would ever need to know.

"How..." I started to say. His eyes danced with amusement.

"I will arrange it."

Of course he would. He was adept at trysting with women.

Eleanor came back then, very flushed and indignant. "I could not find Mama," she complained as she bustled over to the window and grabbed her poem in jealous hands. "You must have misunderstood, Will."

Her brother did not take his gaze from me. "Very likely I did," he agreed. "Your pardon." And he smiled his secret smile, for me alone, and kissed my hand again, and was gone.

I spent the evening in an agony of anticipation. Lady Fenner snapped at me for inattention. Even Eleanor commented that I seemed distracted and asked me if I had the headache. It was the excuse I needed and I seized upon it, apologising to Lady Fenner and asking to retire early. She was at cards with Will and he did not look up once from the hand he was playing. I waited for a sign from him but none came and Lady Fenner raised her brows and asked why I was still standing there.

"The girl acts like a simpleton sometimes," I heard her complain to Will as I was leaving the room. "It is hard to believe her mother was a clever woman."

"We do not all inherit our parents' virtues," Will said smoothly. "If one considers intelligence a virtue in a woman."

Lady Fenner gave him a very unfriendly look.

I could not fathom their relationship. She was proud and possessive of Will, her only son, and yet utterly contemptuous of his weaknesses. He tolerated her sharpness and her interference, more out of laziness than anything else, I believe, though sometimes he would snap back at her and his words always had a sting in them.

Up in my chamber I paced the floor, unable to settle. Will would not come for me. He had forgotten we were to go to the fair. I should go to bed and forget about it. I was half excitement, half dread, shredding my handkerchief between my restless fingers, running to the window when I heard a sound outside, watching the door.

Yet I still missed his coming. One moment I was standing gazing out into the twilight, the next I turned and he was standing right behind me. I drew my breath on a gasp and he pressed a finger to my lips, silencing me.

"Hush! Are you ready?"

It was so very typical of Will to give me no word but expect me to be waiting for him. Which, of course, I was. Reckless excitement possessed me.

"Yes!"

"Come then." He held out a hand to me and led me to the door. Truth is, I was disappointed. I had imagined we would climb down the ivy—except that there was none at my window.

The corridor outside my chamber was empty. Will paused, listening, then drew me towards the servants' stair at the end. We tiptoed. My heart beat like a drum. I think I was shaking.

There were steps, voices. He pulled me into the darkened doorway of Lady Fenner's chamber, pressing me close, his body hard against mine. I could not have breathed then had I wished. Two maids passed by, heads bent close together, giggling. One held a pail. They were so close that some of the water in it splashed my gown but they did not see us.

"I would bed him," one of them said, nudging the other with her elbow, causing more water to splash. "He is very handsome."

"Then you would be a fool, standing in line with all the other fools," the other girl said.

I felt Will's amusement. He bent his head and his lips brushed my hair.

"Come, sweeting."

The maids had gone and I was still standing there transfixed like another of his fools.

The stair was tight and narrow and our footsteps sounded loud on the bare wood but no one came. At the bottom was another narrow passageway I did not recognise. I had never visited the servants' quarters; Lady Fenner would have been horrified. Light and noise at one end of the passage, but at the other there was a chill draught and an open door. We were outside, in one of the small courtyards, and Will was laughing as he pulled me towards the stables.

"We're free!"

The rain had cleared to leave a starlit twilight. We rode east, towards Hungerford, Sir Walter's domain where I had never been before. Will did not speak but hummed under his breath, a tuneless ditty. He seemed in a very good mood.

There were bonfires on the Common Port Down and the sound of music in the air. The crowds were huge, noisy and rough, though good-tempered in the main. The surge of humanity took us hither and thither with no free will of our own, swept along like so much flotsam on the flood. I was constantly pressed against Will's side as we walked through the narrow avenues between the booths. He did not seem to mind one whit and wrapped an arm about me to hold me safe.

I had heard of the Hungerford Midsummer Fair though I had never thought to see it. During the day it was a place where farmers, merchants and men of more dubious means came to buy, sell and barter, but at night they retired to the tents and booths to feast and drink. Then the fair became the province of the minstrels and the jugglers. Strolling players mingled with the crowds, tumblers danced around us, making me jump with their brightly painted harlequin faces, like dolls from an infernal toymaker. I clung tight to Will's arm as the crowds buffeted us. When we came across the bloody remains of a cockfight I buried my face in his jacket and he laughed at me.

"You're too soft-hearted, Mary," he said. "You need to toughen up."

We drank mead that Will swore was entirely proper for a lady but which made my head spin delightfully, and we danced to the music of the lute and the recorders, and watched the fire-eaters, and I felt dizzy and drunk as much on excitement as mead. Many a woman passed by, lady and harlot both, who cast Will a covetous glance but for that one night he was all mine.

Trouble came out of nowhere, violence like a whisper of wind through the corn, growing and spreading. There was a group of men standing outside a booth talking loudly. They were drunk and on the edge of argument already when Will jostled one inadvertently in order to protect me from the lurch of people on the other side. The man spilt his ale and spun around on an oath.

"Watch yourself, you clumsy fool."

I felt the change in Will. He drew himself up straighter,

his arm falling away from me, his hand going to the sword he carried beneath his cloak.

"It's Will Fenner of Middlecote," I heard someone whisper. "God 'a' mercy, it's Wild Will—"

There was a shout away to the left and Will turned instinctively towards to noise.

"Fenner! You whore-mongering bastard!"

A fist flew above my head. Something sharp grazed my cheek. One man was barrelling in from the right, trying to attack Will with fists and feet. Another, the man whose drink he had spilt, had pulled a knife. I screamed.

I was falling down amongst the pounding feet and writhing bodies and I thought I would be trampled for sure, but Will caught my hand and dragged me out from beneath them all.

"This way," he said, in my ear, and we were running, dodging amongst the booths, away from the light and the shouting and the noise. I stumbled over my skirts and heard the material rip. I had a stitch in my side, my face felt sore and I had lost a shoe but I was exhilarated, laughing so hard I had to stop running, and when Will swung me around to face him and the surprise in his eyes warmed into approval, I laughed all the harder.

"You surely know how to entertain a lady, Will Fenner."

He laughed then too, and kissed me.

"Mary," he said, against my mouth. "Who would have guessed you had such spirit."

The stars spun all the more about my head and I thought I had never been happier than I was then, in Will Fenner's arms.

It was as easy as that for me to fall in love.

# FOURTEEN

ALISON CHECKED THE OFFICE SURREPTITIOUSLY to make sure everyone was engrossed in their work and then flipped Internet screens from a luxury lodge on Namibia's Skeleton Coast to a picture of an eighteenth-century map of Wiltshire. It was the earliest one she had been able to find online and was almost impossible to decipher with its cursive writing and strange topographical detail. It showed the north-east corner of the county as it had been in 1759, with all the named tracks across the Downs marked on it: the Thieves' Way and the Sugar Way and the Rogues' Way. She had traced a likely route for Reginald De Morven from Oxford to Salisbury, taking him past his ancestral home at Kingston Parva but she was no closer to discovering at what point he had turned aside from that path and travelled from the past to the present.

She leaned closer to the screen, squinting at the map detail. One plus was that it did show the location of Kingston Manor, which had still been standing in the mid-eighteenth century. It was to the west of the church, as the vicar had indicated, and although the map was far from accurate, she would probably be able to find it using the landmarks shown. At the bottom right of the map was also Middlecote Hall and a huge tree drawn totally out of scale beside a name that read "The Big Stile." In smaller letters, she saw tangled in the roots the words "The Phantom Tree." Any moment she expected to see the legend "Here Be Dragons."

It was not far over the hills from Middlecote to Kingston. Alison tried to measure the distance but the actual scale was impossible to work out. A network of tracks led between the two, however, passing Lambourn Woodlands and Baydon and various other villages.

"Planning a safari into the past?" Charles slapped a set of papers down on her desk, making her jump.

*Something of the sort...*

At any other time, Alison might have laughed since a trip into history was exactly what she planned. This was no laughing matter though. Twice now she had been caught using the work Internet for personal projects. C&D were pretty hot on such transgressions. No surfing the Net, no mobile calls on work time. The trouble was she was becoming suffused by the need to find out about Arthur. It was all she thought about, from the moment she woke to when she went to sleep. The longing permeated everything—not overtly—no one would have guessed her preoccupation—but it coloured her life like a stain. She was becoming obsessed, just as she had been when she first arrived and had been utterly fixated on going back to find Arthur and bring him to the present.

"I..." Alison knew better than to lie. "Sorry, Charles."

"That would be right up Alison's street," Andre said quickly. He had seen the panic in her eyes. He turned to Kate. "D'you remember that time when we were in the pub and she'd had too much white wine and started rambling on about parallel universes and time travel?"

"Yeah." Kate cradled her coffee cup, smiling gamely at Charles. "Alison said it was perfectly possible to travel between different dimensions."

It seemed unlikely to Alison that a rehearsal of her one ill-timed attempt to talk about her life would charm Charles out of his bad mood.

"I think I had flu and was running a temperature," she said. "Clearly I was deranged."

She had been ill, she thought. She had been sick, and bone tired and lonely, because there had been a big item on the news about a baby snatched from its mother. The woman's grief had cut her to the heart and broken down all the carefully erected defences she had built about her emotions. Sometimes it simply was not possible to be strong, to lock away the hurt with all the other old secrets. Sometimes she just wanted to tell someone, to let them into her world.

"Some physicists think time travel is possible," Charles said.

"Special Relativity," Kate said. "Einstein."

Alison felt inadequate. She had had very little formal education. Usually it didn't matter; she was sharp and had discovered that she was commercially aware and she knew she was good at her job. It was only occasionally that she felt lacking, just as she had done as a child.

Charles, however, seemed to be looking at her with something approaching approval.

"I rather like that as a concept for our cultural tours," he said. "Travel through time…the closest thing to Special Relativity you can get in the modern world… Hmm, yes. Good work."

He wandered off, murmuring something about Einstein.

"You owe us," Andre said, sitting back in his chair and grinning.

"What was it this time?" Kate had wandered over to Alison's desk and was looking over her shoulder.

"'A topographical Map of the County of Wiltshire, 1759,'" she read aloud. "What on earth are you looking for?"

"I don't know," Alison said. She felt so tightly wound up she wanted to snap. Reginald's fate tormented her. On the one hand it held out the possibility of finding her way back to Arthur, but it was a false hope because she had no idea how to use that knowledge. Frustration and anger stabbed her viciously in the gut. It felt as though every path to her son was closed to her. She would never find him. Even if Adam helped her to discover the clues Mary had left, what could she do with them? She could never go back.

She blinked hard and picked up the file that Charles had left on the desk, pretending to study it. The last thing she wanted to do was cry in front of her colleagues. Why wouldn't Kate just leave her alone and go back to her desk? She wanted to push her away and had to repress the physical impulse.

She read the cover brief on the file. A family of two adults and three children wanted to plan a bespoke safari to Tanzania. Great. Time to play happy families again. That was all she needed. She hated arranging family trips; one of the reasons she enjoyed the Africa work was that relatively few families made the journey, usually finding the driving distances too great to keep children amused, as well as worrying their offspring might be eaten by leopards.

"Oh, how lovely!" Kate's eyes lit up. "There are loads of family-friendly venues we can put forward for them. Perhaps they could write a piece for our newsletter on travelling with children."

Alison shuddered and saw Kate's eagerness dim at her blatant lack of enthusiasm. She hated herself in that moment. Kate had never understood her attitude towards children and families. How could she? Alison could never explain. Kate had reached out to her a few times, wanting to talk as a friend would, and she had always knocked her back.

Alison's phone buzzed. It was a relief to break the circle of toxic thoughts. She looked around to make sure that Charles was out of sight then checked the caller ID. It was Adam. Suddenly she felt edgy and anxious. As she was leaving Middlecote, Adam had said he would ring her when he had been able to get hold of the box and the portrait for her to have a look at. This was one call she was definitely not going to let go to voicemail.

She pressed the button to answer, gesturing meaningfully with her head towards Kate, who scooted back behind her own desk.

"Hi, Adam. How are you?" She hoped her voice didn't betray her nerves. She saw Kate's lips form the words "Adam Hewer" at Andre, who raised his brows and grinned.

"Good, thanks." Adam sounded a bit abrupt. "Are you free this evening?"

Alison briefly considered and discarded the idea of pretending that her diary was packed. "Yes," she said.

"I'll meet you at the National Portrait Gallery," Adam said. "Seven?"

"Why?" Alison said. She saw Kate roll her eyes at the bluntness of the conversation. Well, they had agreed it was only business.

"The portrait is on show there now," Adam said. "If you want to see it, you'll have to join the queue."

"And the box?" Alison said.

"I can get that for you in a couple of days," Adam said. "Not the contents though, I'm afraid. They're under lock and key in the university lab undergoing analysis."

Alison thought about it. She could go and see the painting

on her own; she didn't need Adam there. The less he knew about why she was interested, the better.

"Not to worry," she said quickly. "I'll wait until the box is ready, thanks."

"Right." Adam sounded put out, as though he was surprised she had refused. "I'll let you know." He ended the call without saying goodbye.

"Don't ask," Alison said as Kate opened her mouth. Kate closed it again.

"Jesus," Andre said. "I can see why you never have a long-term relationship. It's just amazing you have any friends."

"Sorry," Alison said. She saw that Kate was looking flushed and unhappy, and was instantly contrite. "Sorry, Kate. I'm a moody cow."

"That's all right." Kate smiled bravely. "We only want you to be happy, you know that."

Alison bit back the sharp retort she wanted to make. Kate's generosity infuriated her sometimes. It reminded her of Mary's naïveté. Both of them had a gentleness about them that she would never share. Nor would she ever have a long-term relationship. She was mature enough to see now that secrets, lies and love didn't sit well together. There was so much of herself that she held apart. Andre was right; she did it to friends as well as lovers. She made it impossible for people to get close to her.

The rest of the afternoon dragged whilst she contacted the couple that wanted to book the Tanzania safari and made preliminary enquiries into child-friendly activities. There were a number of lodges that had children's pools and jungle playgrounds. There were special visits to animal rehabilitation centres, survival classes and lessons in how to track wild animals. She was forced to admit that it sounded rather fun, but her mind kept drifting to Mary's portrait. Since for the time being it was proving so hard to track Reginald De Morven's path to the past, she was left with only one tenuous lead and that was Mary. She should have looked at the picture more closely when it had been in Richard's gallery, but she had been too shocked to take it all in. So, she would go to the National Portrait Gallery on her own, this evening, and stand in a queue if she had to in order to see Mary's face again and glean what she could from the painting.

She was the last to leave the office at seven-thirty, grabbing a sandwich from the deli by the Tube station and taking the underground to Leicester Square. She'd never been to the NPG before. Art galleries were another sort of culture that she avoided, at least the ones that represented the life and times she had come from. It felt too weird to walk amongst faces and landscapes she might once have recognised.

That weirdness hit her forcibly as she reached the second floor and walked slowly through a gallery that was devoted to fashions in Tudor and Stuart collars and ruffs, and from there through the Elizabethan gallery to the early Tudors. The only way she could process it was to look at those painted faces and see them intellectually, not emotionally. These were the people that the present day considered important, or who represented her time: Queen Elizabeth was one, of course, in all her haughty glory. Odd how those paintings of her were so admired now when Alison remembered the queen as a faintly sinister character, who saw all, heard all and was all powerful. She noted with amusement that the fashion for huge ruffs had grown in the later 1500s. That was something she had not realised. People had been far neater with their collars in her time.

The early Tudor gallery seemed crowded with portraits of King Henry VIII, as dominant in posterity as he had been in life. Alison gazed into those small mean eyes and repressed a shiver. There was no portrait of Mary's aunt, the famous Jane Seymour, but there was one of her mother Katherine Parr. She looked beautiful in a serene, understated way. There was no glimpse of the fine intellect or shrewd wit she had been said to possess. The paintings seemed to Alison like playing cards, telling her nothing.

There were two portraits of Anne Boleyn on display. To Alison's critical gaze they looked nothing like each other. In both, Anne was wearing the famous B for Boleyn necklace, but in the first her hair was dark and her features delicate, whilst in the second her hair was golden and she looked considerably older. Both had captured something calculating in the eyes though. Alison shook her head. Both artists were listed as unknown and it was suggested that the paintings were copies of a lost original.

It was no surprise that the late evening crowds were gathered about the miniature portrait that was framed in the centre of a stand, brightly lit and somehow vulnerable-looking in the open way in which it was displayed. Alison was surprised by a pang of protectiveness for Mary. It felt as though she was at a freak show, where people came to mock and stare. "Anne Boleyn" the board beside it announced. "A recently discovered contemporary portrait by an unknown artist."

A man moved into her field of vision, detaching himself from the edge of the crowd, his head bent over the catalogue he was reading. It was Adam. Alison wondered why on earth she had not had the sense to realise that, like her, Adam might come along to see the portrait tonight. Then, before she could turn and walk away unseen, he looked up, tossed the catalogue aside as though it had no further interest for him, and started to walk towards her.

★ ★ ★

They sat on a long wooden bench in front of Mary's portrait whilst the crowds ebbed and flowed around them. Neither of them spoke but Alison was acutely aware of Adam beside her, his shoulder brushing hers, the restlessness she remembered in him banked down and contained as he studied Mary's picture. He hadn't said anything when he had come up to her, simply smiled as though he had known she would be there, despite what she had said earlier, and Alison hadn't felt like trying to justify herself. So they sat whilst a gaggle of students took photographs on their phones and a father holding a small child in each hand told them the story of Anne Boleyn, and the gallery lights shimmered and Mary smiled her serene smile. Alison felt oddly peaceful and gradually the crowds melted away and quietness enveloped them.

Adam shifted a little and half turned towards her. "It's an odd portrait in a way," he said. "I've never thought about it before but most smaller paintings focus entirely on the sitter's face. They seldom contain any additional detail. This one isn't that much larger than a miniature, yet it has plenty of detail in it. In fact, it looks quite cluttered."

"It's probably symbolic, isn't it?" Alison said. She was certain Mary had insisted on including the box in the picture as a message for her but the other features were less easy to understand. There was an angel in the top right-hand corner and a lion in the bottom right. On the left there was a wyvern—Alison wondered if that was a match for the ones on the gateposts at Middlecote—and in the top left there was what looked like a stick with flowers growing from it. It was difficult to tell at a distance.

"I think so," Adam said. "I did look into it briefly when we first found the portrait but I couldn't tie it into anything specific to Anne Boleyn." He glanced at her. "I know, you're going to tell me that's because this isn't a portrait of Anne so there's no reason why it should be relevant to her."

"I'm saying nothing," Alison said.

Adam laughed. "You don't need to. Okay." His voice changed. There was a note of challenge in it now. "Here's what the symbolism means—you tell me if it's appropriate for Mary Seymour."

Anticipation tickled Alison's spine. "Okay."

"The angel is usually a messenger," Adam said. "The lion has many interpretations, of course." He frowned. "This is all a bit simplistic. But it could represent pride or anger or even fortitude."

Alison barely heard the second part. Her gaze was fixed on the delicate lines of the angel. *A messenger.*

"What is it holding?" she asked. "The angel?"

"A candle," Adam said. "It's a seraph, bringing light in the darkness."

Alison felt a prickle of tears in her throat. She had felt that she was in darkness for a very long time but here, at last, she was sure, was the message she had been waiting for.

She realised that Adam was looking at her expectantly. He was waiting for her to make some informed comment about Mary Seymour, but there was nothing she could say without giving away the very personal nature of the message she was sure was there for her.

"The lion was a part of the Seymour coat of arms," she said. Her voice was husky and she cleared her throat. "Perhaps that's the connection."

Adam looked disappointed. "I suppose it could be. I was hoping for something rather more exciting."

"Sorry," Alison said. "Is that a wyvern?" she added. "There's your connection to Middlecote."

"Yes," Adam said. "They're common in heraldry, of

course, but you don't often see them in art so that probably is a clue to where the portrait was painted."

"It's as though it's saying, 'Mary was here,'" Alison said.

"Or Anne."

"I don't suppose Anne hung around long enough to have a portrait painted," Alison said. "If she was there at all."

"Fair point," Adam sighed. "What about the flowering wand?"

"Oh, that's what it is!" Alison said. "I thought it was a stick. So it's a magic wand?" She thought of Mary, the fey, the seer. How appropriate. "What about the flowers?"

"Flowers can symbolise spring," Adam said. "Was Mary Seymour born in the spring? I can't remember offhand."

"No," Alison said. "It was September."

*And we were sent away in the depths of a cold winter...*

"I suppose it could depend on the flower," Adam said. "Those look like lilies."

"I think they're irises." The gallery had emptied completely now. Alison got up and walked towards the painting, squinting to get a better look at the tiny purple blooms in the corner of the picture.

"Ah, well that makes all the difference." Adam was beside her. "Iris, the goddess, is sent to rouse people from sleep—or death. Her spring flowers symbolise hope."

Alison's eyes met Mary's painted gaze. *Hope.* She could feel it opening like a flower inside her after too many long, barren years. It was terrifying, exhilarating.

*"Look in the box,"* Mary's sideways glance seemed to say. *"Follow the trail I have left for you. Find your son..."*

Adam's hand was on her arm, drawing her back to the real world. "We have to go," he said. "They want to close up."

They went out into the evening. It was cold and there was a hint of snow on the air. It seemed to make the crowds excited; the streets were packed with Christmas shoppers going home and people on their way to and from office parties.

"Are you going to the Tube?" Adam asked, stepping closer to Alison as a group of laughing revellers barged into them. He smelled of crisp night air and faintly of aftershave, very delicious.

Alison cleared her throat. "I get the bus," she said. "Adam—" she touched his arm "—thanks for this evening. I realise I haven't really given you much to go on."

"No," Adam said. He smiled suddenly. "Not as much as you might have done."

"What do you mean?" Alison was startled.

"Only that you know more than you're saying," Adam said. "It's okay." For a moment she was sure the back of his hand brushed her cheek but in the melee she thought she must have imagined it. "I guess you'll tell me in your own good time if you want me to know. Whatever this is about, it seems very important to you."

"It is." Alison blinked back unexpected tears, shaken by his generosity. She knew she didn't deserve it. Somehow the time they had spent together in the gallery had spun a fragile peace between them.

Adam covered her hand with his where it rested on his sleeve. Alison was so surprised she let hers stay there beneath the warm touch of his.

"If you're still interested in seeing the box and its contents," he said, "I should be able to talk to someone tomorrow who could help."

"That's very kind of you," Alison said. "I don't really understand why you're being so nice to me."

"Neither do I," Adam said dryly.

They were so close that she could see the flecks of gold in his dark eyes and the hard, exciting line of his cheek. Her gaze moved to his mouth and she saw a muscle tighten in his jaw.

He drew her closer to him purposefully, holding her still, his eyes, full of questions, searching her face. She put a hand against his chest to steady herself. Suddenly she felt dizzy.

"Adam," she said.

The crowds swirled about them but Alison barely noticed. Adam took her face in his hands and kissed her. She felt stunned. The night, the people, faded away completely. She was aware of nothing but him, the cold air, the taste of him, and the sense of recognition. She felt as though she had been a long, long way away without even realising it, but that suddenly she had come home.

Adam let her go. "Damn," he said forcefully.

Alison gave a shaky giggle. "I've had better responses to a kiss," she said.

Adam ran a hand through his hair. "Yes. Sorry. I didn't mean—" He stopped. "I knew I was going to do that," he said explosively, "and yet I still did it."

"You knew more than I did, then," Alison said. "You don't even like me."

The blaze of heat in Adam's eyes died down. A rueful smile lifted the corner of his mouth. "Really?" he said. "You believe that?"

Alison felt her stomach twist and tumble. "There's a reason why an ex is called that," she said quickly. "It implies that something is over."

Adam did not reply. He was watching her with that steady, perceptive dark gaze and she felt vulnerable beneath it. She remembered that sensation from when she had been with him ten years before. It was one of the many reasons she had split up with him, because it felt as though he demanded honesty from her and she could not give it.

But that had been a long time ago.

"If you're still up for discussing history," she said, "the six-teenth century rather than ours, let's meet somewhere neutral once you've got the box."

"Somewhere neutral?" Adam rubbed his chin. "How about the Travellers Club? I stay there sometimes when I'm in London and we could meet for coffee and it would all be very respectable."

"Fine," Alison said briskly. "Good."

"I'll call you," Adam said.

"I'll call *you*," Alison said. "I've already got your card." Her bus was pulling in. She drew away from Adam and pushed her way through the press of people about the stop. When she had grabbed a seat and looked out, he had gone.

# FIFTEEN

## Mary, 1566

DARRELL CAME TO ME ON THE NIGHT I HAD
been out with Will. He came in my dreams, calling to me.
Perhaps it was because I could barely sleep with excitement and my mind was like an open door and so he slipped
through.

"*Cat…*"

For the first time in my life, I did not want to speak to
him. My love for Will felt so huge and new that there was
no room for other emotions and I wanted to drown myself
in it. Yet at the same time I felt an old loyalty to Darrell. I
could not simply ignore or dismiss him. He had been a part
of my life, a part of *me*, for so long, and if that life now felt
past and gone I at least owed it to him to explain.

There was a sense of animation about Darrell, too and
a thread of pleasure and hope that was bright and excited.

"*Cat. I must tell you…*" The words came through like a
pulse of light, but then, as though he was sensing my reluc-
tance and withdrawal, wariness crept in. "*What is it?*"

"Will Fenner is home."

*"I know."* He sounded flat all of a sudden, the life drained away. I could feel his thoughts mingling with mine. His were dark and shadowed in a way I could not understand whilst mine were so airy and free with love.

*"Cat..."* He called my name again, and I knew he had read me. I felt it then, a blaze of fury and hatred, before he closed his emotions down.

*"You love him. You are in love with Will Fenner."*

It was a blank accusation that left me feeling as much anger as I had sensed in him.

*"Why should I not be?"* I shot back.

Such a welter of emotion came through to me then. There was pity and regret, and beneath it a love and hopelessness that shot me through with grief. I understood then. I had loved Darrell but I had not been in love with him the way I felt towards Will. But he... He had loved me wholly and entirely and had thought that I loved him.

*"Darrell..."*

I did not know what to say, but he saved me the trouble. I got no response only a sense of loss and sorrow like faded blossom falling at the end of spring, and then he was gone.

At first I was upset. I tried to reach out to him again but met silence. Then I felt guilty. This was hateful, so instead I allowed myself to feel a righteous indignation. Who was Darrell to pour scorn on my love for Will? How dare he give me no right of reply? My angry thoughts seemed to do nothing but echo through my mind. I told myself that it did not matter, I did not need Darrell, my future was here at Middlecote and he was gone with my past. Yet still it hurt for all I tried to forget it.

I fell into a different sort of sleep after a while and began to dream. It started with Alison disappearing like a wraith into the thin rain of a Marlborough winter. Then I saw a bird, a peregrine falcon, flying free from a woman's hand, circling high against the piled-up grey clouds of an oncoming storm. The bird was calling but the notes were lost in the buffeting of the wind and then I too was up high, looking down on Alison's upturned face as she tried to trace the falcon's path. Her long blonde hair blew out like a ragged banner and her face was a pale blur and she looked so small and alone.

The scene changed then and Alison was standing in front of a ruined hall. It was not a castle with pennants flying, as I had prophesied for her that night at Wolf Hall, but a manor clad in ivy, thick and close. She reached up a hand towards the engraved stone above the empty doorway. Her desolation was palpable. I could feel her emotions as though they were my own. She was too late.

I woke shuddering to see that it was morning, grey and dull, with the same biting wind as in my dream. I felt out of humour, my head heavy and my eyes tired. The intoxication of the night before, both of my body and my senses, had gone. It felt as though it had been no more than a shred of imagination. Those images from my past, of Darrell and Alison, had both visited me in their different ways and left me lonely. I dressed hastily, eager to banish their shadows in the warmth of Will's company.

He was not there. Eleanor said he had gone to Newbury to buy a horse, but though I waited on tenterhooks all through the day, he did not return. The hours dragged. It seemed astonishing to me that everything at Middlecote seemed to go exactly the same when I could not have felt more different. Lady Fenner had us at our embroidery although the weather brightened into a very fine day. She seemed as fretful as I felt. Only, Eleanor sewed away as placidly as ever.

In the afternoon, I walked across the fields to the remains of the Roman villa and sat amongst its tumbled stones listening to the river run and the hum of the bees. It should have been soothing but it was not; I still fell stirred up and restless. I closed my eyes and concentrated on the sun on my face. I felt drowsy yet still oddly awake. When I opened my eyes, the sky above me was a clear crystalline blue and there was something that looked like a big grey and black barrel with wings flying high above my head, the sun glinting off it. I blinked and saw another and another, and heard a droning sound like none I had ever heard before. Panic leaped in my throat. The sound grew louder until it filled my ears and it felt as though my entire body was vibrating. Then, as quickly as it had happened, it faded, and I was left in a silence so loud it felt as though my head rang with it.

Machines that flew... I had never seen or heard of such a thing. There were legends, of course, of men who dreamed of flying like birds, but that was all they were—myths and stories. Those great, ugly machines I had seen were beyond my understanding.

I felt entirely miserable. I had not wanted the strange events of Wolf Hall to recur here at Middlecote. I had wanted to start a new life, to be ordinary, to belong somewhere. At last it had felt as though such a dream was within my grasp. Perhaps that was why I had cut myself off from Darrell, because I wanted something more earthly and commonplace: a home, a husband, a family. Marriage to Will—for my mind had already leaped ahead from one kiss to the altar—promised that. Not only was it a normality that I craved, it also meant that I would be safe; no accusations of witchcraft or heresy, like my mother. No danger of difference, or threat of death. I clung to the dream tenaciously. I would not beg Darrell to come back. I would forget Alison. I would never see any visions again.

I got to my feet and dusted down my gown, wandering back across the field towards the house. Immediately, I re-

alised that something was different, wrong, and my steps faltered as I stopped and stared. The house… The house was
much bigger than it had been before, and around it were
scattered any number of ugly grey buildings, foursquare and
squat. Men ran between them, men dressed in green and
brown, like a monstrous regiment of ants, bustling, for ever
busy, an army of them.

"*Cat!*"

Darrell's voice burst into my mind like an explosion. A
second later there was shouting, and a welter of light and
sound all about me. The earth was blowing up about my
feet and it sent me tumbling back down into the grass. I was
blinded; clouds of white about me, and in my nose the acrid
tang of smoke. I felt a sharp pain in my arm and saw blood.

Everything was dark and confused. I felt as though I was
falling, tumbling down the centuries as if down a bottomless
well, no longer sure of where I was or even who I was. I put
out a hand to steady myself but it met nothing but air. I was
a creature of no substance, a spirit flying through the night.

"Mary! Mary!"

It was Eleanor's voice. I opened my eyes and saw her face
hanging over me like an anxious half moon. She recoiled
at the sight of the blood. "Oh! What have you done? What
happened?"

I sat up. The world was steady. There was nothing in my
view; nothing but the empty fields and the little manor house
basking in the sun, and the call of the birds.

"I fell," I said. The blood was on my gown. Lady Fenner
would be furious. It was monstrously difficult to get blood
out of any material.

"Come inside," Eleanor urged, clumsily trying to help me
to my feet. "Come within before you take a fever."

I let her take my arm and guide me up, and followed her

inside obediently enough. She took me to my chamber where I allowed her to wash and bandage my arm, and listened to her exclamations over the strange white powder she said was scattered in my hair. I told her a dust cloud had blown up out of nowhere. There was an acrid taste in my mouth and I could still smell the sharp scent of the explosion in my nostrils. It had been so fierce it had closed my throat and set me coughing. Eleanor, of course, saw the cough as a sign I was developing an ague so whilst she brewed a mixture of herbs for me and one of the maids fussed over my gown, trying to remove the blood from the silk with water and salt, I sat peaceably in front of the fire and tried to think about nothing at all.

I did not call on Darrell. I did not thank him.

Will had still not returned by nightfall but late, when it was dark, I was woken from a restless sleep by the sound of hooves on the cobbles outside and the scatter of gravel against the panes of my window.

"Mary!" Will's whisper.

My heart leaped. I padded across to the window and threw the casement wide.

"Will?"

"Hush! Come down to the stables."

I went the way that we had escaped the previous night, down the backstairs and through the chapel, out by the door into the garden. The stables were warm and smelled of hay and horse; in the corner, a bay mare stood tied to a post, looking cross and tired, a pair of bulging saddlebags beside her.

"She's a temper on her," Will said, "just like all the other women I know." He smiled at me, that dazzling smile of his. "Except you, Mary. You are the only one who is different."

I felt a thrill of pleasure at his words, mixed with a gaucheness I could not hide. "She is the one you bought in New-bury then?" I asked, to cover my embarrassment.

"She is." His eyes gleamed with a secret amusement, his gaze travelling over my body, making me feel hot. "Thank you for coming to rescue me," he said gently. "That damn fool of a hall boy locked the door."

I could not see why he, as master of the house, would not rouse the whole of Middlecote if he chose, but I said nothing. Instead, I watched as he moved over to the saddlebags and went down on one knee beside them, unfastening the buckle. Gold gleamed and there was the chink of coin. I stared.

"My winnings," Will said. He looked up, the gold slipping through his fingers. "It's been a good night."

But my eyes were on the tear in the sleeve of his jacket and the ugly gash beneath. "You're injured!" I said sharply. "How—"

"A scratch." He dismissed it with a flick of his hand. "I came across a footpad and had no wish to hand over my prize."

"What happened?"

"A fight," Will said. "I half killed him."

The satisfaction in his tone took me aback. Footpads were thieves, outlaws, and deserved neither sympathy nor pro-tection, but the pleasure in Will's voice chilled and bewil-dered me.

He swayed to his feet and I moved instinctively to catch him, thinking he might fall. Instead, he caught me up in his arms and kissed me. He smelled of wine and woodsmoke, and a sweet scent I did not recognise that caught in my throat. I knew he was half drunk and I did not like it. I tried to per-suade myself that I did, but what had seemed amusing and ex-citing the previous night now felt wrong, careless and cheap. Still I fought the emotion, telling myself that this was Will and I loved him, but it was no good. The kiss repelled me and I struggled to be free. He released me at once. His eyes narrowed; there was a flash of anger in them.

"Tired of my kisses already, my sweet?"

I was trembling, confused. He must have seen it in my eyes for his own expression softened and he smiled again, that wicked, devil-may-care smile that made me sigh with relief, for this was the Will I knew, back again.

"Ah, I'm sorry," he said. "Forgive me, Mary. I am in no fit state to kiss the hem of your gown, let alone your lips." He staggered and I moved to support him again, sliding his arm about my shoulder.

"I am weak from loss of blood," he said. "Damnation."

"Let me get you to your bed," I said.

He flashed me another grin, though this one was frayed at the edges. "Stow the money for me first, sweetness. Under the hay—" he nodded to a corner of the stable "—where it will be safe."

It seemed madness to me; if he had won the money fair and square then he had no need to conceal it. However, I did what he said beneath the incurious stare of the mare who seemed only to wish we would leave her alone.

Somehow we made it out of the stable and across the courtyard to the little door by the chapel that I had left open.

"Let me call a servant to help you," I suggested, but Will only shook his head.

His weight lay heavily against me. He was a tall man as well as broad and I was only small. It seemed to me that we made enough noise to wake the dead as Will dragged himself up the backstairs, but no one stirred. Perhaps they knew better than to enquire when Wild Will Fenner was abroad at night.

I left him at the door of his chamber and went back to my

own. My window was still wide. In my eagerness to help him I had left it open and the night air flowed in. Shivering, I lay down on my bed. It felt as though the new-minted happiness of my love for Will was already confused and tarnished somehow by the events of the night and yet I clung stubbornly to it. I was the one he had called for help when he needed it. I was the person to whom he had turned. I held his secrets.

When we broke our fast the next morning, Will seemed as fresh as a daisy. White linen and velvet covered the injury to his arm. He gave me a wink and a special smile and I glowed with the pleasure of being the only one in his confidence. Halfway through the meal there was a knock at the door and a servant, flustered, said that the constable had called to enquire about a highway robbery the previous night. The man was shown in; a valuable horse had been stolen and its owner robbed and left for dead, he said. Had we seen a bay mare?

Will swore blind that he had returned from Newbury in time for dinner and had not stirred again all evening. He looked at me as he said it, holding my gaze with his. There was no pleading in his eyes but a secret amusement that took for granted my connivance.

I said nothing at all.

The weeks of summer seemed enchanted. Whether it was wilful blindness I was suffering from or painful naïveté, I am not sure. Perhaps it was a little of both. I was determined to love Will, so bewitched was I by the sensation of loving and being loved. I ignored his long absences, excused his erratic moods, and joined the conspiracy of silence. If there were strange comings and goings in the night, voices, raucous noise, laughter, we kept our doors firmly closed and our lights doused. Once, I even heard a woman's voice, soft, pleading, with a note in it I did not recognise, and Will's reply:

"We have all night..."

Then the door shut. I shut the thought of his debauchery out too, such was my infatuation with him.

During the day, all was sunlight and pleasure, riding, walking in the gardens or by the lazy stream, even music and dancing on some evenings when Will exerted himself to play the charming host and his mother was able to find sufficient of our neighbours to invite whom he had not cuckolded or cheated. I knew none of that, of course, or if I did I pretended I did not. I felt worldly; a man was not a gentleman if he did not drink and gamble and take a mistress, I told myself. Besides, when Will stole moments alone with me, I did feel as though I was the only woman he had ever cared for. His kisses were ardent and exciting but he took care not to frighten me as he had done that night in the stables. Degree by slow degree he was seducing me, with sweetness and gallantry, until I ached for him with an abandon I scarcely understood.

Eleanor noticed a change in me. She said I was dreamy. Lady Fenner said nothing at all but she watched me with her sharp, dark gaze. I started to read poetry. I even wrote some bad verse of my own though I would share it with no one. Will brought me small gifts—a bolt of cloth, a ribbon and some lace. I floated on air through those hot summer days. And I had no more visions.

An odd thing happened one afternoon. Eleanor and I were sitting in the gardens, she with her sketching, I with my verse. It was a still day, ripe and heavy as though there was to be a thunderstorm and, sure enough, out of a blue sky came a ruffle of wind, snatching my book from my hand and sending Eleanor's drawing bowling away over the grass. She gave a cry of distress and ran after it but it was Will who reached over and plucked it from where it was wrapped around his boots. He had come out onto the terrace to find us and now he started down the steps and onto the lawn.

All might have been well had he handed Eleanor the drawing back without looking at it but he glanced down at it once, casually, and his expression changed from indulgence to fury in one frightening second.

"What the devil—" He held it out to her. "When did you see him? Did he come here?"

Eleanor seemed to have shrunk into herself. "I haven't..." she stammered. "He didn't... It's only imagination, memory."

With one violent movement, Will tore the parchment across and across again, leaving the pieces to scatter over the grass as he stalked away. The first fat drop of rain fell. Eleanor gave a sob, one hand pressed over her mouth as though trying to hold back the sound. I grabbed at the pieces before they could be blown away in the rising wind.

"Don't tell Mama," Eleanor said, clutching them to her. "Please don't tell her." She looked agonised.

"Of course not," I said. I squinted at the scraps of paper in her hand. It had been a portrait, a man; young, tall, good-looking. In fact, he looked like Will although he was fairer and not as handsome.

"Who is it?" I could not help my curiosity. I thought it unlikely I would not know if Eleanor had a suitor.

She looked evasive. "It's Thomas."

"Thomas?"

"Our brother."

That confused me. I had no notion that Will and Eleanor had a brother. No one had ever mentioned him and I was certain that he did not feature on the vast and elaborate family pedigree that hung in the Great Hall.

"I mean half-brother," Eleanor amended. "Thomas's mother was Mary Fortescue, Papa's mistress."

I gaped. I had heard nothing of this. Lady Fenner had been a widow for a long time and no one spoke of what had happened before. "But... How old is he?" I asked.

"Younger than Will and older than I am," Eleanor said. "Mistress Fortescue was Papa's mistress for over twenty years. I think perhaps he always did prefer her to Mama. Thomas is nice," Eleanor added. "He's the opposite of Will."

That distracted me for a moment. "Will is nice too," I argued hotly. "Will is lovely!"

She gave me a very hard look from her red-rimmed eyes, a shrewder look than I would have imagined Eleanor capable of. "Will is unkind, Mary," she said. "There is a darkness to him."

I didn't want to quarrel with her. Instead, I gestured towards the picture. "But how did you meet Thomas? When did you meet him? Surely he did not grow up with you and with Will and he hasn't been to Middlecote in all the time that I've been here."

"It was before you came," Eleanor said. "Thomas used to live here. Papa left Middlecote to Mistress Fortescue when he died. It was Will who drove her out, pursuing her through the courts to reclaim his inheritance. I heard Mama telling him that he had killed her with his lawsuits and Will agreeing, and saying how fortunate that was."

I sat down abruptly. The rain was starting to fall in earnest now but I did not notice. That was the sort of thing that Will *would* say, I thought, but surely only in jest. And it was right for a man to want to reclaim his inheritance. Will was Sir Edward's legitimate son. Middlecote and all the other Fenner estates were his by right.

"I met Thomas once when I was about nine years old,"

Nell said wistfully. "We were visiting a friend of Mama's and I was playing in the garden with some other children. Thomas was older, fifteen perhaps. He was very kind to me. We talked for a long time. I think Mama was not aware that he was there because when she found out she came bustling out to take me away and we never went back."

I could see Lady Fenner now, sweeping towards us across the lawns, skirts flapping like a great black crow. Will must have told her what had happened. I could not help but reflect that it was no great wonder Sir Edward had shunned her bed for that of another woman. There was no warmth in her at all. And perhaps it was good and right that he had tried to make provision for his mistress and her child. I had heard he had been an honest and respected man.

"You are to come indoors, both of you!" Lady Fenner was looking around suspiciously, almost as though she expected to see Thomas lurking behind a bush. "What are you thinking, to be sitting out here in the rain?"

"Yes, Mama," Nell said submissively. The rain was mingling with the tears on her cheeks and she looked wan and bedraggled. I thought it odd Lady Fenner had come to fetch us herself rather than sending a servant for she hated the rain. She was like a cat in that respect. Then I saw her craning her neck to try to get a glimpse of the picture in Nell's hands. She did not ask for it; she made no reference to it at all but there was a spark of something in her eyes. I thought then:

*She is afraid. She is afraid of Thomas Fenner.*

I waited all day for someone—Lady Fenner, or Will or even Nell herself—to speak more of Thomas, but they did not. Will took himself off to his study with a bottle. Nell went and hid in her chamber and Lady Fenner took out her vicious bad temper on the housekeeper. It was as though a blanket of silence had fallen over Middlecote Hall, a silence tinged with fear. It was most odd. Will was too aggressive a man to scare easily yet there was something here that frightened him, something to do with his half-brother.

I overheard Will and Lady Fenner talking in Will's study that night. I confess I eavesdropped; I was hoping to hear more of the mysterious Thomas. However, it was of something quite different they spoke.

"She should have been married off long before now." Will sounded as irritable as a man could when troubled by business he thought beneath him. "She mopes around here like a pale ghost. It annoys me beyond measure."

"She is only nineteen." Lady Fenner sounded stiff. She was touchy on the subject of marriage, having been an old maid when Sir Edward had plucked her from the shelf. "Besides, it is not easy, William. Not with Nell's lack of dowry and your reputation."

Will gave a bark of laughter. "*My* reputation is a blight on my sister's prospects? By God, madam—"

"You know it," Lady Fenner said coldly. "None of the Hungerfords would have her, nor would the Fettiplaces, or the Bassetts. They do not wish to be allied with you."

Will gave an exaggerated sigh. "Then marry her off into your own family. There must be a lowly Essex cousin somewhere who would be glad of the recognition."

"Or a Seymour cousin might take her," Lady Fenner said waspishly. "They owe us that at least."

"Ah." Will's tone had changed. He sounded amused, mocking even. "Why such resentment, madam? Mary is a little sparrow of a thing—surely she cannot have cost us much to feed and clothe these past few years?"

"I thought to profit by taking her," Lady Fenner said, "not lose by it."

"And so you shall."

"Oh, no." Lady Fenner seldom laughed and when she did it was not a pleasant sound. "Do not imagine for one moment, William, that you are to marry that chit. If that is your plan you must think again."

I was trembling now. To marry Will had been my most ardent hope and it seemed that he wished it too. My breath caught as I waited for his reply.

"Why should I not wed her?" For all the laziness in Will's tone there was a watchful note as well.

"She has no money," Lady Fenner said, her voice cold, barbed. "Nothing other than a ring her father left her and few other worthless baubles. There are no estates, nothing at all." Her voice rose and she deliberately calmed her tone. "She is your pensioner, William, not your honoured guest, and least of all is she a potential bride for you."

The blunt assessment of my situation made me smart. For nigh on two whole months I had been enjoying my new status, easily believing, under the warmth of William's attentions, that I had been elevated from poor relation to noble lady. To see it for the sham it was pained me, but I told myself fiercely that it would make no difference to Will's regard for me. He loved me and if he wanted to wed me he would do so even if I were a pauper.

Swift on the heels of that thought came another quite different one. How did Lady Fenner know of my father's ring? It was the only thing I had of his and though I had no notion of its worth, I guarded it like a treasure, keeping it safe in the box I had had from Alison. Yet Lady Fenner, it seemed, knew where to find it. She knew everything in this house.

The rumble of Will's reply, too low to distinguish the words, brought my attention back. Then I heard Lady Fenner again:

"So that is your plan? You are in a fool's paradise! The

Queen will never restore her lands. Why should she? Mary is no kin of hers. There would be no advantage to her. No, I fear, the Lady Mary is destined to remain another high-born spinster with no looks or fortune to aid her."

"It might still be worth the gamble." Will had moved closer to the door. I, correspondingly, shrank back into the shadows. "With Mary as my wife I could approach Her Majesty and ask for the restitution of Thomas Seymour's lands in this locality at the least. Ramsbury, for instance, is a rich and fine estate and there are others. To ask only for those that are close by would swell our income but would look modest, and stand more chance of success than to claim the whole." He sounded pleased with his calculation.

"Her Majesty would refuse you." Lady Fenner sounded even colder. "Thomas Seymour was a fool, marrying unwisely and gaining little profit from it. You should not follow his example."

*A fool.* I bristled with indignation at the insult to my father, even knowing in my heart of hearts that he had been rash in almost all his dealings.

"I hope you have not seduced her already?" Lady Fenner sounded alarmed now. "Surely not even you could be so imprudent, William?"

"You are correct." Will was as cold as she now. "Not even I would do such a thing."

In my folly and ignorance this pleased me. Sir William Fenner was too much a gentleman to take advantage of me. His attentions were honourable. He wanted to marry me.

Lady Fenner was not equally impressed. "Pshaw," she said. "Don't seek to cozen me. This has nothing to do with Mary. You are still entangled with the Lady Anne Hungerford. You are like your father, intemperate in your affairs."

Will laughed. "There was nothing intemperate in Sir

Edward's behaviour, madam. He sincerely loved Mistress Fortescue."

"Oh, you seek to provoke me," Lady Fenner said impatiently. "Do you think that I do not know how you like to prick at people until they bleed? Well, you will get no pleasure from baiting me." She sighed. "Heed me on this and leave well alone. Leave Mary alone."

There was a pause. I waited for Will to tell her he would not, that we would be wed, but he said nothing.

After a moment I heard Lady Fenner sigh. Her tone had changed.

"What are we to do, William?" she said. She sounded almost afraid. "What are we to do about Thomas?"

"Precisely nothing, madam," Will said. "Thomas cannot take Middlecote back. It is mine by law. His mother suffered when she tried to oppose me. Thomas will also feel my wrath if he troubles us."

I was forced to move away at that point as the hall boy came down the corridor, wiping his hands on his apron. He looked startled to see me as well he might, but bobbed his head and scurried away, as did I, back up the stairs to my chamber. There I opened the box where I kept my father's ring, nestled on a bed of rich sapphire velvet. It was huge, a great lozenge of gold, inscribed with the words "What I have I hold." I had heard that my uncle Edward, the Lord Protector, had given it to my father not as a gift but as a warning. It was, I thought, a suitable dowry for Thomas Seymour's daughter whatever Lady Fenner thought. I slipped into my bed and tried not to think about Lady Fenner goading Will about Anne Hungerford. My jealousy was a hot and horrible thing. In some curious way I thought of Will as mine now, though there had been no declaration from him. Any admiration I had felt for him as a worldly man with a string of mistresses was gone now. I would not share his affections.

I pulled the covers over my head to try to block out the dark thoughts but all I could hear as I fell asleep was Will and Anne's soft laughter ringing in my ears as the bedroom door closed behind them.

# SIXTEEN

ADAM THREW DOWN HIS PEN AND RAN HIS hand through his hair in a gesture that Alison was starting to know well.

"This is all amazing stuff, Ali," he said, "but without any kind of authentication it might as well be fantasy." He took a gulp of his coffee and grimaced. During their discussions they had let it go cold and now a waiter glided up unbidden with a silver pot to refresh the cups.

Alison had to admit that she liked the Travellers Club. It wasn't the sort of place she would normally visit but the hushed elegance of the lounge was an oasis away from the bustle of the London streets at Christmas.

"I realise that," she said. "I'm sorry I can't be more helpful but you did know that before we started."

Adam was looking at her with a mixture of puzzlement and frustration. "I understand that a lot of this is family legend and hearsay," he said, gesturing to the lists of notes and family trees scattered on the table between them, "but who told you about it in the first place? I thought you were an orphan, but someone must have told you these stories about Mary Seymour and Wolf Hall."

Alison shrugged helplessly. Her information came from memory and observation, neither of which she could explain to Adam.

"I had relatives," she said. "Once upon a time. And then… Well, I went to genealogy websites and on to Internet boards."

"So it *could* all be fantasy." Adam shook his head in exasperation. "We all know how reliable those are."

"I told you I couldn't prove much of it," Alison said. "But you know there is often more than a grain of truth in family stories. Besides, you found reference to Mary at Middlecote yourself."

"I don't like it," Adam said. "There's too much speculation. It's as though you want it to be true so much you're trying to fit the facts to your version of events."

The stark accuracy of this stung Alison. "That's rich coming from you after the Anne Boleyn fiasco," she said coldly.

There was a tense pause then Adam laughed. "Okay, you have a point," he said.

"Have you found any more connections between Mary and Middlecote?" Alison asked hopefully.

Adam shook his head. "Not yet," he said. "The Fenner family papers are scattered across various different county records offices. Some of them are lost too. It all takes time." He looked at her thoughtfully. "You really do want this to be true, don't you," he said, more gently. "It seems hugely important to you."

"Yes." Alison knitted her fingers together tightly. "It's a sort of personal quest." She took a breath. "I promised someone," she said carefully. She had thought this all through the previous night when she had been doctoring her documents to remove all references to an Alison Banestre. It had seemed simple when she had planned it: she would tell Adam everything except for her own part of the story. Now, though, beneath Adam's cool, analytical gaze, she felt as though she was treading on ice that might splinter at any moment.

"My grandmother told me the stories of Mary Seymour

when I was very young," she said. That much was almost true: Old Lady Banestre, who probably had not been old at all but in her fifties, Alison thought, had spun endless fairy tales to her grandchildren, mingling fictional princes and princesses with tales of their ancestors' famous deeds. She had been brought up on stories of the illustrious Banestre family and its proud intermarriage with all the great names of the time—the Howards, the Berties, the Devereux. The Seymours had been parvenus in comparison. Even now, with the passage of so many years, Alison could remember the lilt of her grandmother's soft voice as she told the tales by the light of the fire, the red and silver of the Banestre coat of arms rippling in the golden glow.

She had felt secure then. She had understood her place in the world before chaos and darkness had set everything awry.

"Grandmama knew all about the family ancestry," she said. "She knew how we were originally related to all the great families. I don't know where she had gained all her knowledge. I suppose it was word of mouth down the generations, some true, some false, much embroidered to tell a good tale." She shifted. "There was someone she asked me to find: a boy, called Arthur." She swallowed hard. It was odd how difficult it was to lie. She wanted to claim Arthur as hers, not pass him off as some distant cousin.

Adam stirred. "You mean she wanted you to find out what had happened to him?" he asked.

Alison realised her slip. Arthur's fate felt so present to her that it was impossible not to refer to him as though he were alive now. To her he was, and she would find him.

"Yes," she said, "sorry, I meant she wanted me to trace him on the family tree. She said that he had been special and that his story should not be lost. She had been illegitimate, you see, just as he was. She had been erased from the family tree…" Her voice faltered as she embroidered the lie. "I think she felt a kinship with Arthur. So I… I promised her, before she died."

The silence that followed felt to her as though it rang with half-truths and falsehood. Alison could hear all the distinct and separate sounds: the chink of china, the low murmur of voices from the lounge to the right, the hum of traffic outside, even the call of the birds. Adam waited. He was good at silences. It made her feel even more uncomfortable.

"It's strange," he said reflectively, "when you were talking about it just now you sounded quite different, as though you were telling a story. Your grandmother must have been very special to you."

Alison felt a rush of emotion. Colour stained her cheeks. "Yes," she said. "She was."

"I'm sorry," Adam said, leaning over to touch her hand. "Sorry you lost them all."

Alison moved her hand away from his. It felt too dishonest to take his comfort when she was lying to him.

"Thanks," she said awkwardly. "Well…it was a long time ago."

"So it's this Arthur you are particularly intent on tracing?" Adam said, after a moment. "Is there some connection between him and Mary Seymour?"

"He was the illegitimate son of Mary's cousin, Edward Seymour, Lord Hertford," Alison said. "I think Mary knew what became of him."

"Find Mary and you find Arthur?" Adam raised his brows.

"Exactly," Alison said. "Or," she added hastily, "so my grandmother said."

"Was Mary Seymour his mother?" Adam asked.

"No." Alison realised she had spoken too quickly and

moderated her tone. "I mean, I don't think so. Arthur Seymour was born in London whilst Mary was at Wolf Hall."

"So who was his mother?" Adam said.

Alison studied her hands intently. "I don't know. He wasn't called Seymour either," she added quickly, glancing up to see that Adam was watching her. "That's why we can't trace him. Edward Seymour sent him away to be fostered and that's where the trail dies out."

"Right…" Adam said slowly. He rubbed the back of his neck. "Illegitimate children are notoriously difficult to trace. So often they slip through the gaps in the records."

"I know," Alison said, miserably. "I know."

"I've got to be honest," Adam said, "I think this is a wild-goose chase. I know you promised your grandmother and that this matters to you a lot, but I think you're just set for more disappointment if you're pinning your hopes on the portrait and the box telling you anything useful."

Alison bit down on her lips so hard she tasted blood, bit back too her sharp response. As far as she was concerned there was no alternative. The portrait had given her clues. The box *must* contain further evidence of Arthur's story. She could not contemplate a world where it did not.

"I don't expect you to understand how I feel," she said, "and I did promise I would see this through, and so I will."

Adam sighed. "All right," he said. "Well, I agreed I would show you the box anyway." He reached for the briefcase, placing it flat on the table and snapping the catches open.

"Here it is," he said, lifting it out and passing it to her. "Be careful with it."

Alison ignored him. She barely heard him. It was the most extraordinary feeling to be holding the box again. Across the centuries she recognised it immediately. The wood was duller now, polished by time to a grey brown hue. The black initials in the top—AB—were almost worn away. It looked smaller than she remembered.

"It's beautiful, isn't it?" Adam said and she found that she could not speak; her throat was blocked with tears. So she nodded.

She reached out a tentative hand, stroking the wood. She could remember the precise moment she had been given it. It had been before her parents had died. The estate carpenter had made it for her as a natal day gift and her father had given it to her on a morning bright with sunshine and hope. It had been shiny then, the initials a bold black, the wood smelling new.

The sweating sickness had come swiftly after that day, wiping out the sunshine and the hope and the happiness along with her parents and siblings. She had often wondered why she had survived and wished she had not been stronger than they.

She blinked back the tears again and lifted the lid. The box opened smoothly. It smelled faintly of sage and camomile, rosemary and orange. She recognised all the different scents individually.

The box was empty. The disappointment was crushing. *Too easy.*

Hadn't Adam said that there had been items in it when it had been found? It had been stupid of her to imagine they would simply leave them there for her.

"Are you all right, Ali?" Adam was looking at her quizzically. "Do you need more coffee?"

"No, sorry, I'm fine." Alison gave herself a shake. "Just some water, thanks." She poured for herself, splashing the water into her glass. "Sorry," she repeated. "You mentioned that there were some items in the box when it was found," she added. "I don't suppose you know what they were?"

"Yes, of course," Adam said. "They were taken away..."
He unfolded a piece of A4 paper and handed it to her.

Alison's hand was trembling. She tried to conceal it by holding the paper in her lap whilst she read it but the hammering of her heart betrayed her. She knew Adam could see she was shaking.

She read down the list. It was detailed and annotated, as she would have expected an academic document to be:

*A twig of wood, badly rotted, but identified as Rosmarinus officinalis (rosemary).*

*A piece of satin weave cloth of gold, degraded, pinned to a silver button in the shape of a shield with a bear.*

*One hammered silver penny, dating from 1560, showing the profile of Queen Elizabeth I on the obverse and a quartered shield of arms on the reverse. Very worn.*

*One pencil drawing, subject unidentified.*

*One plate from a falcon.*

*One knight from a chess set carved from holly.*

*One woollen thread in green, tied to a piece of catgut.*

"*Catgut?*" Alison said, startled. And then: "What on earth is a 'plate from a falcon'? A serving plate?"

"It was similar to a ring," Adam said. "Falconers used engraved rings to mark the ownership of their birds. As for the catgut, they used that for stringed instruments. It came from sheep's intestines, though, rather than cats."

"The things you know," Alison said. She had had a falcon once, a merlin, which had been the approved hunting bird for a lady. She hadn't cared for it. It had such a sharp predatory gaze and a mean spirit. She had hated hunting in all its forms and hated that she was despised for her soft heart even when she tried to hide her aversion. One of the other children at Wolf Hall had rubbed stag's blood on her face once and she had screamed and screamed.

"It's something of a random list, isn't it?" Adam was watching her. "I guess if the box was a charm against witches they would put all kinds of stuff in there. It's lucky it didn't include urine."

"I don't think it's random," Alison said slowly. "I think it's a riddle." She ran her fingers thoughtfully over the surface of the box again, relishing the satiny surface. "You know, a word game. Weren't the Tudors supposed to be fond of puzzles?"

Adam looked unimpressed. "Were they? I thought card games and cockfighting was more their thing."

Alison shook her head. "Definitely it's a riddle." She had already worked out the first couple of clues, or she thought she had. The rosemary was for remembrance.

*"You see, Alison, I did not forget you…"*

She could almost hear Mary's voice; see her smile. The angel in the portrait pointed to Mary as the messenger.

The inclusion of a penny from 1560 could be no coincidence either. It had been the year Arthur was born, the year before they were banished from Wolf Hall.

The rest of the items, though, were a mystery to her, but one she was determined she would work out.

Adam checked his watch, stretched. "Well, I guess we can try to work it out if you think it's worth a go. Do you want to grab something to eat? Unless you've got plans for this evening?"

Alison hadn't thought that far ahead but now she saw that the afternoon light had gone and it was full dark over Green Park, the lights on the buildings, the cranes and the shops twinkling with a vivid colour to rival the Christmas decorations.

"I was supposed to be going to the cinema with Kate," she said, "but she texted me that she had a better offer."

"Unexpected date?" Adam asked.

Alison shook her head. "A free ticket for *Mamma Mia!*. She's only seen it five times already." She gathered up her bag, still thinking about the list of items in the box. What was the significance of the cloth of gold and the button in the shape of a shield? Cloth of gold was for the rich—it signified wealth and fortune. A shield signified protection.

She gave herself a little shake. It was easy to see how she could become obsessed with this, searching for meanings just as she had been searching for Arthur all her adult life.

"Ali?" Adam was waiting for her answer. "Do you want to go out or not? I'm only suggesting a quick pizza, not dinner at the Ritz."

"Sorry," Alison said. "Yes, that would be nice. May I keep the list," she added, holding out the paper to Adam, "or do you need to return it?"

"Keep it," Adam said.

They went out into St. James's, where shoppers and sightseers vied for space on the pavements. The air was thick with noise and fumes. Unconsciously, Alison squared her shoulders and took a deep breath, only becoming aware a moment later that Adam was watching her.

"You love the city, don't you," he said, smiling. "You kind of come alight when you're out here."

"You feel a part of something bigger here," Alison said. "I've always felt as though I belonged in London."

They ate seafood at a little café in Soho and talked about everything except the past. Alison had thought it would be awkward but it was dangerously easy. It felt as it had done ten years before only better. There was more to talk about, experiences, ideas, interests. She could not imagine being bored with Adam. And underneath the conversation ran the attraction, hot and intense, and the fact that both of them were scrupulously ignoring it only served to make it feel more exciting.

They sat late over coffee, later than Alison had intended, but it was still only eight when they went out into a city just waking up for the night.

"I'll see you home," Adam said.

"You're so old-fashioned," Alison said.

"Yeah." Adam gave her the glimmer of a smile. "I am." He straightened. "No, actually, it's on my way. I have a place in Kensal Rise."

"Very nice," Alison said.

"Not as cool as Camden," Adam said, with a sideways glance at her. "How did you manage that?"

"I got lucky," Alison said lightly. "I had a bit of cash and I bought a bargain."

After her disastrous first attempt to sell the jewels she had stolen from Wolf Hall had ended with her taken into care, she had become much more wary. She had hidden the gems away for several years, eventually taking them to a dealer in South London who had been suspicious, but not enough to refuse to buy them. He had paid her a fair price and that had given her enough for a deposit on a flat.

Theft, lies and a life based on deception... But what choice had she had?

She looked at Adam, at the strong, clear-cut lines of his face and the steadiness in his eyes. She had idealised him as a teenager, she realised. She had thought he epitomised all the honour and gallantry that should have been present in her life but had been so conspicuously lacking. It had been an illusion, a fantasy. She had been trying to find an anchor and it was unfair to Adam to make him take that role. She had needed to find her way for herself and now she had. For the first time in her renewed quest to find Arthur she felt torn. She had friends, a home, a job and a life here now. Did she really want to go back for Arthur? Doubts had crept in somehow when her back was turned. She felt appalled, guilty. She thought of Arthur lying in her arms, his deep blue eyes unfocused and sleepy, his tiny fingers, his scent of newness and milk and sweet baby freshness. Her heart clenched hard. Fiercely, she banished the betrayal. She was closer now to finding him than she had ever been. Mary had kept her vow. She would keep her own promise.

# SEVENTEEN

*Mary, 1566*

THAT SUMMER WE SAT FOR OUR PORTRAITS, Eleanor and I. Eleanor grumbled, complaining that she could pen a better likeness than the artist Will had chosen. He was young and poor but also Italian and exotic. He soon won Eleanor round with his flashing black eyes and facile tongue. He told her she was *bellissima* and she blushed and smiled at him. I was not beautiful, of course. He called me Lady Mary, very correctly, and painted me with touch of mystery that I quite liked.

Will had not said so but I guessed that the portrait was for him, to mark our betrothal. That thought lent a smile to my lips and a sparkle to my modestly cast down gaze. I expected him to speak formally to me any day now, once he had gained the approval of Cousin Edward to our marriage. Oh, I was full of hope and expectation that summer. Will no longer stole kisses from me at the fair or in the stables. I told myself this was because everything had to be formal and proper between us now that we were to wed. I also told myself that I was not like Alison, risking ruin for an hour in a lover's arms but, in truth, I would have given almost anything for a taste of such passion. But Will was preoccupied as the summer days lengthened into early autumn. His study overflowed with documents that went unread: there were lawsuits and mortgages, debts and disputations. Not even Lady Fenner could speak to him without fear of violent reaction. The household tiptoed about him as though on hot coals.

Yet I loved him, or I loved the idea of being in love with him. It seems impossible now, now that I know the truth. Yet then I was blind to it. Will was the most exciting, the most glamorous person I had ever met and that dazzled me.

It was on one of those long summer days that I met Anne, Lady Hungerford, for the first time. We were visiting one of Lady Fenner's many Essex relatives, this time in the village of Lambourn. Her cousin Sir John owned a fair manor there, though not as extensive as Middlecote, as Lady Fenner was pleased to note. His wife Dulcibella was a faded, anxious woman, given to fusses and flusters. She bobbed about us: Had we had sufficient to eat? Was the sun in the solar too bright? Were we too warm, too cold? Lady Fenner treated her with contempt and she seemed to consider it her due, whilst Sir John was bluff and cross and the entire visit was most uncomfortable.

Will did not accompany us, much to the disappointment of the Essex's three giggling daughters who plied Eleanor and I with questions about him when Lady Fenner's back was turned. Was it true that he was in dispute with Jacob Green over some land where he had felled the trees for profit without permission? Had Green accused him of inciting riots? Was the truth of it that he had seduced Green's wife and the man had sworn revenge on him? They giggled and bobbed like their mother until Lady Fenner turned her dark, disdainful gaze on them, when they subsided like pricked bladders.

There was a summer downpour on the way back to Middlecote, a huge heavy shower from out of nowhere that turned the roads to mud within moments. The horses laboured hard to pull us up the hill towards home and, as we reached the crossroads near Lambourn Woodlands, we saw that a fine carriage was stuck fast, with one wheel broken and another entrenched in the mud. It completely blocked the way.

"It is Sir Walter Hungerford's carriage," Eleanor said, catching sight of the shield painted on the side. "Oh dear. Oh, no."

Her mother silenced her with one fierce look. It seemed Lady Fenner would not deign to set foot out of the carriage in the rain, least of all for Sir Walter, but she summoned a groom to bear a message to him to move his coach out of our way. This he did eventually, with much heaving, shoving and shouting from the mud-splashed servants, whilst we sat in frigid silence, waiting. When at last we could pass by the coach was canted at a violent angle up on the bank to allow us room. Sir Walter was glaring out at us whilst at his side sat a slender fair woman with an ethereal beauty that made me catch my breath.

"That is Lady Hungerford," Eleanor whispered to me. The jolting and heaving of the coach as it struggled along the rutted track had distracted Lady Fenner's attention from us for a moment.

"I thought you said she was old?" I whispered back, hot with jealousy.

Eleanor stared at me. "She is. Thirty or more."

"But beautiful still."

"Beautiful enough for Will to want to bed her still," Eleanor said. She laughed. "She wrote him a letter saying that if Sir Walter died she would wed him. It made Will laugh. He showed it to everyone."

"That was unkind of him," I said. I wanted to be pleased that Will did not take Lady Anne's professions of love seriously but I was not. Instead, I felt upset for her.

Eleanor shrugged. "Sir Walter is hale and hearty so Will is spared the trouble."

*Will is free to marry me.*

I did not say it, but I thought it. God help me, I still wanted it, Lady Hungerford and her beauty notwithstanding.

Lady Fenner's gaze turned back to us. "What are you two girls whispering about?" she demanded.

"Nothing, Mama," Eleanor said. "Nothing of consequence."


The portraits were finished. Eleanor's was delightful, a true facsimile of her person, pretty and delicate and sweet. I saw Lady Fenner's smile when she viewed it. She was pleased to have raised such a pattern-perfect daughter, yet at the same time she did not value delicacy, seeing it as weakness. Thus she managed to look both contemptuous and satisfied at the same time.

I was less happy with my likeness. It was true enough, but the artist had made me look secretive rather than mysterious. There was something uneasy about it. Both pictures had a small drawing of a wyvern in the bottom left hand corner to signify the heraldic beasts that snarled at Middlecote's gates. Will glanced at them in cursory fashion.

"Very pretty," he said, dismissively, handing mine back to me when I had hoped he would keep it for himself. I was disappointed. As there seemed nothing else to do with it, I put it in the hiding place up the chimney where I kept Alison's box, the one that was no hiding place at all since Lady Fenner knew all about it.

There was more trouble that day. Will had refused to pay the painter and had kicked him out of the house. The poor man was dragged down the drive, protesting volubly in torrents of Italian.

"I do wish Will would not do things like this," Eleanor said, sighing, as we watched from the window. "It is very bad of him."

Barely had the artist been dispatched when Sir Henry Knyvett stormed around to demand payment of a debt that Will owed him. Will gave him short shrift too and Knyvett left swearing to high heaven that he would be revenged upon Will for his knavish behaviour. Hot on his heels came an agent representing the Earl of Rutland, who was demanding the repair of land in Chilton Foliat that Will had apparently despoiled.

"Lord Rutland will see you hang!" the man yelled as he too was summarily ejected from the house.

This set the tone for the week. Barely a day passed without some luckless tradesman petitioning to have his bills paid and being laughed off the premises. It was difficult to concentrate on my embroidery with such dramatic affairs at every turn. Lady Fenner's thin lips became more pursed with every knock upon the door. Nell shrank in on herself, shuddering at each loud noise. Will had threatened to marry her off to whoever paid the highest price and she crept about the house like a wraith in the hope he would forget she existed.

On the Friday eve, I had retired early with a headache but I had not slept well. The cold cloth on my forehead did not soothe me, and the fretful moonlight skipping across the room kept waking me whenever I did fall asleep. Besides, my ears were attuned by now to the sounds of Will's nocturnal activities. I heard the crunch of his boots on the gravel and the muffled clop of his horse's hooves. I wondered what would be his target tonight—the gaming tables, to win a fortune perhaps, or perhaps a lady's bed.

There was the rattle of stones at my window and my foolish heart leaped with excitement, headache quite forgotten.

"Mary! Come down!"

Why did I go with him that night? Why did he ask me? The answer to the first question was that loving Will made me rash and reckless. The answer to the second I did not know.

It was a fair night and we rode out to the north, along the old trackways that led up onto the Downs, the Thieves' Way and the Rogues' Way, which Will told me were the haunt of highwaymen and footpads, and thus had gained their name and reputation.

"We never ride this way," I said. "Why is that?"

"It's too dangerous." He gave me a wolfish grin. "You will need me to protect you." He patted the pistol in his belt.

I admit it; I was excited, by the night, by the man, by the adventure.

"Whither do we go?" I asked.

"To church." His shoulders shook with suppressed amusement. He was in a merry mood that night. "We go to Kingston Parva. There is a church there, small, rich, well endowed and poorly protected. It holds the De Morven treasure. We go to relieve the priest of his gold and silver plate."

My mouth dropped open. "You are robbing a *priest*?"

He cast me a sideways look. "*We* are robbing a priest. You will distract him whilst I steal the key."

"I? How...?" I was all at sea, fearful suddenly, not simply

because of the enormity of his plan but because, for the first time, the doubts I had repressed were swimming back up to the surface, too dark and persistent to be ignored. I knew Will was a rogue. I had even admired him for it. But this… this was wrong.

"No," I said, "I can't."

He stopped his horse and caught the bridle of mine to make me halt too. We were deep in a holloway where the track passed between high banks. It was very dark, but I could see that he was smiling.

"Mary…" His voice was soft, wheedling. "Won't you do it for me?"

"But why?" I almost wailed the words. *Don't ask this of me. Don't put me to the test. I will fail you.* "You don't need to steal," I said. "I have money."

He looked sad. "Not enough, Mary," he said. "Not anywhere near enough. Taking Reginald De Morven's treasure will enable me to wed you. Help me so that we may be together."

I like to think that I would have refused him though I cannot be entirely sure. For good or ill I never had the chance to find out, for there was a shout behind us and the sound of pounding hoof beats and then Will pushed me, hard. Taken by surprise, I lost my balance and fell from the saddle, landing on the ground with a sickening thud. Earth spattered my face. My head spun. The sound of retreating hoof beats rang in my ears. I tried to sit up only to sink back with a heartfelt groan, closing my eyes. It felt as though my head was about to cleave in two.

There was a lantern. Someone was kneeling beside me, turning me over so that my face was to the light. I opened my eyes.

A man. He was leaning over me. This was not good.

I could not see his face well. The lantern was between us, dazzling me, yet, oddly, there was something about him that seemed familiar.

Then his voice jerked me from my confusion.

"So," he said, "who the devil are you?"

# EIGHTEEN

===

"WOULD YOU LIKE TO COME IN?" ALISON ASKED.
She had not meant to invite Adam back. There were several
dozen reasons why it was a bad idea. She was always cautious
in her relationships these days. She'd made more mistakes in
one lifetime than most people could have managed in ten.
Besides, none of her relationships were serious. They could
not be where there was no honesty.

She saw Adam's eyes widen with surprise and realised he
hadn't expected the invitation. Then, just as she was starting to feel hot, embarrassed and something of an idiot, he
smiled, a proper smile that warmed his eyes and made her
feel even hotter inside.

"Sure," he said. "Thank you."

Alison was very conscious of him as he followed her into
the flat. The staircase was narrow. She could feel his presence behind her and it made her shiver in a way she barely
remembered. She needed to get a grip on herself before she
did anything stupid.

Adam was looking around. "Wow!"

"Do you like it?"

The living room was huge, with a big bay window, the
floors bare wood scattered with colourful rugs. Alison had
always loved the rich colours and elegant plainness of modern classic designs. The one concession she had made to any-

thing personal was that there was a large charcoal drawing on the wall that she had done herself. It was of Wolf Hall, long, low, rambling, a tumbledown manor covered in ivy. That was how she remembered it.

"I love it." Adam's tone was warm. "So often, modern places can be a bit soulless but this has so much character." He turned slowly, taking in the high ceilings and the big windows, the oak bookshelves and the glass wall through to the kitchen. "You've got such an eclectic mix of stuff but somehow it works."

"I love picking bits and pieces up on my travels," Alison said.

"You should have been a designer," Adam said.

Alison shook her head. "Travelling is my thing. I don't settle well in one place."

"And the drawing?" Adam was looking at the picture. "Yours?"

Alison nodded.

"I remember you were always good at sketching," Adam said. "You were studying art at Summer School the year we met, weren't you, along with tourism?"

"I was," Alison said. The memory unsettled her. She already knew that inviting Adam here had been a dangerous mistake. She realised she had not wanted the day to end. She didn't want to lose what felt like the beginnings of intimacy between them. The instinct was so strong and yet it was an illusion. She could never truly be herself with Adam, or with anyone.

Adam followed her into the galley kitchen. "Do you live alone?"

Alison glanced at him over her shoulder. "Yes. It suits me."

"But are you seeing anyone?"

"No." She snapped the kettle on.

"That's it?" Adam sounded amused.

Alison turned to face him. "What else is there to say? No, I'm not seeing anyone. Are you?"

"Why do you ask?"

"Because you asked me."

"Interest, courtesy or objective curiosity?" He was moving towards her. She felt an uncharacteristic flutter of panic.

"The latter of course." She moved away from him, towards the window. It was a small kitchen but it had never felt this small before.

"Of course." Adam smiled. It was devastating. "Well, my work doesn't leave much room for relationships. I'm always travelling, or writing or filming." He cocked his head, looking at her. "What's your excuse?"

"I don't need an excuse not to date," Alison said. "I did all that stuff when I was young."

Adam raised his brows. "There's a difference between dating and being in a relationship."

"Generally, you've got to date in order to find someone you want to be in a relationship with," Alison said.

"And you've sworn off both?"

Alison shrugged. "For now. Who knows about the future, though?"

The silence tingled. The kettle clicked off, sounding very loud. Alison opened a cupboard and took out two mugs.

"Tea or coffee?"

"Coffee, thanks."

Alison splashed hot water into the mugs and dumped a couple of spoonfuls of coffee in the cafetière.

"You make proper coffee," Adam sounded pleased. Then his voice changed. "Ali—"

"No," Alison said, anticipating him. "Let's not make the same mistake twice."

Adam laughed. "Is that all you've got to say?"

"Broadly speaking, yes," Alison said. "I'm sure that there are hundreds of women who would give a lot to be in my place right now, thousands, maybe..." She stole a glance at him. He was smiling.

"You think?"

"I'm sure," Alison said rapidly, "but—"

"You're not interested." Adam closed the space between them.

Alison shook her head. "It would be a mistake, just like it was last week."

"Because we both fell under the spell of the moment? That doesn't make it a mistake."

"We've been here before, Adam," Alison said. "Why go there again?"

"We were eighteen and nineteen," Adam said. "We were too young to work it out."

"It was ten years ago," Alison said. "I don't see any point in going over old ground. Relationships end for a reason." She swallowed hard, reaching for the cafetière, pressing down the plunger. It was probably too soon to have brewed but she needed something to do to distract her from how acute her emotions were.

"I'm surprised you'd consider it for one minute," she said, her back turned to him. "I treated you very badly."

She felt his touch on her shoulder, light but insistent. She didn't want to turn around to face him. She was afraid.

"That's true," she heard him say, after a moment. "It did hurt. And perhaps I don't understand the impulse myself. All I know is that it feels..." He paused. "Important, significant in some way. I want to be with you. I don't know why but I want to find out."

She did turn then to find him watching her with the kind of intensity in his dark eyes that made her breath catch. She remembered how she had felt when she had stumbled across Mary's portrait in Richard Demoranville's gallery and had gone in to find that Adam was there. That had felt significant too, as though it were part of a pattern, but she had interpreted it in a different way, seeing Adam's role only to help her find Arthur. She was using him. Yet that was also disingenuous. It might have started that way but now her feelings were more complicated.

"It was lovely when we were together," she said slowly, "and I was entirely swept up in it, but it wasn't real."

She poured a mug of coffee and pushed it towards Adam.

"Why wasn't it real?" Adam took his mug and wrapped his hands about it. "Just because we were young doesn't make what we felt any less valid."

"No," Alison said. She remembered this about Adam now, the way in which his straightforwardness made her feel she had to be honest in return. It had been inconvenient for someone whose life had been based on a lie.

She picked up her mug and led the way through to the living room.

"You were quite guarded in your emotions in those days," she said. "You were good at debating, but only about facts, never about feelings. You've changed."

"I was a typical boy." There was a rueful smile on Adam's lips. "I knew how I felt about you and it blew me away, but I couldn't articulate it. I went to a school where emotions are repressed, even these days, where they teach you how to hide how you feel behind good manners and charm. My family is the same."

"Well you learned that lesson extremely well," Alison said dryly.

Adam laughed. "Thank you—I think."

"What changed?" Alison sat back on the sofa. "I mean,

I saw your family with you when you did the talk in Marlborough. They were so proud of you. It was obvious and they made no attempt to hide it. There was no stiff upper lip on show."

A shadow crossed Adam's face and she felt a chill. "My father was killed," he said. He put his mug down with a soft click and sat forward. "It...made us all reconsider what was important, I suppose. It could have gone either way—we could have withdrawn into the familiarity of silence or we could reach out to each other and in the end that was what we did."

*The familiarity of silence...* Alison knew that well.

"I'm so sorry," she said. She found she wanted to touch him, to offer comfort but she did not reach out. "You said he was killed," she said hesitantly. "What happened?"

"It was a hit and run," Adam said. He didn't look at her. He was studying the coffee in his mug. "Just before Christmas. A drunk driver on his way back from the pub one night."

"When?" Alison asked.

Adam didn't misunderstand her. He looked up and held her gaze. "The year we split up. I was down from my first term at Cambridge."

"Oh, God, Adam..." Alison felt a flare of misery.

"Yeah." Adam gave her a lopsided smile. "It was a tough time but—" He shrugged. "We came through, you know."

Alison did know. She knew how it felt to lose everything that was important and yet to have to keep moving forward. There was a cold, hard weight of unhappiness that she had kept locked inside ever since she had lost Arthur. It had eased a little when she had had Diana to talk to but now, Diana, the only person who knew her secret, was dying. At the same time, she was digging into the past, exposing those scars she had done so much to hide. It was no wonder she felt vulnerable. And that was why this was so dangerous, she and Adam, talking about their brief, shared history. Yet ignoring it was no longer an option.

"Are you angry with me?" she said directly. "Did you blame me for hurting you too? Is that the real reason you're here? For some sort of closure?"

"Just a minute." Adam looked startled. He held up a hand. "That's a lot of questions." He sat back with a sigh. "I was angry at the time," he said at last. "Hell, I was furious with you, Ali, for being the personification of everything I had ever wanted and then taking it away from me and refusing to talk about it." His hand clenched the handle of the mug. "I didn't know what to do so I threw myself into my studies and then my father was killed…" He hesitated. "I suppose that eclipsed everything else for a time and when I came out the other side I'd changed, and I moved on and didn't think about you any more."

Alison tried not to flinch. It was a straight answer and she should have been glad to hear it. Perhaps it was her pride or her vanity that was hurt. No one liked to be forgotten.

"So this is not about unfinished business," she said.

Adam put his mug down carefully on the table. "No. Unfinished business implies I want it to be over and I find that I don't." He ran a hand through his hair. His voice was slightly rough. "All you had to do was walk into Richard's shop and I felt as though I was nineteen again. I wanted you as much as I had before."

It stole Alison's breath. "That's quite a statement."

"Do you think I don't know that?" Adam said. "It's not a choice I would have made." Now he did sound angry. "I'm being honest here," he said, "because I don't see any other option. I'm not playing games."

"No," Alison said.

"Your turn," Adam said.

Alison swallowed hard. "I don't know," she admitted. "There's something… I don't want to feel like this, but I do."

It was honesty, up to a point, but it was nowhere near to the whole truth. The truth was that there was no point in her embarking on any serious relationship because she felt like a traveller. She was doing no more than passing through. She always had been.

"Walking away would be the best option for both of us," Alison said. "I'm going to tell you some stuff I should have told you years ago," she added. "It's not an excuse for how I behaved towards you but it does explain…" She paused, picking her way through the truth. "It explains why I'm so messed up," she finished.

Adam smiled. "We've all got baggage."

"You have no idea," Alison said dryly. She curled her legs up beneath her on the sofa. "I didn't tell you much about my family or my history when we first met," she said. "By which I mean my background, not this." She waved a hand vaguely towards her genealogy files. "I deliberately kept it from you," she said, "because it wasn't pretty and I thought… if you knew…" She stopped, frowning. This hurt far more than she had anticipated.

"My parents died when I was young," she said. "I was sent to live with some distant relations."

"I thought you grew up in care." Adam was watching her closely now and she knew she had to be careful. She wanted to be open with him whilst holding back that one, impossible truth: that she had come forward in time.

"That was later," she said. She remembered that she had talked to him a little about that, ten years before. "To start with I went to live with some cousins. I was about eight or so. It was a big house and a rambling family. We didn't go to school. It was all a bit mad and informal."

"Were you happy there?" Adam expression was still now, intent.

Alison shrugged. It was impossible to sum up what it had been like growing up at Wolf Hall. "It was fine," she said. "There were quite a lot of us. People came and went. We all got on all right. It wasn't..." She hesitated. "It wasn't a normal family in the way that you would imagine one. We weren't close. It was more like we shared a roof and food and some experiences, but it was all very casual."

"I guess there are plenty of households like that," Adam said. "Working parents, kids essentially taking care of themselves, no time to talk or take meals together."

"Yes," Alison said. "I'm sure there are." She was silent for a moment. "I think what happened next probably isn't unusual either." She looked up and met his eyes.

"My eldest cousin came home. He was very glamorous. I...kind of idolised him."

"What happened?" Adam's voice was very quiet.

"I got pregnant," Alison said. "I was fifteen." She took a deep breath. "We were together for a while but I realised..." She stopped, trying to find the right words. "Well, it was an unequal relationship, you know? He was older and he had money and could do what he wanted, whereas I—" She stopped again, biting her lip. "I didn't have much say in the relationship," she said rapidly. "He dominated me, told me what to do."

She heard Adam swear under his breath. "Christ, Ali."

"It's okay," Alison said. "I'm okay with it now. I talked to someone about it. A counsellor. That helped."

Adam sounded grim. "He abused you."

"He abused the situation," Alison said. She remembered

how Diana had helped her to see the truth of what had happened with Edward. "He took advantage, but I wasn't unwilling," she said. "I was just a girl, in love with being in love. I just didn't realise quite how much of an imbalance of power there was between us until...until he took the baby away."

Adam swore again, very succinct and descriptive. "Bastard," he said, between his teeth.

Alison looked at him. She thought she would see pity alongside the anger in his eyes, but there was nothing there she could understand, no emotion at all, only darkness.

"He was adopted." She had to finish this, quickly. Adam had never seen her cry and she had no intention of starting now. The instinct to bury her grief had started young, when her parents had died, and it was one thing that had not changed when she had entered a different time. "I never saw him again," she said. "In the end, I ran away and that was how I ended up in care."

"When we split up you said, 'It's not you, it's me,'" Adam quoted softly.

"You remember that?" Alison was startled.

"I remember everything you said to me," Adam said.

"And you can see I was right."

Adam gave a shrug. "I'm not saying you were right but I can see why you were so mixed up."

"Messed up," Alison corrected. "I was completely messed up when we met."

She saw the glimmer of amusement in his eyes. "If you like," he said. The amusement faded. "You never tried to find him? Your baby?"

"I looked," Alison said carefully. "But in the end that's his prerogative, isn't it, rather than mine."

It was the first lie she had told and it was odd, as though Adam could sense it somehow in her tone. He frowned and she felt a flash of panic. She had been so careful to tell him about Arthur in a way that would not have any resonance with her search for Mary Seymour. She did not want Adam drawing any parallels. Yet now she wondered if she had underestimated him, or the ties that bound them. Adam did seem to have an uncanny knack of tuning into the things she did not say as much as the ones she did.

"Thank you for telling me," he said, after a moment. "I don't suppose it was easy for you." He pinched the bridge of his nose, still frowning. "It's a hell of a lot to take in."

"Yeah," Alison said. *If only he knew... "Oh, and by the way, all this happened in 1566. My cousin, my abuser, was Edward Seymour, the Earl of Hertford."*

"I'm sorry." Adam ran a hand distractedly through his hair. "So sorry for what you had to go through. God, that's inadequate, isn't it, under the circumstances? I don't know what to say..."

"Forget it," Alison said. Suddenly she was desperate for him to go. She felt horribly vulnerable. Diana was the only person she had ever spoken to about her past and that had been quite different; difficult, loaded with emotion and grief, but somehow she had felt less exposed than she did now with Adam. Her feelings felt naked.

"Thank you," she said, rising from the sofa. "For telling me all about the box and its contents today when I couldn't really help you much in return."

Adam had got up too. She knew he had understood that this was his dismissal.

"You're welcome," he said. He gave her that glimmer of a smile that always set her pulse awry. She could not understand why she simultaneously wanted him to go and yet longed for him to stay. She didn't want to be alone to face this blizzard of memories she had stirred up, but at the same time it was the only way she knew to protect herself.

"You'd better go," she said, when Adam made no move towards the door.

She saw him shake his head slightly. "Take care of yourself," he said. He bent to kiss her cheek. "I'll be in touch." There was puzzlement and anger and pity and a welter of other emotions in his eyes. Alison looked away quickly, fearing her own emotions would be too easy to read.

She closed the front door of the flat behind him and resisted the urge to bang her head against the panels. Tears prickled her throat. She had made Adam leave, had driven him away with the truth just as she had intended to do. The secret of her past was safe at the cost it always exacted, that of isolation.

She sat down on the second step and put her head in her hands. Dry sobs shook her whole body. She stuffed a fist in her mouth to stop the sound.

The shrill ringing of the bell above her head made her jump violently. Staring through the security viewer she saw that it was Adam. Her heart started to thud in long, slow strokes.

"Ali, I know you're there. Open the door."

She took a deep breath. Damn it. She didn't want him to know how upset she felt so she had no choice other than to be cheerful. Her hands shook as she turned the lock.

"Did you forget something—" she started to say, brightly, as she swung the door open, but the words died at the expression in his eyes.

"Yes," Adam said. He took her in his arms and kissed her. It was hungry, desperate, driven by something Alison did not want to question, but still she did. She drew away from him, breathing hard.

"I don't want your pity."

Adam swore. "This isn't pity."

He was kissing her again and this time she allowed herself to become lost in it, the old and the new, familiar sensations, the thrill of rediscovery, the sweet relief of no longer being so alone. She knew she should not give in to the need for solace and yet it was irresistible. She had no idea how they moved from the bottom of the staircase to her bedroom, only that they were there and she was pulling off his clothes far more clumsily and with less finesse than she had when they were teenagers. She would have laughed, but it felt too urgent for that as her hands slid over Adam's bare shoulders and she arched up to kiss him more deeply, more desperately still. Past and present collided. She felt adrift. So she let herself be taken by the tide of it, and it took her apart and left her undone.

# NINETEEN

*Mary, 1566*

I SAT IN THE RUINS OF AN OLD MANOR HOUSE, watching my captor prepare a rabbit for the pot. After Will had cravenly run away and left me, this man had picked me up with somewhat insulting ease, tossed me over the horse's neck, and led us away. I had kicked and screamed so he had tied my wrists and pointed out that all I was hurting was the horse. After that I stopped.

I had no notion what he wanted with me. He had not said. I was frightened. Only a fool would not be.

"You did not answer my question," he said now. "What is your name?"

He did not wait for me to answer, but continued to gut the rabbit, head bent as he worked. There was a ruthless efficiency in his movements. Where I shuddered with sentimental disgust over the fur and the smell and the pile of entrails, he seemed unaffected. I wondered if it was the product of hunger or native heartlessness.

Once again, I did not answer his question. Instead, I drew my knees closer to my chin, hunching forward. He did not know me but I had recognised him at once. There was enough of a look of Will about him to make identification certain. Fair where Will was dark, thoughtful where Will was fiery, he nevertheless had the dark Fenner eyes, the high cheekbones and the long aristocratic nose. There was a stillness about him I had never seen in a man before, a kind of distilled concentration that intrigued me for it seemed a quality far beyond his years. He rushed into neither action nor words.

"I know who you are," I said. "You are Thomas Fenner, Will's brother."

His head came up. "Half-brother," he said. Then: "Does he speak of me?"

"Never," I said.

I saw him smile. After a moment, his hands resumed their work. I watched him; his fingers were elegant, but long and strong, an artist's hands, perhaps, rather than a butcher's.

"Are you another of Will's women?" he asked.

"In addition to whom?" I said, haughty now.

He looked at me. The contrast of those dark Fenner eyes with the fair hair was enough to steal the breath. I do not know why it affected me so but it felt as though my stomach had dropped a long way, almost down to my boots.

"The Lady Anne Hungerford for one," he said. "She bore his child. She is accounted very beautiful."

"She is old," I said. It was a habit now to feel that flash of jealousy, but suddenly I wondered if I truly meant it. Anne Hungerford was indeed a beautiful woman and Will evidently still lusted for her, but what did I want from him anyway? Tonight the scales had fallen from my eyes.

"Lady Hungerford is old and you are young." His gaze appraised me. "Too young. But then—" his mouth twisted

"—no woman is too young or too old for Will. He does not discriminate."

"Thank you," I said politely.

He laughed. "What's your name?" he asked, for the third time.

"Mary," I said.

He waited but I did not add anything further and in the firelight I saw his eyes glint with amusement. He put the rabbit, skinned, gutted, jointed, neatly to one side and got to his feet. Without another glance in my direction he strolled out of the circle of firelight, down towards the stream I could hear running at the end of the garden. I heard the splash of water and saw the glint of steel as he washed the knife.

It was humiliating to be left so, as though I was of little importance, even more so because I was. Thomas knew I could not run. I was still firmly tied.

Eventually, he came wandering back up the slope. He had washed his hands; water dripped from his bare forearms onto the carpet of old beech leaves beneath his feet. He was rolling down the sleeves of his shirt and whistling tunelessly under his breath.

"A fox stole the rabbit while you were gone," I said. "I am sure it was grateful to you for the care you took in preparing its meal. There was nothing I could do." I raised my bound wrists expressively.

His gaze flew to my face and then to the place where he had left the rabbit. He said something very short and very to the point. I said nothing.

After a moment he came across to me and squatted down beside me. The knife was still in his hand. Inside I could feel the flinch but I tried not to show it.

"Would you like some of the stew I have already made?" he asked.

The stew smelled delicious. I had no notion what time it was but I was starving, the hunger gnawing at me, and all my principles about refusing to break bread with my captor were long banished.

"That depends," I said.

He cocked an eyebrow. His brows were dark like his eyes. At such close quarters I could see the flecks of gold in them, illuminated in the firelight. The light and shadow flickered across his face in bars of red and black, highlighting those high cheekbones and the hollows beneath.

"On what?" he said.

"On whether you intend to kill me directly afterwards," I said. "If so then do not waste your food on me."

A smile tugged the corner of his mouth. "But at least you would not die hungry." He raised the knife. This time I did flinch. I could not help myself.

He sliced cleanly through the ties at my wrists. The rope fell away. Even in the dim light I could see the skin chafed red. So could he. For a moment he did not move. I watched the shadow of his eyelashes against his cheek, each lash spiky as a sharp-edged leaf. Then without a word he stood and moved away and I released the breath I had not realised I had been holding.

"There is a plate," he said briefly, over his shoulder. "We are not short of our comforts here. Come closer to the fire."

I had originally thought to run away if he untied me, but given time to cool my heels, I had realised what folly that was. I had no idea of where we were—somewhere below the northern Downs, I supposed. Will and I had been riding towards Kingston Parva on the Sugar Track and the Robbers' Track, so we must be near Ashdown Park. That was a long way from home, especially since Will had taken both horses.

*Take the horse. Leave the girl. Only one is valuable.*

I could easily imagine his thoughts. I knew he had deliberately pushed me from the saddle in order to take the horse and also to slow Thomas down.

"What is in the stew?" I asked. "More rabbit?"

"Chicken," Thomas said.

My stomach rumbled. "Stolen?" I asked.

"Of course," Thomas said. "You have fallen out with one thief and in with another, Mary whatever-your-name-is."

"Seymour," I said. "And I am not Will's mistress. I am his cousin."

He had been rummaging in his knapsack, pulling out a plate and spoon, but now he paused with them forgotten in one hand.

"Cousin to me too, then," he said, in an odd tone, and I had the sense that the news displeased him.

"Not really," I said. "Very distantly, if at all. I do not even know the precise relationship to the Fenners. It may be cousinship three or four times removed, I think, but you know how it is with kinfolk. When they wished to find me a new home they insisted there was a connection and so your brother was obliged to take me in."

"A Seymour of Wolf Hall," Thomas said. He was staring at me, his gaze moving thoughtfully over my face as though considering each feature. I could feel my skin grow hot, though that might have been simply because the fire was fierce so close. "My father's kin," he said slowly. Then: "Why were they looking for a new home for you?"

"It's a long story," I said.

"Are you in a hurry?" He had recollected the plate now and was ladling some stew onto it. The smell of the meat mingled with herbs—wild garlic and chives—and it was delicious. My mouth watered.

"I don't know," I said. "Am I?"

He passed the plate and the spoon to me. "We have all night," he said.

*"We have all night…"* I remembered Will and his woman, the door closing, the laughter and the whispered words. My face flamed.

"What are you going to do with me?" I asked.

I had not meant to blurt it out. It felt too much like begging, even more so when he subjected me to one of those long stares of his and did not answer immediately.

"Would anyone pay to get you back?" he asked. He spoke through a mouthful of stew. He was eating it with the ladle since I had the plate and spoon. I smothered a smile. At the back of my mind I could hear Liz Aiglonby scolding:

"Manners, Lady Mary!"

"No," I said truthfully. I took a spoonful of stew myself. It tasted so good I wanted to gulp it down in one go. There were turnips and mushrooms too and other things I did not recognise, but as they tasted so fine I did not question them.

"And yet you are a Seymour of Wolf Hall," Thomas said, "and the Seymours ride high."

"Not as high as they have done before," I said. "Their time is gone and I am an orphan with no place in the world. When my mother's kin did not want me I was sent to the Seymours and when they needed to be rid of me I came to Middlecote."

He nodded. His gaze was inward looking now and I wondered whether he was thinking of the Fenners and their fractured family. To be unwanted, unloved, rootless was so common a matter. Why else would Thomas make his home here in the ruins of a tumbledown manor and steal chickens and vow vengeance on his half-brother? I wondered about him then; I knew his mother was dead, for Will had harassed her endlessly for the restitution of his lands and rents. Thomas had nothing. How did he live? What did he do?

His voice recalled me to the circle of firelight and the lure of more chicken stew.

"Why did the Seymours need to be rid of you?"

"You ask a deal of questions," I said crossly. My anger was directed more towards myself than to him. I had already said too much. I did not know him; I could not trust him and I did not understand why I should want to confide in him. I only knew that here, now, for the first time in my life, I wanted to share everything about myself with a complete stranger. My own folly made me angry.

Thomas seemed unaffected by my antagonism. "How am I to know if I can profit from you if you tell me nothing of yourself?" he said. He sounded damnably reasonable, but I was sure he was teasing me.

"I have told you there is no profit to be made," I said. "No one will pay a ransom."

"Then do you have any skills?" He cocked his head on one side. "Can you pluck a chicken or make medicines or grease a saddle?"

"I was never taught to do so, but how hard can it be?" I said. "I was brought up a lady."

"That is not a great deal of use," Thomas said.

"I know." I thought of Alison. She had been brought up a lady too but she had skills and cunning, sufficient to survive. I was an innocent abroad.

"I do have one talent," I said. "I see visions. That was why they sent me away from Wolf Hall. I saw things that they did not like." I scraped the last of my stew off the plate and licked the spoon. "So perhaps you could set me up in a booth at the fair," I said. "The Middlecote Witch. I might make you a few crowns before they burn me."

He laughed at that. His teeth were very white and straight and a crease ran down his cheek when he smiled.

"Were the visions true?" he asked.

"Yes," I said. "So you should beware."

I heard it then, the whisper through my mind, as though in speaking of visions I had opened the door a crack.

*"Cat... Catherine."*

I ignored it ruthlessly, closing my mind. I did not want to talk to Darrell now.

"Have you had visions at Middlecote?" Thomas was saying, cutting across my thoughts.

I thought of the fighting I had witnessed and the flashes of light and the machines flying in the air. He would think me mad if I told him. I shook my head.

"No."

He was looking at me intently and it was as though he knew I lied but he did not pursue it. Instead, he gestured towards the pot. "Would you like some more before I eat it all?"

I did not even pretend to think about it. I got up and walked over to the fire. I sat down beside him, holding the plate steady, and he tipped half the remaining stew out onto my plate.

"Thank you," I said, and he smiled.

"You are a proper lady, aren't you, Mistress Seymour?"

"What about you?" I asked. "Are you a gentleman, Thomas Fenner?"

He shook his head, a secret smile tilting his lips. "I don't aspire so high."

"What do you aspire to be?" I asked. "The owner of Middlecote? Is that why you seek to displace your brother?"

He looked up sharply and I felt a shock in my chest at the intensity in his eyes. "I love Middlecote," he said. "I always did."

"Will loves Middlecote too," I said, though to tell the

truth Will had never spoken of the place with even half Thomas's passion.

The scorn in his eyes seared me. "Will cares for nothing but himself and the income his estates can bring him," he said. "He has mortgaged every piece of land he owns, stolen others, lied and tricked his way into a fortune and lost it through his own profligacy."

"I don't think that's true," I said, smarting under his contempt. "Perhaps you do not know him well enough to make that judgement."

"And perhaps your judgement is flawed," he said. He spoke evenly now but I felt cold. I knew I had lost his good opinion. I did not know why it mattered that I had.

"A woman—a girl—" he corrected himself "—who rides about the country at night with a man who is plotting robbery, who thinks it is mere sport…is hardly a good judge of character. And a man who encourages her to do so, who puts her in the way of danger rather than protecting her—" his voice had hardened "—he is worse still."

I jumped to my feet, upsetting the plate with the cooling remains of the stew, which was a terrible waste.

"What do you know of it?" I demanded. "How could you possibly know what I think, how I feel?"

My voice trembled. I remembered how Will and I had laughed together as we had ridden out from Middlecote and how it had seemed the finest adventure of my life. I had been so proud to ride with him, so excited, whereas now I felt chastened, guilty and ashamed.

"I know," Thomas said, and I stared at him, struck dumb, because it did indeed feel as though he knew me through and through.

"Have you engaged in such escapades with Will before?" He sounded implacable, like an inquisitor.

"No," I said. I knew that in contrast to him, I sounded like the sulky child I was as I stood there scuffing my boot in the earth and avoiding his eyes. "We went to the fair once," I admitted, "and it is true he got into a fight—"

"I heard about that." Thomas was watching me. "So you were the woman he was with that night."

"I was," I said. Before I might have felt a thrill of pride. Now I felt miserable.

"It was just the once," I said. I tried to forget the incident in the stables when I had learned that Will had robbed and beaten a man, and all the nights when I had lain awake listening, wondering what other villainy he was involved with.

"I would not tell you anything anyway," I added. "You will not persuade me to incriminate your brother, Thomas Fenner."

"Your loyalty to him is misplaced." Thomas sighed sharply. "Not that telling you so will make any difference to your feelings. Do you love him?"

"I…" I hesitated. There had been a time not so long ago when I would have said yes without question and I would have believed that I loved Will Fenner with a great passion. Now though I felt battered and sore at his abandonment of me. It had been the final blow that had forced me to confront my naivety. So no, I did not love Will Fenner any more. Not that I was going to share that with Thomas.

"At the risk of sounding repetitious," I said, "I would not tell you if I did."

He stood up then, and came towards me, catching hold of my hand to draw me closer.

"Shall I test your loyalty?" he mused. "Test whether you love my brother?"

For all that naïveté, I understood exactly what he meant.

"Half-brother," I said. "And you would not be testing my loyalty to Will but indulging your own whims."

He smiled. "How wise you are for one so young, mistress. It seems your judgement may be better than I thought."

He dropped my hand and turned away. Conversely, I now felt very disappointed that he was not going to kiss me. I hoped it was not too obvious.

"I should like to go home now, if you please," I said.

"Home to Middlecote?" He cocked a brow. "Or home to Will?"

Truth was I was so angry with Will for leaving me that I did not wish to be anywhere near him but I did not have much choice.

"Back to Middlecote," I said. "Nowhere is home to me."

"Do you mind that?" He was standing watching me and although he was not within touching distance it felt as though he were very close indeed.

"No one has asked me that before," I said slowly.

"I'm asking now."

"Yes," I said. I had never been so honest before, with my-self or with anyone else. "I am accustomed to being rootless," I said, "but that does not mean I like it. What about you?"

"This is my home," he said. He gestured towards the fallen walls and broken beams of the house behind us. "One day, when I may, I will rebuild Kingston Parva. My mother's kin, the De Morvens, lived here. I may never regain Middlecote but this I can do."

"Your mother was descended from the De Morvens?" I was impressed. "I heard they were noble."

"Sir Reginald De Morven was the greatest knight of his time," Thomas said simply.

"Until he went mad," I said. Eleanor had told me about the De Morven knights once when we had taken the carriage past Kingston Parva to visit Lady Fenner's relatives in Ashbury.

"He was not mad," Thomas said. He fixed me with his cool, dark gaze. "Sir Reginald saw visions of the future. He was like you, Mary Seymour, only different. He passed through time."

A shiver brushed over my skin. How foolish that I, with my visions and my secret friend, would feel superstitious to hear such words. Yet I had never met anyone else with gifts mysterious like mine. I had never known Darrell as a real person. For all I knew, he could be no more than a figment of my imagination, which was almost how he felt now that I had cut him out of my life and not spoken to him for so long.

*"Cat. Catherine…"* Again it came, that echo. Again I ignored it and concentrated on Thomas.

"Truly?" I looked at him suspiciously. "Or do you tease me?"

"On my honour," he said, "such as it is. Reginald De Morven visited the future and it was that that drove him insane."

It did not sound to me that the future had a great deal to offer if that was the case. "How do you know?" I demanded. "How do you know that was what happened to him?"

I saw a shadow cloud his eyes then, secretive and dark. "I know," he said, just as he had done earlier, and somehow I believed him now as I had then.

"Come on," he added impatiently, as though I was keeping him waiting. "If we are to return you to Middlecote, we must be gone." And he strode away across the paddock to fetch the long-suffering horse before I could reply.

Dawn was breaking as we crossed the river by Middlecote. I half expected to see the house awake, the lights burning and men out searching for me, but it was silent and shuttered.

Thomas jumped down from the saddle and held out a hand to help me down. This time he did not let me go.

For a moment we did not speak. He was very close to me, so close I could smell the leather and the cold night air on him. Then he leaned down and touched my cheek lightly with his gloved fingers.

"Goodbye, then, Mary Seymour," he said. He kissed me, very gently, but I felt it deep in my bones. When I opened my eyes, I saw he was smiling at me.

"I wish you good luck, Thomas Fenner," I said. "I think you will need it."

He laughed. "A man makes his own luck," he said. The smile died from his eyes. "We'll meet again. Soon."

I watched him ride away and after he had gone I stood there until the cool night breeze reminded me that it was still early and I was cold.

The door of Middlecote stood open. Will pounced on me as soon as I was inside, pulling me into the parlour, shutting the door so that we were trapped in the dark. I was taken by surprise, my head still full of Thomas, my body still singing from his touch. I could just see Will's face in the dying light of the fire. He had been drinking. The room was so full of heat and alcohol fumes that my head spun.

"What did you tell him?" His hands gripped my shoulders like claws. His face was so close to mine I could smell the brandy on his breath. He sounded angry, his handsome face contorted by drunkenness and fear.

"Who?" I shook him off. I was furious with him. For the first time I almost despised him. He had abandoned me and returned here to the comfort of his wine bottle.

"Don't toy with me, Mary." There was a quality of violence, barely suppressed, about him that sent ripples of fear over my skin. I knew the brutality Will was capable of inflicting. I edged around until my back was to the door.

"You were with Thomas tonight." He slopped more wine into his glass and a good deal of it over the desk. An empty flagon already lay by the grate.

"I was not *with* anyone," I flashed back at him. It would have been politic to hold my tongue but I had had enough. "You left me. Your half-brother brought me back. I cannot be held responsible for that."

"What did you tell him?" he repeated. His voice had risen slightly. Violence rippled along the edge of it. "God damn it, what did you say about me?"

"Nothing," I said. "I don't know what you mean. What should I tell him?"

He came towards me and I backed up against the door, feeling for the latch, my heart missing a beat as my anxious fingers searched in vain.

"He wants to ruin me." Will was crowding me now, pressing me against the wooden frame, his body hard against mine. I had the impression though that I was of little importance; his anger and aggression were focused elsewhere, beyond me and that hot little room where the air buzzed with hatred.

"You can do that yourself without Thomas lifting a finger," I said. "You are halfway there already."

His gaze focused on me. Astonishingly, he laughed. "Wise little Mary," he said. "All I need is for Thomas to deal the final blow." Suddenly the tension left him. His body slumped against me, his head lolling on my shoulder.

"Ah, Mary," he said. "You are so sweet and so honest. I should wed you. I really should, even though you have no money."

"You're drunk," I said, pushing him gently away, half exasperated, half afraid he would fall. "I'll not hold you to it."

"Hold me to it. Please." His grip was tight, his eyes urgent, the change in him as fickle and sudden as the veering wind. "I need you to save me."

I stifled an insane desire to laugh. How recently Will professing his need for me would have had me swooning. Yet it seemed like years ago now, and I a green girl who had known no better. I felt cold and disillusioned and so very stupid.

"Will," I said, "go to bed."

He slumped into the fireside chair. "Aye," he mumbled, the spittle dribbling from the side of his mouth. "Sleep."

He was already snoring when I slipped out of the door.

I did not expect to be able to sleep myself, but, as the light started to strengthen, I fell into a doze, and dreamed of Thomas Fenner. In my dream he was not as I had seen him that night, but was dressed as those soldiers had been long ago when I had seen them in Savernake Forest, in a buff-coloured coat with a red sash. He was part of a small band of mounted troops fighting a bitter skirmish before my very eyes. I watched the engagement through my dream: Thomas proved a skilful swordsman, elegant and economical in his movements, and it would have been a pleasure to watch him had the fight not been so brutal and bloody. In the end he and his men won out, and, as they rode away, he turned back towards me. In the background I could see Middlecote Hall and before it Thomas, sword in his hand and blood on the sword.

"Men will always fight," he said, speaking directly to me through the dream. "Remember that, Mary. Will and I are kin but we will always try to take from the other the one thing that counts the most."

# TWENTY

ALISON WOKE TO FIND THAT ADAM HAD GONE. The room was light and the sheets were chilled. She supposed it saved her the trouble of wondering what would happen next. She had never had a one-night stand before and it felt strange to realise that she had no idea of how to handle the morning after. Then she heard the sound of a key in the lock and Adam's tread on the stairs.

"I borrowed your keys," he said. "I hope that's okay." He had a bag of croissants in one hand and a tray with two coffees on it in the other. He put them down on the chest of drawers and came over to kiss her. His face was cold. He smelled deliciously of fresh air but the kiss was warm and confident, and Alison felt her stomach drop. It felt secure and weirdly good. It was almost as though they had been together for ten years rather than apart. She stifled a giggle.

"What's funny?" There was wariness in Adam's eyes even if he was smiling. He was not as sure of her as he had seemed. That made her feel a bit better. Everything had seemed to be moving far too quickly.

"Nothing," Alison said. She smiled too, pushing the hair away from her face. "That was nice of you. The coffee smells great."

Adam seemed to have lost interest in the coffee. He kissed her again, more slowly this time, very sweet and hot. His hand came up to tangle in her hair.

"You're so beautiful, Ali," he said, against her mouth. "You do know that, don't you?"

Alison broke away from him. "It was the only thing about me that was valued when I was growing up," she said.

"Sorry," Adam said slowly. He sat down next to her on the bed. "I'm sorry if it upsets you. But it is a fact."

The chill within Alison eased slightly. "No, I'm sorry," she said. She touched his cheek, the stubble rough against her fingers. "Thank you," she whispered. Inside, she was feeling warm and it was lovely, a lambent sweetness that filled her head and her heart. She could not let herself think about it too much because she knew if she did she would want to pull back from the brink of intimacy. She shut the thought out. There would be plenty of time to think later.

Adam was running the strands of her hair through his fingers. "I think that was what scuppered me at Middlecote," he said ruefully. "I was so annoyed that I had found some evidence to support your theory about Mary Seymour living there that I felt I had to go down and revisit the place. And there you were, having tramped across the fields in your city clothes, and you still looked gorgeous and then you took off your hat and shook out your hair and I wanted to take you straight inside and—"

Alison pressed her fingers to his lips, then turned his face to hers and kissed him. "Show me," she whispered, lying back, pulling him down with her into the tangle of bedclothes.

The coffee went cold so they brewed some fresh in the cafetière.

"You're looking very well," Diana said.

It was a chill day. The water rushed down the stream at the end of Diana's garden. The bare twigs and branches looked even more desolate than they had done two weeks before. So did Diana; she seemed to have diminished since Alison had last seen her, skin translucent and paper-thin, her whole body seemingly brittle.

"I'm so sorry to trouble you," Alison said. She felt very awkward. Diana was the only person who knew the truth, the only person she could talk to, but it felt like imposing on her when she was so sick.

Diana smiled and beckoned her inside. "It's no trouble. So many people keep away when someone is dying. It's nice to have a visitor."

The interior of the cottage was very bright and cheerful. Hector the cat was curled up on a cushion in one of the armchairs. He raised his head, gave Alison a long, thoughtful stare from his glassy green eyes, then went back to sleep.

"Tea?" Diana asked.

"I'll make it," Alison said hastily.

"There's biscuits in the silver tin," Diana called after her. "Christmas ones."

"You said in your telephone call that there was something urgent you needed to discuss with me," Diana said, when they were settled with the tea and ginger biscuits shaped like fir trees. "What can I do to help?"

"I need you to tell me I'm sane," Alison said.

Diana raised her brows. "Are you starting to doubt it?"

"I don't know," Alison said in a rush. "I don't know anything any more."

It was true, she thought. She felt helpless, buffeted by conflicting emotions and desires. For so long finding Arthur had been her guiding light. Now though there was so much more: Adam, her life in London, the promise of the future. She felt guilty and horribly conflicted.

Diana waited, brows raised, blue gaze steady and clear.

"A few weeks ago I stumbled across a painting of Mary Seymour," Alison said. "There were some artefacts associated with it. I didn't tell you last time I saw you, because…" She stopped again. Diana waited again. She was a killer with silences as well as with questions.

"Because it involved Adam," Alison said, in a rush, "and I didn't want to open up all that again."

"I see," Diana said.

Alison thought Diana probably did see far too much. She had always challenged her to tell Adam the truth about herself and Alison had always resisted, seeing it as impossible.

"Adam thought it was a portrait of Anne Boleyn," she said, trying to focus on the facts and blot out the conflicting emotions.

"I read about it in the paper." Diana gestured towards a pile of newspapers and magazines stacked on the table beside her. "Everyone seems very excited at the discovery."

"So was Adam until I told him he'd got it wrong," Alison said gloomily. "Perhaps I should have kept quiet, except that I needed to find out where he had discovered it and what else he knew."

"In order to see whether Mary had left you any clues to Arthur's whereabouts," Diana said. "I remember you telling me about the agreement the two of you had made." She sat forward. "But this is wonderful! Have you found anything useful?"

Alison studied the swirling pattern of colours on the rug, scuffing her boot over the thick pile, wondering why it did not feel as wonderful to her as it should.

"I think so," she said. "There are some clues in Mary's portrait and also in a wooden box." She looked up. "I know it all sounds quite ridiculous."

"Is this why you are questioning your sanity?" Diana asked. She stirred her second cup of tea very precisely.

"Yes," Alison said, looking up and meeting Diana's perceptive blue gaze. "I can't quite believe it, and I'm scared I'm imagining the whole thing because I want it so much. You know—that I'm so obsessed that I'm trying to force the facts to fit what I want them to be."

"And what are the facts?" Diana enquired. She sipped her tea, her eyes, still very bright, watching Alison over the rim of her cup. "What have you found out?"

"First there's a box that belonged to me when I was a child," Alison said. She sat back in her chair, relaxing a little as she told Diana the story of the wooden box with her initials inlaid in the lid.

"I left it behind when I ran away in Marlborough that day," she said. "There wasn't much in it—a few pins, a ribbon... Mary must have taken it with her to Middlecote Hall and when she discovered news of Arthur she left clues in the box for me to find."

"Why would Mary make it so complicated?" Diana asked. "Why not just leave you a letter?"

"I've thought about that a lot," Alison admitted. "Mary didn't know where I was or how to contact me." She swallowed painfully. "And I couldn't get back to find her. Perhaps she thought a letter could get lost more easily, or be destroyed, or that it wasn't very durable."

"Or perhaps she wanted it to be a secret," Diana said thoughtfully, "something that only you would understand. After all, you must have impressed upon her that yours was a confidential arrangement. No one was to know."

"Both of us were keeping secrets," Alison agreed.

Diana stretched out a thin hand and stroked Hector's head very gently. The cat started to purr extremely loudly. "So what were the clues that you think Mary left in the box?" she asked.

Alison opened her bag and took out the piece of paper Adam had given her with the list of items. She had added to it her notes on the images in Mary's portrait.

"First of all, the box was featured in Mary's portrait," she said, "which could have been a coincidence or a deliberate inclusion. Then there were four little symbols in each corner of the picture." She checked the paper. "One was a wyvern, which I think is the symbol of Middlecote. There are carved wyverns on the gates. Then there was an angel. Adam says they are usually messengers."

Diana nodded. "That seems plausible."

"The other two are more open to interpretation," Alison admitted. "One is a lion. It's a symbol of fortitude and endurance—of waiting, if you like. And the fourth is a magic wand decorated with irises."

"The symbol of the goddess Circe raising the dead," Diana said, nodding. "That's clever. Mary was trying to tell you to keep faith and that the answer to your quest was at Middlecote."

Alison's heart leaped. "That's what I hoped," she said. Her hands shook a little as she picked the paper up again. "This was the stuff that was in the box," she said. "First, there was a coin dated 1560. That's the year of Arthur's birth. And a twig of rosemary—for remembrance, I thought. Mary wanted me to know she had not forgotten me." She stopped, a lump in her throat. It felt as though she could cry at almost anything these days. She found it very irritating.

"I haven't worked out the other clues yet," she said. "There was a button engraved with a bear. I thought it might be a play on the name Artorious—King Arthur?"

"Or perhaps it's from a family crest?" Diana suggested. "This is like a cryptic crossword. Find the hidden meaning."

"Exactly," Alison said. She glanced at the list again. "There was also a plate from a falcon—" she looked up "—like a ring on its leg, according to Adam. I've no idea about that. Then there is a knight from a chess set carved from holly, and a woollen thread in green tied to a piece of catgut."

She stopped, waiting, and realising as she did so that she had expected Diana to come up with the solutions. Diana always helped her; it was what she did. In this case she had come to Diana expecting answers, which had been rather naive of her. That was not Diana's job.

"Have you told Adam that you think it's a riddle?" Diana asked.

"Yes," Alison said. "I've told him I'm on a bit of a quest as part of my family history research."

"So you've lied to him." Diana's tone was unrevealing.

"Well, yes…" Alison floundered a little. "I mean, I had to tell him something. But obviously that couldn't be the truth."

She stopped. This felt like every other conversation she had had with Diana about Adam over the years. "Nothing's changed," she said, spreading her hands wide in a gesture of appeal. "I still can't tell him who I am, can I? He'd never believe it."

"I believe it," Diana said reasonably. "Why shouldn't Adam?"

"Other people are not like you," Alison protested. "Adam thinks of time as a linear thing. Most normal people do."

"How do you know?" Diana said. "You've never asked him."

Alison rubbed her forehead. "Because I knew that if I did he would think I was certifiable and would walk away!"

"Does that matter now?"

There was a small, sharp silence. "Yes," Alison said. "It always mattered."

"So you walked first," Diana said precisely. "And you'll do it again. You'll do it because you think there is no alternative and that Arthur has to come first."

"I... Yes." Alison laughed reluctantly. "You're just too good at this, you know? I thought I was asking for help about the contents of the box but you guessed about me and Adam."

Diana smiled serenely at her. "Perhaps you wanted to talk about both," she said. "And for what it's worth, I think I can help you. The holly for the chess piece represents hope. Holly is the queen of the white wood in Celtic mythology. She governs the dark part of the year just as the oak governs the light. In the darkest hours, holly shines bright to give you hope."

Alison was horrified to find the tears stinging her eyes. *Hope...*

"I think Mary wanted to sustain you and give you encouragement," Diana said. She shifted in the chair as though she were in pain. "It's an educated guess. Of course, it may have another meaning as well." She gestured towards the pile of magazines and papers at her elbow. "I do a lot of cryptic crosswords. It passes the time and keeps my mind active." She smiled. "If I come up with any suggestions for the other clues I'll let you know. The ring on the falcon could be a clue to a surname. Falcons were ringed to denote ownership, if my memory serves me right. And the catgut... An instrument, perhaps? A violin?"

"With a green thread," Alison said. "Fiddler's Green? Is that a place?"

"It could well be," Diana said. Her blue eyes were still vivid and bright but Alison realised suddenly how pale and drawn the rest of her face was, lined and tight with pain. She got up.

"I'm so sorry," she said. "I've exhausted you."

"It's no problem," Diana said. She got to her feet too. "I won't see you again," she said, taking both Alison's hands in her own. Hers felt warm and surprisingly strong. "Take care, my dear. And always think twice about what it is that you truly want."

For a moment, Alison clung to her. She did not want to cut the mooring to her past life. Yet it was inexorable, as though Diana was slipping from her even as she stood there, and a moment later she found herself out on the path, and the door was shut, and Hector was weaving about her ankles. He followed her out to the car.

"*Shoo,*" Alison said. "Don't wander about on the road. Go home."

She opened the driver's door. Hector leaped gracefully into the passenger seat. "No," Alison said. She went round to the other side, opened the door and tried to pick him up. Hector dug his claws into the seat. An undignified tussle ensued, which Alison lost. She stood there, scratched and undecided. She could go back and tell Diana that her cat was trying to run away but she doubted Diana was strong enough to come and move Hector herself. Perhaps if she walked back towards the cottage, Hector would follow her...

She was halfway along the path and Hector was still curled up in a tight, disdainful ball on the passenger seat of the car, when her mobile rang.

"Miss Bannister?" She did not recognise the number or the male voice. "I'm so glad I caught you. This is Hugo Green, Diana's nephew."

Alison stopped with one hand on the picket gate. She looked at Diana's cottage. The mullioned windows winked back at her. Nothing moved behind them.

"I wanted to be there to meet you today," Hugo was saying. "I saw that you had an appointment with my aunt—it was in her diary. The thing is…" He cleared his throat. "I'm sorry, Miss Bannister, but Diana died last night. I've just been over to sort out a few things and I popped out to talk to the vicar and was longer than I expected…" He paused. "Are you still there?"

"Yes," Alison said. Her legs felt shaky. She tightened her grip on the gate. "I'm outside the cottage, as it happens. But I don't understand."

"It wasn't unexpected of course," Hugo said, "but it was quick at the end."

"Yes," Alison said faintly. Her head was buzzing.

*Other people are not like you. Most normal people see time as linear…*

Had she really spoken words to that effect to Diana less than half an hour ago, when Diana was supposed already to have passed away?

"I'm sorry," she said, realising that she hadn't uttered the conventional words. "I'm shocked."

"Of course." Hugo sounded heartily comforting. "I'm sorry I wasn't able to get hold of you sooner to let you know."

"No, please don't apologise." Alison made an effort to pull herself together. "Diana's cat's here," she said, a little at random. "He's in my car."

"Ah, yes, Hector." Hugo said. "That's fine. Diana left a note. She said you would take Hector to his new home. It sounds as though he's already settling in."

# TWENTY-ONE

*Mary, 1566*

WE WERE ALL WALKING ON EGGSHELLS THAT week. I did not see Will for two days and when he did emerge from his study he had a grey pallor and bloodshot eyes and stank of the bottle. He swore he was ill but he was only sick with the drink and it served him right. He was also morose and in an evil temper. Those servants unlucky enough to take him his food would be fortunate to get away with only having a flagon thrown at their heads.

Meanwhile, I tried to find out all I could about Thomas Fenner from Eleanor. It proved to be precious little.

"How would I know where to find him?" Eleanor asked, casting a furtive glance over her shoulder to make sure that her mother was not listening. "I know nothing of him."

And that was that. Thomas had told me we would meet again and soon. All I had to do was wait yet I chafed at the delay. Besides, if he were like his brother, soon probably meant never.

Eleanor was in a miserable mood, for Lady Fenner had told her she was to be married. The chosen suitor was Egremond

Ratcliffe, son of the Earl of Sussex. It was a great match for Eleanor, for which she had the influence of her mother's family to thank, but she did not appear thankful for her good fortune, if that was what it was.

"He is a violent brute," she sniffed into her lace handkerchief. "Will likes him and that is no good recommendation. He says he is a doughty fighter."

"Why not wait until you meet him and draw your conclusions for yourself?" I asked, but it did not pacify her.

"It will be too late by then," she wailed. "I will have to run away."

It seemed unlikely to me that Eleanor would prosper if she chose that course of action. She had absolutely no resources for survival. She was the opposite of Alison, whom I thought about often, wondering what had become of her and whether I would ever hear from her again. I did not know that Alison had survived, of course, but I had a stubborn feeling that she had. I also had not forgotten my pledge to her, but had no notion how I might accomplish it. I never went anywhere or saw anyone new. I had no letters from the Seymours, no news from court, no prospect of ever discovering what had become of her child. Yet I felt the promise weigh heavy on me.

I am not sure what imp of mischief it was in me that prompted me to seek out Lady Fenner and ask her about the plans for my future. Perhaps it was because I was nineteen now and, as Eleanor was to wed, I was fearful that the Seymours and Fenners would seek to marry me off too. Or perhaps I was equally afraid that they would not, and I would be left with Lady Fenner, an ageing spinster. I had no illusions any more that Will wished to marry me, still less any desire for him to do so. I felt embarrassed at how foolish and naive I had been. Mostly I felt determined to take back what I saw as mine; my father's estates that Will and his mother had discussed on the occasion I eavesdropped on them.

Lady Fenner greeted me civilly enough and bade me sit. She had a private parlour on the south side of the house where the afternoon sun slid through the windows and warmed the room. Even so there was an icy chill about her that defied closeness. She watched me carefully with her unreadable black gaze.

"What may I do for you, Lady Mary?"

"I have come to ask about my future, madam." I sounded as bold as brass despite the quaking of my heart. "I have trespassed on your hospitality a good while now and I wondered whether my cousin, Lord Seymour, had indicated how long I might continue to stay with you?"

Her finely plucked eyebrows arched. "What makes you think that his lordship would concern himself over such a matter?"

It was a thrust straight to the heart, as was her wont. There was no kindness in Lady Fenner. If I were to fight her I had to show her I was her equal.

"Because we *are* first cousins," I said politely, "and I am both a Seymour and a Parr, and Edward has always shown himself solicitous for my care."

Even though this was a lie, Lady Fenner's eyes narrowed at this reminder that I was better born than she and more closely related to the Seymours.

"Are you unhappy then, here at Middlecote?" she asked silkily.

"Not in the least, madam," I lied again. "But I would not wish to be a burden upon your household for any length of time."

"How very thoughtful of you, my dear," she said. She flicked an imaginary piece of thread from her elegant skirts.

"I hate to disabuse you of your fine ideas, but I doubt that your cousin Edward has any plans for your removal from Middlecote any time soon. You are without looks or fortune—" her tone was bored "—and your noble relatives have no interest in you at all."

"And yet all my relatives seem to take an interest in my father's estates," I said sweetly. "Including William. He contemplates marrying me, does he not?"

Lady Fenner stiffened. I could sense her discomfort and feel the lightning quick calculation of her thoughts.

"He may have toyed with the idea." She had clearly discarded the option of denying it outright in case Will had told me himself. "However, I am sure you are aware, my dear, that Will is not a man that Lord Hertford would approve of as a husband for you. He is far too wild."

"I did not say that I wished to wed him," I said, "only that I knew he wished to marry me and so I must have something to recommend me. The estate at Ramsbury, perhaps?" I added. "I hear it is a rich one."

My barb hit home. Lady Fenner drew back from me like a snake preparing to strike.

"Your father forfeited that manor along with all his others," she said. "The Queen holds it now and is unlikely to give it up."

"She might be persuaded to grant it to me," I said. "If I asked her nicely."

Lady Fenner was not the sort of woman to display agitation but the tap of her fingers on the arm of her chair betrayed her.

"Understand this, Lady Mary," she said, "you are nothing and no one. The Queen will not concern herself with your small matters. Nor will my son. You possess nothing but a misplaced pride and your father's feckless temperament."

That very feckless temperament she referred to caught fire and burned. "At least I am not a gambler, a lecher or a drunkard, madam," I said, "unlike your precious son, who is still so tied to your apron strings that he runs to his mama at every turn."

"No, but you are an ingrate." A spot of colour came into each of Lady Fenner's cheeks. "You have been our pensioner here for six years with barely a penny from the Seymours to keep you. The Parrs cut you off long ago. If it were not for us, you would have starved in the street—or burned as a witch."

The word cut through my fury and killed it stone dead. Never had Lady Fenner referred to the monstrous rumours that had driven me from Wolf Hall. I had not even been aware she knew of the reason for my banishment. Cousin Edward must have betrayed my situation to her when first he had sent me. After all, she had known of Alison's besmirched reputation. It seems she had also known of mine.

I stood up. The sheer frustration of my situation, my powerlessness, burned in me. What was it that Alison had said?

*"I want to be like a man and determine my own fate."*

Women could be powerful too, I thought, widows like Lady Fenner who had status and fortune and ruled her son's lands because he was too lazy and feckless to do so himself. But they were few and far between. Most women were like Eleanor, who expected little and yet were still disappointed. Eleanor would marry Egremond Ratcliffe. Of that I had no doubt.

I wanted more than that and yet I felt boxed in at every turn. Lady Fenner knew it too. There was spite and triumph in her eyes.

"Yes," she said. "Cause me a moment's trouble, Mary Seymour, and I will not hesitate to use your scandals against you."

For a long moment we stood there, our gazes locked, and

it felt as though our wills battled it out in silent fury. She held all the cards and yet I was stubborn and angry.

"You should have a care, madam," I said, as steadily as I could. "Fortunes can turn. You will not always hold the power."

With that I swept from the room, only slightly denting the drama of my departure when my skirts caught in the door and I had to wrench them free.

That night I sat down at the desk in my chamber and wrote to the Queen, addressing the letter to Liz Aiglonby, whom I hoped might make my case to Her Majesty.

Once again, I was foolish. I should have waited and allowed my fury to cool, taken a little time to allay Lady Fenner's suspicions of me. Yet I was too fired up with indignation and anger to wait. I was also unpractised in deception and so I entrusted my letter to the hall boy to take to Hungerford. I did not know it at the time but he pocketed the bribe I gave him and took the letter straight to Lady Fenner. Thus it was that only a day after I had last crossed swords with her, I did so again.

She confronted me in her parlour. Will was there too, lounging in an armchair, looking dishevelled and bad-tempered like a schoolboy who has been summoned by the headmaster but would far rather be elsewhere.

"You write a fair hand," Lady Fenner said, waving the letter at me. "I am glad that your education was not entirely wasted." She thrust the parchment into the fire and I stood there, watching it burn to ashes. I waited for her wrath to fall on my head but when she turned to me it was with a cold smile and words of great prevision.

"Sir William is to write to the Queen on your behalf," she said. "It is appropriate that the letter should come from him, not from you."

I was astonished; then I was suspicious.

"Sir William will write on his own behalf, not on mine," I said. "Do you think I do not know that? Those estates are *my* inheritance. Who has a better right to petition Her Majesty?"

"It is not seemly for you to do so," Lady Fenner retorted. "You, a woman—"

"To write to another woman," I said.

Will started to laugh. "I told you, Mama," he said. "The Lady Mary is a Seymour through and through."

"Foolish, reckless and ignorant," Lady Fenner said coldly. She turned on me like a hissing snake. "You stupid girl! Your cousin Lord Hertford still languishes in the Tower of London for marrying against the Queen's wishes. Your name is not in good odour at court."

Will stirred. "Enough, madam. The Lady Mary has learned her lesson. Have you not, Mary? She will leave the matter with me." He smiled at me, patronising, like an adult to a wayward child. "Run along now," he said. "Run along and sew, or whatever it is you do all day."

I went up to my room, threw myself on the bed and indulged in a most childish tantrum. It was sheer frustration; I was thwarted, trapped, imprisoned in what felt like an empty future. My sheer misery must have communicated itself to Darrell because when my sobs had diminished I felt his presence slide into my mind like it had done when we were children. No words, only comfort and warmth, no demand, only giving. Naturally, his gentleness made me feel much worse. I had treated him dreadfully and I did not want him to pity me. Nor in my vanity did I want to have to admit my folly. But there was no escape.

*"I am sorry."*

*"Cat."*

*"I've been so stupid."*

I felt his smile. It was wonderfully comforting.

*"Yes, you have."*

There was love, and teasing and all the reassurance I remembered. It made me want to cry all over again.

*"I do not deserve your friendship."*

*"No you do not."* Still teasing, but then I felt him hesitate. The thought patterns, the sensations, changed. My heart started to thud.

*"Cat, you have my love. You always did."*

Now I felt afraid. I had spurned his love before, thinking that whilst I cared for him I could never love him in the sense that I thought I had loved Will. But both Will and my feelings had proved quite illusory. There had been no depth to them and no worthiness in Will. I had been infatuated, in love with the excitement and glamour. As for Thomas, I did not know how I felt about him. I had sensed in him a kindred spirit and the potential for love but what did I know? I was confused and inexperienced and had made too many mistakes of which I was ashamed.

I sent Darrell a very small, shamefaced acknowledgement and felt again that rush of love surround me. It was both frightening and exhilarating at the same time. I knew he wanted more than I thought I could give; his was a mature love. Suddenly I realised that he had been waiting for me for a long time and that he did not want to wait any longer.

*"When will I see you?"* I asked.

*"Soon."* It was a promise that sent a skitter of anticipation down my spine, part confusion, part excitement.

Will had a woman in his chambers that night. This was not unusual in itself; whether the woman was a servant girl or a drab from the town or even the lady wife of some local squire, they came and went and Will made no secret of it. Lady Fenner also treated it as of no moment, as though to acknowledge that her son turned Middlecote into a bawdy-house would be beneath her notice.

I stuck my fingers in my ears to block out the noise and fell into a restless sleep full of vivid images of Darrell, whose face I never saw, and Will, who rode hell for leather through my dreams as he had that day he came back to Middlecote. Then the images changed and I dreamed of Alison again, but oh so differently from the vision I had had of her with the falcon. Perhaps everything was confused and jumbled up in my mind, but when I saw her I knew at once she was somewhere far, far from me. She looked different. She even sounded different, as though the Alison I had known was half the same, half transformed. She was standing outside Middlecote but the house was different too, much larger, tumbledown and dark, shuttered in ivy. Alison was sitting on the front steps, her head in her hands. At her side sat a large black dog of a breed I had never seen before.

"I need you, Mary," she said. "I'm still waiting. Where are you? Mary, where are you?"

I woke trembling, with Thomas Fenner's words in my ears.

*"Sir Reginald De Morven saw visions of the future… He passed through time…"*

And suddenly I knew where Alison was, and what I had to do in order to find her son and get word to her.

Eleanor was appalled when I told her that I wanted her to alter the portrait.

"I can't!" she said, aghast. "It was painted by a proper art-ist!"

"And you have as much skill," I argued. "Besides, no one wants it. It is hidden away here, so what's the harm?"

I saw she was still hesitating and added, with cunning, "I

only wish for the painting to feature one small angel—and a lion. Religious symbols, Eleanor, to affirm my faith."

I should have felt guilty using such deception but I did not. Eleanor was very devout and her brow cleared and she smiled at me. She did not even query when I added a magic wand garlanded with flowers to my requirements, so that there was a picture in each corner of my portrait. I thought Alison would like the wand; it was a nod to both of us and to the discussion we had had about my powers as a seer. A portrait, I felt was more durable than a letter or some other form of communication. It might last for centuries. Besides, mine already had Alison's box amongst the background details. I was not sure why the artist had chosen to represent it but perhaps because he had realised how precious it was to me as the place I stored everything that reminded me of my parents, pitifully few as those items were. One day he had come to paint me and seen me poring over my father's signet ring. I had not known he was there and slammed the box closed fast enough when I saw him but he must have guessed its significance to me. Now it was to be significant to Alison too. It was to be the repository of any information I found about her son. That, and the portrait together would be my message to her.

Of course, I still had the difficulty of discovering what had befallen little Arthur Seymour but I had a very vague plan. I rode out the following afternoon. I did not have permission and no one accompanied me. I slipped into the stables and took one of the mares and rode north over the Downs along the Sugar Way and the Thieves' Way, until I was lost amidst the green lanes. I saw no one. Eventually, I dismounted and sat in the sun, eyes closed, feeling the warmth on my face. I waited—I suppose I may even have dozed, as the minutes stretched into hours and no one came.

There was movement beside me, sudden and unexpected, and I opened my eyes and made a grab for the knife in my boot.

"Can you use that?" Thomas Fenner asked, as I levelled it at his throat.

"I've never tried," I said, "but how difficult can it be?"

"Surprisingly difficult to spill blood the first time," he said. He moved the blade away from his throat carefully. "After that, easier each time, I am sorry to say."

"How do you know?" I asked. I put the knife down between us and it lay, glinting in the sun.

"I've been a soldier." He was looking out across the downland, his gaze distant. "After my mother died and we lost Middlecote, I went away to fight."

"I didn't know," I said. "Why did you come back?"

His gaze came back to my face and I felt a flash of emotion that I did not understand, as though I had missed something important, but all he said was, "There's a time for everything. It was time for me to come home."

"To live in a ruin, and steal chickens and watch your brother despoil the lands you love?"

He smiled then. "Middlecote will never be mine again," he said, "but this—" he gestured to the rolling land that encircled us "—this William cannot take from me." He picked up the knife, where it lay in the grass.

"This is a fine blade," he said. "It's not a woman's knife, nor is it English. Where did it come from?"

"It was my father's," I said. "I inherited a few—a very few—useful things from him."

Thomas had the knife resting on his palm now as he admired the balance of it. "It looks Swiss to me," he said. "Does it have a sheath decorated with the dance of death?"

"Yes," I said. "How did you know?"

He looked at me sideways. "Your father would have had just such a knife. It's expensive, high status, possibly the most useful thing you could have inherited from him, apart from your reckless spirit."

"I'm not reckless!" I protested.

"Of course you are," Thomas said. "You are here, aren't you? Alone?"

"I'm with you," I said. "How is it that you are here, anyway?"

There was a pause. "I ride this way each day," he said, "waiting for you."

I stared at him. The sun was in his eyes, lifting the dark brown to golden. A steady light burned in them. That was the difference between Thomas and his brother, I thought suddenly. Will was mercurial, quicksilver, never to be trusted. Thomas was resolute.

*"When will I see you?"*

*"Soon..."*

The man I had seen in my dream turned around and at last I saw. He had Thomas Fenner's face.

*"Darrell..."* I don't know if I said it aloud but he smiled and spoke.

"Cat..." Then: "Mary."

He moved so fast then, catching me to him, holding me close. I could feel the material of his jacket against my cheek and the beat of his heart beneath that. It mingled with mine, two hearts beating together as they always had from the very beginning. He kissed me and I clung to him, losing myself in the sensation, coming home. It was a long time before he released me and then it was only to push the tumbled hair back from my face with shaking hands so that he could look at me.

"I've been so slow," I said. "So stupid."

His mouth curved into that smile I loved. "You have," he agreed gravely.

I raised a hand to his cheek and felt the stubble rough beneath my fingers. "You," I said wonderingly. "But how?"

He shook his head. "I know not. But you said our families were connected generations back. Perhaps others had the gift and passed it down to us."

"When?" I asked. "When did you know it was me?"

He paused. "I worked it out years back," he said. "You gave me lots of clues. Grimsthorpe, Wolf Hall…"

"Whereas you told me nothing," I reproved.

He looked shamefaced. "Secrecy is a way of life for me."

I thought then of his family history: his illegitimacy, his mother thrown out of Middlecote, hounded by Will, his struggle to survive. I could understand his reticence. He trusted no one.

"You have me now," I said, as I reached up to kiss him again.

"I always had you," he said, against my mouth. "You were always mine."

He kissed me again. It was lighter this time but not careless, gentle yet demanding. Kissing Thomas was not like kissing Will. It felt like standing on the edge of a precipice, waiting to fly.

I saw the heat flare in his eyes but then, just when I thought I would tumble right down there in the bracken and grass with him, he smiled at me and simply lay back, looking up at the blue sky above our heads.

*We have all the time in the world…*

I smiled and lay back too. I felt warm and happy and very loved.

"You did not tell me," he said, "how you came to be up here alone."

"I wanted to escape," I said, "just for a little."

He propped himself up on one elbow and looked at me. I could see him out of the corner of my eye but kept staring up at the scudding clouds.

"Is it very bad?" he asked.

"No," I said. "No one ill treats me, I suppose. It is boring and I feel trapped, and Will is unpredictable and Eleanor is sad and Lady Fenner is…" I stopped. "Dangerous," I said, after a moment. "Sometimes I think she is more dangerous than Will is."

"She is certainly cleverer," Thomas said.

"People lead worse lives than mine," I said. "Much worse. I do realise that."

"And more fulfilling ones," Thomas said.

"I tried to write to the Queen," I said, "but Lady Fenner stole my letter and burned it. I wanted my lands back. I wanted to build a life for myself elsewhere."

"Alone, again?" Thomas asked.

"Not now," I said. "I want to live with you." An idea took me.

"*You* could go!" I rolled over and faced Thomas. "You could carry a message to London for me!"

When he smiled the lines deepened at the side of his eyes. "You want me to be your messenger boy now?" he asked. "You do not ask much, do you, Mary Seymour? It's a long way to London and it costs. Can you pay me?"

I had spent my last coin on bribing the faithless hall boy. "No," I said.

Thomas shook his head. "Well, then…"

This time it was I who, daring all, leaned forward to kiss him. I took the leap. It was how I imagined flying might be; my stomach dropped, there was a rush of excitement. I felt dizzy.

"I'm not sure exactly what it is that you are offering,"

Thomas said, a long time later, "but perhaps we should stop this, at least until we are wed."

I sat up, feeling hot and dishevelled and wonderfully wanton. My hair had come loose from its hood and lay about my shoulders. A part of me was mortified at my behaviour whilst the other half of me wished I had taken matters a great deal further. I started to straighten my clothes, picked up the knife and tucked it back in my boot.

"My parents left me a dowry," I said, not meeting Thomas's eyes. "A golden ring, a quantity of other jewellery, a psalter, a few small items. But if we were to regain my father's lands I would be an heiress—"

Thomas caught my wrist and tumbled me back down into the grass beneath him, disarranging my carefully tidied hair so that it spread about me again. There was a fierce expression on his face.

"When I take you, Mary Seymour," he said, "it will not be for the money."

He kissed me again. It was fierce this time, catching alight, like a wildfire, but he released me with a groan before it had barely started.

"I'll ride to London for you," he said. "Damn it, you must know I would do anything for you."

I had known it, in my heart of hearts, that he and I were inextricably linked, destined from the first. That feeling surged in me now, growing and expanding inside me all energy and excitement. I pressed a hand to his cheek, revelling in the touch, the warmth and roughness of it. The sensations were all new to me, and glorious.

"I do know," I whispered, "and I feel the same."

There was a shadow in his eyes. He shook his head and moved back, putting space between us. "Is there anything else I can do for you," he said, "whilst I am there?"

I remembered then, through the haze of my happiness and my new-found feelings.

*Alison.* Only that morning, I had hatched the plan of asking Thomas to seek word of her.

"Yes," I said. "Yes, please. You can make enquiries after a Mistress Alison Banestre. And you can ask after her son by Lord Hertford. He is called Arthur. I need to know what happened to him."

Thomas nodded. He seemed unsurprised. "Whom should I address?"

"Go first to Mistress Elizabeth Aiglonby," I said. "She is in the service of the Queen. I will give you a letter, and a token for her."

He gave me a glimmer of a smile. "That means that I shall need to see you again before I go."

"Alas," I said, "it does." I looked at him from beneath my lashes. "Tomorrow?"

Thomas nodded. "Meet me at the Phantom Tree."

I shuddered at the name. "Where?"

"It is the huge oak that stands on the track just to the south of Middlecote Hall," Thomas said.

"I know the one." I had ridden that way with Will. "But why the name? Why so macabre?"

He shrugged. "I know not. Some say it was because a dead man walks there. He materialises from nowhere and vanishes as quick. Superstition, I expect."

*A dead man walks there…*

I shivered again. I had seen a dead woman on horseback once. I, more than most, should believe in such dark tales. I wished Thomas had not chosen to meet there though.

It felt ill wished.

# TWENTY-TWO

"A CAT," ALISON SAID. "WHAT AM I TO DO WITH a cat?"

She had rung Adam from the car as she drove slowly back towards the motorway along the country lanes. He had sounded sleepy and warm, as though she had stirred him from falling asleep over the Sunday papers, and she had felt a sudden and terribly strong urge to be there with him, curled up in the flat together, talking and laughing and making love, relearning each other, as they had done the previous day.

Adam had offered to come down to Wiltshire with her but Alison had wanted to go alone. When she rang, she had told him that Diana was dead and the warmth had fled his voice as he had asked how she was.

"I'm fine," Alison had said. Then: "No. I don't know. I'm shocked. But…" She had hesitated on the edge of telling Adam everything, but had drawn back.

"Hector can't live with me," she said now. "I can't have a cat in London. There's no garden. It's impossible."

Hector, asleep on the passenger seat, ignored her. He had woken briefly when she had tried to put the seat belt around him, and had then promptly turned his back on her.

"Take him to Richard," Adam said. "He likes cats and the shop has a long back garden that goes down to the river. Hector would like it there."

"I thought Richard was looking after Monty," Alison said. "Dogs and cats don't go together."

"Monty gets on fine with cats," Adam said. "Marlborough is on your way, isn't it? I'll ring Richard and tell him to expect you. He's always taking in strays. He'd love to have Hector."

"Well, if you're sure…" Alison looked dubiously at the cat who was snoring now. "It seems an imposition."

"I'll call you back," Adam said, "but I'm sure it will be fine."

It only took ten minutes to get to Marlborough and Alison parked directly outside the portrait gallery. There was a yellow line on the road but it was a Sunday and she thought it unlikely there would be a traffic warden on the prowl. A couple of doors down, the sign of the White Hart jutted out over the pavement. The shop, unlike many others in the High Street, had a closed sign in the window, but when she tried the door it opened.

She rang the bell and stepped inside. Today the bright lights were out and the gallery full of pale shadows rather than colour. It was silent. Adam had said Richard was expecting her but there was no sign of him.

"Hello?" Alison walked towards the counter at the back. Behind it, a door opened into what looked like an office. The building was long and thin. Alison could picture it as Adam had described, stretching back from the road like the rambling medieval houses she had once seen, a garden behind it, each tenement plot a small piece of land carved out to support a family.

The office door seemed to sway on its hinges for a moment and it was as though the scene before her changed, dissolving and reforming into a different picture, a room with an earthen floor and a rough wooden table. She could hear the clash of pots and the sound of voices and in her nose was the smell of roasting meat...

"Ah, Miss Bannister." Richard was coming out of the office towards her. "I'm so sorry, I didn't hear the bell."

"Please, call me Alison," Alison said, "and I do apologise for simply walking in." She gave her head a little shake, trying to clear it. The office looked perfectly normal now, but just for a second she had glimpsed, or thought she had glimpsed, something very different behind that door. No doubt the shocks of the day were making her feel a bit confused. There was a smell of roasting meat though: Richard's Sunday lunch, she assumed.

"I'm looking forward to meeting Hector," Richard said. "Adam said he needed rehoming."

"It's very kind of you," Alison said. "He was sort of bequeathed to me, but my flat isn't suitable for him and I'm not sure..." She hesitated. "Well, I don't think he was meant for me, anyway."

Richard didn't ask her what she meant. He smiled. "Animals often know." He followed her out to the car where Hector graciously deigned to be picked up and carried into the shop. Once there, he inspected the premises carefully, looked thoughtfully at Monty, who wagged his tail, then wandered through to the office door and disappeared.

"Oh dear," Alison said, "I hope he'll be all right."

"The garden is walled," Richard said.

"But cats can climb."

"I think Hector knows exactly what he's doing," Richard said. He gestured to the office. "Would you care for a cup of tea? I know you have to get back to London, but if you have time..."

"That would be lovely, thank you," Alison said. "I'm sorry I don't have any of Hector's belongings. Everything happened

rather oddly. I'll ring Hugo Green—that's Diana's nephew—
and ask if he could drop anything of Hector's off with you."

"Adam mentioned that you were hoping to see your friend
but that she had died last night," Richard said. The kettle
was starting to buzz. He took two mugs from a neat little
antique cupboard and placed them on the tray. "I'm so very
sorry. That must have been quite a shock for you."

"The whole day has been completely bizarre," Alison said,
with some understatement. She felt again a wash of confusion and puzzlement. She had seen Diana. She knew she had.
She could not have imagined the entire episode.

"I'm going to need some time to think it all through,"
she said.

"And to talk about it, I'm sure," Richard said, adding water
to the mugs. "Take a seat on the window cushion. Just shove
those papers out of the way. Adam can help if you want to
talk about it with him," he added. "He's good at that sort of
thing these days."

"He told me about his father," Alison said. "I'm sorry."
She took the mug from Richard. "I imagine you and he were
close friends. How hideous for you all."

"Peter Hewer and I only met when we were in our twenties," Richard said, opening a packet of biscuits and offering one to her. "But we immediately connected as friends.
You know how sometimes you meet someone and it feels
as though you have known them for ever?" He raised a
brow. "I sometimes felt we could not have been closer even
if we had been blood relations. It was a bad time when we
lost him." He sat down in the wing chair opposite her. The
cushions gave a protesting squeak. "I must get this thing re-
upholstered," Richard said vaguely.

"Did Adam tell you about us?" Alison asked. She hadn't
meant to discuss Adam but it felt awkward not acknowledg-

ing their relationship when she was here with Adam's god-father.

Richard's eyes twinkled. "He said you were a friend, which is a step forward, isn't it?"

Alison blushed. "I suppose we were a bit antagonistic when we bumped into each other here that time," she said.

"Just a bit," Richard said mildly. "Adam didn't mention it," he added, "but I realised who you were. You were always…" he paused as though trying to find the right word "…important in his life."

Alison was startled. "Me?" she stammered. "How? I mean surely he didn't tell anyone about me at the time—" She stopped.

"I knew he had had a very serious relationship when he was very young," Richard said, "and that it had ended badly." He looked at her, but his blue gaze was opaque, as though he were thinking of something quite other. "He never told us your name," he said, "but we all realised he had loved you. Very much."

There was no reproach in his tone but even so Alison felt a rush of guilt. "I loved him too," she said. "But it was… complicated."

"It often is," Richard said.

"And I was too young to handle it," Alison said. "Although," she added hastily, seeing the flash of some expression in Richard's eyes, "I'd never belittle it by saying it was a youthful thing and not important." She sighed. "Oh, you know what I mean."

Richard smiled at her. "You have a second chance now. Not many people get those."

Alison's sense of guilt intensified. Richard was right, of course, which only made it all the more painful that she felt so torn between the past and the present. The feeling had haunted her for the whole day, first in her conversation with Diana and now here.

"It's very new," she said cautiously. "I don't know..."

*"You will walk away again..."*

Diana's words seem to echo in her mind. When had she started to want to belong somewhere rather than to be for ever searching? It confused her. Finding Arthur had been her sole purpose for so long. She had never imagined she might want something else, something that challenged the foundations of her belief.

"Well, it's up to you," Richard said. "Or Adam. Or both of you. At any rate, it isn't my business. Sorry. This is very tactless of me. I'm an interfering old man and I should keep my mouth shut."

Silence fell, but it was a comfortable silence broken only by the hopeful beat of Monty's tail on the floor as he begged for a biscuit.

"I haven't had the chance to thank you for telling me about Middlecote," Alison said, after a moment. "It helped me a lot to know where to go for my research."

Richard lifted one shoulder in a half-shrug. "I sensed you were looking for something," he said. "If I helped then I'm glad."

"You obviously have a keen interest in the place," Alison said. She had seen the pile of books teetering on the edge of one of the shelves. They had titles such as *Wiltshire Airfields in the Second World War* and *101st Airborne Division* and *Berkshire Battlefields*.

"Middlecote played host to a succession of British and US troops during the Second World War," Richard said. "It's an interest of mine."

"Middlecote has a pretty war-torn history down the centuries, hasn't it," Alison said. "Adam mentioned that a regiment of parliamentarian troops were based there during the English Civil War."

"Ralph Hopton's men," Richard said. He moved sharply, as though something pained him. "Yes, there was a great deal of action in this area during the 1640s. Vicious fighting, some of it." He stood up a little abruptly. "Well, I imagine you'll be needing to get home…"

"Yes, of course." Alison could take a hint. The atmosphere in the office had changed; it felt awkward, painful in some way as though their conversation had taken a wrong turning though she had no idea how or why.

She gathered up her bag. "Thanks again," she said.

"No problem." Richard's smile was back but his eyes looked strained and the lines ran deep in his face. "Interesting name, Bannister," he added, apparently at random. "Very old. Norman French, isn't it?"

"Yes," Alison said. "My ancestors came over with the Conquest and inter-married with the Saxons."

"The Hewers were stonemasons, I believe," Richard said. "They took their name from their occupation. Good working stock, though like so many people they did have noble connections way back in the medieval period. Fascinating subject, family history."

Alison stood up. "I'd better go before I get a parking ticket," she said. "Thank you for the tea as well as for taking Hector. Please, will you let me know how he gets on?"

"Of course," Richard said. He walked with her back to the gallery door and held it open for her to go out onto the pavement.

"This feels like a very old building," Alison said, turning to look at the frontage. "Do you know when it was built?"

"It's seventeenth century," Richard said. "It was built after the great fire that gutted Marlborough in 1653."

"Oh," Alison said, "I thought it might be earlier." She felt disappointed; so much for the glimpse through the open door into an earlier world. Suddenly, she realised how tired she was; tired, sad, and imagining things. She was going to need to be very careful driving home.

"I believe it was rebuilt on earlier foundations," Richard said. "This bit of the street was once part of the White Hart Inn. It was much bigger in the Tudor period. The stables and outbuildings were located somewhere around here. In fact—" he looked around vaguely "—I have a sand clock somewhere that was originally in the Tudor inn. I bought it about ten years ago when they turned the place into a gastro pub and got rid of a lot of the old fixtures and fittings."

Alison felt as though the polished boards of the gallery were shifting slightly under her feet. "What's a sand clock?" she asked.

"An hourglass," Richard said, diving back into the office, then calling over his shoulder, "like an old-fashioned egg timer. You know the sort of thing—the sand runs from one segment to the other."

*The sands of time…*

Alison felt a cold shiver rack her. She remembered her utter despair on going into the White Hart ten years before and finding that her route back to the past was denied to her. For so long, she had cudgelled her mind to try to work out what had changed, when the pub, whilst different in decoration over the years, had been essentially the same.

Except it had not. Something had been lost, sold off, missing…

"Here it is." Richard had emerged from the office in triumph holding an hourglass in his hand. It was smaller than Alison had imagined, the bronze and silver gilt of the wooden stand worn away in places, the sand inside the glass a pale golden colour.

"It's a pretty little thing, isn't it," Richard said. "Not so fragile that it hasn't survived for five hundred years. It used to hang on the bar but as you can see it was originally designed to stand on a flat surface like a table."

"I've seen something like it recently," Alison said slowly. She chased the elusive memory. It had not been in Diana's cottage, yet there was some connection there, tugging at the edge of her mind.

"I'll be in touch about Hector," Richard said. "Give my best to Adam when you see him."

He closed the door of the shop, locked it and waved to her through the glass. Alison watched as he walked back through the display of paintings and disappeared through the door into the back room, the sand clock in his hand. Further down the street the door of the White Hart opened and a group of people came out, chatting and laughing.

Alison remembered then. She saw the open hall of the old inn and the spiteful landlady stirring the pot of beef stew and on the table at her side a wooden hourglass with the sand almost run through. She felt a little faint. She turned back to the gallery, a mad idea possessing her that she would simply run back in and snatch the sand glass from Richard's hand. But it was too late. The showroom was dark and no light gleamed beyond the office door. She would have to wait. But now she knew. She knew she had found the key.

# TWENTY-THREE

*Mary, 1566*

THE END OF SEPTEMBER BROUGHT DISASTER to Middlecote, if disaster it was to see Will dragged away to Salisbury gaol. Others might disagree and see it as a blessing. I see it as the beginning of the end, the start of the long unravelling of Will's fate and the short unravelling of my own.

To tell the truth, I was more concerned with Thomas than with Will that day. I had met him at the Phantom Tree a full fortnight before with a letter for the Queen, to be delivered by Liz Aiglonby on my behalf, and since then there had been no progress. I knew he had reached London safely. That much he had vouchsafed to me when I had called on him. Now he kicked his heels at the Queen's pleasure. Whilst he waited, I fretted. As each day passed exactly like the last, I fretted a little more. I wanted Thomas back, I wanted to make a fresh start with him and I wanted it immediately. I had no patience, another quality I had no doubt inherited from my reckless father.

It was a night of winter storms. The house creaked and groaned like a foundering galleon. Branches tapped against the window. The wind hurled rain against the panes. It was no time to be venturing out in the dark and the wild weather. Despite that, at past midnight, I heard the peal of the bell at the door and a violent knocking. Accustomed now to nocturnal disturbance, I simply heaved a sigh and turned over in bed, burying my head beneath the bolster. A moment later, though, there were voices upraised and the sound of footsteps on the landing outside, then the rasp of Will's chamber door opening.

A burst of desolate weeping dragged me from beneath the covers to sit bolt upright in horror. There was such misery and hopelessness in it.

"I had to come! Where else might I go?"

Then Will's voice, slurred with drink and malice: "I have no notion, nor do I care. You cannot be here. Not now. For pity's sake go home."

Another door slammed violently close by and I started. There were shouts and a babble of voices, swiftly hushed. Were those Lady Fenner's sharp tones I heard, raised in heated argument with her son? It was impossible to tell through the maelstrom of sound outside and the confusion within.

After throwing back the covers, I groped for my mantle and found my way to the door. Out in the corridor was Eleanor, huddled, barefoot and shivering. A line of light showed beneath Will's door.

"What is going on?" I asked her.

"I heard sobbing." Eleanor was practically sobbing herself, with fear and anxiety. "Someone is in there—" She stopped and grabbed my arm tightly as the most pitiful scream I had ever heard rent the air. There was another, and another. It sounded as though someone were being gutted alive.

"Merciful heavens," Eleanor gasped whilst I stood frozen with horror.

The door opened.

"Where is that bloody midwife?" Will's voice bellowed from within.

Lady Fenner appeared in the doorway with the light behind her. She was fully dressed, neat as a pin, an incongruous sight in the middle of such chaos. She closed the door swiftly behind her but not before I had seen the room in all its vivid horror: Will, dishevelled, pacing before the fire, a woman on the bed apparently convulsed in agony. A maidservant, white and shaking, with a pan of hot water and evidently not the slightest idea of what to do.

I thought Eleanor was going to faint. She swayed and I caught her instinctively, then Lady Fenner was by my side.

"Come away," she snapped. "This is no place for you."

Eleanor was drooping in my arms, weeping softly. She was a broken reed.

"What in God's name goes on here, madam?" I burst out. I could not help myself. Not even Lady Fenner's most quelling expression could hold me silent.

"The poor soul went into labour whilst travelling," Lady Fenner said, her hand on my arm like a claw dragging both Eleanor and I away. "We have sent to Mother Barnes, the midwife. I pray God she comes soon."

It was a tissue of lies, all of it. I knew it at once. William would never have given succour to any woman in her hour of need. Most likely he would have turned a stranger from the door. Besides, I had heard her words, and his. They had known one another.

I wanted to argue, but Eleanor had started to snuffle and sniff again by now and all my energies were taken with encouraging her back into her chamber. Together Lady Fenner and I got her into bed and then Lady Fenner ushered me out and turned the key in the door on the outside, pocketing it.

"I do not want Eleanor disturbed by anything else," she said. "She is of a most sensitive disposition."

"Certainly she can be of no help to you in this situation." I agreed.

Her eyes narrowed on me. "She will keep her mouth shut. That is all the help I need." She gestured to me to precede her into my own chamber. "Can I trust you to do the same?" She must have read the answer in my eyes for she replied to her own question. "No, of course I cannot. You are as slippery as an eel, Mary Seymour. I will lock you up too whilst I think what to do about this."

"I've seen nothing," I said, "other than a woman in your son's bedchamber, which is in no way an uncommon occurrence."

I saw her lips twitch and thought she would smile but in the end all she said was, "You are too sharp. Your wits will bring you into danger."

I knew she meant to lock me up and God knew what she would do to me after that, but before any of it could happen there was an urgent call from the landing.

"My lady, the midwife is here!"

With an impatient exclamation, Lady Fenner hurried away, leaving me on the threshold of my room.

All good sense should have prompted me to go inside and shoot the bolt myself. That way I could have pretended for ever that I had seen or heard nothing of import that night. But I was done with pretending. I was done with closing my eyes to Will Fenner's misdeeds. So I waited a breath or two and then, my heart thumping, I slid from the room and silently followed her, hiding around corners, sliding into shadows, making sure I was neither heard nor seen this time.

The door of Will's chamber was firmly shut. The sound from within was muted. I waited, but nothing happened.

I felt my heartbeat settle a little and the tense knot of fear in my chest slowly started to unravel. Then I heard the thin wail of a baby's cry.

The child had been born and it was alive.

"God be praised," I whispered. There was some good news in Middlecote Hall this night.

Yet something was wrong. Even as a feeling of nameless dread began to swell in my chest again I saw it all happen before my eyes, slowly, oh so slowly, each moment in agonising clarity. The door opened and the little maidservant ran out. She was screaming, loud and shocking, her mouth a wide gape of fear and horror; Lady Fenner was hot on her heels.

Behind her, the firelight illuminated a scene from hell. Will, in his shirtsleeves, bloodstained and dishevelled, his eyes glazed with a blank madness; a pile of white sheets on the floor, similarly stained with streaks of blood, and on the bed, the woman, not screaming now, but sobbing as though her heart would break, a great sodden heaving mass of misery, from her white tear-stained face to the disjointed tumble of her limbs.

"You killed him!" The maid was panting. She blundered about the landing like a terrified animal, backing away from the bedroom door, stumbling in her haste. Lady Fenner caught her arm and slapped her, very hard. The screams died abruptly. I saw a red smear on the girl's cheek. The smell of heat and blood and sickness caught at my throat.

"Not a word." Lady Fenner was shaking the poor creature as though she were a rag doll.

I turned to creep away and one of the boards creaked, loudly, beneath my feet. I saw Lady Fenner freeze then she darted across the landing. I had the sense not to run.

"You again," she said, pulling me into the pale pool of

light thrown by the candle in the sconce. "Spying?" Her tone was vicious.

"I thought I heard a baby crying," I said, aware of the frantic battery of my pulse as I tried to keep my voice steady.

"You did not." Lady Fenner stared at me fixedly. "The babe was born dead. The midwife has taken the body away. A tragedy, but perhaps for the best under the circumstances."

The maid snivelled.

"Go away, you foolish creature," Lady Fenner snapped at her, "and remember to say no word or your family starves."

The poor girl dragged herself away and her mistress turned back to me. "Well," she said silkily.

I had already decided how I was going to deal with this. I knew that she was lying, and she knew that I knew. I was no servant to be demeaned and bullied, but that made me more dangerous to Lady Fenner than her maid would ever be. I had to disarm her, persuade her that I was no threat. I was not sure I was that good an actress but my safety, my life, depended on it.

Lady Fenner was examining me like a specimen, cold-eyed, dispassionate. "What am I to do with you, I wonder," she mused. "Perhaps I will have to marry you off to Will after all. That should at least clip your wings and silence your tongue."

"There is not the least need to do anything with me, ma'am," I said smoothly. "We are kin and blood is more important than all else. Anything that hurts Will would damage us all."

She stared at me. It felt as though her dark gaze was probing my soul.

"It is not like you to put practicality before principle, Mary Seymour," she said. "I thought you had more integrity than that."

"I want to survive," I said bluntly. "And on my own I have nothing. I have come to realise that. Foolish, then, to cut myself off from you."

I was halfway to persuading her. I could tell.

"Which does not mean," I added truthfully, "that I like you. You and your murderous son can go to hell for all I care but I will not go with you. So we must all stick together."

She did laugh then and I saw that through my straight talking, my words had rung true where lies would not have convinced. I had satisfied her that I would not betray them. My heart thumped uncomfortably at the deceit but I kept my voice steady and my gaze on hers and eventually she nodded again.

"We will talk in the morning," she said. "Go to your chamber now."

I lay huddled beneath my bedcovers, unable to feel any warmth. When I closed my eyes I saw it all again, the bed-chamber, the fire, the blood, and in my nostrils was the scent of death. Will had been drunk, that much was for sure, and violent with it. I knew that he must have killed the newborn child. His viciousness was not out of character but he had never displayed it so nakedly before, and in his own home.

*"Cat. What's happened?"*

Thomas had felt my distress. The pattern of thought was urgent, edged with fear. I hurried to reassure him.

*"Nothing. Will is drunk and violent but I am safe. Have no fear."*

His response was a violent burst of sensation; fury at Will, reassurance, comfort all intermingled.

*"I will come back."*

*"No!"* I sought to reassure him. What he was doing for me was the most important service of all, to me and to Alison. I told him I needed him to stay, to see it through.

*"I am safe,"* I repeated. *"Take care, my love…"*

I felt bereft when the patterns faded and he was gone. Realising that I would never sleep, I kept my eyes open instead, to block out the memories of the things I had seen. Everything now depended on Thomas. All I had to do was keep Lady Fenner fooled until Thomas returned. Then I would have protection and Thomas and I together would bring down William Fenner once and for all.

By the following morning, Will's chamber was swept clean and bright as a pin. A great deal of scrubbing must have gone on in the small hours of the night to remove those bloodstains. The woman had gone too. I never knew her name. It had not been Lady Anne Hungerford that was for sure.

By mid-afternoon, the High Sheriff had come to question Will on the events of that night. The midwife, he said, had laid against Will a shocking charge of infanticide. He must answer for his crimes.

But Will was gone. No one knew where.

"You, girl." Henry Sherington of Lacock Abbey was a small man who made up in the volume of his voice what he lacked in stature. On finding his bird flown, he had been furious and had insisted on interviewing Lady Fenner instead. She had chosen me to accompany her; Eleanor was prostrate with nerves that day.

"You girl," the High Sheriff said again to me, taking me for a servant. "What did you see and hear last night? What do you know of this outrage?"

"This is the Lady Mary Seymour, Sir Henry," Lady Fenner said, steel in her voice. "She is the daughter of the late Queen Katherine. You do not question her so roughly."

Sir Henry blinked crossly, but he did moderate his address. "Well? Lady Mary? What do you know?"

"I know nothing, Sir Henry," I said. "I saw and heard nothing out of the ordinary last night."

Lady Fenner raised her brows infinitesimally at that and I repressed a smile.

"There was a woman here," Sir Henry barked. "Visiting Sir William."

I cast my eyes down modestly. "That may be so, sir. As I said, it would not be out of the ordinary."

One of Sir Henry's men smothered a guffaw.

"I have already told you," Lady Fenner interposed. "There was a traveller, benighted here because of the weather. We gave her shelter. This morning she departed for Marlborough. That is all."

"Mother Barnes reports attending the birth of an infant," Sir Henry said.

"Then she was not here but at some other house," Lady Fenner said. "The midwife is old; she becomes confused."

"Your daughter is sick and abed," Sir Henry said sharply. "Perhaps she is the woman Mother Barnes was summoned to help."

Lady Fenner looked down her nose at him. "My daughter is affianced to the son of the Earl of Sussex," she said. "They are not wed yet. You are premature in your suspicions."

"A babe was killed!" Sir Henry bellowed. He was cherry red with frustration. "Murdered on the fire! The midwife saw it!"

"She saw no such thing," Lady Fenner said, cold as ice. "This is no more than a tale cooked up to cause trouble for Sir William." She swung around to confront the other men. "Do you think I do not know it? That Sir Walter Hungerford and Sir Henry Knyvett and many more seek to bring William down through false accusation? No doubt they paid this woman to lie." She straightened. "You waste your time, gentlemen. Search the house if you must. You will find nothing. As for Sir William, he is away on business and, if you seek to arrest him on these flimsy matters, you will be shown for the fools you are."

She was magnificent. Even I, who hated her, had to admire her steel. They went then, grumbling, and searched Middlecote from top to bottom, and found nothing. They grew filthy with dust and thirsty and short of temper, and in the end they rode away empty-handed. Lady Fenner and I watched them go.

"I will write to Sir John Hopton," Lady Fenner said. "He has seen Will right before and will do so again."

"Who is Sir John Hopton?" I asked.

She let the curtain fall and moved away from the window. "He is a friend to our family. A lawyer."

"A useful friend to have," I said.

"He is influential." Lady Fenner nodded.

"I imagine he makes certain...difficulties disappear?" I asked.

She gave a small secret smile. "You and I understand one another very well after all, Lady Mary. Who would have thought it?"

I was not going to contradict Lady Fenner if she thought that we were allies. I settled down to learn more. Anything that could be useful to me—and to Thomas in future—was valuable.

"Lawyers are expensive," I said, "and Will is mired in debt."

"We found a way to retain Sir John's assistance." Lady Fenner said. "It was not what I would have chosen, but without Sir John's help, Will would already be imprisoned or very likely dead." She sighed. "Now that Eleanor is safely betrothed and dowered..." She let the sentence hang. "Besides, it was a way to ensure the future security of the estate." She was speaking quietly now, almost to herself.

I do not know how I guessed the truth. Perhaps I had remembered Thomas's words:

*"Middlecote will never be mine..."*

He had seen the future that Lady Fenner was revealing to me. Somehow Thomas already knew.

"You have given Middlecote away," I whispered. "You have promised it to Sir John in return for his help."

"It was the only way to protect William," Lady Fenner said. "It is no more than bricks and mortar for a man's life."

I struggled to conceal my feelings. I had no love for Middlecote Hall but I knew that Thomas had. He would never have bartered away his past and his future in so shoddy a fashion.

"You are loyal in your affections, ma'am," I said. "You do much for Sir William and I am not sure he deserves your generosity. Have you noticed how he seeks your advice and yet always goes his own way?"

She shifted. I felt her antagonism. We might be allies now, or at least she thought we were, bound by mutual silence over Will's misdeeds, but that did not mean we liked one another. Nor did I understand why she tied her fortunes so tightly to Will's wayward star. She was ruthless and clever and calculating. Will was reckless and unpredictable and could ruin all her work at a stroke. Yet she loved him. It was the only explanation. She loved him with so fierce a maternal love that she was, if not blind to his faults, then prepared to tolerate them.

She did not answer me, turning her back, reaching for the ink pot and paper to summon Sir John Hopton.

Sir Henry's men found Will in an alehouse a few miles outside Wilton. He had been gambling on a game of shove ha'penny and could not pay his debts. Of course, there was a fight. They threw him in Salisbury Gaol and we all waited to see if Sir John Hopton could save him.

# TWENTY-FOUR

"HEY." ADAM'S VOICE WAS WARM. "I KNOW WE hadn't made any plans but I wondered if you'd like to get something to eat? I'll cook for you—I've got some research I wanted to show you."

"You don't need to bribe me." Alison reached up and kissed his cheek. Her heart had leaped when she had seen him waiting for her outside the office that evening and the realisation terrified her. In theory it should have been possible to walk away now, to draw apart again as abruptly as they had come together. Sex with the ex, she'd heard people call it, but it didn't feel like that to her. Already it was too complicated, too intimate, simply too special to write it off as unimportant and cut Adam out of her life again. Yet she knew she was going to do it. She had found the sand glass, and with it, the way back to the past and to Arthur. She was already planning how to use it.

Adam was laughing. He folded his arms about her and kissed her properly. Over his shoulder, Alison could see Kate emerging from the office door and pausing in the act of wrapping her scarf about her neck as she stopped to stare. Then she grinned, gesturing that she was getting her phone out to take a photo. Alison waved her away, closed her eyes and kissed Adam back, forcing herself to forget about her planned betrayal, living only for the moment.

"Get a room, you two." Andre hustled Kate away down the street and Alison tucked her hand through Adam's arm as they walked slowly towards the Tube station.

"Busy week?" she asked.

"Yeah," Adam said. "I'm starting to prepare next term's syllabus, planning a couple of guided tours to Italy for Easter, plus there are plans for another TV series." He glanced down at her. "Strangely, though, all I seem to be able to think about is researching Mary Seymour—and spending time with you."

He drew her a little closer as hurrying passers-by buffeted them in their rush to get home. It felt nice; cosy, comforting, as though they *were* a couple, as though, for a moment she had seen a different past in which they had by now been married for ten years and were totally at ease in each other's company. It was as though a whole vista opened up in front of her then: children, an extended family, a whole web of links and connections, work, travel, a settled home she could always go back to at the end of a trip... The regret shot through her, the sense of loss, of what could have been. It was a moment before she realised she was seeing an idealised vision of what her life might have been like. It had not happened, but even so she felt the regret, as though she had lost something precious.

"Ali?" Adam said, and she realised that she was standing blankly at the ticket barrier, holding up all the impatient people behind her.

She loved Adam's house as much as he had loved her flat. It was Georgian, combining elegance with a modern colourful vibe. There was a study overflowing with books and a state-of-the-art kitchen.

"You're surprised," Adam said. He was watching her reaction.

"I wonder if you really can cook," Alison said, "or whether this is just for show."

"You'll find out," Adam said.

"I was expecting something plainer, more minimal," Alison said. "This is so vibrant."

"You're the minimal one in this relationship," Adam said, a little dryly.

Alison put her bag down slowly and slid off her coat. "What do you mean?"

"Only that sometimes it feels as though you're just passing through," Adam said slowly. He pushed the hair back from his forehead. "You seem to travel light with few commitments. I was surprised when I saw your flat because it felt more established than I was expecting. Sometimes I have the feeling you'll just disappear."

His acuity disturbed Alison. When she had first arrived in the present that was exactly what she had intended. The fact that she had not been able to find her way back had forced her to rethink but she had never intended this life to be the defining one. Even now, ten years later, she felt almost like a trespasser, treading lightly, because she had always intended to return to the sixteenth century if she could. She shifted in the comfortable chair, thinking of Richard's shop and the glimpse she had had of the White Hart Inn, the past lying behind the present. To her, time had always felt like that, non-linear, layers you could find your way through if only you knew how to do it. That was what she had always been searching for: the way back.

Adam handed her a glass of chilled white wine. "Hector is settling in well," he said. It was almost as though he had read her thoughts. "Richard says that he's quite at home and he and Monty are getting on fine."

They ate pasta with lemon and basil, which Adam served with a crisp salad.

"It's basic," he said.

"But delicious," Alison said.

They did not talk about the research until they had finished, when Adam cleared the table, made them coffee and spread out some papers in front of Alison.

"You'll see here that I managed to find two other possible references to Mary at Middlecote in the 1560s," he said, pointing to a sheet neatly annotated in his writing. "This is in addition to the one referring to payment for the upkeep of the 'late queen's child.'" He glanced at her. "This is very significant. I think you'll like it. There was an obscure Italian artist called Francisco Estense, who came to England in the mid-1500s. He had no success at court and in the 1560s became an itinerant painter and teacher who travelled the country taking commissions where and when he could. There's a note in his diaries for the year 1566, when, apparently, he went to Middlecote Hall to paint 'Mistress Eleanor Fenner and the Lady Mary.'" Adam waited and looked at her expectantly.

"That could be the portrait you found," Alison said. Her heart leaped. "Is there any way of comparing it with existing works by Estense?"

"It's already in hand." Adam sounded smug. "I've got a specialist on the case. Unfortunately, Estense doesn't have a large body of work. He was considered third-rate. A lot of his portraits have been lost or destroyed and he died only a few years later from the plague, but even so it might be possible." He smiled. "The best bit is that apparently he was never paid. There's a very terse note in the diary to the effect that Sir William Fenner does not honour his financial commitments, which sounds about right since Fenner was always fathoms deep in debt."

"Poor guy," Alison said. "It must have been desperate to be dependent on people like that and to be let down." She looked at him thoughtfully. "You seem quite pleased. I thought you'd be furious to find that the portrait probably wasn't Anne."

Adam shrugged. "I'll admit that I'm not thrilled, but in the end I'd rather be right." He ran a hand through his hair. "All those bloody books will have to be pulped."

"You could rewrite it as a sensational story of discovery," Alison said lightly. "Not Anne Boleyn but something even more astonishing. The secret life of Katherine Parr's lost daughter."

Adam laughed. "Yeah, I suppose I could. I need to find out a lot more before I could do that, though. It's all pretty circumstantial." He stopped, scowled. "Yes, I know, it didn't stop me before."

"Don't beat yourself up," Alison said. "Tell me instead what else you've discovered."

Adam sat down beside her. "Look at this." He opened a file. "Will Fenner in the flesh."

It was a wonderful portrait in the sense of being a great example of the artist's skill but even so it chilled Alison to the bone. All the arrogance of an Elizabethan nobleman was captured there in the tilt of the head, the narrowed eyes and the faint smile that curled Will's lips. He was dressed in black but the heaviness was lifted by the sparkle of diamonds. In the background sat Middlecote and its lush acres as a testament to his wealth.

"Handsome?" Adam asked, looking at her quizzically.

Alison shook her head. "No. Too cruel." She closed the

folder and pushed Will Fenner away. "Presumably that wasn't painted by Francisco Estense?"

"No," Adam said, "Federico Zuccari. He visited the Elizabethan court in 1574 and was commissioned to paint the Queen and Lord Leicester."

"Typical of Will Fenner to want the best," Alison said.

"Here's something from the Elizabethan court records," Adam said, passing her another sheet of paper. "Apparently, in the summer of 1566, William Fenner petitioned Elizabeth I to grant him various manors local to Middlecote on the strength of being affianced to a Mary Seymour. They had belonged to her father and Fenner claimed them in her name."

Alison's mouth fell open. "Will Fenner planned to marry Mary?"

"It would seem so," Adam said. "It doesn't seem to have come off, though. I mean, there's no record of such a marriage and he didn't get the estates either. Elizabeth threw out his claim and called him a greedy knave."

Alison laughed. "It sounds as though she had his measure."

"What's really interesting, though," Adam said slowly, "is that only a couple of months later, Elizabeth received another petition for the restitution of Mary Seymour's lands and fortune, this time allegedly from Mary herself."

"Mary wrote to the Queen?" Alison said. She tried to work it out. Mary would have been about nineteen in 1566, she supposed, plenty old enough for Will Fenner to plan to marry her if it was to his advantage. He seemed to have been the sort of man with an eye to the main chance and if Mary were ever restored to her father's estates she would be a rich heiress indeed.

"The letter doesn't survive, unfortunately," Adam said, "or we would know for sure that this is the same Mary Seymour who was Katherine Parr's daughter. As it is, the evidence is circumstantial but strong since she is claiming the estates that were once the property of Thomas Seymour. She made no mention of Fenner, apparently. He was in gaol at the time and it was his half-brother, Thomas, who presented the petition on Mary's behalf, which is odd since Will and Thomas Fenner were violently opposed in just about everything."

Alison's lips twitched. "Maybe Mary traded in one brother for the other," she said. It seemed unlikely that the meek and mild Mary she had known would do anything so calculating, but she liked the idea. Perhaps Mary had outgrown her naivety.

"It's interesting that you should say that," Adam said slowly, "because later in his life Sir Thomas Fenner, as he became, *did* receive some of the former Seymour lands from the Queen. It does feel as though there had to be some connection to Mary."

"What else do you know about Thomas?" Alison asked.

Adam shook his head. "Very little. He's an elusive guy. It's odd the way that right from the start he drops out of the record for years at a time and then reappears. There's a book of local legends that even suggests he possessed magic because he was said to appear and disappear all the time. It's only in later life that he settled down, tended to his estates and became a respected local gentleman."

"And what about Will Fenner?" Alison asked. "What happened to him? Didn't you say he fell off his horse or something?"

Adam laughed. "Oh, there is a great story about him. He went thoroughly to the devil, mired in debt, hated by his relatives and enemies alike. You remember me telling you he was reputed to have killed his illegitimate child? Well, it's said that Will Fenner died one day when he was out hunting because the ghost of the slain infant appeared and startled his horse, which threw him. Legend has a way of meting out justice."

Alison shuddered. "How horrible."

"They were an unlucky family all round," Thomas said. "Eleanor Fenner was widowed young and the mother, Agnes Fenner, née Essex, drowned. Apparently she slipped on the frozen grass one winter and fell through the ice on one of the Middlecote fishponds. A nasty end. It was said that no one heard her cries for help, but I wonder." He tapped his pen on the table. "She was reputed to have been a very unpleasant woman. Perhaps no one wanted to help her."

Alison shuddered. "As you say, fate has a way of meting out justice," she said.

Adam opened his tablet and tapped to call up an image. "Thomas Fenner," he said. "You can see a resemblance to Will."

"Nice," Alison said. "He's better-looking than Will. Will was more classically handsome but something ugly inside him spoiled it. Although I suppose it's easy to say that with the wisdom of hindsight."

She looked at Adam. "Are there any other records for Mary?"

Adam shook his head. "Nothing but conjecture. As is often the case when someone disappears, there are ideas and myths. One has Mary joining a band of pirates in Ireland, another that she married a nobleman at the court of King James I. Neither seems likely. The only artefact ever found that was said to belong to Mary is a golden ring which was once Thomas Seymour's. It is inscribed with the words 'What I have I hold.'"

"Where is the ring now?" Alison asked. She remembered it; remembered Mary sitting on the bed at Wolf Hall counting out her pitiful belongings. How she had scorned Mary for her attachment to her dead parents' meagre legacy. How jealous she had been to be so unkind to her, how lost, how unhappy.

Adam was reading from his tablet. "The Seymour ring was in the possession of the Seymour-Hart family for many generations. It was given to a museum in the 1920s."

"The Harts," Alison said. "I've heard of them. I think they were yet more cousins. I'll check the family tree." She stirred. "But you don't think either of those stories about Mary are true," she said, "yet there's no record of her death, or a grave."

It was only what she had found when she had been trying to discover more about Mary Seymour's life but still she felt disappointed. If there had been anything to find she was sure that Adam would have found it. It was starting to feel as though in chasing Mary to find Arthur, she was searching for two phantoms not one.

"I've been thinking about the box as well," Adam said. "And the riddle of the contents. Had you had any more ideas on that?"

"Not really," Alison said. "I still think it is a puzzle of some sort and I've been trying to decipher it." She hesitated. "There was the green thread and the wire, for instance. I wondered if it could be a place name like Fiddler's Green, or something, but when I looked it up I couldn't find any family connection to any villages called that…" She stopped, feeling the hopelessness of it overwhelm her. To start with the challenge had almost felt like fun, a riddle she could solve and each step would bring her closer to Arthur. Now, though, she felt as though she had hit a dead end.

"Let's play a game," Adam said. "It might prompt a few ideas."

"A game?" Alison stared at him.

"Yeah." Adam was smiling at her. "A game of chess. There was a chess piece in the box, wasn't there? Perhaps a bit of thought association will help you." Then, as Alison still hesitated, "Don't pretend you don't know how. We played it before, do you remember? You said your father had taught you when you were little."

"Did I?" Alison felt the brush of time over her skin. She had had no recollection of telling Adam anything at all about her childhood before she had gone to live at Wolf Hall. Suddenly, she was scared. She was walking such a fine line in what she disclosed and what she kept secret. If there were something she had forgotten, if she made a mistake, Adam would guess. It laid a layer of guilt over the discomfort she already felt at deceiving him. The closer they became the worse it made her feel.

She followed him into the living room and watched as he took out a chessboard and set it up on the low table in front of the fire. It was a nice set, wooden like the piece in the box, and obviously a family favourite as the pieces were worn smooth from years of handling and the squares on the board had faded over time.

"It was my father's," Adam said, looking up and seeing Alison's look of appreciation.

They played for a little while in silence. Adam won the first game easily. Alison was trying to remember, reaching into the past, memories flickering through her mind, the fire, the dogs sleeping, the peace in the house, her father moving the pieces.

*Chess is a game of skill and cunning.* She could hear his voice. *You need a strategy to win, as you do in life.*

If only he had lived, matters would have been so very different, but he had left her. Both her parents had. It had not been so notable in those days but it had been as painful as any loss. She swallowed hard and concentrated on watching

Adam move the knight across the board. Two squares horizontally and one square vertically. She stopped.

*Two squares horizontally and one vertically…*

"Ali?" Adam touched her hand. "What is it?"

"The knight in chess is unusual, isn't it?" Alison said. "I mean, it can move in different directions?"

"It can go either the way I moved it or it can go two squares vertically and one square horizontally," Adam said. He picked up the piece and demonstrated. Alison grabbed her bag and took out her tablet, her fingers shaking a little in her eagerness. Diana had said that the holly chess piece symbolised hope but that it also might be a clue to something else, a family name or a location…

Two counties horizontally from Wiltshire to the west was Devon. There was nothing to the north but the sea. Two counties to the east and one vertically took her to Hertfordshire. To the south was Surrey. But what would happen if she travelled one county vertically and two horizontally? That threw up plenty of other options…

She started to key in the name Fiddler's Green and Hertfordshire, then realised that she had already checked the location of all the villages of that name in England and found nothing that connected any of them to Arthur. It didn't matter which counties she checked. She did not know the name of the place she was looking for.

She slammed the cover of the tablet shut in frustration. If Arthur had been fostered with a family in any of those counties there was no way to find him, not without their name or a definite location.

"It was just an idea," she said, in response to Adam's look of enquiry. "I thought the way that the knight moved might be a clue to the location of the person the riddle is about."

Adam looked intrigued. "Where are you starting from?" he asked.

"Wiltshire, I think," Alison said. She tried to imagine what Mary might have done when laying her clues. Surely she would start from the place where they had both grown up?

"That would take you into Wales in the west," Adam said, "or Buckinghamshire to the east."

Alison doubted that Edward would have sent their son into Wales. He had no connections there.

"What other stringed instruments were around in the Tudor period?" She asked. "Viols, rebecs, dulcimers..." She was keying them rapidly into the tablet. None of the them came up as place names.

"Psaltery," Adam said. "Lute...um...cittern?"

There were various places names that began with 'Lut' but none of them were musically related. Alison rubbed her forehead. She felt as though she was missing something.

"Harp," Adam said suddenly. "I think harps could also be strung in catgut."

Alison felt a little shiver along her spine. She typed the name Harper's Green into the place name finder. One location came up. Her heart leaped with excitement and then she saw it was in Northamptonshire, not in any of the counties they had identified.

"What's wrong?" Adam was watching her.

"There is a place called Harper's Green," Alison said slowly, "but it's not where I'd hoped. It's Northamptonshire, not Buckinghamshire. My guess about the chess piece must be wrong."

"They're next door to each other," Adam said. "Perhaps there was a boundary change? I mean the counties have all changed quite a bit since the sixteenth century."

Alison's fingers were shaking. She typed in 'Buckingham-shire boundary changes' and checked the list that came up:

"Transferred to Oxfordshire 1884… Transferred from Hertfordshire 1843…"

There it was: Harper's Green, transferred to Northamp-tonshire under changes made in 1884, but, in the sixteenth century, firmly within the county of Buckingham, as it was known then.

Alison could hear her heart beating in long slow strokes now. It felt as though it shook her entire body. She could barely click on the link to the village, she felt so faint and breathless.

Harper's Green was a deserted village, she read. There was a long history of the place from pre-Conquest to the nineteenth century. The manor house had been built in the Elizabethan period to an E-shaped plan with gabled wings and a battlemented central porch. It had been gutted by fire in 1875 and subsequently left as a ruin. The thirteenth-century church still stood and was the burial place for many members of the Tercel family, who had originally come to England after the Conquest and remained lords of the manor of Harper's Green for seven hundred years, only dying out in the male line in 1776.

*Tercel…*

It was an unusual name. She typed it into her tablet and waited what seemed like hours for the results to come up.

A tercel was a peregrine falcon.

With crystal clarity Alison recalled the wording of the list Adam had given her:

One plate from a falcon.

It was curious how the unravelling of one clue suddenly seemed to spin out into a pattern, the links finally weaving together to create a fragile whole. Almost she did not dare to examine it in case it vanished beneath too close a look.

A twig of wood, badly rotted, but identified as *Rosmarinus officinalis* (rosemary). *For remembrance. You see, Alison, I did not forget you.*

A silver button engraved with the shape of a bear. *For your son Arthur, named for courage.*

One hammered silver penny dating from 1560, showing the profile of Queen Elizabeth I on the obverse and a quartered shield of arms on the reverse. Very worn. *The year your son was born.*

One woollen thread in green tied to a piece of catgut. *For Harper's Green.*

One knight from a chess set carved from holly. *One county north, two east.*

One plate from a falcon. *For the Tercels.*

So now she knew. Mary had not forgotten her promise. After ten long years, she knew where Arthur had gone.

She sat quite still, the tablet forgotten in her lap while she thought about it. For a moment she felt nothing, no emotion at all, and then a huge burst of elation swept over her and she turned to Adam, hugging him tight.

"Hey." He sounded surprised, then pleased, at the ferociousness of her emotion. He put his arms round her and hugged her back. The tablet dug into her ribs, but she ignored it. She was swept by so many feelings she could not identify and separate them: relief, joy, excitement, hope and a love so fierce it shook her.

"Ali," Adam said, his voice changing into tenderness and she realised that there were tears on her cheeks and he was wiping them gently away with his thumb. She didn't want him asking her questions. She did not want to explain anything of how she felt. She could not.

"I think we've done it," she said shakily. "I think I know where to find him. Arthur Tercel, Harper's Green."

Adam was smiling. He could have no concept of what this really meant to her, but she realised that the reason he was so happy was because she was happy.

"We'll go and find him," he said. "We could go to Harper's Green tomorrow. There's bound to be something left of the ruined village, perhaps even the manor. We can check out the history of the Tercel family."

He sounded so pleased for her. Alison's heart swelled with love and gratitude and utter misery. She could not bear it, could not endure Adam's happiness when she knew what it truly meant. Now she could go to find Arthur. Now she possessed the knowledge and soon she would have the means.

She did not want to think about it so instead she kissed Adam, putting all she was feeling into it, and the emotion blazed between them and it was beautiful. It left her reeling.

Only, later, when Adam was asleep and she wasn't because her mind was too active to rest, the sadness came back. She slid closer into the curve of Adam's shoulder and heard the steady beat of his heart and inhaled the scent of his skin. She loved him. She thought he might love her too. And that was enough to shatter her heart because all unwitting, Adam had helped her to find Arthur, the one person for whom she would leave him.

# TWENTY-FIVE

*Mary, 1566*

THEY LET WILL GO. WHEN IT CAME TO THE murder of the child it was the midwife's word against his. Mother Barnes had never met Will before, nor had she ever been to Middlecote Hall. In addition, she was old and poor and Will, despite the wrath of his enemies, had powerful friends. They said she was confused, mistaken, and that there was no evidence to support her wild accusations. Will rode back to Middlecote on a new horse and a wave of defiance and pride. No one, knowing him, would have expected him to go quietly and he did not. That evening he called his cronies around, those he had left, and drank and gambled late into the night.

It was impossible to sleep. Not only was the house in uproar but also I was too afraid. There was such a febrile atmosphere at Middlecote. Eleanor was to depart for Yorkshire and her wedding in only ten days' time and after that I had no notion what might happen. Lady Fenner had intimated she might leave Wiltshire to return to her own manors in Kent. She could not control Will, nor did I have the sense that she wanted to any longer. She, like the rest of us, saw he would go to hell in his own way.

It was as I lay tossing and turning, trying to block out the sounds of debauchery from below that the first whisper came through to me.

*"Cat..."*

It was very distant but I caught it immediately. I had been waiting for him, longing for him. The joy burst from me.

*"Darrell..."*

What came back were patterns of relief and joy, and immediately I felt more hopeful and whole again.

*"Where are you?"* I asked.

*"Close. Soon..."*

The promise comforted me. I drowsed, ignoring the raucous shouts and laughter from below until some unidentified time later he woke me from my dreams.

*"I am here. Outside."*

I ran to the window and peered out. The night was clear but the new moon cast very little light. It was a winter night, cold and dark. I could see nothing and no one.

*"You are not."*

*"I am."*

A shadow moved beneath the bare branches of the oak on the lawn. I grabbed my cloak and ran, along the corridor, down the stairs, past the half-open door, where Will entertained, the noise loud, the air thick with drink... Someone caught a glimpse of me, shouted. I did not stop. I pushed the startled hall boy aside and whirled out of the door, down the steps, tripping, tumbling, across the grass.

Thomas caught me to him and spun me around and I felt lighter than thistledown, lighter than the air, and I laughed aloud. I put my arms about his neck and slid down and pressed myself against him as I kissed him. It did not matter that my feet were bare and cold. I did not feel it.

*"I have missed you so much..."*

We were speaking some of the time, our thoughts sliding into one another the rest, and kissing in between. He drew me away from the house, to the corner of the knot garden where the arbour cast its shadow. It was not the easiest or most comfortable of bridal beds but I did not care. When Thomas kissed me again it was gentle but I sensed the heat running deep beneath. I clung to him, alive to him in every way, and when we came together it felt easy and right and the most natural thing in the world. This time I had no thought of holding back, no sense of modesty or convention, and I gave myself to him wholly and took him to me as completely in return.

"Mary..." He buried his face in my neck. I felt the press of his lips against my skin. He was breathing hard.

"Thomas." I was smiling.

"That was..." He sounded dazed.

"Delightful?" I offered.

I felt his chest move as he laughed. "I do love your lack of artifice, Mary. Was it delightful for you?"

I stretched. I felt different. My body felt more rounded somehow, fuller, knowing. It made me feel wicked and excited. Gone were the constraints of my position and my upbringing, scattered like chaff in the wind.

"It was lovely," I said.

A frown touched his eyes. I felt as though I had said the wrong thing.

"You were a virgin."

"Of course I was." I rolled onto my side to look at him. The air was cold on my bare skin. Goosebumps prickled me uncomfortably. It was odd how I noticed these things now when before I had thought of nothing but him. I pulled my nightgown towards me, covering my nakedness.

"You thought I had slept with Will," I said, and it came out as an accusation. I sat up, started to dress quickly, throwing on my clothes haphazard to protect myself.

"It would not have been so surprising." He was watching me steadily and he did not sound defensive. "You were in love with him."

"But I…" Despite my indignation that he should believe such a thing of me, I stopped. There was no point in protesting that I was a lady born and bred. Alison had been that too and she had fallen. If it came to that, Thomas's mother had been no whore and the Lady Anne Hungerford the same, at least not by profession. Such matters were not simple. If I were even more painfully honest, I would admit that there had been a time when I would have given myself to Will with gladness, believing myself so deep in love with him.

Even so I felt hurt that Thomas would believe it.

"We should wed." He spoke abruptly, following a line of thought of his own.

All the remaining pleasure drained from my mind as swiftly as a snuffed candle.

"Because I was a virgin?" I spoke coldly. "Don't be ridiculous."

He looked annoyed now. "You might be with child."

"That could be the case whether I was a virgin or not." I sat up, hugging my knees to my chest. It was odd and confusing that in some ways I felt so close to him, so intimate with him, body as well as soul now, and yet we were still so capable of saying completely the wrong thing to one another. "Are you feeling guilty, Thomas?" I asked. "You should not."

He made a noise of exasperation and pulled me down into his arms. I struggled with genuine resentment. "Let me go!"

"No." He kissed me. "Never. You're mine, Mary. Why do you think I was so angry when I discovered you loved Will?"

I pushed ineffectually against his chest. "Because you are a man and so you think with your c—"

He silenced me with another kiss. "You are my soul's star," he whispered against my lips. "You know it. Since the beginning of time and beyond the end of it."

It was pretty enough to steal my breath and the heat and longing I saw in his eyes even more so. Nevertheless, I was not going to give in so easily.

"I belong to no one," I said haughtily.

"No." He smiled. "You are your own person. But Cat and Darrell have loved each other a very long time."

I placed a hand against his bare chest. "Not like this," I said.

"Not until now." He was solemn. "Yet in all ways and for all time, I think."

I did not answer. Instead, I allowed myself to relax into his embrace, my head against his shoulder.

"Can I come away with you?" I asked. "Now?"

He smiled and pressed his mouth to my hair. "Of course," he said, as though it were the most natural thing for me to run away with him, barefoot and half-clad. "For now and for ever."


I took very little with me from Middlecote, only the clothes I stood up in and Alison's box with my meagre dowry stored within. I was happy to forget the place, at least for a short while, and indeed the first night I spent with Thomas in the tumbledown manor at Kingston Parva we did not speak of Will and I told Thomas nothing of what had happened in his absence. In truth, we were too happy to let the shadow of murder besmirch us. We were cosy enough curled up together in his bed, talking, making love, thinking nothing of the future but only of the joy of the present. At some point, Thomas went to fetch us some food, apples and bread and cheese, and I wrapped my cloak about me as I ate and finally remembered all the questions I had for him.

"Did you see the Queen?" I asked eagerly, and felt my spirits plummet when he shook his head.

"No," he said, "but Mistress Aiglonby carried your letter to her and, as a result, I spoke to William Cecil. He has the Queen's ear and will help us. Once upon a time he had some fondness for your father's family."

"He ingratiated himself quickly enough with our enemies," I said hotly, for Cecil had abandoned my godfather the Protector when he fell, as a rat would desert a house on fire.

Thomas laughed. "That is what politicians do," he said. "Trust me, he has your interests at heart, but it will take time." He sighed. "We do need money, that's true." He was talking half to himself. "I must see what I can do." He propped himself on one elbow to look at me. In the half-light I could see that his dark gaze was very earnest. "Would you trust me enough to come with me anywhere, Mary?"

"Of course." I was astonished he would doubt it. "To the ends of the earth itself," I said. "But you have no need to provide for me. You know that I have a small dowry—"

"You're to be my wife," he said firmly, "and I will find a way. I don't want your money."

I grumbled a little at his pride but he was soon able to turn me to good humour with his kisses and eventually, some considerable time later, I lay in his arms and looked up at the gaps in the manor's roof and felt a warm contentment that one day soon we might be able to restore Thomas's manors as well as regain my own. I pressed closer to his warmth and turned my head against his bare shoulder.

"What of my other commission?" I asked.

Thomas was playing with my hair, running it through his fingers, and seemed disinclined to talk. He started to kiss the curve of my neck, my bare shoulder, his lips trailing lower towards my breast. I was astonished that he seemed to want to touch me all the time, that he took pleasure in looking at me, plain little Mary Seymour. Yet with him I did feel beautiful on the inside and it did not matter how I looked on the outside.

"Alison," I persisted. In my happiness I felt a sudden sharp desire to see Alison happy too. "Mistress Banestre. What news was there of her?"

Thomas sighed and drew away from me a little. "No news. No one knows anything of her except that she was once Lord Seymour's mistress. No one has heard of her in years."

"Lord Seymour," I repeated. Something clicked in my mind then and I felt an absolute fool. Alison had never told me the identity of her lover and I had never seen him in the light. I thought of their clandestine meetings, her misery when she had told me he could not wed her, the secrecy that had forced her to keep quiet. Who better placed than Edward to seduce and manipulate. The first time she had gone away it must have been to be with him; then he had discarded her, planned to marry her off.

*He had taken their son.*

My heart bled for her.

"You did not know?" Thomas asked idly.

I shook my head. "No I did not. Lecher!" I thumped the pillow with force. "Vile, horrible man! To pretend so!"

Thomas soothed me. "Perhaps she is his pensioner now," he suggested. "Perhaps he has provided for her and she lives retired. That may be why I could find no word of her."

But I knew better than that. I knew Edward, weak and

manipulative, would never have shown generosity to Alison once he was done with her. He had shown no kindness to me either. I wondered then how Alison had persuaded him to send us away from Wolf Hall in safety, what persuasion she had used.

So I was no further on in finding her. I supposed it was not surprising; Alison had said that she was going to disappear, go to a better place. My dreams had suggested that the place she had chosen was a long way away both in time and space. Yet she had always planned to come back, to find Arthur, to take him away with her. That was why she still troubled my dreams. She was waiting. She needed my help.

"There was a baby," I said to Thomas. "Arthur. I suppose there was no news of him either?"

"I must find the priest this afternoon." Thomas was following a train of thought of his own. His hand swept over my belly and I knew he was imagining that I too might already be with child.

"Thomas..." My protest was already half-hearted, for his fingers had moved to stroke the inside of my thigh, rising higher still.

"There was nothing," he said. "No mention of a child. You will need to draw on the Sight to find the truth," he whispered in my ear. "For, believe me, Mary Seymour, you possess powerful magic."

He was scattering little kisses across my breasts now and I could feel my body rising to his touch. I knew he was teasing me but I did feel powerful then. Something had changed in me; perhaps it was belief in myself. I do not know. I thought about the visions I had had before and whether in future I would be able to summon them and bend them to my will. Thomas's lips brushed the skin of my belly and I shivered.

His tongue was tracing patterns lower, then lower still, to the soft inside of my thigh.

I thought about how, if I did see the future, I might leave word for Alison, carefully, secretly, so that neither Edward Seymour nor anyone else would ever know. I would do it with cunning and skill, I thought, using the box to hold the clues...

"Mary?" Thomas sounded amused. "I do believe you are thinking of something else."

The tip of his tongue touched the very core of me, stroked in sly caress, and my entire body sang in response.

"Thomas!"

I heard him laugh to hold me so completely in his thrall. There was pure masculine triumph and satisfaction in it. I wanted to smack him for it yet at the same time the ache in my body demanded more.

"Beautiful Mary," he said. "I love you."

"I love you too." I arched as he slid up me and entered me in one hard thrust, claiming me as his now, before, and for all time.

And I thought no more.

Thomas left early the next morning. I sulked to be parted from him so soon but he kissed me into a better humour.

"Next time I go, you are to come with me," he said. "There is a great adventure ahead. I go only to make everything ready for us."

It sounded exciting so I forgave him and kissed him again.

"Stay within the protection of the manor," he told me. "Will does not know I am here, still less that you are too, but should you need to hide there is a cellar beneath the buttery." He frowned and touched my cheek. "I don't like to leave you, Mary, but I will be back soon and you should be safe enough. Promise me you will not wander far, though."

I promised and kissed him back but then, at the last moment, when he would have gone, I drew him back to me.

"You are not going to find Will are you?" I asked anxiously. "Promise me you will not hurt him, Thomas. I know you hate each other but you must never act upon it. I could not bear to see you hang."

Thomas's expression lightened and he laughed. "Sweetheart," he said, cupping my face tenderly, "don't fear for me. Will Fenner will never be my death, even if one day I am his."

That was not good enough for me. I shook him. There was a shadow on me and I wanted to lift it. "Promise me," I repeated and saw him smile with resignation.

"I promise," he said.

I watched him ride away down the road to Marlborough and then I went down the orchard to the river where we had first eaten the stolen chicken together. It was a cold day and the frost lay sharp on the grass and the mist rose from the water.

I had no idea how to summon a vision, for I had never tried other than on the night at Wolf Hall when I pretended to scry for Alison. I sat down in the spot beneath the trees where I had sat with Thomas and closed my eyes, concentrating on the sound of the water and the wind in the trees. I tried to clear my mind and think about Alison and her son, but other thoughts kept intruding and, finally, when I was able to banish them, my mind remained obstinately empty of all but the sensation of cold and damp.

With a sigh, I rose to my feet and smoothed my wet and crumpled skirts. This was hopeless. I saw visions when I did not wish to and when I tried to call them up I saw nothing.

I walked back up the orchard thinking of Arthur Seymour. He would be six years old now and I hoped he was growing into a fine and strong boy though it made me sad to think he did not know his mother. It was odd how my feelings about Alison had changed. It felt to me now that in all the time I had known her she had never been a child. She had had to learn too young how to protect herself because there was no one else to help her. Her beauty, that luscious fairness that I had so envied, had been more of a curse to her than a blessing. I hoped that, wherever she was, she had found some measure of happiness. Then too, I tried to imagine what it might feel like to bear a child and have it taken from me. Here my imagination failed me though. I only knew, in the revelation of my new-found love for Thomas, that if I bore his child I would fight for it to the death, and for him too.

It was then that I remembered the dream I had had of Alison that night at Middlecote, of the peregrine falcon flying from her wrist, and the ruined hall. I stopped dead with the cold of the hoar frost chilling my feet to numbness. Had I held the key all this time but been too slow to realise? Did I already know where Edward had sent Arthur?

I hurried up the slope towards the house, dodging between the apple trees, making for the library. I had only set foot in it for the first time that morning and it was a sorry place—the plaster crumbled from the walls and the remaining books were mildewed and damp. Thomas said that there had once been a fine collection of manuscripts there for his mother's family, the De Morvens, had been great scholars. All I found was a broken desk, more suitable for firewood than for writing, and a pile of elaborate lineages. These had been popular in the days of the Queen's grandfather, when the new Tudor dynasty had sought to excuse its taking of the throne through demonstrating its legitimate claim, or so

Liz Aiglonby had told me once in one of her more astringent and less discreet moods. As a child, I had loved all the brightly coloured lines and decorations on the manuscripts, the shields and roses, the lions and lilies.

The book I drew towards me was a poor specimen of the craft but it had what I needed, a list of all the noble families of England and their connection to one another. It made me smile that when this list had been compiled the eminent family of Seymour were no more than gentry. They were included only because Sir John Seymour's wife, Margaret Wentworth, was a connection of the Howard Dukes of Norfolk. On the Wentworth side of the family though, I found what I was looking for. Lady Seymour had cousins called Tercel and their main estates lay in Northamptonshire, at a place called Harper's Green. Just as Edward had lodged me with the Fenners when he needed to call on his cousins for a favour, had he lodged his illegitimate son with the Tercels?

I closed the book carefully. I had no notion of whether I was following a true vision or my own imagination but it was all I could devise. The peregrine, the tercel, had been so fierce and vivid in the dream, clinging to Alison's wrist. As for the ruined hall, I tried to recall the details, the date stone above the door, but all I could see were holly trees pressing close.

I opened a drawer in the old desk and searched for the means to write it down, but there was nothing either to write with or on. If I were to leave word for Alison I would need to devise a different way, and the idea I had had before, of items that carried a double meaning, seemed the only way. I would use the box. It would be more durable, it would be safer and I would put it aside somewhere Alison and I both knew and set on it a prayer and a charm that she would one day find it. The minute I thought that I laughed, for the idea of me casting a charm was a foolish one. Once again, I had no notion how to do it.

First of all, I went to the chamber I shared with Thomas and emptied out the contents of Alison's box. The ring from my father I put on a golden chain and hung about my neck. The other items—my mother's pearls, the crucifix, the jewelled psalter—I set aside under the bed, wrapped in one of Thomas's shirts that I had found. I had long before used the silver pins, the pomander and the ribbons that Alison had left behind, but I had kept the little drawing she had made of Wolf Hall all those years ago. It had been the place of our shared childhood. Looking at it now I felt a sudden pang of sadness and folded it up and replaced it in the box.

Then I set about collecting the clues for her. I took a sprig of rosemary from the overgrown herb patch so that she might know I had remembered her, and a silver penny from the year of Arthur's birth. There was already a button in the box with the image of a shield with a bear on it. It had once belonged to Lady Fenner—her mother had been of the Baring family, whose device it was.

I found an old plate from a falcon that I found lying on the cobbles of the empty stables. I was pleased with that piece of cunning. Even if Arthur had not taken the Tercel name, it would tell Alison with which family he had been fostered. I thought long and hard about the name Harper's Green. The green element was simple enough—I snipped a thread from my gown—but I had no harp, or any other musical instrument. What I did find, however, was a rotting, broken bow lying beside archery butts in the outhouse, so I took a string from that and hoped the meaning would be clear enough. I was not entirely satisfied with my choices but by now the late-afternoon sun was starting to pale and my stomach rumbled with hunger. I realised Thomas had been gone a long time, far longer than I would have expected. The first shaft of anxiety pierced me then and I ran to the gate, checking the lane in both directions but there was no one. Then I heard the sound of hoof beats and saw the cloud of dust rising on the track.

"Thomas!" I was so happy. My heart soared. Without a thought, I ran out into the road, the box still clutched tight in my hand. The horseman was getting closer now. I waved, screwing up my eyes to see through the dust and the fading winter light. He did not respond but still he came on.

Something was wrong. I sensed it before I saw that it was not Thomas who was coming but Will. A chill ran through my entire body. It was like the vision I had seen of Will approaching Middlecote Hall, his black cloak flying, the devil at his heels. I felt the same sick nausea and my vision started to blur until it was full of darkness. I turned and stumbled, wanting to run, needing only to reach the house and safety, but it was too late. He was beside me. I felt him lift me and, even as my mind screamed out for Thomas, I was carried off into the dark.

I awoke to light and warmth but also extreme discomfort. There was a pain in my head that felt as though my skull had been split in two with an axe. I was lying on my back, my hands bound behind me. I tried to open my eyes but could not. Shadows moved behind the closed lids; the buzz in my ears resolved itself into voices.

Will and Lady Fenner were talking about the box.

"Put it in the aperture above the fire." Lady Fenner's voice was sharp. "Quickly. Push it in as far as you can."

I had forgotten that she knew the hiding place where I had kept my treasure. I had forgotten that she knew everything that went on in this house.

"Why can we not simply destroy it?" Will sounded sulky and I heard her turn on him, snap.

"Because we have already told everyone she has run away. It must appear so. She has run away and left her belongings behind."

A faint trace of rosemary hung on the air. I tried to hold on to the scent, to bring clarity to the nightmare darkness in which I lay, but my mind felt as hazy as mist. I had been gathering clues for Alison, I thought. Rosemary for remembrance, a thread of green… My head ached sharply again and my mind drifted away.

"Are you sure?" I heard Lady Fenner speaking again. I tried to concentrate on her words. "Are you sure he was not there?"

"I told you." Will sounded querulous in response. His mama could always reduce him to such childishness. "I searched everywhere. No one has seen him."

"You saw him yourself," Lady Fenner said.

"That was weeks ago." Will was impatient. "He's gone again, I tell you. Like he always does, a will-o'-the-wisp. He has nothing to do with this."

They were talking about Thomas. Through the pain in my head I tried to reach out to him.

*"Thomas…"*

Nothing. No returning echo of emotion, no response.

"I still think he is involved in some manner." Lady Fenner had turned towards me now. I lay very still. "You said Eleanor had been telling her about him," she continued. "What if she ran to him, with all she knows? What then?"

Their words and the pain in my head and the jumble of my thoughts were interfering with my attempts to reach out to Thomas. Each time I tried I felt nothing. Yet I could not give up. I kept trying to shape my thoughts, drawing strength from the thought of him, the memory of love. It sharpened my determination.

Will walked over to the bed. I sensed it, caught the movement and smelled his odour of stale sweat and soap. Then I felt him touch my cheek, running a finger over the curve of it. I wanted to shrink from that touch but forced myself not to move.

His hand fell lower, slipping beneath the gold chain where my father's ring lay between my breasts. He drew it out. I felt the chain snap.

"My little brother always takes from me what I want the most," he said and a shudder ran through my blood at his tone.

"There's no time for your whoring now," Lady Fenner said sharply. "She has to go. You do see that? She knows too much."

Will turned away abruptly. "I do not see that, no."

I heard Lady Fenner sigh. "Yes you do. It is your fault— you were the one who involved her in your crimes. Besides, she saw what happened that night, with the babe."

"And she said nothing."

It was Will who was defending me, Will who was trying to save my life, but at what price? I did not want to think on it. Nor did I want to think about the fact that in our happiness together neither Thomas nor I had spoken of Will at all. I had not told Thomas what I knew and now it was too late.

*"Thomas…"*

At last there was the faintest tremor of a response. I felt it. *"Mary…"*

He was a long way away. I knew at once. He was separated from me not in distance but in time. I felt his anguish, and it met my own like a tide, rolling over me, dark and deep, full of love and despair.

*"Mary…"*

He was not coming for me. He could not. I saw my dream again, the men fighting in the forest, father against son, brother against brother, a time past and a time still to come. Thomas had been there, I thought. Like Alison, he had found a way through the different layers of time. That was how he had known to warn me of the danger that day I had seen the soldiers in the forest when I was still a child.

"There will always be the chance that she will speak out." It was Lady Fenner's voice. She sounded implacable. "Do you not see, William? We may count her as nothing but others will not dismiss her so easily. She is a Seymour. That is the one thing they cannot take from her. If she were to talk then I doubt even Hopton could save you." She was coming towards me as she spoke. Though I kept my eyes tight shut I could feel it. Lady Fenner, always the driving force, always stronger than her son. Why had I not understood sooner? I had known she was dangerous to me, yet still I had been careless, too slow to realise that when I was of no further use to her she would snuff me out as easily as she had taken the life of the child. I could see the vision now, through that closed door, now that it was too late. Will had had blood on his hands that night, but he had not been the one to throw the baby on the fire. His mother, always more ruthless than he, had seen the threat and destroyed it.

In a blinding flash of clarity, I understood. That was why the one thing Lady Fenner feared was Thomas. She could not control him. She could not even find him. Thomas was her nemesis. In one manner or another he would bring them all down.

There was one last thing I had to do. The charm. It was the final thing I could do for Alison. I thought of the box in its resting place above the fire and I prayed.

My head hurt so badly. I sensed a flutter of love through my mind, soft and gentle. Thomas was with me. I had thought the end would be fierce but it was so mild. A weight pressed down. I could not breathe and then all was dark.

# TWENTY-SIX

ALISON STOOD OUTSIDE THE ART GALLERY ON Marlborough High Street. Two weeks before Christmas and the streets were packed, shops open even though it was a Sunday, pavements full of people searching in a rather harassed fashion for last minute presents. It was the perfect time to stage a break-in because no one was paying any attention. Not that she was breaking in. Not really. She had taken Adam's key. He didn't know, so technically she had stolen it, but she really did not want to think about that now. She could not think about Adam or she would start to question herself. She would falter and then she would fail when most she needed to be brave.

She put the key into the lock. The gallery was closed, all the lights out, the pictures in shadow. Adam had said that Richard was away that weekend visiting friends in the run-up to Christmas. She hoped, belatedly, that there wasn't a burglar alarm. There ought to be in a place like this and yet she could not see one. Carefully, she closed the door behind her and made sure that the latch was dropped.

She picked her way cautiously through the displays. The office door was shut and suddenly she wondered if it was also locked. She should have thought of that. There were so many things she should have considered and prepared for, instead of this headlong flight into the past, but she felt desperate now, so close to her heart's desire, within touching distance. And she also knew that if she did not go now she would never go at all.

She did not know how she had got through the past week with Adam. It had all been a pretence, each day more painful than the one before, because she had known she was going to go and she had laid her plans, and Adam had known nothing. He had thought she was happy; they had agreed to go to Harper's Green the following weekend and in the meantime he had promised to try to find some information on Arthur Tercel for her to help with her family history research. Her grandmother would have been so pleased, he had said. He hoped it helped her to feel more connected to the family she had lost. Alison had felt wretched. That morning he had headed off to the British Library and she had come here.

Her hand was on the office doorknob when she heard the sharp rapping on the outer door. Turning, she saw Adam on the pavement outside, one hand pressed against the glass to shade his eyes so he could see inside, the other beating against the wooden panels.

"Alison! Open the door!"

She froze. How had he known where to find her? Why was he here? The doorknob turned in her hand and the office door opened a crack. She almost turned her back on Adam then. It would be so easy to slip through. She was so close. But when she had planned on leaving him behind she had not planned on this. She had not realised how difficult it would be to look into his face, to hear his voice, and then to walk away.

She hesitated. In front of her the office was shrouded in darkness. She could see the desk, the window seat where she had sat that day she had delivered Hector. Paper cascaded from a tray onto the desk and from there to the floor. It stirred in the draught from the open door.

The hourglass was on the bookcase directly in front of her. If she reached out a hand she could take it. She could at last step back into the past...

"Alison!"

Adam again. She stopped.

She could not go. Not yet.

She shut the door and turned back. Adam was still standing outside, a piece of paper in one hand, the other still resting on the doorframe. As though in a trance she walked slowly back through the gallery and opened the door, and he came inside and closed it behind them. The sudden silence seemed loud.

"I took your key," Alison said. "I'm sorry."

"I know," Adam said. "That's how I knew where to find you."

He was staring at her, and from her to the blank panels of the office door. There was anger and bewilderment in his eyes and suddenly she could feel again, with raw intensity. The sensation of grief burst through the cold determination she had cloaked herself with and pierced her to the heart. She had loved Adam. She had loved him ten years ago and she loved him now. Yet she had deceived him and stolen from him and crushed everything that was between them in her single-minded quest to find Arthur. It was as though she had seen nothing else, had valued nothing else.

"You were going back," Adam said.

That stopped her. She had no idea how he could have guessed.

"I..."

"Don't bother to deny it," Adam said.

"No," Alison said, "I won't." Then: "I am sorry. Truly—"

"Save it," Adam said. He was still staring at her as though

she was a complete stranger to him, which perhaps she was. "So it is true," he muttered. He ran a hand over his face. "Shit. I thought I was imagining things."

"Understandably," Alison said. "But how did you know?"

Adam blinked. He seemed to recall the piece of paper in his hand. "This," he said. He came to stand next to her and snapped on one of the spotlights, holding the paper out to her. It was small and faded almost to the point of being illegible. There was a grid pattern to it. Alison could see the lines on it made by the wire. When she had been young paper like this had been her greatest luxury and she had used it with her charcoal, drawing and rubbing out, designing and painting... With a gasp she jerked back, for she too had recognised the picture now. Tiny, pale, worn, it was a miniature version of the painting on the wall of her flat, Wolf Hall, all sloping roofs and jumbled gables, with the wood at its back and the gate that led to the fields.

She looked at him.

"It was in the wooden box with the other items that Mary left," Adam said. "It was on the list I gave you as a drawing, subject unknown." He took it back from her. Their fingers brushed. Alison swallowed hard, blocking out the warmth of the human connection. Too late now...

"I arranged to have it dated," Adam said. "The test results came through this morning." He was watching her almost clinically now. The anger had gone to be replaced by something more distant, something cold. "It's sixteenth-century laid paper made from linen pulp spread on a wire grid," he said. "But I think you know that, don't you, Alison? You drew the version that is on the wall of your flat. You told me so." He dragged a hand through his hair. "Somehow you drew an identical picture to this one."

"Yes," Alison said, "I did."

"This is Wolf Hall!" Adam said, explosively. He took three steps away then turned sharply back to face her, as though he could not repress all the pent-up emotion inside. "It fits the physical descriptions," he said, "even though there are no paintings of the original house—and, of course, it was demolished many years ago."

Alison swallowed hard. He had not guessed, then. He had worked it out logically, based on the evidence. That, she thought, with a rush of love and utter misery, was totally Adam.

"My conclusion," Adam finished softly, as though reading her thoughts, "impossible as it is to believe, is that either you had seen the original before—" he brandished the little sheet of paper at her "—or you drew it. You drew both of them." Then, whilst she groped for an answer: "Tell me. Tell me I'm right. Because otherwise I'm mad, which I may be anyway."

"You're right," Alison said. She took a shaky breath in. "I drew it. Mostly I stole the paper for my drawings because it was so expensive. I stole a lot in those days."

"You still have the talent," Adam said dryly, and she felt a little sick.

"AB," he added. "AB for Alison Bannister—or Banestre. The whole bloody thing makes perfect sense when you suspend disbelief and look at it from a different perspective. The box was yours all along and you wanted it back."

"I needed to find it," Alison corrected him. She reached out a tentative hand. "Adam—"

Adam took a step back, the movement rejecting her more clearly than words could ever have done.

"Okay," Alison said. "Let me explain?"

"This should be good," Adam said. "Shall we sit down?" He gestured towards the office door, opening it and stepping back to allow her to precede him inside. The room looked exactly the same as normal. Adam switched on the light and it gave the place a dusty glow. Alison took the window seat as she had with Richard whilst Adam moved a pile of books off the armchair and sat opposite her.

"Go on then," he said.

He wasn't making it easy for her but then there was no reason why he should. This was not simply a case of what seemed on the surface to be a mad fantasy; there had been deceit on her part at every step. Adam had believed she had told him the truth that night at the flat when she had spoken about her past and it had been true as far as it went. He had trusted her, opened up to her, given them a second chance, only to discover that the biggest secret of all she had kept from him.

She swallowed, her throat suddenly dry. She wasn't going to beg him to understand or to ask him to forgive her. There was no point now in asking him if he would have believed her had she told him. She would give him the facts and let him make of them what he willed.

"I was born in about 1545," she said, "in Leicestershire. I don't know my birth date for sure but my parents both died of plague when I was about eight years old. We were kin to the Seymours so I was sent to live at Wolf Hall." She looked down at her hands, entwined in her lap. "Everything I told you about my childhood was accurate," she said. "It was chaotic at Wolf Hall. We were a great sprawling family, who were tenuously linked and who depended on the patronage of our rich relatives to survive. Children came and went. When I was about eleven years old, Mary Seymour came to Wolf Hall."

Adam shifted. "That would have been in 1555, when the Duchess of Suffolk fled abroad to escape the Marian persecutions." His tone was objective, the academic, neither believing nor disbelieving, simply weighing the evidence.

"I suppose so," Alison said. "All I knew at the time was that I had to share a chamber with this little plain dab of a girl whose parents were so much more famous than mine. She had a gentlewoman who acted as governess, Elizabeth Aiglonby, who had been appointed by her mother, and her father was Thomas Seymour, of course, brother to the Lord Protector himself, of whose wit and charm and daring men spoke with admiration."

"But both brothers were dead by then," Adam said.

"Yes," Alison said. "It was my cousin Edward who became Lord Seymour shortly after." She glanced at him. "I told you about him too."

She saw Adam's jaw harden. "He was the father of your child?"

"Yes," Alison said again. "I was his mistress." She did not want to talk about Edward now. This was about Mary—and Arthur. And it was her story, for better or worse. Adam did not have to believe it. Very likely he would not, but at least the truth would be out between them at last.

"I hated Mary Seymour at first," she said. "Children can be very cruel and I was vile. I had had no discipline, I suppose, and no example to follow. There was no kindness in me at all."

"You had had no love, I imagine," Adam said.

That got through Alison's defences. She blinked back the tears that stung her eyes. She couldn't answer.

"Mary was strange," she said. "She was quiet and clever in some ways, naïve in others. She was…" she paused, searching for the right word "…otherworldly, somehow. She saw visions and talked to people who weren't there. I thought she had the sight and could foretell the future."

"Did you think her a witch?" Adam asked.

"I didn't believe in witches," Alison said. "But others did. That was how Mary came to be banished from Wolf Hall. They said she caused the death of one of Lord Seymour's servants on a hunting party. I saw it happen. It was an accident but they blamed Mary. I think they would have hanged her for it, superstitious fools that they were, except that I blackmailed Edward into allowing us both to go away."

For the first time, Adam smiled. "Oh, Alison," he said. "Yes, you would do something like that."

"I told you I wasn't a nice person," Alison said.

"You'd been badly treated," Adam said roughly. "You were barely more than a child."

Alison fixed her gaze on the light streaming in through the high windows. Outside was the walled garden that stretched down to the river, with its herbs and its vines, its parterre and raised beds. She could imagine Hector patrolling his territory much as cats would have done down the centuries: mousers, house cats, pets. It all looked so normal and yet there stood the sand glass on the desk and here, once, had been the kitchens of the White Hart Inn, layer upon layer of history.

"Edward was planning to marry me off once he was finished with me, but I had had enough of being told what to do," she said. "I knew about his marriage to Catherine Grey and I threatened to tell the Queen. Edward was a weak man," she added, thoughtfully, "but paradoxically a powerful one. He agreed to send Mary and me away if I kept quiet; but he would not tell me where."

"He sent Mary to Middlecote," Adam said, "but what happened to you?"

Alison hesitated. "I jumped out of the carriage in Marlborough and ran away," she said baldly. "I didn't want Edward dictating my life any more."

"You ran a long way to escape him," Adam said dryly. "How did that happen?"

"I had already found a way through to the future once before," Alison said. "I knew it was possible although I was not clear how it worked. But I was so desperate that I was prepared to risk everything for a better life. I made one mistake, though. I thought I would be able to come and go at will."

She looked up and met Adam's eyes for the first time, willing him to understand. "I was going to go back and find my baby," she said. "Once I knew what sort of place we were coming to, once I had had a chance to prepare. I intended to find Arthur and bring him back with me." Her voice cracked. "But when I tried there was no going back. I was trapped in the present and Arthur...he was...lost to me."

Her fingers were knotted together so tightly they were white.

"You've been looking for him ever since," Adam said, and it was not a question.

"I wanted to know what became of him," Alison said. "I had asked Mary to leave word for me if she could, but then I could not find trace of Mary let alone of Arthur. It never occurred to me that Mary would disappear. The daughter of a queen, lost from history. It seemed so unlikely."

"So when you saw the portrait in the window of the shop here you thought there was a chance that might be the clue you were looking for," Adam said. He shifted, turning slightly towards her.

"It all happened by chance," Alison said. "Although it felt...meant...in some way."

Adam let that go. "And what followed?" he said a little grimly. "Did you deliberately get involved with me again in order to find out as much as you could about Mary and the box?"

"Adam," Alison said helplessly.

"Did you?" Then as she did not answer: "Just tell me the truth, Alison."

"No," Alison said. "I love you. I loved you ten years ago and I still do. I just didn't know how…" She stopped.

*I never knew how to make it work. I didn't see how it could.*

She did not know if Adam would believe her. She did not know if it would make a difference. The only thing she knew was that she had to be open with him now as she had not been in the past.

"I won't lie this time," she said. "I did want the box. You knew I did just as I knew you wanted to know more about Mary Seymour. That was always clear between us. But I wanted you as well."

"The difference between us," Adam said, "was that I was straight about needing to know the truth for the benefits of my research, whereas you made up some cock and bull story about a deathbed promise to your grandmother and your family tree." He sounded coldly angry.

"All right," Alison said, holding on to her own temper by a thread. "Yes I did. I did lie. Because what was the alternative, Adam?" She threw out a hand. "If I had said, 'I need to know this because I'm a time traveller from the sixteenth century, looking for my son,' you would have thought I was mad. *Wouldn't* you?" she added fiercely, when Adam said nothing. "You're probably thinking that now anyway."

She felt exhausted all of a sudden. From the very first with Adam, it had felt like an impenetrable mess. That was why she had pushed him away the first time, because she had not known how to deal with it. Nothing had changed. She was still utterly lost now.

"I'd like to think that was the explanation," Adam agreed. He smiled, that lopsided smile that made her heart clench.

"But that would be flying in the face of the evidence. And sometimes…" He sighed. "Well, hell, sometimes you have to believe, not question."

Hope flared in Alison. "You mean—"

Adam shook his head. "I need to think."

"I'm still the same person you always knew," Alison said.

"That's the trouble, Ali," Adam said, "I never did know the real you." He stood up, looking around the office. "Besides, you're still going back, aren't you? That's why you're here. You've found a way somehow, something to do with this place, and you're going back to find Arthur."

"It's the hourglass," Alison said. "I only discovered recently that that was the key."

"The sands of time?" Adam said. "That figures, I suppose." He stretched out his hand towards the sand clock, almost as though he might take it and smash it, then let his hand fall.

Alison remembered then where she had seen the image of the hourglass before, on Reginald De Morven's tomb, and the Latin inscription that she had later discovered translated as "Grasp your time before it runs out."

"I have to try," she said. She stood up too, facing him. "This was what it was all about, Adam, from the very start."

"I know," Adam said. He sighed. "God damn it, this is beyond unreal. If the evidence didn't fit the facts so beautifully I'd think I was dreaming."

"Welcome to my life," Alison said shakily.

Adam took her wrists and drew her towards him. His gaze searched her face. "How did you survive?" he said wonderingly. "Jesus, Alison, how *could* you survive?"

Alison laughed shakily. "I'll tell you one day, if I get the chance." She shook her head. "It was hard. It still is."

"Fuck," Adam said. "I don't want this." He gave her wrists a little shake. "I want to walk away, but I can't." He took her face in his hands and kissed her. "I'd never ask you to choose."

"Come with me," Alison said suddenly. She held on to him tightly. "Come back with me."

She saw the excitement flare in Adam's eyes, as the thought took hold, then just as swiftly the light there was doused.

"I belong here," Adam said. "And no matter how fascinated I am with the past, I don't believe in changing it."

"You wouldn't," Alison said. "You wouldn't need to do anything—"

"You can't know that," Adam said. "That's why you should leave it too, Ali. You know enough now to find out what became of Arthur. You can find out his story. What are you planning to do—snatch him back? Bring him to the present, like you always planned to do?" He shook his head. "It doesn't work like that, or it shouldn't do. The hourglass is a blunt instrument—you said so yourself. You couldn't get back to the time you wanted before. Why should it work now? What if you arrived at some other point in history? What then?"

"I only want to see him," Alison said. The sheer aching loneliness at the heart of her, the loss that had not healed, felt as though it would consume her. "Just once."

"If that were true," Adam said, "it might be possible." He drew her carefully into his arms. They felt strong and sure. "It's a dream you cling to," he added softly, his lips pressed to her hair. "Seeing Arthur once would never be enough. He's your son and you would want to know him. You would want him to know *you*. It's natural, but whatever you find will never be enough for you." He kissed her again and released her. "Good luck, Ali," he said. "I hope you find what you are looking for."

He went out of the office, closing the door softly behind

him. Alison waited. He did not come back and she did not know if what she felt was relief or regret.

It was time. She stood quite still in the centre of the office, looking around carefully at the battered old desk, the sagging cushions of the wing chair, the setting sun showing up all the dust and dirt on the windowpanes. She listened and heard nothing, waited and smelled nothing but the scent of old books and damp paper, saw nothing but the fading lines of stacked-up paintings. Then she took the hourglass in her hand.

# TWENTY-SEVEN

*Alison, Middlecote, 1589*

SHE KNEW AT ONCE THAT SHE WAS IN THE wrong place, in the wrong time. Adam had been right, of course. Time was not easy, pliable, an instrument to be bent to her will. Knowing where she wanted to be and when was not enough. The sand glass had a will of its own. Time was no easy medium to control. She felt instinctively that she was late, but how late: days, months, years? She had no notion.

What was familiar was the absolute silence, the absolute blackness, of the night, especially on a night like this when no stars shone. She had forgotten. There were no streetlights, no glow in the sky from distant towns and cities, no moving lights of aeroplanes or satellites, no car headlights breaking the blackness. As her eyes adjusted, she could see distantly the dark shape of a house crouching over to her right at the bottom of the hill. It looked familiar. With a jump of the heart, she realised why. She was standing at the stile at the top of the park where she had been only a few weeks before on her first visit to Middlecote, beneath the Phantom Tree.

There was no sound, no movement. Yet she was certain

that she was being watched. The feeling sent a long shiver down her spine. In her past life her instincts had been sharper, but now they had been weakened by a world where survival was so much less dependent on one's wits. She kept quite still, her heart racing, her thoughts tumbling over one another. This had been a mistake. She knew it now, now that it was real, now that it was too late. She was woefully ill equipped to survive. She had acted on instinct, full of impulse. Time had changed her beyond recognition. Had she truly believed she could find Arthur and tell him who he was, who *she* was? She felt as though she was waking from a long dream.

Movement caught her attention, then a faint noise and a light, which turned out to be the wavering glow of a lantern. The noise was incongruous, an insouciant whistling. It was the sound of a man without a care in the world. Alison drew back into the concealment of the trees.

In the lantern's gleam she saw him and recognised him at once. He was holding the light in one hand and the horse's reins carelessly in the other, a fine horse, coal black. Shadow hid half his face but the other was clear, the dark hair greying now, falling across his brow, the wickedly handsome face, older than in the portrait she had seen but still compelling, and the cruel line of the mouth.

*Wild Will Fenner, thief, rogue, lecher, murderer...*

Alison felt ice cold. Her fingers slipped to the knife in her pocket and clenched tight about the handle. It was all she had brought with her, along with a torch and some coin. Not that they would be much use with the head of a queen long in the future and a date four hundred years from now.

The whistling stopped. She saw Will Fenner come awake, his head tilting as he listened, poised like a hunting dog. Slowly, he turned towards her. He had sensed her presence.

Everything happened very fast then. A man stepped out

from the trees on the other side of the path. There was a knife in his hand. The horse, nervous, highly bred, gave a squeal that was so loud and unearthly that Alison jumped. Will realised his danger a second too late. He swung around in the saddle to face this new threat and the horse shied, rearing up onto its hind legs and unseating him with one fierce movement that sent him tumbling beneath the descending hooves. His head hit the ground with a sickening thud.

The horse bolted. Will Fenner lay still, the lantern tumbled from his outstretched hand, his body lying disjointed like a broken puppet. There was blood, Alison noted numbly. She could not move. She wanted to run, but her limbs felt frozen. All she could think was that this had been the moment that had become the myth, the story that Adam had told her about. Will Fenner had not died through a child's ghost taking its revenge but because of a man intent on murder.

The stranger came forward and knelt beside Will's body. In the glow of the lantern his face was very still and grave. He turned Will's head towards the light then let it fall back on the ground in a gesture that said more clearly than any words that Will was dead. Then he got to his feet and turned towards Alison again. He was very tall, fair with dark eyes, not young. None of them were young any more. The realisation jolted Alison. She remembered that Will Fenner had died in 1589. Had she stayed in the sixteenth century she would have been almost fifty years old by now, had she lived.

*Thomas Fenner.* She did not think she spoke aloud, but his gaze narrowed on her as though he had heard her, the lantern's spark catching the darkness in his eyes and lighting it with flecks of gold. Alison studied him. This was the man she suspected had loved Mary Seymour, who had petitioned the Queen to restore Mary's lands, not as Will had done, greedily seeking them as his, but, she suspected, for Mary alone.

"Fate cheats us of our revenge." He spoke slowly, thoughtfully, as though he had recognised her too and assumed her mission there was the same as his.

"Not so," Alison said. "Fate has saved you the trouble of killing him."

The man nodded, standing up, wiping his hands on his jacket as though to rid them of the dead man's touch. "A violent end to a violent life," he said. "I suppose in the end it is fitting."

He was watching her as calmly and dispassionately as he had watched the death of his half-brother. This was a man, Alison thought, who had learned the measure of all things and did not rush to take action but was considered, thoughtful.

He inclined his head. "You are Mistress Alison Banestre," he said. "Mary Seymour spoke of you to me once. I recognise her description. Hair like the spun sunshine, she said, and an unquenchable spirit." He shifted a little. "I never thought to see you," he said. "I thought that you had gone, like me, to a different time."

Understanding came to Alison in a blinding rush of sensation. "You too?" she said. And then with a leap of hope: "And Mary?"

He shook his head slowly. His expression was unreadable. "Not Mary Seymour. She never left Middlecote."

There was a silence. "What happened to her?" Alison asked.

Again there was a long pause.

"She vanished," Thomas said. "I never knew for sure what became of her." His gaze was distant. "She cried out for me but I was too late." His voice was gruff. "She was gone and I could not find her. Many times—so many times—I have looked for her."

"You were a long way away when she disappeared," Alison said. She was guessing, feeling her way, the story coming together piece by piece. Thomas had been like her, like Reginald De Morven, a traveller through time. It seemed that that had been his downfall, his and Mary's.

She waited, conscious of Thomas's thoughtful gaze resting on her, horribly conscious of the dead man a mere few feet away, Will Fenner, gone to account for his sins at last.

"I was a hundred years away when it happened," Thomas said at last. "A hundred years in the future. I had gone to find work so that I could wed Mary. I had nothing and I wanted to be able to offer her so much, a future to make her proud." His voice fell. "I planned to take her with me the very next day."

Alison remembered Adam reading aloud the description of Thomas Fenner from the book of legends: *There were those who called him a magician, a warlock, for the way in which he could appear from the mists and disappear... His brother's men sought him in vain..."*

"You were trapped in time and could not get back," she said. "You could not find a way back in time to save Mary."

"It had always been easy before," Thomas said, "but not that night. That night I bet the hourglass in a foolish game of chance. I lost it. When I needed it the most I could not use it and there was no way back, and Mary's voice screaming in my head, and then nothing more."

The hourglass, Alison thought. Like Reginald De Morven years before, like her, Thomas had had a sand clock too.

"You reclaimed it though," she said. "You must have done for you are here now."

"I half killed a man for it," Thomas said. "We fought. The glass ran back and forth between us until I thought it must surely break. It brought us both back here but at the last moment he snatched it from me and disappeared. And I—" His voice fell. "I was too late. I was too late to find Mary." He turned his face away from the light.

Alison's heart ached for him. "I'm sorry," she said. Then: "I loved her too. I did not realise it when we were children, but I did. She was gallant and true."

A smile lit the sombre darkness of Thomas's eyes. "It pleases me you think so," he said. The smile died. "Will killed her," he said. He looked down at the dead man, stirring the body with his foot. "He swore it was not so, but I know he did. Many a time I would have killed him for it. I wanted to kill him."

"And tonight you intended it," Alison said. "Why, after all these years? Why had you not done it before?"

Thomas was silent for a moment. "I promised Mary," he said quietly. "The very first night we were together she made me swear I would never touch Will. She knew we hated each other. She knew we could easily come to blows and she was afraid I might hang for it. For myself I would not have cared, not with Mary dead. But I gave her my word and I would not break it. For so long I did not waver. But tonight—" He sighed. "Tonight she felt closer to me than ever before. I could not bear it. I no longer wanted to live with the shadow of Will Fenner taunting me."

He knelt beside his brother again and raised his arms so that the light caught the flash of gold on Will's hand.

Alison stared. "That's Mary's ring," she said. The long-faded memories of Wolf Hall came to her then, of Mary furtively rummaging through a box in the room they had shared, counting up her pitifully small possessions—her mother's pearls, her father's engraved ring: *"What I have I hold."*

"I will hold it now," Thomas said, "in memory of her."

He raised his gaze abruptly. "Why did you come back, Mistress Banestre? Was it to find your son?"

Alison nodded. "I too have been searching for many years."

Thomas gave her a faint smile. "You are in quite the wrong place."

"I know," Alison said. "Like you I have never found time bends well to my will."

"He is a fine knight now, your son," Thomas said. "A great man." He looked at her. "Are you sure you wish to change that?" He waited. "Perhaps," he said slowly, "you should go back. Before it is too late for you too."

He dipped his head in farewell and walked away.

The lantern flickered and went out, leaving Alison in darkness. Somewhere in the wood an owl hooted. The house still stood, a dark shadow against a darker sky.

*You should go back...*

Thomas had been a kindred spirit, she thought, searching for Mary just as she had searched for Arthur, through time, through space, looking, longing, failing in his quest. She had the chance to succeed though. She was here, now. She could find a way. She could go from here to Northamptonshire, begging a ride on a cart as she would have done in the past, trading her money for food and drink if she could persuade people to take the foreign coin, until she came to Harper's Green and found Arthur Tercel.

Yet still she hesitated. Arthur would be in his late twenties by now. She had no idea of the form that his life would have taken. It was such a difficult adjustment to make. All of her thoughts had been focused on reclaiming her baby not on what he might have become. She had never imagined that when she found him he would be an adult man.

She shivered. Everything felt tilted off its axis, different from how she had imagined. She rested her head back against a tree trunk and closed her eyes briefly. What had become of Arthur in adulthood? A fine knight, Thomas had said, a great man. She wondered what it would be like to have an adult child and her mind felt empty, unable to grasp the concept. Arthur was the same age that she was.

She realised with a shock that she belonged to a different time now, a different place. Thomas had spoken the truth. She could not set history on an altered course. She did not have that right. She no longer had a place here. Everything had changed.

Even so, she still hesitated, breathing in the cold night air, feeling the touch of it against her cheek, knowing that she would never stand here again in her own time. Then, catching her breath on a sob, she took her bag from over her shoulder and groped inside it until her hand closed about the hourglass. She closed her eyes again and wished harder than she had ever done in her life before.

It felt as though she was falling, through time, through space. She opened her eyes and saw the stars spin crazily over her head and then someone caught her and held her tight and she recognised his touch and held on to him and thought:

*This time I will not let you go.*

"I knew I said I wouldn't interfere," Adam said fiercely, "but in another moment I was coming to find you."

Alison raised her head slightly from his shoulder. They were standing under a streetlamp, bathed in its orange light, directly in front of Richard's gallery. Cars swished past through the dark. The Christmas market was shuttered, the shops closed. She let out her breath in a long sigh and held on to Adam more tightly.

"You couldn't," she said, against his chest. "You'd have needed the hourglass."

"Fuck the hourglass," Adam said savagely. "I would have found a way."

"You said you would never follow me," Alison said.

"I lied," Adam said. "I got as far as the motorway and knew I had to turn back." He drew back a little, tilting her chin up so that she was looking at him. "Why did you come back, Ali?"

"Because of lots of things," Alison said. "Because of you."

*Because of Thomas and the things he said. Because love should be stronger than time.*

She could feel the tears running unchecked down her face and for once she did not try to hold in the emotion nor did she feel ashamed of it.

"I've a lot to tell you," she said, stepping back but keeping a hold on his hand. "Let's go home."

She saw a shadow touch his face then and felt the happiness wither in her. She was too late.

"Adam," she said desperately, but he shook his head.

"No." But his grip on her hands had tightened rather than pushing her away. "It's my turn. Listen."

She waited, holding her breath.

"If we do this," he said roughly, "if we are going to be together, then I don't want to mess it up again. Once was bad enough."

"You didn't mess it up," Alison said. Her throat was thick with tears. "I did that. Not once but twice, through not trusting you."

Adam nodded. "I need to know that will never happen again, Ali, that I can trust you and you can trust me. I don't want to come back one day and find you've gone." He caught hold of her tightly. "This is our reality now. It doesn't mean that what happened before doesn't count. It made us the people we are. But now we go forward, not back."

Alison put her arms about his neck and pressed close. "Yes. I promise." She snuggled into him and felt the love and reassurance flow from his body into hers and did not turn from it. Here she had found her still centre and her peace. There would be no more travelling, at least not into the past again.

The hourglass was still in her hand. She opened her fingers and watched it fall. The glass smashed and the sand fell in a soft cloud that seemed to vanish into the air.

"Thank God for that," Adam said, looking at the splinters of the empty wooden stand.

"There are two of them," Alison said, "but I don't know where the other one is." She pressed her hand against Adam's cheek. "Now can we go home?"

Adam unlocked the car and she slid inside.

"Do you want to talk about what happened?" he said.

Alison sat there silently for a moment, conscious of his gaze on her face, the contained patience of him as he waited. There was so much she wanted to say, a tumult of emotion fighting within her.

"I'll tell you everything one day soon," she said. "I promise. I need to think about it first."

Adam nodded. "Arthur?" he said.

"I know now what he became and where to find him," Alison said shakily. "But I will go and look for him in the present, not the past."

Adam put his hand over hers and squeezed it gently. "*We'll* go and look for him," he corrected her softly.

There was a tap at the car window. "Traffic warden," Adam said, reaching for the ignition.

"No," Alison said, "it's Richard." She opened the door and Monty pressed a wet nose into her hand.

"Hello, my children," Richard Demoranville said, as though to find the two of them sitting outside his gallery at night was a perfectly natural occurrence. He tilted his head to one side and fixed Alison with his bright blue gaze. "Did the sand glass work, my dear? Would you like to come in and tell me all about it?"

# TWENTY-EIGHT

"YOU'D BETTER EXPLAIN WHAT YOU KNOW about this," Adam said.

They had followed Richard back into the gallery, watching as he moved between the displays, placidly turning on the lights, banishing the past in the bright reality of the present. It amused Alison to see how pugnaciously Adam was looking at his godfather. Poor Adam, he had had a lot of shocks to deal with in a single day. She wondered if this would be the one to push him over the edge.

"Shall we go upstairs?" Richard suggested, his blue eyes twinkling benignly as he took in Adam's confrontational stance. "You can be indignant in more comfort up there."

"Thanks," Alison said hastily, scuttling through the office and up the stair, following Monty before Adam could refuse.

The first floor contained an elegant sitting room with a bow window that overlooked the High Street. Hector was sitting curled up in an armchair. He raised his head and regarded them solemnly with his very green eyes.

"Take a seat," Richard invited. He seemed in no hurry to talk. Adam's seething impatience only seemed to amuse him. Alison settled into a deep armchair with plush silver and gold cushions but she was too wound up to relax. Instead, she perched on the edge, watching Richard.

"How did you know?" she asked directly.

Richard laughed. "About the sand clock? Because, my dear, I had taken the same journey as you."

Alison's stomach dropped with the shock of realisation. "You too?" she said. Then: "Of course. How else—" She stopped as another, greater shock hit her. "Wait," she said slowly. "You were Reginald De Morven."

Richard spread his hands in a little gesture, half apologetic, half acknowledgement. Hector rose from his chair, arched his back and leaped elegantly onto Richard's lap, looking at Alison with an expressive flash of his green eyes.

"Holy shit," Alison said, staring. "I wish you'd told me," she said, as the thought sank in. "I've been searching for you everywhere."

"Who the hell is Reginald De Morven?" Adam interrupted. He ran a hand through his hair, ruffling it to agitated spikes. "Will someone tell me what the fuck's going on?" He looked wildly from Alison to his godfather. "You're saying that you're some sort of time traveller too? Am I the deranged one here, or is this a conspiracy?"

"Dear boy," Richard said calmly. "Did you think that Alison was the only one?"

"Yes!" Adam said explosively. "Call me simple but I didn't imagine it happened that often." He glared at them ferociously then threw himself down in the armchair opposite. "I'm not sure how much more of this I can deal with," he muttered.

"You'll be fine." Alison waved a hand towards him. "It's just the shock." She turned back to Richard. "Did you know I had come from a different time?"

Richard smiled. "Dear child, I knew nothing." He paused, head bent, studying the cat on his lap. "I thought perhaps there was a chance," he said, after a moment. "There was something about you. I could scarcely ask, though, could I?

It's not the sort of question one *does* ask without risking an accusation of madness." He looked at her directly, his blue gaze suddenly acute. "Which answers your previous question. There was never the slightest likelihood that I would tell anyone I was Reginald De Morven." He stroked Hector's ears gently. "How many people did you tell the truth of your identity?" he asked. "I doubt it was many."

Alison was silenced. She remembered the utter isolation and the sense of dislocation she had suffered. Of course Richard would not have approached her directly. It was impossible.

"I told Diana," Alison said. "Just as you did."

"Yes, Diana," Richard said. He sighed. "I was so very sorry to hear she had died. She helped me a great deal. Not in the beginning, perhaps. I was too disturbed and confused to understand what had happened to me. But in time—" He gave a rueful half-shrug at his choice of words. "Well, in time her wisdom helped me find my way."

"I did ask," Adam said, recalling them to his presence in the room, "who Reginald De Morven was?"

"Sorry," Alison said. "Reginald De Morven was a fourteenth-century knight in the service of Duke Humphrey of Gloucester. He disappeared one day on his way to the French wars and when he reappeared he raved of seeing metal birds and diabolical machines and of having paid a visit to hell."

"As in, the twenty-first century?" Adam said. There was a spark of amusement in his eyes. "That's pretty apt."

"Diana told me." Alison turned back to Richard. "I'm sorry. She broke confidentiality to try to help me." She frowned. "We thought you had died, though. Your tomb is at Kingston Parva."

Richard was shaking his head. "The tomb in the church at Kingston Parva is a *memorial* to Reginald De Morven," he corrected gently. "There is no body." His gaze turned opaque, inward-looking. "I can only assume that the De Morven family wished to give the impression that I—that Reginald—had died," he said. "They would not have been able to explain it when I vanished for a second time. Had I run mad again? Had I taken my own life? There would have been shame in it for them and confusion." Rueful affection warmed his eyes. "It was another world we occupied, a world of superstition and magic and fear. My family—" His voice caught a little. "They were not people who would have understood."

"Is that why you chose to come back?" Alison said. "To the present, I mean. Because they could not understand and you were alienated from them?"

"In part." Richard's gaze was shadowed now. "Having seen the future, I felt disassociated from my own time. But in the end it was curiosity that took me on my journey. I longed for a time when my talents as a soldier might be recognised."

"The English Civil War," Adam said softly. His dark gaze was riveted on his godfather now. "You always were a dab hand at sword-fighting and building fortifications when Rob and I were kids."

"Dear boy," Richard said, "you have no idea how lucky you were. That was genuine medieval technology we used on those sandcastles."

Adam grinned. "You provided my inspiration for studying history," he said. "So thank you for that."

Richard smiled in return. "A pleasure," he murmured. He reached out and opened the rosewood cabinet to the left of his seat, leaning over to take something out of the display. Alison's breath caught as she saw it was a sand glass, a match for the one that she had taken from the office downstairs. This one looked different, though. It was far more battered and worn and, even as she looked at it, it seemed that the glass shivered. Then she saw there was a crack running down the side and almost all the sand had run out.

"You had them both," she whispered. It was then she remembered Thomas's words:

*"I half killed a man for it... We fought. The glass ran back and forth between us until I thought it must surely break. It brought us both back here but at the last moment he snatched it from me and disappeared..."*

"Oh!" She looked from the sand glass's battered frame to Richard's steady blue gaze. "That was the glass that belonged to Thomas Fenner," she said slowly. "You took it from him in a fight."

Richard's gaze darkened with memory and pain. "They had both been mine at the beginning," he said. "The sand glasses were identical, matched. I left one behind at Kingston Parva when I fled that time. When I saw it in the possession of Thomas Fenner I wanted it back."

"You met Thomas Fenner during the English Civil War?" Adam leaned forward. "At Middlecote?"

"We were strangers," Richard said. "I saw him in a tavern, gambling one night. He was reckless; he offered the sand glass as a prize. I wondered about him then, how it had come into his possession, whether he, like me, had used it to travel from one time to another. I could see he never thought he would lose it. He was lucky with the cards. But I was luckier and I won it and then I knew he did not wish to give it back."

"Thomas needed it," Alison said. "He needed it to go back to find Mary Seymour. She was in terrible danger. Will Fenner killed her that night."

She felt rather than saw Adam move sharply at her side but he did not speak. He, like she, was watching Richard, seeing the lines of grief and unhappiness deepen on his face.

"So that was why Fenner fought like the devil," Richard

said. He closed his eyes briefly, as though absorbing the horror of it. "Dear God, if only I had known." He looked up, his gaze shadowed with pain. "The glass took us both back to his time but I wrenched it from his hand and it brought me back here."

"And in the process it broke," Alison said, looking at the wicked little crack that ran down the side. "The sand had all but run out."

"Time had all but run out," Richard said. "Thomas Fenner was too late to save his Mary." He rubbed a hand across his eyes. "Why gamble with something so precious?" he burst out. "Why risk losing everything?"

Alison was not sure whether he meant the sand glass or Mary. They had been beyond price and Thomas had lost them both.

"Thomas wanted money so that he and Mary could wed," she said. She touched Richard's hand lightly. "Do not reproach yourself. You didn't know."

It did not seem that her words could reach him. There was a shadowed, inward-looking expression in his eyes, the heaviness of spirit of a man who had perhaps seen and done too much.

Adam shifted a little beside her. "I'm very sorry to hear Mary was killed," he said gently, to her.

Alison nodded jerkily. "I am too," she said. "I'm going to find her, though. I won't let that vile man Will Fenner erase her life as though it never happened."

"Arthur first, then Mary," Adam said, with a wry smile. "I'm proud of you, Alison Bannister."

Hector yawned widely, got up, and stretched. Alison looked at Adam and stood up too. "I think Hector wants his tea," she said. "Monty as well, I expect. And we need to get home." It all felt so odd, so prosaic, after everything that had happened. She looked at Adam again for support. "We'll come back soon, Richard," she said. Then, hesitating, "You will be all right?"

"Dear child." Richard smiled as he eased himself to his feet. "Of course I shall." He kissed her; shook Adam's hand.

"Come back on Saturday," he said. "We can talk some more."

They went out through the gallery. The bright colours of the paintings were muted and everything was a monochrome. It fascinated Alison that Richard had embraced modernity so wholeheartedly. One day, she thought, she would ask him about that. There was so much she wanted to ask: Why he had never chosen to go back when he was the one of the three of them who could have done so? What had been the origins of the two sand glasses... She stopped walking so abruptly that Adam almost cannoned into her.

"Sorry," she said. "I've just remembered something I wanted to ask Richard about. I'll only be a second."

She hurried back through the office and up the stairs. Her hear was beating hard. She felt breathless, as though she had been running. The same thought kept hammering through her mind.

Reginald had had one of the sand glasses. Thomas had had the other. Yet she had seen a sand glass on the table in the White Hart Inn, and it was that one that had taken her forward and back through time.

*The power of three...*

From long ago, Mary's whisper reached her.

*"Light the other candle, Alison. The strongest magic is summoned by the power of three."*

Even in her haste she still paused to knock on the closed door of Richard's sitting room. There was no response and no sound from within. She opened the door. It looked exactly the same: the lamps lit, a dent in the seat of the chair in which Richard had so recently sat. Hector wove around her ankles, purring. Monty dozed on the rug.

"Richard!"

Alison's voice sounded shrill in the quiet. A moment later, she heard a step on the stair and felt a rush of relief, but it was Adam who was hurrying to join her and even as she saw the question in his eyes she knew he knew the truth and he knew she did too.

Richard had gone.

# TWENTY-NINE

———

"DO YOU THINK HE'LL EVER COME BACK?" ALISON
said.

It was the morning after and they were driving up the M1
towards Northamptonshire. Monty was in the back of the
Land Rover, curled up and snoring contentedly. They had
left Hector behind in Marlborough in the care of the landlady of the White Hart, who had seemed very excited to be
looking after him. Hector himself had appeared unmoved.

"Richard?" Adam looked up from his phone. "I'm sure he
will when he's ready." He reached for the map. "I've texted
Charles for you and asked for a couple of days off on your
behalf. I've implied—" he grinned "—that it's for romantic
reasons. The whole office will be agog."

"What it is to be a celebrity," Alison said, sighing. "If I'd
asked him for some time off he would have told me to get
straight in there."

"It's not far now," Adam said, checking the satnav. He shot
her a look. "You okay?"

"Yes." Alison's hands tightened on the wheel. "I'm fine.
But Richard—" She came back to the thought that was troubling her. "I mean, where has he gone? *Why* has he gone?"

"Ali." Adam's voice calmed her. "We talked about this
last night. Richard's always been travelling, ever since I've
known him." He gave a rueful laugh. "That bloody gallery

was closed so often it was a family joke. We just didn't realise where it was he was going."

"Oh." Alison felt a little reassured. "I suppose that he has had plenty of experience at it."

"A few hundred years," Adam said dryly. "I almost wish he had taken Rob and me with him when we were kids. That would have been better than teaching us how to build sandcastles."

"You've changed your tune," Alison said, without rancour. She sighed. "I just wish I knew where he was—"

"You're worried he's going to do something that may alter the course of history," Adam said, glancing at her sideways. "Something to do with Mary, or indirectly with Arthur?"

"I suppose so," Alison admitted. "He seemed so gutted when he realised what had happened to Thomas."

"Yes," Adam said, "and I think you're right. Richard went back to make his peace with Thomas. But that's between the two of them and I doubt he would do anything foolish. Richard knows all too well the dangers of tampering with time."

They had left the motorway behind and were travelling down a lane between two high, bare hedges. A sign at the side of the road welcomed them to Harper's Cross. It was a new village and seemed to have sprung up close by the original abandoned village of Harper's Green. It was a busy place with a school, village shop and tearoom. The pub, festooned with Christmas decorations, proclaimed itself one of the few remaining bits left from the original settlement, the second oldest inn in the county and a hotbed of plotting during the English Civil War.

They parked in front of the Co-op and took the dead-end road that led towards the canal, Monty plodding along with true dogged spirit behind them. The hoar frost hung from the trees that surrounded the ruin of the Tudor hall. It looked impossibly romantic, the jagged walls stark against the pale blue of the winter sky, the tumbled chimneys, the empty hearths. Ivy cloaked the ruin, stealing the shape of the original Elizabethan manor, transforming it into something dark and strange. Holly trees stood sentinel all around.

There was a barbed-wire fence surrounding the site. It ruined the atmosphere.

"Private land," Adam said. "That's a pity."

Alison stood with one hand resting on the gate. Through it she could see the overgrown path to the front door and the stone carving above the lintel. There were the initials "WT," a date of 1575 and a coat of arms, too eroded for the shape to be clear.

"Walter Tercel," she said. "He built the manor house here during the reign of Elizabeth I."

She had read as much as she could find about the Tercel family but still she had not found any mention of a child called Arthur in connection to them. This was her last hope, coming here to see what she could find.

"It could do with some TLC," Adam said. "Maybe one day, when I make a fortune, I'll buy it and do it up."

Alison poked him in the ribs. "I'll hold you to that."

The church was set across the field from the manor on a footpath that led down to the canal. In the summer, Alison imagined it would be the sort of place for picnics beneath the willows. Now, the houseboats were locked up and frost-bound. Everything looked cold.

The church *was* cold. It felt like stepping into a freezer, encased in darkness. There was no friendly vicar here to give a potted history of the place, no light, nothing that felt living at all. Never had Alison felt so disconnected from the past.

She had read on the Internet that the Tercel family graves were here and, looking around, she could see the dark humps and bumps of the monuments. There was some ancient-looking stained glass too and wall paintings that still retained their bright colours despite the damp and the cold, but the whole place looked in desperate need of restoration.

"Amazing triptych," Adam said. He flashed his torch in her direction. "Come and see this."

Alison joined him in the side chapel, where a three-panelled monument commemorated Walter, Lord Tercel and his family. He and his wife lay side by side, sons kneeling to the right of their parents, daughters to the left, ten of them in all.

To the left of the triptych was a square stone plaque in the wall. Alison read it once casually to herself and again, this time out loud, with a sudden rush of disbelief:

"'Near here lies the body of Sir Arthur Browne of West Woodhay, knight, beloved cousin to the Lords Tercel and beloved husband of Anne Paget of Blakemere, three times Lord Lieutenant of Northamptonshire, soldier, builder and philanthropist, known as the Knight of Woodhay for his renown. 1560–1645. *Audax at fidelis*.'"

Adam was standing at her side. "'Bold but faithful,'" he translated softly. "That's quite a tribute. A long life and one of great renown."

"Just as Thomas said," Alison whispered. She felt herself trembling and slid down to sit in the nearest pew. A sob bubbled up from her chest. She could not catch her breath. She pressed a hand against her mouth to try to quell the tears but this time she could not. The weeping came, great, undignified gulps of sobbing that seemed to wrench her chest and tear her apart.

Adam said nothing. He sat beside her and wrapped his arms around her and let her soak his coat with her tears. He was stroking her hair and murmuring words of comfort to her, and she felt such a blazing tangle of emotion, of grief and loss but also of such pride. Eventually, she caught a steadying breath and got to her feet.

"I expect I look a state," she said, unsteadily.

"I won't lie," Adam said, "you've looked better." He kissed her.

Alison held his hand tightly as she reached out to touch the lettering of the plaque, feeling the hard edges of the carving against her fingers. "I wonder where they buried him," she said. "It says near here, not where."

Adam was holding a dog-eared guide to the church. It drooped, looking as though it had absorbed the damp of centuries, just as the building had. "It says here that Sir Arthur Browne is buried in the graveyard." He paused, reading. "He requested that he be interred outside of the church, 'beneath the green earth and the tall trees, where the winds blow and the spirit is free.'" He looked up and smiled at her. "That's rather nice, isn't it? Poetic. I like the fact that he didn't want to be hemmed in. It feels as though he inherited your wanderlust."

It was sunny outside now. The frost was melting on the grass. The graveyard was neat and tidy, well kept. Adam stood with his hands on the wall, looking out over the fields whilst Alison wandered amongst the stones, looking, searching. She knew he had sensed she had to do this alone, to say a final goodbye. She walked along the rows of stones, some upright, others fallen, all worn by wind and time. There in the grass beneath the yews she found a plain white stone, a name, dates. Alison knelt down in the grass and shielded her gaze from the low morning sun.

*Arthur Edward Banestre Browne, 1560–1645.*

She caught her breath sharply. "Banestre," she whispered. "He knew. How could he know?"

She felt joy and lightness of spirit spreading through her entire body.

"Perhaps he searched for you," Adam said. He had walked over to join her and she looked up at him, smiling through renewed tears, of happiness this time. "I imagine he wanted to know his mother," Adam said. "And when he found out who you were, he was proud to take your name."

Alison looked down at the stone, at the clear edges of her name carved with such care and pride. Arthur had known of his ancestry and had added her name to his. Arthur had known about *her*.

She closed her eyes and touched the warm stone of Arthur's grave. *Sleep well. We will meet again one day. Until then, all my love, always.*

Adam drew her to her feet, tucking her hand through his arm, pulling her close. For a moment they stood, heads bent, looking at the grave of Sir Arthur Banestre Browne and then they walked together down the path into the sunlight, as high above a peregrine circled against the cold blue winter sky.

"We'll come back," Adam said. "As often as you like."

"We'll get to know the pub quite well then," Alison said, "just like Arthur probably did. We'll walk in the places he walked."

Adam's mobile rang.

"It's Richard," he said, checking the caller ID. He pressed to take the call. "Hello, Richard. Where are you?" Alison thought he sounded extremely calm but then she supposed his godfather was hardly going to be calling them from the seventeenth century.

"Right," Adam said, listening intently. He glanced across at Alison. "Yes, I'll tell her. We'll see you later. He wants his dog back," he said, as he ended the call and slid the phone back in his pocket. Monty wagged his tail enthusiastically.

"Where has he been?" Alison grumbled. She felt a mixture of relief and anxiety.

"He wouldn't say. All he would tell me was that he has something for you." Adam took her hand. "Let's go and find out what it is."

"You came back!" As soon as Richard emerged from the office at the back of the gallery Alison threw herself into his arms. "I was so worried!"

"Dear child." Richard seemed rather amused. He patted her back gently. "Of course I did. There was never any chance I would not. Do you think I would have let Monty and Hector starve?"

"Humph." Alison wiped away a surreptitious tear. "You could have told us there was another sand glass."

"I'm sorry." Richard didn't sound as though he meant it at all. His eyes twinkled. "How did you know?"

"I worked it out," Alison said. "Maths isn't my strong point but I realised that you had a glass, Thomas had a glass and I had a glass all at the same time. Plus, there were three hourglasses on your memorial in the church at Kingston Parva. The power of three."

"What's the power of three?" Adam asked.

"It's natural magic," Richard said vaguely. "The number three has special powers." He ignored Adam's disbelieving snort. "Not your sort of thing, dear boy, not at all. Now." He drew them over to an artist's easel that stood beneath one of the bright spotlights. "I wanted to show you something. I went to Middlecote to fetch this for you."

It was a map. It reminded Alison of the seventeenth-century county map she had studied on the Internet, quaintly drawn, the writing almost impossible to read, illustrations as well as names scattered across the parchment. But this looked much older than the map she had seen. It was also beautifully preserved, jewel bright in the spotlight. She could see a house that looked like a child's lopsided drawing, and the huge spreading branches of a tree. There was a church, a wide blue river and even a windmill.

"But that's—" Adam fell silent, looking up at his godfather in disbelief.

"The Middlecote Map," Richard said. "Yes, it is."

"What is the Middlecote Map?" Alison asked.

"It was one of the first estate maps drawn in England," Adam said. "It dates from the mid-sixteenth century and—" he glanced at Richard again "—it was lost during the English Civil War."

"Just think what a stir the rediscovery of it will create," Richard said contentedly.

"Bloody hell," Adam burst out. "You can't just claim to have found this!"

Richard looked affronted. "Of course I can't, dear boy," he said, "but you can. It will make up for your debacle with the portrait. Besides," he added, "it *was* found at Middlecote, so where's the harm?"

Alison took in his deadpan expression and Adam's explosive one and tried not to laugh.

"All the same," she said, "you'd better get it authenticated properly this time."

Richard's lips twitched. "Yes indeed," he said. "Although strangely enough I didn't bring it here so that you could perpetrate a historical hoax." He turned to Alison, his expression sobering. "I understand that it is important to you to discover Mary Seymour's resting place," he said. "If Will Fenner truly did murder her and conceal the body then it would be likely to be close by, on the estate. Since there is no record, all we can do is search."

Alison turned back to look at the map. It was so vivid and beautiful that she wanted to touch it. Was it also the key to Mary's tomb? She thought of Will and the dark deeds he had perpetrated, his callousness, the arrogant way he had taken and worn Mary's ring as though it were his by right.

She thought of Arthur and the clues Mary had left for her that had enabled her to find her son. Mary had not failed her. She had kept her side of their bargain and as a result Alison knew that her life had been renewed, imbued with peace and fresh promise.

Mary had not been so fortunate.

The determination hardened in her. It might be four hundred years too late but Mary would be found at last and Will Fenner would be indicted for the evil he had done.

The Phantom Tree looked bare and stark as Alison and Adam stood at the top of the hill above Middlecote Hall in the following dawn. Mist hung over the grass of the deer park. Every blade of grass was a spiky white. Middlecote sat in its hollow, the stone pale pink in the rising sun.

"It looks beautiful," Alison said, shivering, "but I wouldn't want to live here. Even if it isn't haunted it feels as though it is."

They walked slowly down towards the house, the frozen path crunching beneath their boots and the air chill on their faces. To the east the fishponds lay dark and secretive behind the garden walls. In the growing light, Alison caught the flash of silver where the river ran.

"The house was pretty thoroughly surveyed when we catalogued the contents," Adam said, as they came to a halt in front of the imposing oak door. "That's how we found the box and the portrait. If there had been a body concealed somewhere in the building I'm sure they would have found it at the time."

"Yes," Alison said. They had talked about this the previous night; where Will Fenner might have hidden Mary's body if he was in haste and did not want to be seen. There would have been no time to dig a grave. He had needed somewhere quick and easy.

"There was the remains of the Roman villa," Adam said. "Although I'm not sure how much of that was visible in the sixteenth century. The famous mosaic they found there was only discovered in 1727." He paused and rubbed a hand over the nape of his neck. "Oh, but it was excavated in the 1970s. I forgot. If they had found any skeletons then they would have been recorded."

"Let's go over there anyway," Alison said. "It might give us some ideas."

Rather than take the drive along the west front of the house, they cut through the gardens to the east, following the overgrown gravel paths, the yews that had once been sculpted into extraordinary topiary designs, but were now a tangle of branches and sharp spiny leaves. Beyond the formal gardens, the fields spread between the house and river. Mary would have walked here, Alison thought, ridden out over the Downs perhaps, or sat beside the river on a fine day and watched the water run.

The field where the villa lay was flat, the grass neatly cut around the site. A gravel path led away in the opposite direction to a car park. A sign noted that the villa remains were in the care of English Heritage and were open all reasonable hours and free of charge. Adam took out a photocopy of the Middlecote Map—having refused point blank to take the original with them—and placed it on one of the interpretation boards so that they could study it.

"We're here," he said. He pointed to a green field beyond the house. The villa was drawn on it with the word "antiquitie" written beside it. Beyond it was another field that looked as though it was littered with stone. "Old Middel Cote," the map said.

"There was a village here until the fourteenth century," Adam said. "They used the stone from the villa for building material. It was one of the places that was devastated by the Black Death."

"So it would already have been abandoned by Mary's time," Alison said. She raised a hand to shield her eyes from the rising sun, scanning the fields. "It's impossible to see where it was now."

There was layer upon layer of history here, she thought. It had been old even in Mary's time, her time.

Adam stood head bent, studying the map. He took a little leather-bound book from his pocket and flipped it open. "This is a gazetteer for Hungerford from the 1950s," he said, in answer to Alison's questioning look. "It's full of little snippets of useful stuff you don't find in the official histories... Ah, here we are..." He read. "Yes, there was a village already here in the Domesday Book and in the thirteenth century a hunting lodge was built, and—" He stopped dead. "And a chapel," he finished softly.

"I thought the chapel adjoined Middlecote House," Alison said.

"Yes," Adam said. "It does now. But that one wasn't built until the 1650s. The old hunting lodge and the chapel stood here until 1780, when they were both demolished. The chapel probably wouldn't have been in use by Mary's time, although I don't know. It might have been..."

"But even if it had been superseded by one in the house it would still have existed," Alison finished. Impatience gripped her, she started to run, stumbling a little over the rough ground. Then she realised she did not know where she was going.

"Let's see the map," she said. Then: "Yes, there—look." There was a modest cross on the map next to an old building that said "King John's Lodge."

"Of course," Adam said. "I don't know how I missed that before."

"She's there." Alison grabbed the map. "I can feel it." Excitement possessed her and with it a painful sort of urgency. She set off across the field.

"Wait!" Adam was hurrying after her. "It's that way," he said, pointing to the west corner of the field. He took out his phone and keyed in a number. "I'm going to call in a favour from a friend." He looked at her. "Are you sure?" he added. "I mean is this just a guess or do you have an instinct? Only I don't want to request permission to excavate a chapel and get some help in if it turns out we're on the wrong track."

"I know it," Alison said firmly. The urgency was a fizzing in her blood now. "Can you hurry?" she added. "I know Mary's probably been here for over four centuries, but now we're so close."

"You seem very sure," Adam said.

Alison stood, turning towards the west of the field, where a scattering of stone from a low wall was just visible through the frozen grass.

"I am," she said. It felt as though something of Mary's gift had touched her, she who had once scoffed at soothsayers and their visions.

*I am coming*, she thought. *I am coming to find you at last.*

*Mary, Middlecote, the present day.*

I soared. Above me was a sky so blue it reminded me of the best of Middlecote summers, cloudless and bright. Below me I could see them gathered by the grave, see the broken slab and the freshly turned earth, and the coffin of the woman whose resting place I had secretly shared for so many years. They were looking down at me, at the nest of crumbling silks and lace, at the tumbled bones. All but one; she was kneeling in the grass but she was looking up at me where I soared, reaching for the sky.

*Alison. My enemy. My friend.*

"Mary." I saw her lips move, as though she could see me, as though she knew I was there. The sun was on her face and her hair was spun gold as I remembered. She was smiling.

*You escaped. Now I do too.*

I left them behind. Over the Downs, along the Thieves' Way and the Rogues' Way to the old manor at Kingston Parva...

"*Darrell!*" I called his name. It burst from me with joy, spilling out in a blaze of emotion and light.

"*Cat...*"

From now until the end of time, he had said to me, and so it proved because love was stronger than time.

He had been waiting. He came to me. We were free.

★ ★ ★ ★ ★

# Author's Note

═══════════════

THE STORY OF MARY SEYMOUR IS SHROUDED in mystery. She was born on 30 August 1548. She disappeared from the historical record in 1550, which has led to much speculation about her life—and death. In The Phantom Tree, I take the known facts of Mary's life and weave them into a broader framework of the history of the Seymour family. Middlecote House is based on Littlecote, near Hungerford, and the inspiration for the Fenners of Middlecote was the Darrells, cousins to the Seymours. Alison's story is entirely fictitious.

# Acknowledgements

MANY, MANY THANKS GO TO SALLY WILLIAMSON for working so hard to make this book the best it can be, and for her ideas, her good humour and her patience. I am also so grateful to the wonderful team at HQ for all the work that goes into publishing my books. I am sure I don't know even a quarter of it.

A special thank-you goes to Tony for sharing with me his portrait of Anne Boleyn, which sparked the idea for Alison's part in this story.

I am indebted to everyone at Safari Drive, to which I am sure Cleveland & Down bears no resemblance at all, but to whom I am so grateful for introducing me to the glories of Africa and the original phantom trees.

Thank you, as always, to my family for the endless encouragement and support, to Andrew for being wonderful and to the dogs for their patience when walks or meals are delayed because I lose track of time.

This book owes a great deal to a group of old friends with whom I spent a memorable evening discussing the plot for this story. Sadly, many of our ideas, including the donkey, have not made it into the finished version, but I value your input and your friendship very much.

Finally, thank you very much to my readers for choosing my books and sharing a passion for history.